when we paid for paradise

j.a. jernay

PLOTWORKS PUBLISHING

"*The greatest piece of urban design in the United States today is Disneyland. It took an area of activity—the amusement park—and lifted it to a standard so high in its performance, in its respect for people, that it really has become a brand new thing.*"

—Real estate developer James W. Rouse, in a keynote speech before the 1963 Urban Design Conference at Harvard University

"*Prosperity breeds monsters.*"

—Victor Hugo

prologue

. . .

THE CAR SPED down the darkened corridor of the expressway. Three inches of crusted snow lay on the frozen sides of the earthen embankment. Nothing moved in the predawn blackness.

Inside the car, the driver glanced at the clock on the dashboard. It read six-thirty a.m. He was expected to be at the attorney's office at seven o'clock.

For the reading of the will.

His *dead wife's* will.

The man felt his stomach tighten with guilt.

So began the morning after her funeral, and the newly widowed Stephen Craving—or Sharpy, as he had been called for the lion's share of his forty-two years—was headed into downtown Indianapolis. He ignored the brown branches blurring by the windows, the streetlights craning over the lanes. It was easy to look past the scenery, he thought. After all, Indiana was so utterly *average*. He thought of classic Hoosier heroes like Ernie Pyle, Dan Quayle. Both native sons; both remarkably unremarkable. Then he remembered another Hoosier, vice-president Thomas Marshall, saying that Indiana had created "more first-grade second-class men" than any other state in the nation.

Was Sharpy one of those second-class men?

Not yet. At the very least, he'd mucked up his life in a first-class way. Badly enough for his dearly departed wife to send him to probate after her death.

He chewed over his predicament for what felt like the thousandth time. He was going to probate for his wife's estate. To *probate*. This was unheard of. Everybody knew that when a spouse died, the estate passed to the survivor. Simple. Like peanut butter and jelly. Right?

Not his situation. A year earlier, when her aged mother had finally given up the ghost, Felicia had inherited just under three hundred thousand dollars in cash. A disorganized mess of stocks, bonds, and real estate added another six hundred and eighty thousand. All told, her inheritance totaled almost a *million* dollars—almost *seven* figures—and because it had been so complicatedly structured, she had postponed rolling up her elbows and plunging into it.

Then the cancer had struck. Sharpy had assumed that the inheritance would pass on to him—but he was mistaken. His wife hadn't transferred the windfall to any of their joint-title accounts. Every penny of it remained in her name.

That was because she'd found out about Vivian.

Vivian Talon.

Sharpy's stomach winched itself shut again. Why had he ever taken up with that woman? Why had he thought he needed a mistress? For outrageous sex? Not really. To escape the ordinary? More likely. Living in the middle of middling Indiana for so many years had dulled his senses. He'd feigned interest in too many antique furniture stores and Mennonite-quilted blankets for far too long. He'd itched for something more sophisticated … more luxurious … expensive …

All of which he'd *certainly* found in Vivian.

But all the pain and recriminations could've been avoided if only he'd hidden that trifling silver bracelet someplace less obvious than in his underwear drawer. How *juvenile*. It'd been a toss-off gift, a thin clasp with a pendant featuring Vivian's initials, purchased at a jewelers' shop safely on the other side of town. He'd been planning to sneak it to Chicago the next morning on his so-called business trip, that time-honored feint of the cheating and cowardly. So why had his wife chosen *that one afternoon* to fold his boxer shorts and lovingly tuck them away in his armoire?

In the ensuing disaster, he had defended himself with all the skill of the craftiest defense attorney. He'd evaded, shifted, omitted, fabricated, and perjured himself a hundred different ways. He'd launched a thousand lies into the air like weather balloons. Felicia had shot them all down. She'd been a sharpshooter, that one.

All of which explains his presence on the freeway this morning. He had no other option but to go to probate. He simply had to grit his teeth and discover what kind of revenge she had plotted for him.

Downtown Indianapolis slid past his windows—the Central Canal, Monument Circle, the neoclassical dome of the state capitol. Finally he arrived at the office building, a twelve-story tower, and parked in a nearby municipal garage. Pulling his trenchcoat tightly around his body, burying his cheeks in his lapels to avoid the icy, stabbing wind, Sharpy trudged four blocks through the gray frozen cityscape.

Towards the attorney's office.

He had already figured out that this attorney was very shrewd. In Indianapolis, nobody set appointments at the ungodly time of seven o'clock in the morning, especially not during the winter. This was a stunt designed to subtly remind Sharpy who held the moral high ground.

He entered the building lobby and nodded to the security guard warming his gloved hands over the hot aluminum slats of an electric space heater. He scanned the mounted directory, the white letters on black felt behind glass, and found his destination: *The Law Offices of John A. Montgomery, Esq.*

He stepped into the elevator on the first floor, stepped off at the ninth floor—and immediately spotted the dreaded doorway at the end of the hall. Oaken and heavy. An in escapable reality.

A sudden wave of panic flashed through Sharpy's body. He aimed for the nearest men's room, pushed through the swinging door, and beelined for the urinal. Standing with his feet spread, he gripped his cold, shriveled penis between his trembling fingers and waited for the stream to come. He tilted his head back and pushed the air out of his lungs. *Don't let them see you like this. Think about something else.*

The bedroom mattress. He needed a new one. His wife had expired on their orthopedic, by her own wishes, and though he was willing to pay penitence, he sure as shivering shit wasn't going to sleep on the downstairs couch for the rest of his life.

Then there was the question of her wardrobe. He needed to do *something* with her clothing—the silk blouses, skirts, scarves, wool sweaters, pantsuit outfits, and especially that horrible pair of purple sweatpants with the sequined fish. The only bright spot in this whole disastrous affair was that he wouldn't have to pretend to like *those* anymore. Still, the wardrobe weighed in silent judgment upon his soul. What would he *do* with it? He couldn't give it to their daughter, D.L. She was fifteen years old and only wore hoodies and utility pants. Maybe he would store some of it in the basement until her tastes changed. Maybe he would dump all three hundred pounds of the stuff onto the Salvation Army's lap. That would guarantee him at least one Christmas card every year.

Maybe he would just throw it all away.

The way he had so much else.

He looked down at the floppy little appendage dangling out of his slacks. Nothing was forthcoming. Frustrated, he yanked up the zipper, moved to the sink, and surveyed himself in the bathroom mirror. Not even six feet tall . . . stooped posture . . . a head of thinning blonde hair … rheumy blue eyes . . . a flabby apron of meat growing where his flat abdomen used to firmly stand … and now *jowls*. Were those for real? He lifted his chin, turned it sideways. No doubt about it. He was growing wattle.

He left the restroom and turned down the hallway. The silhouette of a man waited behind the frosted glass of the door.

It was the attorney.

Sharpy brushed his lapels, straightened himself, and strode as confidently as possible. He would pretend to be casual. If he just acted breezy enough, if he just swung his arms loosely enough, the gathered family members might overlook his trembling knees, his perma-grinned face—and his desperate soul.

The door swung open before he could knock. There stood Montgomery—tall, thin, implacable, wearing a conservative charcoal gray business suit.

"Stephen," the man said.

"John," Sharpy said.

They shook hands cordially. The attorney's palm felt cold, thin, but strong. "Glad you could make it so early," he said.

He and Sharpy had been casual acquaintances for years, greeted each other perfunctorily at cocktail parties. Montgomery possessed a calm, imperturbable temperament that drove Sharpy completely bonkers. His conversation was carefully measured. His syntax was letter-perfect. Even his clothing was tailored within a stitch of its life. On the whole, Montgomery's monkish dedication to precise living made Sharpy feel like a stupid piece of livestock.

"Everyone's already gathered in the conference room," said Montgomery.

"All six?"

"Yes."

Sharpy hemmed and shuffled his feet. "I gotta be honest with you, John. I feel like I'm being fed to the wolves here."

"Nobody's blaming you for her death," Montgomery said. "It was simply unfortunate timing." They passed his secretary's desk covered with needlepoint samplers (*Lord grant me patience—but do it NOW!!*) and pictures of adorable gap-toothed children with happy, slobbery dogs.

But Sharpy paid no attention to either the attorney or the decor. His blood pressure had skyrocketed, and a little voice was nagging inside his head: *You're screwed you're screwed you're screwed…*

As Montgomery reached for the door of the conference room, Sharpy grabbed his elbow. "Can I ask you something?"

"You can try."

"Is it good news or bad news?"

Montgomery waved his hand in the air dismissively. "Stephen—"

"My wife and I were married for *nineteen years*."

"I'm very aware of that—"

"—and they were *good* years."

"No," said Montgomery firmly. "Not the last one."

Sharpy reluctantly agreed. The last year had been excruciating for him and Felicia. It had been an inverted honeymoon, a trip into the ninth circle of hell. Each week featured a worse sin brought to light, a more devastating lie unmasked, a grimmer prognosis from the doctor. But he'd *made it*. He'd passed through the trials. He'd paid the price for his misdeed. Hadn't he?

He grabbed the attorney's arm. "Can't you just tell me before we go in there?"

"Tell you what?"

"You can't keep me in the dark like this. I don't need to get sandbagged."

The attorney tilted his head quizzically. He was playing dumb and Sharpy knew it. Finally Sharpy chopped a hand into his palm. "*Did she cut me out?*"

His passion disappeared as the attorney's clear, cold eyes pinned him down like a wriggling insect against a board.

"You have bigger problems than money," said Montgomery. "Your family has suffered a huge loss, the worst possible, and you are a very convenient target for their grief. Try to be sympathetic with them. Feel their pain, Sharpy. You have common ground."

Chastened, Sharpy stood with his arms hanging at his sides. "She did it," he said glumly. "I knew she would."

Montgomery sighed in the condescending way of someone who knows better but is forbidden from discussing it. "Are you ready to hear the will? Or would you rather continue your clairvoyant theatrics?"

Sharpy shrugged. "I guess I'm ready."

"Are you *positive*?"

"Sure."

Montgomery nodded slightly. "Then let's go inside." He placed a cool hand on Sharpy's shoulder and opened the door.

Sharpy entered the room feeling as though it were his execution chamber.

You're screwed you're screwed you're screwed you're screwed.

———

The conference room was dominated by a large gray sectional table surrounded by eight chairs. Long bookcases stretched along three sides, their shelves groaning under the weight of brown leather law books with gilded lettering: *Contracts, Corporations, Tort Law*. A green plastic rhododendron drooped in a brass pot in the corner. One tiny window afforded a small view of the first fingers of a cold pink dawn reaching across the Indianapolis skyline.

There were six grim faces already assembled around the table. They belonged to his three sisters-in-law and their three respective husbands. Sharpy couldn't help but notice the sour expressions of distaste on the women's rouged faces. They looked at him as if being forced to swallow rat poison at gunpoint. The husbands weren't any warmer. They sat dutifully by their wives' sides, chins bowed to their chests, unwilling to meet his eyes.

Montgomery seated himself at the head of the table. He motioned for Sharpy to take the remaining chair at the opposite end. Sharpy blanched at the seat. It was a rolling number from the early seventies, with rusted casters and squared-off arms and lime-green vinyl cushions spotted with cigarette burns. As Sharpy sank down, he realized that it was nearly a foot lower than the other chairs. Cruddy little mind games, he thought.

He propped his elbows onto the edge of the table and surveyed the three sisters in hopes of finding a glimmer of sympathy. Pam—she was his best chance. Poor hypothyroidic Pammy, the heaviest sister, the homeliest sister, the one who'd always faithfully joined his family for Thanksgiving. When he nodded at her, however, she tipped her nose into the air like a seal balancing a beach ball and looked in the other direction.

No sympathy there.

"Thank you all for attending today," Montgomery said. "The passing of Felicia Cantrell Craving four days ago was a serious loss for everybody in this room. It was a loss for the world as well. She was a beautiful woman in both heart and mind."

The attorney paused while the sisters squeezed handkerchiefs and touched each other on the forearms. Sharpy felt tears gathering in his eyes for the hundredth time that week.

God, his moods were pinging wildly. He'd gone from confident to nervous to angry to disconsolate in less than ten minutes. Now he was entering self-pity: How could he have been so selfish? He'd loved Felicia. They'd boasted a model marriage for most of their nineteen years.

Montgomery continued. "We are gathered here today to hear the private recitation of Felicia's last will and testament. I have been named the executor of her estate, at least until the directives contained within the document have been carried out. Please hold all questions until the end."

The attorney reached into his attaché case, pulled out a black leather binder, and removed a document consisting of five sheets of creamy stationery. Removing a pair of silver reading glasses from his coat pocket, he placed them on his nose and cleared his throat with conspicuous formality:

"The Last Will and Testament of Felicia C. Craving. I, Felicia C. Craving, currently residing at 4810 Chatlahatchee Drive, City of Indianapolis, County of Marion, State of Indiana, being of sound mind and disposing memory, do hereby declare this to be my Last Will and Testament…"

Sharpy's eyes glazed over as the voice faded in and out … *"revoking all former wills"* … *"respect my wishes"* … *"cremated"* … *"station in life"* … He already knew all of this. She'd decided it during the illness. Why didn't Montgomery skip over the preamble? Why didn't he just plunge into the meat of the thing? That's what they were assembled for. His wife had secretly redrawn her will a mere three weeks before her death without allowing anybody to see the new terms. It had been infuriating. Sharpy had pondered the efficacy of filing some kind of counter-claim—though legally he didn't even know what recourse he had—before deciding against it. There was no possible way his wife would *take revenge*. Would she? There was a lot to lose.

That was *his* money, Sharpy thought bitterly. It *had* to be. She had *assured* him it would be.

Sharpy refocused his attention just as Montgomery hit the crucial bits. "…and so I hereby direct that all real and personal property of which I have an interest at the time of my death be placed into an irrevocable trust. I name John A. Montgomery as sole trustee."

In a half second, Sharpy couldn't see. He couldn't hear, couldn't think. Not over the enormous thrumming of blood vessels inside his head. *You're screwed you're screwed you're screwed…*

"Excuse me," he said, "but do you think you could you repeat that?"

"Please allow me to finish," said Montgomery. He continued: "Next, there is the important matter of my husband, Stephen S. Craving. I have chosen to exclude him from this will in retribution for the pain that he has inflicted upon our marriage. I am referring to his longstanding extramarital affair with Vivian S. Talon, of Chicago, which was revealed to me shortly before my death. I hope that I will have enough grace to forgive him in my next life.

"*However,*"—here, the attorney paused dramatically—"I am not *permanently* excluding him from receiving his share of my estate."

Every muscle on Sharpy's body tensed itself. He waited intently. Why was the attorney pausing so damn long? Why didn't he get *on* with it? Couldn't Montgomery see that he was near to popping an artery? Only a sadist would keep a mourning husband in so much suspense!

"By succumbing to his wanton lust, Stephen has torn apart what was once a stable family. For this, he must pay a penalty."

Sharpy leaned forward in his seat, thumbs and heels tapping.

"If my husband performs the following directive within six months following the date of my death, I direct John A. Montgomery to transfer stewardship of the *entire* trust into his hands. Should he prove unable to accomplish this directive, I hereby direct the trust to remain in John Montgomery's stewardship until my daughter, Donna L. Craving, reaches twenty-five years of age, at which time one half of my estate shall be given to her. The other half shall remain under the stewardship of John Montgomery for the purpose of providing for our son, Timothy W. Craving, for the duration of his life."

The attorney paused again, cleared his throat, sipped water from a round glass. Centered the knot of his necktie.

The room lay silent. Sharpy waited, breathless.

"For the past fifteen years, my family never experienced the joy of a family vacation to Florida. It is something that my husband has purposefully avoided, like so much else in his life."

Then the attorney delivered the final judgment:

"Therefore, I, Felicia Craving, hereby direct my husband, Stephen Craving, to undertake a family vacation to Walt Disney World in Orlando, Florida. He must travel with his children, his parents, and his mistress and her daughter."

The entire assemblage swiveled toward Sharpy. He was perched on the edge of his chair. His round eyes glistening like new coins.

"This journey shall last not less than one week. This journey shall be made entirely by automobile. Most importantly, he must return with evidence of the vacation: specifically, one photograph of the entire family, including my remains, before the storybook castle. If he fails to meet this challenge, he will fail to receive my estate. My husband has broken apart this family. *He must make it whole again.*"

The document meandered into the thickets of legalese ... *"compound claims"* ... *"aforesaid purposes"* ... Sharpy's attention, however, had drifted away. He found himself shaking his head in admiration. His wife had actually *done* it. She had denied him the largest part of the estate! The incredible nerve of that woman! *That* was why he had married her! His right hand clenched into a fist. She knew exactly how much he *hated* the idea of visiting that tutti-frutti amusement park. God, they'd waged that argument for years. Each winter she'd pestered him to book plane tickets to Orlando, and each time Sharpy had ducked his head and mumbled something about the possibility of looking into an off-season trip when the rates were lower.

Now he'd have to gather the whole stinking brood. He ran through the list in his mind. His children wouldn't put up any fights. Vivian would complain at first but would quickly see the financial value in such a journey. His elderly parents in the assisted living home would be the toughest carrots to peel.

But for a million dollars, he would *make* the vacation work.

No matter what.

Montgomery finished reading and closed the will. He removed his silver glasses, returned them to their case, and gazed across the table. Like a Pharisee atop a granite bench.

"I have a question," Sharpy said.

"What is it?"

"Do you think I could *pay* somebody to take this trip for me?"

"Excuse me?" said the attorney.

"You know," Sharpy said, "give somebody five thousand dollars, or whatever, to satisfy these conditions," he said. "This way, I wouldn't have to go." This seemed perfectly logical. Sharpy already paid people to do nearly everything for him anyways. He paid a company to babysit his children, a company to clean his house, a company to clean his pool, a company to cut his grass, a company to fix his car, a company to care for his parents, a private school to teach his daughter, a private clinic for his son, and (he thought ruefully) for almost three years he had essentially been paying Vivian to be his mistress. The only real, tangible actions he committed these days were conducted on his desk: writing checks, paying bills, managing financial data. Why not pay someone to take the trip too?

Montgomery shook his head. "Stephen, payment in lieu of pilgrimage is not an option. This is a journey designed to bring your family *together* again. You *must* be present. So must your entire family. As well as Miss Talon and her daughter."

Sharpy sighed loudly.

The attorney drilled deeper. "You've been successful in financial terms, Stephen. But money destroys families who don't respect its power. Today, you have to choose whether or not you want to repair the damage it's done to your family."

Sharpy made his choice. He decided that he hated John Montgomery, that tweedy know-it-all, that perfect moral arbiter, that—

He caught himself. This was no time to be vindictive, least of all towards the very attorney who held the reins of power. This was the time for penitence. He needed to earn his wife's estate back.

Sharpy composed himself into the very picture of humility. He arranged his fingertips in the shape of a cathedral. He hooked his thumbs under his chin and pressed his forefingers against his nose. Then he closed his eyes. To all appearances, he seemed deep in reflection.

His sisters-in-law and their silent husbands angled their heads sideways.

"Well?" said the attorney.

Sharpy opened his eyes as if returning from a long period of cross-legged contemplation upon a mountaintop. He lowered his hands until they hovered an inch above the table … then lightly thumped his palms on the surface.

"Yes," he said.

"Are you sure?" said Montgomery.

Sharpy nodded. "Absolutely. I *will* take my family to

Disney World. I will make this family whole again. It was my wife's final wish."

There were protests from the sisters, rolled eyeballs, pointed fingers, theatrical outcries, slammed doors. Sharpy ignored all of it. He was picturing the storybook castle, the charmingly outdated rides, the pink cotton candy, the ecstasy on his children's faces. A week of pure harmony. He would earn everybody's respect, gratitude, and love.

And he would also earn a million dollars.

one

. . .

IN A HIGH SCHOOL PARKING LOT, a charter bus slowed to a stop. It was a squat, hulking vehicle that featured the awesome wind resistance of a shoebox pushing through chilled molasses. The words *Heartland Royal Coach Lines* were penned across the side in an elaborate purple scrawl.

Surrounding the school's campus were acres of neck-high cornstalks into which a pair of green athletic fields had been shaven. A boys' soccer scrimmage was in full rehearsal.

The door pistoned open and a flood of cheerful but groggy teenagers spilled out. Near the end, apart from the others, a girl of fifteen descended the rubber-matted steps, placing one tentative foot onto the asphalt. She held a book over her eyes while squinting against the fearsomely bright afternoon. She wore a sweaty pink t-shirt, a pair of green camouflage cargo shorts, and yellow flip-flops. She wore no makeup, but her skin bristled with the crab-red tint of sunburn. It felt sticky from too much insect repellent and not enough showering. She held a blue nylon duffel bag whose seams were fit to burst. She'd slung it over her right shoulder; under her other arm was a rolled-up sleeping bag.

The girl watched the other teenagers hugging their

parents. The mothers clasping the children into their sweaty bosoms. The fathers hauling their luggage out of the bin, potbellies swinging low. *Welcome home.*

But she wasn't expecting any mother to greet her.

Her mother was dead.

As she surveyed the crowd, her heart sank—her father wasn't there either. Her left foot turned inwards, girlishly, toe digging into asphalt. Had he forgotten her return date? Or was this a conscious snub?

The bus driver, his short-sleeve burgundy polyester uniform ringed with sweat around the pits, closed the baggage bin with a brassy clang. As he wiped his face on his sleeve, he noticed the girl. "You ain't got anybody waitin' on you?"

"My dad's not here yet," she said.

"Waiting," the driver said to himself. "Yeah. That's about all I do in this job."

The girl had nothing to say to that, so she shifted her weight to the other foot. He noticed her again.

"What's your name?" he said.

"D.L."

"That's it? Two letters?"

"Yep," she said.

The bus driver nodded again, as though he'd expected that very answer. Then he pushed a toothpick into the gap between his teeth, leaned against the bus, and watched the joyous reunions taking place. "Always nice to see people get back to they loved ones."

D.L. was five feet three inches tall and weighed one hundred and thirty pounds. She was enormously self-conscious about this. She looked down at the folds and fissures of her midsection. Eight weeks at summer camp—and yet she'd barely lost two pounds. Maybe it was because during recreational swim, she'd sat on the beach wrapped in a towel. She was afraid that she would've looked too much like a seacow floundering in the water. At night, in the cabin, her bunkmates complimented her—on her oval face; on her small, upturned nose; on her wide brown eyes that seemed to constantly drink in their surroundings. But she never heard any of it.

It was easier not to.

A high-pitched squeal drew D.L.'s attention. A thin, gangly girl—the other campers had nicknamed her Flamingo —had thrown her long twiggy arms into the sky and was skipping through the crowd. D.L. watched her figure with jealous eyes. There are few words in the English language to describe just how acutely skinny the Flamingo was. She was six feet tall, weighed just under one hundred and ten pounds, and possessed no breasts or hips whatsoever. She could play hide-and-seek behind a rake.

To make matters worse, the Flamingo was now flinging her arms around a tall, handsome striker who'd loped in from the soccer field. His yellow mesh pinnie was tilted sideways with outrageous flourish.

D.L.'s heart sank. That was the Hope Diamond. His real name didn't matter. The Hope Diamond had been her private nickname reflecting her *hope* that he might be a *diamond* in the rough. She had liked the way his sweaty hair bounced on the soccer field—layered nicely and tinted burgundy. She had liked the way he swaggered through the halls of their school. Most of all, she had liked the time she literally stumbled upon him in the mystery section of the school library, glancing through an Agatha Christie novel, and how her breast had accidentally pressed into his forearm, and how the electric tingles had zinged down towards other unmentionable parts.

She treasured that memory like a valuable locket.

But now the promise of romance was gone. She averted her eyes as the couple giggled, cooed, and mashed lips. How had the Flamingo landed the *star forward* on the varsity soccer team? D.L. allowed herself a moment of cattiness. The

Flamingo's scythe-sharp farmgirl's face was pretty, sure—but her corncob-yellow hair was flat and shapeless. And then there was her knobby skeleton frame. Hugging her probably felt like hugging a tray of silverware.

And yet there the Flamingo stood, liplocked with one of the most attractive boys at school. A spasm of anxiety wracked D.L.'s body.

It seemed like *everyone* was finding somebody to love.

Except her.

The parking lot was emptying fast. The bus driver noticed the pained expression on D.L.'s face. He didn't say anything. Instead, he lightly pounded the aluminum side of his coach to announce his intentions. "Well, young lady, you'd better step back. I got to take this baby on home to her yard. She needs some grease an' oil an' all kinds a other love."

D.L. walked to the opposite curb and dropped her things on the concrete. The last of the other campers were driving off with their parents. Now the coach rumbled to life and drove off too. She heard the powerful engine muscle forward, and then doppler lower as it disappeared into the corn stalks—and a moment later there was no sound at all except the locusts singing in the weeds.

Scowling, she picked up her bags and began the long walk home.

Alone.

two

. . .

D.L. TURNED into the subdivision and trudged down the sidewalk, luggage in hand. The air was dripping with moisture, and little parabola of sweat had spread across her lower back. She tried to keep underneath the trees but the maples were too young, the branches too sparse, and shade never really stopped humidity anyways.

She noticed the neighborhood homes—the sprawling ranches, trilevels, Tudors, plus a whole buffet of styles she didn't know the names of—as though seeing them for the first time. Eight weeks at camp had given her a new outlook.

Instead of feeling grateful to be home, for the first time she felt *bored* with the neighborhood.

The people were so ... comfortable. The men were hospital administrators and accountants and farm equipment salesmen and basketball coaches, and the women did whatever jobs that the men didn't want or couldn't do, and everybody was blessed with full medical coverage and investment portfolios. Nobody thought too much about the things that didn't seem to affect them. The parents ate ice cream on Saturday nights and rented movies and sat in their living rooms after the movies were finished and listened to the cicadas chirruping outside in the darkened lawns. The children were strong and played competitive sports and were accepted by good universities when they deserved it and were still accepted even when they didn't deserve it.

Above all, the neighborhood lived secure in the knowledge that they had somehow become *victorious*. They had triumphed. They'd leapfrogged over the great mass of idiots whose tics, bloats, hiccups, marginal opinions, cockeyed murmurings, erratic ramblings, substance abuse, and other irregularities rendered them unfit for custodianship of the finer fruits of civilization.

This neighborhood was her home. These were *her* people.

Sighing, D.L. kicked a clod of dirt and watched it skitter down the cement. She passed a middle-aged couple sitting on yellow nylon-webbed folding chairs in the middle of their lawn. The woman wore a pair of unflattering khaki shorts and a severe blonde bob that signaled her sexual unavailability. The man was reading *Money* magazine with crossed legs.

"Welcome back, Donna Louise," said the woman. D.L. hated the way the neighborhood women used her full name —always with that disapproving lilt in their voice.

"Hi," said D.L.

"Have a good time at camp?"

"I learned how to make lanyard keychains."

She meant it to sound boring but the woman didn't catch on. "How *fun*. Guess you won't even have time to unpack then, huh?"

D.L. didn't understand. "Why not?"

The woman tried unsuccessfully to contain a smile around the edges of her mouth. "I heard your family's going on that trip."

"Which trip?"

The woman covered her hand with her mouth. "Oops, spilled the beans." Her shoulders shook as she giggled. D.L. felt the sidewalk lurch and split apart under her feet. Surely her dad would've told her about their vacation plans, even if she were at camp.

The woman's husband lowered his magazine. "D.L., I noticed your father's let his crabgrass grow awfully high on the front lawn, near the marigolds. Tell him he should think about taking care of that, will you?"

"Honey," his wife scolded.

The man got defensive. "Everybody's talking about it. Might as well get it out in the open."

D.L. hung her head and walked on. Her family had been grist for the town gossip mill for over a year. Most of it had centered upon the inheritance. Frankly, D.L. couldn't care less. The botany of finance, the potting and watering and trimming and repotting of huge sums of leafy-green investment money, wasn't yet on her radar.

However, the one thing that she cared even less about was the prospect of spending a week of quality time trapped inside an automobile with her family.

She quickened her pace, and soon the Craving residence came into view around a curve. Its plot was slightly larger than an acre, situated inside a small cul-de-sac. It offered a green, striped lawn; beds of petunias and tulips and marigolds; and young trees dripping with small clusters of thick, curled leaves. The house itself was a classic white colonial—its slim white pillars rising to the second-story eave, where a black lantern hung from a heavy chain above the double front doors.

In the driveway were parked three different cars—a dinged-up, decades-old Ford truck; a spotless but modest white sedan; and a brand-new blue minivan.

First: the truck. She knew it well. These were the Ladies of Suds, the housekeepers who visited every Friday and maintained the nearly five thousand square feet of parquet floor, pile carpet, flagstone tile, polished mahogany, and glossy linoleum that constituted the Craving house. During her mother's final illness, the Ladies of Suds had been perfect models of sympathy. They'd changed the sheets while her mother suffered through chemotherapy treatments. They'd left Tupperware bowls of guacamole in the refrigerator. D.L. had always thought that they deserved an award.

Second: the white sedan. It was a mystery. She'd never seen it before.

Third: the minivan. An Enterprise Rent-a-Car license plate frame pricked up her antenna. Next to it, a pile of objects were heaped on the cement. A pair of blankets. A sleeping bag. A cooler. Two folding chairs. Three pillows. A handheld video game player. Road maps. A small plastic bag from AAA that hangs off the window knob for trash.

Her father was on all fours inside the minivan, engrossed in the preparation. D.L. stood behind him for a short eternity, waiting to be noticed.

"Dad," she finally said.

Sharpy turned his head around and looked at her underneath his armpit. "D.L.? What in the—"

He thunked his head on the edge of the roof as he twisted and tried to clamber out of the vehicle.

When he finally emerged, his face was sweating and his skin was reddened and bursts of hot breath curled out from his nostrils like a bull's. A look of confusion had clouded his face.

She kept her calm. "You were supposed to pick me up."

"I was?"

"Yes!" She threw her arms into the air. "The twenty-third at five p.m., remember?"

"I thought you said eight," he said.

"Five o'clock. We stood *right here when you said that*!" she said.

Sheepish: "I don't remember."

"Well, you did."

"I guess I must've forgot." The father studied his

shoelaces, and one rough hand ruffled the hair on the back of his head. "Goddamn it," he said. "Goddamn it." He lifted his head up but his eyes kept a wide circle around his daughter. "You get a ride from someone else?"

"No."

"With all the preparation for the trip, I just…" The thought trailed off. His hand ran along the smooth side panel of the minivan as though it were a great stallion. Then a look of alarm rang inside his head. He swiveled towards his daughter.

"Did I tell you about the trip?"

"The neighbors just told me."

He scruffed the back of his head again, harder this time. "Goddamn it." He breathed out like a man who has reached the end of himself. "Which neighbor?"

"I don't know their names."

"Were they on that street?" He pointed to the way she'd walked. "Sitting on the front lawn in a pair of beat-up chairs?"

"Yeah."

He balled his fist and pounded the minivan lightly. "Neal and Jan. Goddamn it. That means the whole neighborhood knows."

One half of the Ladies of Suds team emerged from the house carrying a bucket filled with cleaning supplies. She was built as solid as a Mexican credenza, with hips that could birth a vacuum cleaner sideways, no waist whatsoever, just a straight edge up and down either side of her torso. Her shoulders were sharply cornered like a coffee table. Even her head was square.

She set down the supplies. "Es-*cuse* me," she said.

Sharpy didn't look at her: "What is it."

"I can' find *eet*."

"Find what?"

"I can' find the money." The Lady of Sud pointed inside. "You say you leave the money on the table but I can' find *eet*."

Annoyed, Sharpy rolled his eyes. Then, as he turned, he walked towards her with a smile on his face, grandness in his gestures, and false love in his heart.

"Of course it's not there," he said. "Of course it's not." He spread his arms out as though he were giving a lovely performance. "It's not there because I don't pay you until *next* week."

Though she stood immobile, her thick tricep bulged slightly. "You say that las' week too."

His mouth worked itself around frantically. "You're right," he said. "You're absolutely right. And *that* is because . . . I pay you once a month."

She tilted her head like a dog that hears something curious. "But we get pai' ev'ry week? *Ees* always ev'ry week, you know? For t'ree years *ees* always ev'ry week."

Sharpy laughed as though they had just come to the end of a long, exhausting, but good-natured game that nobody in their sober mind would take very seriously. "This family is leaving on a well-deserved vacation first thing tomorrow morning. You will get paid when I return. That's a *promise*. Deal?"

He offered his hand. She stared suspiciously at it.

"You've been with us a long time, Consuela," he said. "You're almost part of the family."

"My name *ees* Mar-*ee*-a."

Mortified, D.L. couldn't tolerate watching her father making a fool out of himself. "Dad, where's Tim?"

"He's downstairs with Brandy," he said.

D.L. felt a twinge of jealousy in her belly. "Who's *Brandy*?"

"His therapist."

The twinge rapidly became a giant knot, and her jealousy erupted into a full-fledged fountain of self-importance. Tim didn't *need* a professional therapist. Tim only needed *her*. Nobody else could possibly know him the way *she* did.

Sharpy read his daughter's mind. "With you gone, I couldn't handle him alone." Then he added: "Don't worry. Brandy's nice."

But he was talking to a cloud of dust. D.L. had already streaked through the garage and into the laundry room, where she kicked off her flip-flops and inhaled the scent of home. It smelled both the same yet different—a sterile, entropic deadness had entered the home since she had been gone.

Then she heard a strange sound like a child being pushed in a rusty swingset. *Squeak squeak squeak squeak*. The sound was coming from the basement. She stuck her thumb and forefinger into her mouth and wolf whistled. That was their secret signal. Her brother always responded.

Sure enough, there came a weird, high-pitched, seagull-like squawk from the basement.

Tim.

She rushed towards the basement stairs.

three

. . .

HIS FULL NAME was Timothy Weller Craving. He'd been given his middle after the Weller mutual fund had offered his father an amazing yield during the nine months preceding his son's birth. Sharpy had assumed, at the time, that his son would someday enjoy the very same fruits of modern success.

It had been many years, though, since anybody had labored under any illusions of success for him.

The reason: Tim was autistic.

Oh, his life had been well cushioned thus far. He enjoyed the very best care, his mother worried that anything less might result in Tim's being found running naked through the woods and eating dead bugs. That was the way Victor, "The Wild Boy of Aveyon", the first recorded case of autism, had been found shortly after the French Revolution.

Still, despite everybody's efforts, there was no overlooking the fact that Tim was flat-out bizarre. Even D.L. felt her heart skip a tentative beat as she descended into the cool darkness by running her fingertips over the painted walls.

There was the sound again:

Squeak squeak squeak squeak.

In contrast to the upstairs sumptuousness, the Craving

basement was an unfinished expanse of cold-floored linoleum. Rows of shelving were laden with board games, Christmas wreaths, unused hibachis, and what seemed like an entire department store of out-of-season clothing.

As her eyes adjusted to the darkness, D.L. quickly noticed a young blonde woman in jeans and sneakers with rolled-up sleeves squatting on her haunches. Next to her was a red cloth hammock, strung between two I-beams. The shape and the saggy weight told D.L. that her brother was inside. The woman was slinging the contraption back and forth with her muscular forearms, on which sweat beaded despite the dankness. *Squeak squeak squeak squeak.*

As soon as she saw D.L., the woman stopped slinging and stood up. "Are you Tim's sister?" She presented a firm handshake. "I'm Brandy Kernwood. We didn't get a chance to meet before you left for summer camp."

D.L. narrowed her eyes. Tim was her only brother. She had protected him for all twelve years of his life, shielded him from cruel neighbors, explained his eccentricities to strangers with perfect matter-of-factness, even saved him from his own weird excesses. She had *earned* the right to be her brother's caregiver. Who did this *intruder* think she was?

Biting her tongue, however, the teenage girl simply shook the therapist's hand. "Nice to meet you," she said.

"Your brother is awesome," Brandy said sincerely. "He has such an amazing personality."

"Then why did you zip him inside a freaking hammock?" D.L. heard herself say. There was a tinge of hysteria in her voice.

Brandy froze for a moment—and then the ice cracked and her laugh was a gorgeous cascading tinkle of tiny ice crystals. She answered the question with good humor: "This sling is very useful, actually. It stimulates his powers of speech."

"I don't believe you."

"Trust me. All the literature recommends it." Her eyes

were round and bright, and her head nodded up and down affirmatively.

D.L. started to move toward the hammock but Brandy laid a soft hand on her shoulder. "I'm sorry," she said, "but you can't touch him yet."

"Why not?"

"It might compromise the continuity of our session."

D.L. could barely keep a straight face. *Compromise the continuity of the session*? Who *was* this woman? Just then, a high, arching, pterodactyl-like shriek sounded from the bag.

"Oh, never mind," Brandy said. "Looks like we're finished anyways." She unzipped the sack, and the twelve-year-old boy tumbled out of the cocoon. Seeing him, D.L. felt her heart leap. His body was composed of the usual gangly limbs, sunken sternum, and Auschwitz ribcage of prepubescence. But he also possessed more exotic looks. His blonde hair was the color of elfin-spun straw; his face the shape of an isosceles triangle; his eyes an exotic half-inch too far apart. Then there were his cheekbones: high, otherworldly, crescent-shaped, like a Slavic male model. But all these features paled next to his eyes. They were a pale whitish blue—the color of a piece of unreachable quartzite at the bottom of a limpid mountain pool.

"Time to finish," said Brandy.

The boy didn't answer.

"Tim? I know you're in there." Brandy produced a soft brush and stroked his hands with it.

"What's *that*?" asked D.L.

"It stimulates his sense of touch," she said. "He really likes it. See?"

Sure enough, Tim's eyes had rolled backwards in his skull and his eyelids were fluttering lightly. Brandy's brush kept on scraping. After a while, she nodded to D.L.: "Call him."

"Why?

"He might respond."

D.L. doubted this would work. Tim was like a cat; he *never* answered to his name. Long ago, there had been family discussions about whether he was even aware of the concept of naming. Nonetheless, she cleared her throat and said, "Snooker." That was his family nickname. It had started three years ago, when he'd found the word God-knows-where and repeated it *ad infinitum* for an entire winter. The only way to keep their sanity had been by flipping it back on him.

To her surprise, Tim opened his eyes and turned in her direction. He'd never done that before.

"Snooker?" she said.

"Who is that?" said Brandy.

"Who is that?" Tim echoed.

Brandy grabbed the boy's wrist and pointed it at his sister. "Who is *that*?"

"Who is *that*?" he repeated with perfect intonation.

She swatted him with the brush and commanded him to say his sister's name. Instead, a long, atonal croon escaped his lips. His eyes focused and unfocused on the light bulb in the ceiling.

The therapist looked disappointed. "Oh, I get it. Back to your old tricks now that your sister's here." She checked her watch, then tossed the brush aside. "We're finished, buddy. Say hi to your sis."

Thank God. D.L. rushed across the basement floor and threw her arms around her brother's shoulders. He never responded to such embraces, but she held it anyways, even though he smelled like sweaty vinyl.

"Two months," D.L. said. "Two months with no Snooker." She pushed the hair out of his eyes. The autistic boy stared straight at the bulb—

(*light bright light bright light*)

—and blinked.

D.L. took Tim's limp hand and guided him towards the staircase. Her brother always walked with a loping, spastic gait during which his head bobbed in a lonely, queer, anapestic rhythm. It looked like he was being mildly electrocuted.

"Nice meeting you," said Brandy. As she escorted Tim upstairs, D.L. didn't reply. Nobody, *nobody*, told her that she couldn't touch her brother.

four

. . .

LATER THAT AFTERNOON, Sharpy stood in the center of his expansive kitchen, surrounded by an acre of tiled counter-top. A double-wide industrial-size refrigerator. A spotless stovetop range with six burners, vented stainless-steel hood, and practically every appliance known to the culinary world. It was an enviable spread. A talented chef, such as his wife, could serve two hundred people from it.

Sharpy, however, was not a talented chef. Aside from the juicer, he hadn't the vaguest idea how to work any of the equipment.

Instead, he was using a fork to scrape kung pao chicken out of a paper pail from a Chinese restaurant. Sharpy duti-fully distributed the food across three plates, stretched plastic wrap over each, and then admired his handiwork. *That* was dinner. He may not have cooked it, but he had at least made it look nice. He slid the first plate into the mounted microwave oven and pressed three minutes.

D.L. padded into the kitchen with her freshly showered hair piled in a knot on top of her head.

"Dinner's almost ready," he said.

"I'm not hungry."

He took this in stride. "That's okay. You've had a long day. How was camp?"

The teenage girl emitted a blast of exasperated air from her mouth. Sharpy winced; he'd probed too far, too fast. You had to be careful with her sometimes. Approach her from oblique angles.

The microwave beeped twice: the modern dinner bell. Sharpy craned his head around the corner and hollered his son's name. There was no answer from upstairs.

"I guess Tim's not eating tonight," he said.

"Tim never answers," she said. "You have to go get him."

"I know, I know."

Sharpy thumbed through the mail while climbing the stairs. He thought about how touchy adolescents could be. Girls in particular—something dramatic happened to them during early adolescence. At best, they were giddy; at worst, they crashed into a hormonal Bermuda Triangle. D.L. hadn't sunk that far. But she did waver between moments of supreme self-confidence and moments of crushing self-doubt.

He knew that D.L. regarded him as pretty much useless. After all, he'd been a zero, a cipher, a familial punch line, until her mother had died. Since then, he'd claimed an authority that, if he was being honest, he'd never possessed in the first place. He'd begun monitoring her bedtime. He'd instituted a rigid schedule of busywork. He'd even clipped movie reviews from the *Indianapolis Star*, crossed out forbidden titles with a black marker, and posted them on the refrigerator. Maybe these new controls hadn't been very well received. But at least he had preserved the possibility of a future relationship with her.

Tim, on the other hand, was a very different creature. His autism wedged itself between *everything*. It made even the simplest tasks impossible.

He arrived in the doorway of the boy's room. Tim was sitting on the coverlet of his simple twin bed—no posts or sleigh frame, those were too dangerous—with his weirdly arched back towards the door. He was plucking invisible lint from the air with a thumb and forefinger, like a Zen master picking at houseflies.

"It's dinner time, Snooker," he said.

"You've got mail," Tim replied. It was an eerily precise imitation of the welcome voice on the Internet service.

Sharpy looked down at the envelopes in his hand. Then his he caught sight of the reflection of his son's face in the window. Without fail, Tim would use reflective surfaces, such as mirrors or glass, to watch what was happening in the room. But he refused to make eye contact.

"Not just any mail," said Sharpy. "This is very special mail called *bills*. Bills are how you know that people care about you."

"People care about you," Tim echoed.

"Time to eat," he said.

The boy plucked another dust mote from the air. Sharpy felt himself growing frustrated. "Downstairs, *now*."

The boy kept right on plucking. Forget it, Sharpy thought. Tim had been eating on his own for five years. He wasn't going literally lead his son by the hand. If Tim didn't want to eat, he wouldn't. The boy's stomach pains would pull him towards the kitchen sooner or later.

Downstairs, he sauntered into the kitchen and said to D.L., "Just you and me tonight, kiddo." When he raised his head, his daughter was pinning him with an accusatory eye.

"Snooker doesn't eat dinner anymore?" she said.

"Well, he won't come downstairs."

"Since when?"

Sharpy thought back. "Since you left for camp."

"You could at least *try* to help him."

"I have." He paused. "When he's hungry, he'll eat."

She sighed impatiently. "No he *won't*. Sometimes you still have to help him, Dad. Sometimes he gets *moody*."

"I know all about moody," he said. "Believe me."

"*Jee*-sus."

She stomped heavily upstairs. She returned a moment later, leading Tim by the hand. "You can't let him starve, Dad."

five

· · ·

AS THE SHADOWS lengthened across the backyard, the three people silently swallowed their reheated meals. They were arranged at the kitchen table of their air-conditioned home. Tim rocked back and forth, picking at his rice at odd intervals. D.L. sullenly pushed the food around and stared out the window, avoiding her father. In the empty fourth place, where their mother used to sit, resided an artificial plant.

Sharpy finally wiped his mouth and crossed his hands behind his head. "D.L., you've been home for three hours. I can't wait any more. How was camp?"

"I don't know," she said.

"Did you get my letters?"

"Yeah."

"I didn't get yours."

"Yeah." Then she explained. "I didn't have much time to write. And my pen ran out."

Sharpy shrugged; he'd let it slide. "So what exactly did you do?"

"I don't know," she sputtered. "I mean, it was pretty much the same as last year. Archery, horseback riding. You know…"

Her voice trailed off as she noticed her father not really listening, his tongue bulging through the side of his cheek. His absent eyes were fixed somewhere on the wall above her head. He was always losing attention like that.

Then Sharpy snapped back. "Wow, sounds great," he said, interrupting her. "Brandy says that Snooker made friends with the cleaning lady Consuela today. Didn't you, Snooker?"

"Her name is Maria," said D.L.

"Of course. Maria." He turned to his son. "Right, Snooker?"

Tim plucked a dust mote from the air and said, "Citrus."

Sharpy sat back and stroked his chin. "Citrus. Interesting."

"Why is that interesting?" said D.L., annoyed. "We were talking about something totally different." She loved her brother, protected him fiercely, but she wasn't deluding herself. He usually didn't make a lick of sense. Tim lived on some faraway astral plane where everybody spoke an unending stream of *non sequiturs*.

"What do you think goes on in that brain of his?" asked Sharpy.

"Maybe she was using that lemon polish on the furniture," D.L. said.

Tim waved his fork in a circle in the air. "While California grows citrus to eat, Florida grows citrus to juice." He began to swing the fork in wide circles, knocking a salt shaker to the floor.

"Settle down, Snooker," said Sharpy.

"Historians have noted that many varieties of citrus fruits were killed in the Great Freeze of eighteen-ninety-five, including lemons, limes, grapefruit, and—"

To D.L., this rattling off bizarre facts could only mean one thing: her brother had read a Florida travel guide. Tim's memory was nearly photographic. He could read anything and, a week later, quote whole passages verbatim.

Now Tim was gripping the fork so intensely that his

knuckles had grown white. "By the 1940s," he said, "new technologies, such as heat lamps and thermal blankets, helped to protect Florida's most famous product from the ravages of winter frost—"

D.L. also knew that, if this progressed, he'd have to be physically calmed. She looked at her father. Shoveling pork fried rice into his mouth and pretending everything was hunky-dory. Is this how he'd handled Tim's crises while she was gone? No wonder he'd hired Brandy. Just as she hazarded the idea of producing the unthinkable from a hallway closet (a strait jacket, kept for exactly these types of moments)—

Rap rap rap rap rap. Someone at the front door. Tim stopped his weird motions. His eyes—

(*ding dong it's the paperboy give him the money ding dong it's the paperboy give him the*)

—danced about crazily.

Then he suddenly bolted from his chair.

six

. . .

NOBODY KNEW how Tim picked his obsessive-compulsive rituals. Over the years, he'd conducted intense affairs with the weirdest subjects. The history of sherpas. The manufacture of electric violins. Cult bandleader Spike Jones. Chicken rendering.

Lately, his most intense obsession was paying the paperboy.

Twice a week, an ink-smudged ninth-grade boy stumped up their front walk with a sack full of copies of a skinny local newspaper called *The Gazeteer*. It wasn't much of a read. The front section offered a smattering of community articles, followed by fourteen solid pages of advertising. Sharpy still subscribed to the newspaper, mostly because he always had.

The paper boy collected the dues on the last Friday of every month. In response, Tim had developed an ironclad ritual: He opened the door, then ran to his father's safe. Sharpy had taught him the combination to the dull, putty-colored box beneath the bookcase. Inside the safe lay a single envelope, stuffed with a five-dollar bill. Tim chose it, closed the safe, and handed it to the paperboy.

The envelope was the only thing that Sharpy kept in the

lockbox. After all, he didn't have much dough to be squirreling away anyways. He never needed to worry about theft, since autistic people didn't usually understand the concept of money. No, Tim just needed the ritual of reaching into the safe and handing the money over. A long-ago therapist had taught the Cravings that they needed to support these bizarre obsessions. They were the pillars of Tim's perceived world.

And so it happened. Tim heaved open the heavy oaken door, its hinges oiled to perfect silence. On the stoop stood the pimply neighborhood kid. His sweaty, babyish palm lay open. "Hi-I'm-here-to-collect-for-the-Gazeteer."

Tim darted into the study, kneeling down to the safe—

(*ding dong it's the paperboy give him the money ding dong it's the paperboy give him the*)

—and opened it. The single envelope lay there, the words GAZETEER printed on it. Tim loped back to the front door with his weird gait and shoved it toward the paperboy. His eyes were looking at the sky.

Accustomed to this ritual, the paperboy took the money and left without a word. Tim stood at the door and waited until the boy had disappeared—

(*now*)

—around the brick edge of the garage. Then he shut the door.

Ritual accomplished.

seven

. . .

AFTER DINNER HAD ENDED, Sharpy cleared the table and packed away their three plates and three glasses and three forks into the dishwasher. At the sink, he spotted D.L. on the back deck—a twelve-hundred square-foot pine indulgence that cost him, each spring, hundreds of dollars in cleaning, stripping, and re-staining. His daughter was gazing over the carpeted lawn, past the row of hedges, and at the Tyco playscape in the backyard of their neighbor's house.

He poured a glass of iced tea, slid open the glass doorwall, and stepped onto the deck. Streaks of dusky purple and orange stretched above the Midwestern plains as the sun plunged towards the earth.

"Rick bought that right after you left," he said. "Little Kenny loves it. You can hear him whooping at all hours."

Without looking, D.L. moved further down the deck.

Sharpy casually sauntered to the place where his daughter had been standing, as if he had picked that spot by pure chance. He pointed to a bare spot next to the barbeque. "And we took out that rhododendron bush too. I figure maybe after we get back we could put a jacuzzi there. Whaddya think?

Wouldn't you like to go hot tubbing with your friends?" Grinning, he waited for her answer.

It came in a small voice: "I don't want to go to Florida."

That was more than a surprise. It stunned him. He felt like she'd shot him with a beanbag. "I don't understand," he said. "Talk to me."

She shrugged.

"Why don't you want to go?"

She shrugged again.

"You don't know why?"

"I just don't want to." Her voice had shrunk down to almost a whisper.

He picked his words carefully. "Your mother wanted us to go. It was her last wish."

D.L. picked a leaf off a rhododendron and was shredding it into ever-tinier pieces. She was biting her lower lip, trying not to cry.

Sharpy rubbed the bridge of his nose. "I know that you haven't been too fond of me lately." She flashed a dark gaze at him; eye contact, a small victory. "And with good reason too. It's not easy getting used to the idea of a new woman in your father's life." He took a couple steps closer. "But this trip will bring our family closer together. You, me, Tim, Grandma and Grandpa, plus Vivian and Brittany—you haven't even met them yet. We're going to be a *happy family*." He rubbed his hands happily on his pants and looked to the sliver of horizon visible between the neighbors' houses.

"Even if it kills us?" she said.

He snort-laughed. "Yep. But nobody's going to die."

"What happens if we don't go?" she said.

"Then we don't get your mother's inheritance."

Her eyes rolled up and left. She was thinking. "But I would get it someday, wouldn't I? Isn't that what the will said?"

At this point, Sharpy approached his daughter very delicately, the way you would approach a toddler with her finger in the pin of a hand grenade. "That's true, D.L. But wouldn't you rather have me take care of the money? I'm older. I know investment. I know how to handle it." He finally reached out and touched her shoulder. "Money brings problems, sweetheart. Do you really want more problems?"

Sharpy was all softness and sympathy. Better not to burden her with knowledge of the family's debt, he thought. Better not to crush her under the psychic weight of his monthly expenditures, which consisted of a $3721 mortgage payment, a $640 automobile lease, a $438 insurance payment, a $519 heating bill (which seemed to double every year), and nearly three hundred a week at the grocery store. That was just for starters. Tim's new in-house assistant was running upwards of six thousand a month. The lawn care and housekeepers cost another grand. And then there was Vivian. She was gulping his open credit like a hungry mouse swimming through a sea of cheese. By God, she had racked up nearly $13,000 at Saks Fifth Avenue last billing cycle alone. But that would be taken care of later.

D.L. breathed out. She sat down on a decorative bench, which creaked under her weight, so she stood up again. "Okay," she said.

"You'll come?"

"I guess so."

"Thatta girl," Sharpy said, clapping her on the shoulder. Then he paced the deck and verbally outlined his plans for the evening. "First we do a grocery store run for snacks, then we finish organizing the minivan, then—"

D.L. looked towards the abomination parked in the driveway. "Why did you rent that thing?"

"Don't you like it?"

She made a face as though someone had just offered her a plate of pigshit hors d'oeuvres. "Ew. Are you *crazy*?"

"That's a nice minivan. Best on the market. It's got four

captain's chairs and a bench seat for you three kids. Besides, I'm already over my mileage limit on the Cadillac."

"Whatever. It's your trip."

Sharpy nodded in agreement. "So in the morning we're going to fill the tires, then we'll get a great breakfast at Denny's—"

"I hate Denny's," she said.

"Then we'll get a great breakfast wherever you and Tim want."

"I don't want breakfast," she said.

"Say, could you help your brother pack tonight? Make sure he gets some clothes into a suitcase? You know what he needs better than I do."

"Fine."

In his excitement, Sharpy missed the resentment swirling below the surface of her voice. He clapped his hands. "Lots to do tonight. Early call tomorrow too. I'll wake you up. Welcome home, D.L."

He opened his arms to hug his daughter. She stiffened her body and focused her eyes on the grass, the air conditioning box, the pastel plumes of clouds overhead—anywhere but on her father.

eight

. . .

LATER THAT EVENING, beneath a blanket of stars, Sharpy gingerly stepped out into the driveway. In his hands was a very important object.

The urn.

The vessel was made of white ceramic, etched with silver decorative curls, and was about the size of a coffee pot. It was surprisingly heavy, considering there was nothing but ashes inside. A terrible scenario entered his mind. He was treating his wife's mortal remains with extreme reverence, but still ... what if she somehow *spilled out*? It was entirely possible—especially in a crowded minivan. All those bumps, jostles, and reckless bellmen could wreak havoc.

Sharpy laid the vessel on the ground, then ran back into the garage and emerged with a roll of silver duct tape. He wrapped it around the entire urn twice, crossways, intersecting at the top and the bottom. Then he opened the minivan's side door and gently laid her in the place of honor—the top of the pile of luggage in the trunk. Like a dead queen being carried high at the rear of the royal train.

Sharpy wiped his forehead and leaned backwards against the automobile. He lit a cigarette and took a deep drag.

Publicly, he maintained a strong puritanical hatred of all vice; privately, he usually tore through three packs of Marlboro Lights a week.

He stared up into the night. A sliver of moon hung like a clipped fingernail in the dark sky.

He thought about his mistress. Her flight arrived the next day from London, where she and her daughter Brittany had no doubt enjoyed a week of shopping and footloose frivolity. The murderous exchange rate wouldn't deter her. No, Vivian carried several of *his* credit cards, and so her spending wouldn't slowed by a penny, or a shilling, or a pound, or a euro, or whatever currency the British used these days.

When had they last seen each other? Sharpy thought back. It'd been almost a month. Christ. He slowly became aware of his intense sexual frustration. Sweet Jesus, she was sex incarnate. He pictured Vivian prowling towards him across her bed, the way she had that very first night, like a panther, with tendrils of black hair and thin lines of gold jewelry swaying against her shoulders and breasts. He felt sweat popping out under his scrotum. When you got right down to the nub of the matter, Vivian was a predator. That luxuriant plumage, that dazzling smile, those red nails—she was a bird-of-prey, and he was a mouse. Tomorrow she would swoop down from the sky, claws outstretched …

But this time, the tables would be turned. The predator would become prey. Vivian would find herself encased in a cocoon of perfect contentment. There would be no way out—too comfortable. Sharpy smiled as he slipped into this new fantasy. They would be on a beach. Their children playing cheerily together in the surf. Building perfect sandcastles with turrets and crenellated walls. He and Vivian would recline on striped canvas folding chairs, sipping muddled cucumber-and-watermelon rum drinks, reading useless British novels of manners. Calling each other *lovey*. Chatting with undisguised boredom about the latest run on the stock market.

Everybody happy, everybody free.

This is what his wife had wanted, in her final act of self-lessness.

He would *make his family whole again*.

He really would.

Then the reverie ended as suddenly as it had begun. Sharpy dropped the butt of his cigarette onto the cement and ground it beneath his heel. He locked the minivan and wearily returned across the dirty pavement to the house.

Tomorrow morning felt like it would never come.

nine

. . .

IT WAS EIGHT-THIRTY A.M., and the sun was lifting awkwardly from the horizon like a heavy cargo plane struggling down on a runway.

Sharpy checked his watch. He was wearing khaki shorts, a gold-and-black Geoffrey Beane polo shirt, and brand-new Reeboks. Behind him, the minivan was packed, provisioned, and oiled.

He watched D.L. stow her suitcase in the trunk and then prepare to close the hatch.

"Gently," he reminded her, mindful of her mother's urn.

"I *know*, Dad."

She closed it without difficulty. He looked back towards the house. "Could you get your brother?"

"He's already here."

Tim had appeared in the garage. He was dragging two heavy-duty black trash bags behind him on the ground, tied together in a knot.

"Tell me that's not his luggage," Sharpy said.

"I don't know."

"Dammit, I told you to help him!"

"He wouldn't *let* me!"

Frustrated already—and the minivan's wheels hadn't even moved yet—Sharpy spat on the grass. "Forget it. I'll get him a real suitcase."

He disappeared inside the house and reemerged with a battered leather understudy. When he reached for Tim's knotted polyurethane bags, the boy clutched them to his torso and fell to the ground. He howled as though being prodded with a pitchfork.

"Give me those bags," said Sharpy. "You'll never make it to Disney World with bags like that."

"He won't listen," said D.L.

Neither did Sharpy. "I said stop it!" He smacked Tim on the bottom. The autistic boy rolled back and forth, hollering out loud.

"Dad, you can't stop him from being himself," said D.L.

Sharpy calmed down. He walked away from the boy, ran a hand through his hair, squinted into the unforgiving sky. His daughter was right. *He* was the one who needed to adjust. For twelve years he'd known this. He'd always been spared the need to change his behavior because his wife had always controlled the children.

"I'm sorry, Snooker," he said. "You can bring your trash bags." He turned to his daughter. "Let's take this extra one anyways. Just in case."

Tim slid open the door, hopped inside, and—

(*a-bee-cee-dee-ee-*)

—began singing the alphabet. He always sang them when he entered an automobile.

Sharpy took his place behind the wheel, raised his seat, and adjusted his mirrors. Then he noticed D.L.'s lower lip quivering. He crooked his head. She was on the verge of tears. "What's the matter?" he asked.

"I still miss her," she said, sobbing. "I can't help missing her! She should have been here *with* us."

Sharpy touched her forearm. "She *is* with us. Turn around."

D.L. turned. There was the urn, resting in its place of honor at the top of the luggage in the back of the minivan.

Suddenly the urn was gone. In its place was her *mother*, the dead woman's corpse stuffed up in the back of the minivan like a softshell duffel bag, her cancerous skin a bright gold. Her face was grinning.

Horrified, D.L. whipped forward again. When she peeked at the rear again, her mother's corpse was gone. The urn had reappeared.

"See?" said her father. "She's right there. Watching our every mile."

D.L. turned back in her seat, pale and shaken, and said nothing. Her fingers twisted the hem of her shirt.

Tim finished the alphabet, then started again.

Sharpy peered into the rearview. "That's enough, Snooker," he said. "You've mastered the alphabet."

"Just let him *talk*," said D.L. "Don't you get it? He can't *help* himself."

Sharpy bowed his head.

"D.L., I know that he can't help it," he finally said. "But I'm not a patient man. And I admit that your brother really bugs the hell out of me sometimes. There are times, when I'm fed up, or stressed out, and Tim pulls some of his bullshit, I just ..." His fists pounded the steering wheel lightly. "I just want to smack the hell out of him."

D.L. listened closely. Her father's words were frightening but understandable. "He makes me frustrated too," she said. "Just promise me that you'll never hurt him."

"I promise," said Sharpy.

"Do you mean it?"

"You bet."

D.L. blew air out of her mouth as though she were

exhasted. She settled back in her seat. "I think we're ready to leave now."

With Tim's alphabet ringing from the backseat, Sharpy closed the garage door using the remote control that was clipped onto the sun visor. He shifted the minivan into reverse, turned out of the driveway, and drove down the street.

In the rearview mirror, D.L. watched their home shrink into nothingness.

ten

. . .

THE INDIANAPOLIS INTERNATIONAL AIRPORT is located on the southwest outer fringe of the metropolis, so that recurrent flight paths disturb the sleep of the fewest possible residents below. Planted in a brown field dotted with patches of grass and flecked with yellow dandelions, the airport swallows a continuous stream of automobiles from a nearby freeway exit.

The Craving minivan parked at the side of the concrete curb in the arrivals area.

"Shouldn't we go into the parking garage?" asked D.L.

"Their flight arrives in ten minutes," said Sharpy, looking at his watch. "We'll be fine here. I'll just put the flashers on."

The trio entered the grimy bowels of the building. D.L. hated this place. The baggage area was a long room with a tiled floor and rows of orange molded plastic Saarinen chairs and four dirty luggage carousels along the wall. Strips of radium-blue fluorescent lights ran down the length of the room. The sour smell of dirty aluminum invaded her nostrils.

Sharpy disliked it too. He'd spent more hours than he cared to admit beneath this roof during his many jaunts to Chicago. For decades, there'd been talk of building a new terminal in a nearby field, but he hadn't seen so much as a single cement mixer. It didn't matter. He wouldn't be traveling to Chicago anymore.

Not if everything went as planned with Vivian.

They passed quickly through the area and upstairs to the gate. A mass of people was already there, waiting.

"Tim wants to look at the planes," D.L. said.

"Go ahead," Sharpy answered. He was happy to be alone for a moment. He needed to prepare and rehearse his opening line. It needed to be something swift, punchy, and, above all, *domineering*. He needed to regain the upper hand over this woman—immediately.

Meanwhile, at the full-length Thermopane window overlooking the tarmac, D.L. watched as Tim developed a new ritual. He drew a square with his finger; then tapped on the aluminum partition three times. He moved to the next windowpane; drew a triangle; then tapped the next partition twice.

Following the thread into the labyrinth that was her brother's head always proved to be fruitless. So D.L.'s thoughts turned toward Vivian. She hadn't ever met her father's mistress, but she felt more skeptical nonetheless. After all, Vivian had been the object of her father's infidelity, which had indirectly led to her mother's death. There could be no rapprochement with someone who had wreaked so much havoc upon her family. And yet D.L. still felt a smidgen curious. What kind of person was Vivian? Was it possible that a teensy sliver of her was *excited* by the prospect of spending a week with an older woman? Someone who wouldn't have any of the usual moralistic hang-ups that mothers feel around their daughters?

A voice announced, "Flight 285 from New York La Guardia now arriving." People jammed themselves along the metal railing and waited for the passengers to emerge from the accordion-like gangplank.

One by one, the travelers straggled out into the arrivals area, prompting shouts from relatives in the crowd. Sharpy peered over shoulders, trying to glimpse the doorway. His palms were slick with sweat.

Then she appeared. Amid a mob of wheezing, overweight Hoosiers wearing sweatpants, windbreakers, grubby t-shirts, and running shoes, Vivian Talon looked like something else entirely—a creature from another continent, a queen of another galaxy. She was wearing a white miniskirt and a square-shouldered white jacket with three black buttons and tasteful fringe around the bottom. Underneath the jacket was a white silk blouse open to the middle of her cleavage; a string of white pearls ringed the base of her throat. D.L. admired her shapely legs—and then gasped when she saw the stunning pair of white four-inch heels on Vivian's feet. They were the most expensive pieces of leather she'd ever seen. They probably cost more than a compact car. Most impressively, she walked with a firm-lipped no-nonsense buttock-jiggling gait that was meant to provoke the sexual interest of every man within eyesight.

She was holding the hand of her daughter, Brittany, who appeared to be about four or five. Brittany was dressed in a yellow starched dress with a picture of a Royal British soldier across her tummy. Underneath a mass of blonde curls, the little girl's round face was slack and dazed. Her dainty black patent leather shoes, however, were a blur as she ran alongside her mother's brisk stride.

Sharpy made his way through the crowd and touched Vivian on the arm as she passed. She gave him a withering glance and never stopped. As though he were a leering, boil-covered wretch on a streetcorner.

"Vivian!" he shouted.

She turned—and recognized Sharpy. Immediately a wave of lightness and charm lit up her face. "Stephen!"

"Thanks for the greeting," he said.

She rolled her eyes. "Sweetie, I thought you were some-body *else*. I would never intentionally treat you like that." Her heels clickety-clacked on the floor as she flung her arms around his neck. They shared an enormous kiss. Her lips were full, soft, and rouged.

"How was the flight?" he asked.

She sighed. "Horrendous. This old woman next to me kept asking me to help with to her silly crossword puzzle. So when she finally falls asleep, Brittany's *tummy* starts hurting. Then, when Brittany finally falls asleep, I suddenly remember that I left my Chanel No. 5 on the vanity at the hotel in Piccadilly. I couldn't get a wink of sleep after *that*."

Sharpy squeezed her shoulder. "At least you're with us now. Things will get better."

She lit a cigarette. "Maybe."

He deflated. Not only had he forgotten his opening line, but she'd also wrenched the power in the relationship with one measly five-letter word. *Maybe*. He stewed with resent-ment. She'd set the relationship context, subordinated him, and implied that he needed to re-earn her favor—all in ten seconds flat.

Sharpy felt an insistent tugging on his shorts. It was the little girl. He kneeled down. "How's my little Brittany? Did she like London? Did she like the land of chipped beef?"

The little girl's eyes were overwhelmed by the huge, moonish face that now loomed inches from her own. Then her eyes wandered elsewhere. She was already, at the early stage of childhood development, displaying the attention span of a chocolate wafer. Sharpy seized her tiny hand. "Brit-tany? Did you like London? Did you see the soldiers in the fuzzy hats? Did you see them?"

But the little girl had spotted something over his shoulder. "I want one," she said.

"You want what, lovely one?" Vivian said. She bent solici-tously down toward her child.

"I want . . . one of *those*," she said, and Sharpy saw her tiny index finger extended towards a rack of spiral-shaped rainbow-colored lollipops in the gift shop across the concourse.

"You bet," he said, reaching for his wallet.

"Sugar-plum, are you sure you want one of those little ones?" Vivian said, glancing sternly at Sharpy. "We can get you a bigger lollipop later."

The girl broke into tears. "I want one of *those*!" she screamed. "I want one of *those those those those those those*! I want—"

Vivian threw her eyes upward in disgust. "Jesus, just buy her one," she said. Sharpy obediently went to the vendor, bought a lollipop, and brought it back. The little girl cried again when her tiny prehensile fingers proved unable to unwrap the treat, so Sharpy relieved her of that difficult duty. It was only when the little girl finally popped the lollipop into her mouth that her crying ceased.

"Thank God," Vivian said, unwrapping a breath mint. "Did you ever spend two straight weeks with your kids, Stephen? Twenty-four hours a day?"

"Can't say that I have."

"It's hell. Call me self-centered, but it's how I feel. And now *another* week." She sighed, looking around as her haughty cheeks sucked themselves inwards upon the candy. "Speaking of which, where are *your* children, Stephen? I can't *wait* to meet D.L." Her eyes flashed with life.

Where *were* they? Tim wasn't at the window. Scanning the concourse, Sharpy spotted his son's awkward figure spinning himself in circles, arms held straight out, like a wine bottle opener. He groaned. Those were known in the family as *whizzies*. Tim usually only performed whizzies in public places. He would spin until he fell down, and then everybody had to wait for him to regain enough balance to walk again.

"I don't know if you're ready for Tim," he said.

eleven

. . .

THIS WAS Vivian's very first visit to Sharpy's Hoosier country. Over the three years that they had been conducting their clandestine affair, the visitation had been entirely one-sided: Sharpy always traveled to Chicago. Business perks, he came to think. The traveling was hell, and in any other situation, he would have asked to be moved to the Windy City itself—but he realized that he would be robbing himself of the perfect pretext, a made-to-order alibi. It had truly been a double life, in both geographic and sexual terms.

He had met Vivian at a fundraising event in a hotel in downtown Chicago. It was one of those old-fashioned palaces built during the nineteen-thirties, when the city by the lake was riding colossally high on its architectural reputation. The elaborate cornices, the hardwood baseboards, the gilded chandeliers, the heavy mahogany—all the ornamentation had been beautifully preserved over the decades and still signaled High Society. Inside the grand ballroom, Sharpy had sucked down liver pate, swallowed three Manhattans, and shook the hands of dozens of strangers. Then . . . out of the corner of his eye . . . a swift movement . . . a flash of black hair . . . the piercing cry of the hawk as it spots the field mouse in the underbrush a thousand yards below . . . and this woman had suddenly been *right there*, in his face, smelling of the sweetest vanilla perfume, the soft light of the chandelier gleaming off her white teeth.

"Stephen Craving? My name is Vivian Talon," she had said, taking his hand. "My acquaintances"—she gestured to a knot of wealthy cosmopolites in a corner—"told me that you are an important man."

"I'm really not," he said. It was the truth.

Vivian laughed. "It must be *exhilarating*," she said, "to work inside such a profitable industry. Obviously high-tech is going to keep growing, but do you see the *rate* of growth continuing to increase for much longer?"

Sharpy had been taken aback. This splendid piece of tush could actually talk.

Which, he found out later, could also be a liability.

Nonetheless, from that point, things had followed their usual sordid course. With one exception: for the first three months, Vivian had refused to take any presents or cash offerings from her new conquest. She explained to Sharpy that Brittany's father was a high-level executive with a famous jewelry chain who had *more* than provided for her and her daughter's needs. This, of course, was highly calculated. By taking no money, she created the perception of independence, and had thus planted in Sharpy an incredible, nagging insecurity. By the time she'd finally accepted his first gift (a pink cashmere scarf), he was absolutely *burning* to cement the relationship through a display of his wealth.

Oh yes—the fish had been hooked but good. In the following years, he'd slowly grown accustomed to spending anywhere between twenty and forty thousand dollars per year on his personal piece of Chicago real estate. However, he'd also stopped believing that story about the huge child-support payments from the mysterious jewelry executive. He was pretty sure that that had been a load of blarney to throw him off the scent. Still, he couldn't figure out how Vivian really did earn her money. He certainly had never given her enough to afford the swanky two-bedroom condo on Lake Shore Drive where she lived with Brittany. (Of course, the unit was on the third floor, and overlooked a dry cleaner instead of Lake Michigan, but still . . . *Lake Shore Drive*.) How *did* she support herself? You couldn't say that she sold herself entirely. And yet no jury would believe that she was a Sunday school teacher either. As deeply as he was enraptured by that creamy flesh, those juicy bosoms, those Greek gams . . . he was forced to entertain the possibility that he was not her only slavering suitor.

That's when the realization had dawned on him that Vivian was very, very clever—craftier, in fact, than any other woman he'd ever met.

He'd gotten it partly right.

The truth was that she was smarter than *anybody* he had ever *known*.

twelve

. . .

IN THE AIRPORT CONCOURSE, she approached the spinning boy just as he fell backwards onto the tiled floor. D.L. was standing next to him with her arms still folded and her eyes cocked upwards towards the ceiling and her lips pursed tightly.

"D.L.," her father said, "I would like you to meet Vivian. Vivian, D.L."

"It's a pleasure to finally *meet* you!" Vivian said in a super-friendly voice, offering her hand. With some women you could see through that voice, hear the phoniness beneath it, but not hers. She was an amazing actress.

"Hi," the teenage girl said. She couldn't meet Vivian's eyes, so she stared down at the floor.

"You're thinner than your father led me to believe."

"Yeah, Dad thinks I'm fat."

Sharpy exploded. "Donna Louise Craving I *never*—"

"You did too!" A note of hysteria climbed into the girl's voice and hovered there. "Remember the time when you came into the kitchen and I was eating and you said that if I wasn't careful our food bill was going to double? Remember? *Remember*?"

Sharpy dug deeply into his memory vault. He vaguely remembered saying something like that to her years ago, but it had been because she'd been digging into some very expensive tapenade that Felicia had been saving for Sunday dinner. His remark hadn't had anything to do with the *quantity* of the food she was eating, it'd had to do with the *quality*... Oh forget it. This was a lose-lose situation. D.L. *had* gained a few pounds, but at times like these you couldn't comfort girls using logic. There were no reasons, no explanations, no syllogisms that could reassure them. You just had to offer hugs and hope that they would eventually become more secure in their own skins. Even his own daughter.

"I can't believe you remember that," he said.

"How could I forget when my father calls me a fatso?"

"I think you're beautiful," Vivian offered, and the ruthless smile appeared on her face. "But a woman can always stand to lose ten pounds."

D.L. looked at her father's mistress. She had no weight to spare whatsoever. She'd have to surgically remove her liver to lose ten pounds. What *had* her father done to land this fish? She was *gorgeous!* And her clothing was top-notch, the couture found in glossy magazines. That black-and-white ensemble had cost at least a thousand dollars. D.L. thought about her own clothing and felt a touch of embarrassment. She was wearing a gray t-shirt, military-issue cargo pants (she owned ten pairs), and Teva sandals. Her blonde hair was pushed up onto the back of her head with a black clip.

Meanwhile, at their feet, Tim was rolling helplessly like an upside-down beetle. Sharpy pulled him to his feet, while Vivian formally presented her hand.

"I'm Vivian," she said. "What's your name?"

The boy stared out the window, his face averted.

"Go ahead," said Sharpy. "Shake her hand."

"Timothy, you handsome boy," Vivian said, "why don't

you let me see your face." She touched him lightly on the shoulder—

(*ah ah ah*)

—and a deafening scream suddenly escaped his throat. Vivian jerked her hand back and stuffed it into her pocket. The scream ended as abruptly as it had begun. The boy's finger was furiously drawing intricate patterns in the air.

Vivian quickly walked away. She pulled out a pair of jet-black glossy wraparound sunglasses from her purse and placed them on her face and looked the opposite way.

"I don't know what's wrong with him," said Sharpy. "He's usually good with strangers."

"I'm sure he is," Vivian said coldly.

"Mommy," Brittany said, tugging at the hem of her mother's blazer, "I want one of those." She was pointing at a jewelry stand.

"Finish your lollipop," Sharpy said, "and then we'll see what we can do about buying jewelry."

"I think you should get her what she wants, Stephen," said Vivian. "You can consider it a down payment."

Sharpy understood immediately. As a reward for participating in the journey, he had promised Vivian an immediate ten thousand dollars out of the inheritance. Which is why he found himself shelling out three dollars for a low-grade imitation gold necklace at the jewelry cart.

He put the trinket around Brittany's neck and he fumbled with the clasp at the back.

"Isn't it pretty," he said halfheartedly.

"It's *beautiful*," Vivian agreed.

"D.L., this is Brittany," Sharpy said.

"Hi, Brittany," the teenager said, bending down to the little girl. Brittany was adorable—she'd probably turn out to be gorgeous—but D.L. was already astute enough to recognize a future bitch when she saw one. It didn't take a counselor to see that Brittany was flat-out, no-holds-barred, unredeemably *spoiled*.

"We should probably get on the road," Sharpy said.

thirteen

. . .

THEY STOPPED at the carousel to retrieve Vivian's luggage, which consisted of four pieces of chocolate-colored leather with cream-colored suede trim. Brittany had three tiny floral bags. A porter piled all six onto an aluminum cart and followed the family out to the curb, staring lasciviously at Vivian's twitching rear end as she walked.

Sharpy threw an arm across Vivian's shoulders. "Have you thought about what we talked about the other night?"

"What was that?"

"About spending more time with us."

She crinkled her eyebrow. "I'm here, aren't I? For a whole week. Isn't that enough?"

"I mean, *after* the trip."

"Not really."

He pulled her closer, angled his head, and whispered into her ear: "I'd love to make this a very *special* trip for the two of us. Do you know what I mean?"

She lit another cigarette and couldn't meet his eyes. "It's been a long flight—"

"Do you know what I mean?"

The corner of Vivian's mouth turned up in a cruel manner. "You're quite the Casanova this afternoon."

"No," Sharpy said, "Casanova only seduced them. I'm a more ... *permanent* kind of guy. Do you get me?" He attempted a suave grin.

Vivian stayed diplomatically vague. "Maybe."

Maybe. That devilish two-syllable word again. He shook with resentment. If they were playing poker, then she was dealing all the cards—and she knew it.

———

When they reached the outside curb, the minivan was still there, its orange flashers blinking. "See," he said to D.L., "I *told* you it would be okay to park there."

As he said this, an airport security van pulled up behind the minivan and a guard wearing an official black windbreaker hopped out. He was carrying a clipboard.

"Hey there," Sharpy said.

"You're parked illegally," the guard replied.

"We were just leaving."

"Been there for twenty-five minutes, unattended," the guard said. "I ignored it the first time cause I'm in a good mood today." He held his radio up to his lips, called for a ten-twenty, then gave a description of the minivan and its license tag number.

Vivian stared daggers at her paramour. Sharpy knew that she always expected red carpet treatment, and that most definitely didn't include public citations. She wordlessly swept past the guard and flounced into the front seat, slamming the door.

"We're just leaving," Sharpy said. "We're actually on our way to Florida."

"Oh, I've heard all them stories," the guard said. "It's a funeral in Virginia. A wedding in Minnesota. An earthquake in Los Angeles knocked out power to your father's hardware store. This here ole dog used to be a traffic cop and believe me it was like sittin' in grade school story hour every day of the week. I'm gonna write a book someday." He was looking at the license plate and copying down the number onto his clipboard.

"Thanks for your advice," Sharpy said. He motioned for the porter to start stowing the luggage in the back. Then he helped the three children into the back seat and got in the driver's seat.

The security guard wasn't fazed. He walked around the car and lowered his face to the open driver's side window. "Be advised, sir, that if you decide to leave before the tow truck arrives, you will be charged the cost of the service."

"How much is it?"

"One hundred and thirty-seven dollars."

Sharpy smirked. "Send me a bill. We're on our way to make a million dollars."

His foot jammed on the accelerator, the tires screeched, and the minivan pulled away from the curb.

The guard watched the family disappear towards the interstate. He adjusted his cap and walked over to the porter. "Coulda used the boot, but that woman was lookin' like she was fit to kill somebody."

The porter wiped his nose. "I wasn't lookin' at her face."

"Did you see that boy? Somethin' queer there."

"They were assholes," the porter said with finality. "You couldn't pay me enough to take a vacation with them peoples." He thought for a moment. "'less, of course, it was just me and the missus."

fourteen

. . .

THE FAMILIES ARE ON VACATION.

They rush down from the industrial north, from Dover, from Albany, from Boston, down that two-thousand-mile-long ribbon of black, I-95—thin, cold-blooded families with Old World pedigrees and stiff diplomas and silver tongues plated in irony, passing down through Philadelphia and Washington and Richmond.

They rush down from the shuttered manufacturing plants of the Great Lakes, from Illinois, from Michigan, from Ohio, down I-75—plump, cheese-fed families with reddened cheeks and hair the color of hay bales, passing down through Dayton and Lexington and Atlanta.

They rush down from points west, from Little Rock, from Tulsa, from Houston, down I-10—the sunburnt crewcut families with ballots in their Bibles, passing down through New Orleans and Mobile and Biloxi, their windows rolled down to inhale the sad, sweet, fishy smell of ruin.

A handful of locals turn onto the freeways for a few miles, but they quickly turn off. For it is the *families* who own the interstates.

They are on vacation.

The families pump fossil fuel into their vehicles—their quiet sedans, their robust sport utility vehicles, their snouted minivans, their high-chested cruisers, their recreational vehicles, their Fords, Pontiacs, Chevrolets, Hondas, Toyotas, Winnebagos. They drag Coachmen trailers behind full-throated trucks. They drive through the day and half the night, snatching sleep on unfamiliar mattresses at roadside motels. And when the first rays of dawn peek between the musty curtains, they drive on, fast-food breakfasts settling inside their bellies like lumps of clay.

They are on vacation.

Other families, families with higher incomes—those families climb into silver airliners that lift them into the sky, and as the descent begins, the children press their noses to the glass to peer down at the alien blue lakes, the emerald green jungles. On the ground the fathers pay for shiny rented automobiles with firm, clean, unused seats—and they too join the rush on the interstates.

And still other families come from nations much farther afield—from Germany to Jordan, from Seoul to Sydney, from Quito to Qatar.

The state of Florida—especially the Orlando area—is the number-one tourist destination in the world. Sixty million visitors every year. Enough to eliminate the state income tax. Just skin the tourists. An extra five percent here, six percent there.

Spain weeps.

Paris protests.

New York shrugs.

It is the Santiago of the century, the Xanadu of the *zeitgeist*, the Jerusalem of the jet age.

It is Orlando.

fifteen

. . .

THE MINIVAN BLAZED SOUTHWARD from Indiana
for two straight days. Sharpy became an absolute terror
behind the wheel, weaving through clumps of cars, passing
stragglers in every lane, pushing the needle to lands far
beyond eighty. They passed the night in a seedy motel in
southern Georgia for thirty-two dollars, and Sharpy hadn't
slept even an hour. He'd lain there awake all night, aware of
the leggy heft of Vivian's slumbering thighs, while their three
children lay snoring all around them. There was no remedy
for that situation except a cold shower.

Early in the morning they blazed on. Now the minivan
was finally pulling off the endless freeway.

They turned onto a quiet two-lane road. Passing overhead
were thick, beautiful strands of blue-gray Spanish moss that
hung from the branches of magnolias like the hair of a four-
teen-year-old debutante.

They'd arrived in the turpentine-stained heart of backwater Florida.

"What's your father's name again?" Vivian asked, as the
sunlight from the trees dappled across her thighs. She had
assumed the front passenger seat, displacing D.L. to the

back bench—an insult which glittered clearly in the girl's eyes.

"Frederick," said Sharpy.

She nodded. "Just like the king."

"Who?"

"Frederick I. He was king of Prussia."

Sharpy thought hard, trying to remember his geography lessons. "Prussia? Isn't that one of those old Soviet states?"

He saw Vivian wince. Then she said, very evenly, as though trying to control her temper: "No, Prussia doesn't exist anymore. It broke up after the First World War, almost a hundred years ago."

He felt a faint twinge of embarrassment. Were you supposed to *know* where Prussia had been? Was *not* having an encyclopedic knowledge of European states considered a social gaffe? He was sure that none of his friends would be able to say the first thing about Prussia. Sharpy decided that Vivian was intentionally trying to make him feel inferior. That was a fool's errand, however, since he controlled the checkbook. He would *never* again be ground beneath her heel.

Around a curve, he spotted the home's sign. *Village Palms at Winter Haven: An Assisted Living Community.*

It was a long, rambling one-story spread, constructed without any consideration for the indigenous history of the southern region—simple walls of red brick, surmounted by a black shingled roof. The driveway you would pass without noticing. It was the architectural equivalent of tuna casserole at a potluck dinner.

Sharpy parked the car along the retirement home's circular drive. He stretched his hamstrings on the pavement. Vivian was pawing for more breath mints in her purse. When the back door slid open, the three children tumbled out of the back seat onto the green lawn.

"Wake up, gang," said Sharpy. "We're in Florida. Isn't that exciting?"

"How long is this going to take?" D.L. complained.

"Not long," he said. He sensed the displeasure in her voice. "I know that an old folks' home isn't exactly our favorite place. But let's all try to act happy to see Grandma and Grandpa."

"I don't really want to go inside."

"Your grandparents are waiting for us."

Her lip curled and her toe dug into the pavement. "Grandma probably doesn't even remember me anyways."

That was entirely possible. She was losing her mind, after all. Plus, neither Sharpy nor his children had seen, heard, or even mentioned the family's grandparents since the funeral six months earlier. You couldn't say that their relationship had been especially cordial to begin with.

"Maybe so," he said, "but we have to look sharp because…"

His voice trailed off as he noticed that the buttons on Tim's shirt were misaligned. The buttons and the eyes were misaligned.

"Snooker, fix your shirt," he said.

"He always does it like that," said D.L., inspecting a fingernail.

"Since when?"

"It's Tuesday."

"He always screws up his shirt on Tuesday?"

"Yep."

His daughter was invaluable. No matter how much attention he paid to Tim's habits, she would always know him better. "Well," he said, "we should still always try to look our best." His fingers pushed his already-tucked shirt further down into the recesses of his pants.

He turned to Vivian. "Are you almost ready?"

She was reapplying her mascara in the mirror of her compact makeup case. "In a minute. I have to look my best." She moistened her lips. "After all, I *am* meeting your parents."

He took her compact from her hands and closed it. "You're *beautiful*."

She grabbed it back. "I don't believe you."

"I'm serious. My dad is going to completely fall in love with you."

She stuffed the compact into her luxurious purse and zipped it shut. "Fine. Flattery will get you everywhere."

Together, the five members of the group stepped beneath the shaded portico. The double doors opened automatically.

sixteen

· · ·

IN THE AIR-CONDITIONED VESTIBULE, a woman behind a small secretary desk looked up from a magazine. "Welcome to the Village Palms, how can I help you today?"

"We're here for Frederick and Maya Craving," Sharpy said.

"Are you family?"

"I'm their son."

"Really?"

"Yesss," Sharpy said testily.

"Hm." The woman squared her folder. "Your father has never mentioned you."

Meanwhile, D.L. surveyed the sunny atrium. There was a large tree growing in a planter covered in woodchips, and a waterfall tinkled into a small flagstone pool. A few ancient residents toddled by—their crooked, swollen hands clutching the handles of their walkers with split-open tennis balls on the back bottom ends. The decaying odor of slightly fetid cheese was everywhere.

This was the place where time got tangled up in its own feet, she thought, where people lay down like sun-beaten dogs and gave up the struggle.

Then she felt a peculiar prickling at the back of her neck, as though she were being watched.

Behind her, four elderly residents—all women—were studying the newcomers through cloudy cataract eyes. They wore crocheted cardigans, and the wispy white hair floated above their heads like cumulus clouds. Two of them were sitting in motorized wheelchairs. A third was knitting with unsteady hands what seemed to be a diseased kidney. The fourth was holding a plastic bottle to the mouth of an infant doll.

Embarrassed, the teenager glanced away.

"Somebody's got visitors," mumbled Number One.

There was a long pause while the broken synapses jerked and fired up inside the other three skulls.

Number Two piped up: "Who do you think they're here to see?"

Number Three looked up from the knitting. Her pupils focused on D.L. "Now she's a pleasant-looking girl."

Sheer panic flashed through D.L.'s body. *Pleasant*? She looked *pleasant*? Why couldn't she look *vivacious*? Or at least *pretty*? Some other adjective!

By this time, the secretary had signed in the family, and D.L. found herself following her father down a long gray hallway with two railings conspicuously bolted along the sides. The better to hang from.

The doors of the private rooms were decorated with fond remembrances of youthful days; "Welcome to the Woods" read one, with twigs glued around the peephole. New arrivals displayed posters titled "About Me." The elderly resident filled in her favorite food, color, music, television show, every little cherished piece of her world—and then tacked it outside her room.

The posters were enough to take D.L.'s breath away. To a teenager who'd never seen the inside of a retirement home, they looked *exactly* like kindergarten assignments. The shape of a person's life was like a sandwich, D.L. thought. The middle years could be filled with anything, but ages three and eighty-three were the same thin slices of bread. They were the bookends holding up the story of your existence.

"Here we are," Sharpy said, coming up to a door marked *Frederick and Maya Craving*. The mere sight of his father's printed name sent his stomach into loop-de-loops. His hands clenched and unclenched.

D.L. noticed rivulets of perspiration running down the creases of his face. "Dad? Are you all right?"

"I'm fine," Sharpy said. "Couldn't be better."

"You're not nervous?"

He wiped his upper lip on the banded edge of his yellow short-sleeve polo shirt. "No. Yes. I don't know." What an idiotic answer. He was supposed to be their *leader*! Father knows best! Right?

Instead, he stood looking dumbly at the door, gathering up his courage.

"Do you want me to knock?" said D.L.

"How's everyone feeling?" he asked, turning away from the door. "Snooker? You've been so quiet. And Brittany? How's my little pooky-wooky bear?"

Vivian planted a sassy foot sideways. "Stephen, stop stalling and knock on the goddamned door."

But he was dandling Brittany in his arms and conveniently didn't hear her order. Huffing, his mistress reached over and rapped on the door herself.

Inside, a faint voice said something indistinguishable.

"It sounded like Grandma," said D.L. "She said come in."

The teenager pushed down the stainless steel handle. It opened. A second later, she entered her grandparents' room.

seventeen

. . .

INSIDE THE CHAMBER, the sunlight was transformed into a muted glow as it swam through the heavy yellowish lace curtains that had been drawn across the windows. There was an acidic, mummified smell from the brocade Queen Anne's furniture: a double bed with yellowing dust-ruffles; a sagging curio cabinet with dusty ceramic figurines of circus animals; an ornate dresser with cracked finish; a pair of nightstands.

"Hello?" said D.L.

There was a noise behind the musty dressing partition in the corner—and then an elderly woman in a wheelchair rolled out.

Grandma Maya.

She was wearing a pink pillbox hat and a cement-colored trenchcoat. Blue eye shadow was smeared across her eyelids as though a toddler had tried to color them. Most glaring, however, was the old woman's osteoporosis. Grandma Maya was curled up like a boiled shrimp. She probably needed safety straps to keep from falling out of her chair. D.L. winced compassionately. Her grandmother was still hanging on. You had to respect that.

D.L. turned and beckoned to the family. Sharpy gingerly stepped into the room—

then brightened up as he realized Grandpa Frederick wasn't there.

"Mom!" he said.

"Who's that?" she said.

"It's me. Stephen."

The old woman squinted. Sharpy burst out in aggravation: "Your *son*, Mom. Remember? We were coming to pick you up today?"

"Your father's not here," she said. "He'll be back from the office at noon."

"Dad doesn't have an office anymore."

"Don't you tell me your father doesn't have an office!" She shook a stern finger up towards Sharpy's face. "He's had an office all his life! Now give me a hug!"

She opened her arms, and Sharpy grudgingly embraced his mother. She felt even more fragile than the last time he'd seen her. He couldn't detect any muscle tone whatsoever. Her arms were withered. She'd become a bag of bones and guts.

He took his daughter by the arm. "Ma, you remember D.L.?"

Grandma Maya squinted her eyes at the teenager and said, "Are you a boy or a girl?"

"Ma, she's your *granddaughter*!" said Sharpy.

The old woman grew annoyed. "She's wearing a boy's pants!"

"These are cargo pants," said D.L. "Everybody wears them."

The old lady dismissed her with a wave of her hand. "They're *hobo* pants."

Sharpy diplomatically switched grandkids and grabbed his son's arm. "And this is Tim. Do you remember Tim? He was born autistic. Remember?"

Tim was flapping his arms—

(*It smells like gravy in the Retire Ease home where we will pick them up. It does not smell like gravy outside the Retire Ease home where we will not pick them up. It smells like gravy in the*)

—and moving his lips silently.

Grandma Maya fell into a reverent hush when she saw the boy. She wheeled her chair over and peered into his face. "He's one of God's children," she said.

D.L. could see her brother taking quick peripheral glances at the elderly woman in the wheelchair.

"Can you see me?" Grandma Maya said.

"He can see you," said Sharpy. "But he probably won't talk."

The boy sandwiched himself in the corner of the room, between the large rosewood dresser and the musty wall. Like a dunce.

"Give me your hand," Grandma Maya croaked.

"It's okay, Snooker," said D.L.

"Give me your hand," the old woman said.

The boy was screwing up his face tightly. "Can't," he said.

"Why not?" said D.L.

"Only two."

Tim didn't comprehend language with metaphorical meanings, such as idioms or connotations; he only understood literal meanings. He thought that his grandmother was asking to chop off one of his hands.

Grandma Maya finally succeeded in touching his palm and holding it. He started flapping his other arm like a trapped bird. Sharpy watched them with interest. He knew that his mother had been gifted with a certain degree of psychic ability. She could size up people with incredible intuition. Now, as Grandma Maya held on to her grandson, he slowly quit flapping.

The old woman squinched her eyes shut. Then she shivered as though a frightening surge of energy were shooting through her arm, and her eyes widened—

(*that Bear is gonna get you*)

—as though she were having a vision. She suddenly dropped his hand. Her eyes grew immensely wide. Panicking, she turned her wheelchair around and rolled behind the partition on the other side of the room.

"That boy's touched," she said.

Sharpy wondered what had been exchanged between them. But then the door opened, and he forgot everything except for the fact that the last member of the group—the final piece of the puzzle, the key to the inheritance—was entering the room.

Grandpa Frederick.

eighteen

. . .

"THE ATTENDANTS TOLD me that my son was here," the old man's baritone announced. "Now, why he arrived at eleven-thirty is inconceivable. I specifically told him that we wouldn't be ready until after one o'clock."

Grandpa Frederick was hanging his thin jacket onto an antique freestanding coat rack. A silver-haired man with the slim physique of a protractor, he wore a checked-plaid shirt with a sturdy pen clipped squarely in the pocket. From his belt descended a pair of Sansabelt slacks that had been ironed to an obedient crease, and which ended squarely upon a pair of immaculate brown Rockport loafers. His eyeballs were magnified by the lenses of the steel eyeglasses that were perched at the end of his nose. His face was severe.

Then he set down a briefcase on the ground. D.L. wondered why her grandfather carried a briefcase if he was retired.

Sharpy trembled behind his mother's wheelchair. Vivian kicked him in the ankle.

"Sorry, Dad," he said. "I guess we just couldn't wait to see you."

Grandpa Frederick finally looked up, as though he were

finally prepared to acknowledge the existence of other people in the room. "Stephen," he said, looking over the tops of his glasses, "it's good to see you too."

He proffered his strong hand. Sharpy moved forward and gripped the old man's palm. The other family members watched their awkward handshake. When they separated, he quickly stepped back with his eyes cast upon the ground.

"Dad, you remember your granddaughter, D.L.," said Sharpy.

"Of course. It's been a while since I saw her last." The old man's eyes traced the outline of D.L.'s figure. "It's good to see a girl who's not afraid to carry some meat on her bones."

Not again! D.L. felt her shoulders slump down again. Everybody in this bone locker was hell-bent on destroying her self-esteem! First she was *pleasant* looking. Then she was indistinguishable from a boy. Now she's packing on weight like a Christmas ham.

Grandpa didn't notice the distress he'd caused. "If I could give awards, you'd have 'em all. Quite attractive, young lady."

"She's got enough awards," Sharpy said. "You should see the top of her dresser at home. Tell Grandpa about academic decathalon." He stopped as he noticed that D.L. was fighting back tears.

The old man turned to Tim, whose fingers were compulsively twisting his pants into little corsages of fabric. Grandpa crossed his arms and cocked his head while studying the boy. "Timothy." Finally he turned to Sharpy: "Is he getting any better?"

"It doesn't get any better," Sharpy said.

"Still?"

"Never. There's no cure."

Grandpa harrumphed. "There's always a cure. We just haven't worked hard enough yet to find it."

Vivian couldn't tolerate being ignored any longer. She

stepped forward. "Frederick, I'm Vivian Talon," she said, shaking Grandpa's hand with a fierce grip, "and it is an *absolute* pleasure to finally meet you. Sharpy has told me *all* about what a *challenging* father you have been."

Confronted with the dazzling white smile, the curvaceous figure, the powerful mane of black hair, Grandpa Frederick did what hundreds of men before him had done to that iron fist beneath the feminine glove. He submitted.

"It's . . . a, a, a ... real pleasure, Miss Talon," the old man stammered, obviously flustered. "You look like . . . what was the name of that movie star?" He turned to his wife. "Maya? What's the name of that movie star. I can't remember."

"Which one?" said Grandma.

"The one that we saw in the, you remember, the, uh—" His memory failed him.

Vivian interrupted. "I'm sure she was beautiful," she said. "Movie stars of yesteryear were the most elegant creatures on earth."

"Absolutely," said Grandpa.

"I'd like you to meet Brittany, my daughter."

Grandpa Frederick took off his glasses as he stared down at the blonde cherub. "What a beautiful little girl," he said.

"Tell him what you want to do when you grow up," ordered Vivian.

"I wanna make bracelets," said Brittany.

Grandpa Frederick chuckled in the fake, hollow way of someone who is tolerating somebody else's stupid idea. "Jewelry is a cutthroat business, little girl. Tell you what." He crouched down. "You just stay beautiful, and everything will be just fine. How's that?" He pinched her cheek and winked.

D.L. felt a little sick. Her own grandfather was a cultural dinosaur, condescending and paternalistic.

Vivian apparently felt that way too. She scooped up Brittany and spoke to her face-to-face. "Don't listen to him, sweetheart. You can always have whatever you want because you *deserve* it. Even if you were ugly."

Grandpa faced his son's mistress directly and pulled himself up to his fullest height. "Don't knock being beautiful, young lady. It's worked pretty well for you."

A brushfire leapt up in Vivian's eyes. Sharpy quickly stepped between them to head off the argument. "Is anybody hungry? Does anybody want some lunch?"

"No," said Vivian.

"Me neither," said D.L.

There was silence. Then Grandma said, "I could use some hashbrowns."

Sharpy clapped his hands. "Let's get some hashbrowns for Grandma. Let's have a nice lunch. Come on, everybody."

Reluctantly, the family filed into the hallway and prepared for lunch at the assisted-living home.

nineteen

. . .

AFTER BUYING meal tickets from the woman in the vestibule, the seven members of the Craving family walked to the dining room. They passed televisions playing laundry detergent commercials to entire rooms of snoring senior citizens. D.L. crossed her arms over her chest. She felt uncomfortable here. These decaying specimens, their heads blanketed with white furze, sleeping away their precious time left on earth—they made her feel perversely *ashamed* of her health.

In the spacious dining room, there were about fifty mahogany tables underneath soft-lit chandeliers. Lunch had just started, and the residents—mostly female—were staggering into the room like slow zombies in a horror movie. The few male residents of the home were crowded into a small ghetto near the kitchen doors.

Grandpa Frederick pushed Grandma to their regular table where her silverware with extra-large wooden handles had already been laid out. "Son, you and Vivian and I can eat over here with Grandma. The children can have their own table."

D.L. helped Tim and Brittany to an adjacent table. A

chunky black girl dressed in whites glopped their food onto white china plates.

"What's for lunch?" D.L. asked.

"Pork loins, mashed potatoes, green beans, and apple-sauce," she replied. Her bored tone said that she'd rather be pulling the slots in Vegas.

Over at the adults' table, Sharpy and Grandpa Frederick were eating with the mechanical silence of men who have nothing to say to each other. Across the tablecloth, Vivian put a teensy morsel of pork into her mouth, made a face, and pushed her plate away.

The old man noticed. Chewing like a stockyard animal, he pointed to her plate with his fork. "What's the matter? Don't like meat and potatoes?"

"She's on a diet," Sharpy said.

"What for?"

He shrugged. "She always is."

"I can speak for myself, Stephen," said Vivian. She faced her tormentor with dignity: "Frederick, a woman can always stand to lose ten pounds. That's why I don't eat."

The old man didn't reply. He just looked at her queerly, as though she were the neighborhood weirdo fashioning a swan out of aluminum foil. Then he shook his head and scooped applesauce into his mouth.

Grandma noticed Sharpy pushing around the mashed potatoes on his plate. She leaned forward and gripped his elbow with her gnarled fingers. "I remember you pushing around your mashed potatoes just like that when you were a little boy," she said.

"I still don't care for them," he said.

"Land o' goshen, there's so much to reminisce about. Isn't there, Frederick?

Mouth full, Grandpa Frederick only grunted.

"Oh, your father never has liked to discuss the past. He's always looking into the future. Not me." She settled back in her chair with a contented, ambrosial expression on her face. "Remember when you got into that big fight in high school, Sharpy?"

Sharpy was startled. Of all the paths crisscrossing memory lane, this was one that he hadn't expected his mother to tread.

"Skally McCready," he said. "That wasn't a fight. That was an attempted murder."

"It sure was. You almost killed him, the principal said."

Sharpy lifted his hands in the air. "He almost killed *me*! He started *every*thing! I was just defending myself!"

Grandma chuckled. "Oh, they said you just kept hitting him with a soda bottle, over and over—"

"You never told me about this," Vivian said.

"He attacked me with a crowbar!" Sharpy protested. "Besides, this was almost thirty years ago. What does that have to do with anything today?"

"Your mother brought it up," Vivian said.

The elderly woman in question was peering at the black-haired vixen as though for the first time. "Who the hell are you?"

"I think I forgot to introduce you earlier," said Sharpy. "Ma, this is Vivian."

"It's my pleasure," Vivian said. She shifted uncomfortably as the old woman's probing eyes bore deep into her soul.

"She's a whore," announced Grandma Maya.

Sharpy threw down his silverware noisily. "Ma, please! You don't even know her."

But Grandma was unrepentant. "I feel it in my bones. She's let in more men than a turnstile."

"Maya, that's obscene!" thundered Grandpa Frederick.

The argument was interrupted by a woman in whites pushing a medicine cart through the dining room. She pulled up alongside Grandma. "Hello there, Maya. How's my favorite bright young thing this afternoon?"

"Who's there?" said the old woman, trying to twist around.

"It's Darlene, with your medication," the woman said loudly, putting one hand on Grandma's shoulder. She marked something on a chart.

Grandma grimaced and motioned Darlene away. "You can keep your poison," she said.

"Maya, this medicine is keeping you healthy," said Grandpa.

Grandma Maya sent her husband a contemptuous look.

"Frederick's right," said the nurse. "Swallow this pill, dear." She was holding out a small paper cup. Grandma shook her head.

"Maya, swallow that pill," Grandpa instructed. "I'll do it too." He turned to the nurse and said with a broad wink, "Darlene, give me one of those." The nurse handed him another paper cup, winking back. Grandma Maya watched her husband as he placed the pill into his mouth and swallowed it with a long swig of water.

"You're trying to trick me," she said.

"No ma'am," Grandpa said. "I just want you to be happy and healthy."

Hearing this, Grandma softened. She accepted the pill with trembling hands, lifted her water glass to her lips, and swallowed the medication.

Meanwhile, Grandpa leaned into Sharpy and whispered, "Don't worry. I've got it all arranged."

Sharpy cocked his head. "What do you mean?"

Grandpa smiled wickedly. "Your mother won't take her anti-depressant unless I do, so the nurse gives me a placebo. She gets the real thing." He winked and smiled.

"So you're not on any medication?"

"Are you kidding?" the old man boasted. "I don't need that stuff."

twenty

. . .

LATER, after the plates had been cleared, Sharpy and Grandpa Frederick remained alone at the table. The three children had decamped to the game room. In a surprising departure, Vivian had volunteered to push Grandma Maya around the dining room to visit with her friends.

Sharpy felt himself chomping at the bit. They'd arrived at eleven-thirty, and it was now almost two o'clock. He'd chatted for hours with the old coot, avoiding the conversational elephant in the corner of the room, and now his thoughts—like moths to the flame—were flitting back to the real reason underlying this trip. That is, the thousands of dollars that his checkbook was hemorrhaging each month. How much longer could he last? Two months? Three? Without his wife's inheritance, his entire estate would sink into the quicksand of bankruptcy.

He interlaced his fingers behind his head in an exaggeratedly relaxed fashion. "So, Dad, we'd like to leave this afternoon, if that's okay."

"Fine by me," said the old man, "but your mother may not be ready to go."

Sharpy bit his lower lip and felt impatience gathering.

"When we talked, you said she was fit enough to travel anywhere."

"That was two months ago," his father said.

"You said the same thing last week."

"She's very unstable," said Grandpa Frederick. "Her blood pressure is extremely high. And there's always her diabetes."

"Do you know how much this journey is worth to this family?"

"Yes," Grandpa said. "But here's my question." He leaned forward: "What's it worth to *me*?" His eyebrows furrowed, and his face had become hawklike.

Sharpy couldn't believe it. Was he being *blackmailed* by his own father? This man was at the end of the rope of life! Five minutes to midnight! What could Grandpa Frederick *possibly* want with more money? He had few expenses, bought no clothing, took no vacations, no longer even ventured past the front porch of the retirement home.

"What are you saying, Dad?"

"I'm saying that taking your mother out of this home is a risk her health. So it better be for a damn good reason."

Sharpy crumbled. Coming clean, being honest, playing for pity—these were the best possible options. He sighed loudly. "I would be able to keep my house," Sharpy said. "I would be able to keep my car. I would have money for D.L.'s college education—"

"You would pay off your credit card debt."

"That too."

"Vivian's got you over a barrel, doesn't she?"

"You could say that."

"How much do you owe?"

Sharpy couldn't admit exactly how high she'd rung his balances. It was too painful to even think about. He squirmed uneasily. Grandpa Frederick's entire life had been lived with a single purpose in mind: earning money. Maximizing solvency.

Maintaining financial rectitude. Other people might shrug off Sharpy's worries, but his father would *feel* the urgency.

As it turned out, Sharpy didn't even need to answer. His father banged his palms down onto the table. "It doesn't matter," he said. "You're my son, and no matter how prodigal you may be, I can't stand to see you like this. But there is one condition."

Sharpy had felt this coming. His father was renowned for delivering gifts-with-a-catch.

The old man pointed a thick, callused finger at Sharpy: "You have to stand up to that woman! Take charge! Let her know that you are the man—and that you won't be led around like a dog on a chain!"

"I will."

"The woman has to do what the man says!"

"Absolutely, Dad."

Sharpy was spared any further macho cheerleading by the return of Vivian pushing a slumbering Grandma Maya. "I didn't know what to do," Vivian said.

Grandpa Frederick touched his wife's arm gently. "Maya, wake up. We have to get ready to leave."

The old woman stirred in her chair. "Where are we going?"

"We're going to Disney World. We'll sit on the benches together."

"No, I don't think so," she said.

"Well, you ought to get ready anyways."

"I don't feel like going," she said. "The boy . . . he showed me about that."

"About what?"

"He showed me," she said.

Grandpa shrugged at Sharpy. "I don't know what she's talking about."

"Mom," said Sharpy, "we need your help so we can win some money for the family."

The old woman shook her head. "I don't want to go anywhere. I feel sick."

"But you look great!" said Sharpy.

"Come on," Grandpa said, "let's get you ready for the car ride." He stood up and, gripping the handles of her wheelchair, started to pull her away from the table.

But her wizened hands suddenly landed with such great force on the table that the coffee cups rattled.

"I want to stay *here*!" she said.

"Do you want everybody to hear you?" said Grandpa, clamping a hand on her shoulder. "You're embarrassing us!"

"Don't touch me!" she protested loudly.

The few remaining diners had grown quiet. Their rheumy eyes watched Grandpa as he pushed her into the hallway.

Sharpy and Vivian exchanged glances. Darlene the medication nurse had watched the exchange and approached them. "For the record," she said, "I have *never* seen your mother act like that before. What did you tell her?"

"We told her she was going to Disney World," Sharpy said.

"So odd," she said. "Maya's usually so well-behaved."

Sharpy touched her arm. "By the way, I guess I owe you a big fruit basket for cooperating with my father."

"About what?"

"That trick."

She cocked her head. "What trick?"

"The placebo trick." Sharpy winked at her. "You know."

"No, I don't."

"He told me how you give him placebos to get my mother to swallow the real pills."

"He told you that?" said Darlene. She chuckled to herself. "I thought he would have realized by now."

Sharpy's eyebrows lifted. "Realized what?"

"It's not a placebo," the nurse said. "Their doctor prescribed anti-depressants to both of them. But Frederick wouldn't take them, and when your mother saw him refuse, she refused too. So now we tell him that his pill is just a placebo."

"Really?"

"Absolutely, Mister Craving," the nurse said, smiling. "Both your parents are on Zoloft. They always have been."

twenty-one

. . .

"WE'RE ALL READY," Grandma Maya announced.

The old woman was in her wheelchair, a cardigan sweater draped across her shoulders. She had rouged her cheeks, applied some strawberry-colored lipstick. Her fingers clutched a raggedy purse that appeared to have been made of pieces of other people's ugliest bathroom throw rugs.

The rest of the Craving family was assembled outside the room. Grandpa stood with two suitcases in hand, ready for travel. "Everybody here?"

Sharpy did a headcount: *One two three four five six seven.*

"Everybody's here," he said.

"Then we're off," said Grandpa.

As they stepped forward together, Sharpy felt a surge of emotional electricity jolt the group. Each of the family members seemed genuinely excited. Grandpa and Grandma were grinning at each other. Brittany skipped happily. Tim seemed upbeat. Even D.L. betrayed a spring in her step.

Sharpy looked at his sultry mistress, who hooked her hand into the crook of his arm. "You're doing it," she whispered.

"Yep," he said.

She squeezed his arm even more tightly. "My man. My handsome, *rich* man."

During the good cheer, at the end of the hall, there appeared a cluster of Village Palms staffers. Included were the medication nurse, the activities director, another woman —and two hulking kitchen staffers. The group held a brisk air of authority.

"I wonder where they're going," said Grandpa Frederick.

"Somebody's in trouble," Brittany said.

Much to his dismay, Sharpy realized that the staffers were aiming for him. *His* family! The unidentified third woman— the leader of the group—caught and held his eyes.

"Mister Craving," the woman said.

"Yes?" answered Grandpa and Sharpy at the same time.

Both groups slowed to a stop and faced off. It was West Side Story for the over-70 age group.

"My name is Anne Marie Potts," the woman said briskly, offering her hand, "chief director of this facility."

"Pleased to meet you," Sharpy said.

"I understand you're taking this fine woman off the property."

"That's correct," said Grandpa Frederick.

"Unless you're taking her to a physician, we wouldn't recommend that she travel anywhere at this time."

"We're going to Disney World," sang Brittany, spinning around on her foot.

The chief director struggled to contain her alarm. "We *especially* wouldn't recommend taking her to an amusement park."

Grandpa Frederick narrowed his flinty eyes and stuck out his stubborn jaw like a battering ram. "Excuse me—I pay the bills here, and my wife and I can go wherever we please. Have a good afternoon." He pushed his wheelchair-bound wife straight into the gang of staffers. The director stepped aside.

The Cravings headed down the hallway, the white-frocked staffers trailing behind. "It is the opinion of the staff, sir," the chief director said, "that your wife is not in sufficient health to enjoy such a trip."

"Do the words 'thirty-seven hundred dollars' mean anything to you?" Grandpa said over his shoulder. "Because that's what I pay you every month. This isn't the kind of treatment I expect from my employees."

"I'm not speaking to you as your"—and the chief director slapped extra bitter sauce upon the word—"*employee*, Mister Craving, I am speaking to you as someone concerned about the health of your wife."

She was carrying a file folder under her arm. Now she pulled it out and opened it.

Ever curious, D.L. traipsed alongside the director and craned her neck so she could see the contents. It was Grandma Maya's medication chart. There was Metoprolol, a beta-blocker, to control hypertension. Lipitor, a statin. Insulin, for diabetes. Prilosec, for acid reflux. Xalatan eyedrops, for glaucoma. A calcium channel blocker whose name was unpronounceable. And Zoloft.

Underneath the picture was the acronym DNR written in large red letters.

DNR? What did that mean?

Then D.L. understood. *Do Not Resuscitate*.

"It looks as though she has some pretty serious circulatory problems, Mr. Craving," the chief director said.

"That is correct," Grandpa said.

"We really think you ought to leave her here." They were approaching the front atrium.

"Thank you for your opinion," Grandpa said.

The chief director nodded to the hulking kitchen staffers. Immediately, the pair sprinted around the Cravings' procession, turned at the front doors, and crossed their arms menacingly.

Sharpy was intimidated. Those men could *move*, the way football players on the Colts' starting line could move. D.L. took her brother's hand. Anything might happen.

As Sharpy opened his mouth to talk with the chief director, Grandpa Frederick shouldered him out of the way. The old man brought his stubbly chin inches from the woman's face.

"You could lose your job for this," he warned.

"It's possible," she said.

"Do you really want that?"

The chief director clutched her folder to her chest. She thought of the mortgage she'd taken out on her new house four months earlier. Was she willing to thrust herself into serious debt for a doddering seventy-eight-year-old woman? Maya Craving had too many needs to stay in an assisted-living facility much longer anyways. She would probably need to move to a full-blown nursing home by the end of the year. It wasn't worth trading her career for the Cravings.

"No," she said, "I don't. But I did feel that it was my responsibility to warn you of the dangers."

She nodded to the kitchen staffers, who reluctantly stepped aside. They'd been spoiling for a fight, and the men cast glowering looks at Sharpy as the Cravings passed through the doors.

"Nice lunch, boys," said Sharpy.

As they rolled Grandma Maya under the portico, she blanched at the intense Florida heat that lapped across the driveway. "It's quite warm," she mumbled.

"You'll be in the car in a minute," said Grandpa. "Give me a hand, son."

They were loading Grandma into the front seat when D.L. noticed that Tim had disappeared. She ran back inside the Village Palms to look for him.

In the vestibule, the chief director was conferring with the medication nurse near the front doors. She held Tim by the hand. "Looks like you're looking for somebody," she said.

"Yeah."

"It'd be a shame to lose two members of your family."

D.L. ignored her. "Snooker, come on."

The medication nurse stopped D.L. with a light touch on the shoulder. "Young lady, one moment." She dug inside the medication cart and produced a small amber bottle. "Your father and grandfather may not have any sense, but I'm hoping that you do. Take these." She handed it to the teenager. "She might need them."

"What are they?"

"Nitroglycerin tablets."

"The stuff they make dynamite with?"

"It also relieves angina. Chest pains. Put one under her tongue. It works fast. Trust me."

D.L. thanked her, stuffed the bottle into her pocket, and led her brother outside towards the minivan.

twenty-two

. . .

WALT DISNEY'S decision to build a second theme park is spurred by his frustration with the commercial sprawl that engulfed his first one.

The original Disneyland opened in Anaheim in the summer of 1955. It had been built upon 160 acres of land that had been almost instantly swallowed by hundreds of seedy lime-green motels with hot magenta neon lights and faux-British names like *The Twickingham Arms West* in blinking cursive scrawl.

Walt is powerless to stop their mushrooms-after-a-rain flourishing. He grumbles about their honky-tonk presence for years. He often wishes aloud that he could purchase the surrounding land to insulate the park from eyesores.

Determined to perfect his vision, Uncle Walt scouts promising locations for a second theme park somewhere nearer to the East Coast. This project becomes known as Compass East. Early candidates include Niagara Falls, Georgia, even St. Louis—though the last ends when the Busch company discovers that beer would be prohibited inside the park.

None of these locations tickle him. Legend has it that an

irritable Walt was flying over central Florida in a corporate jet when he looks down at a large undeveloped piece of land southwest of the intersection of I-4 and I-535, leans forward in his seat.

"That's it," he declares.

The *it* in question is a massive gray swamp, the most undesirable parcel of property south of the Appalachians, the type of uninhabitable muck which had given Florida real estate its bad reputation for decades. Local old-timers regard it as the sorriest piece of land that God ever put together.

A few days later, five of Walt's most trusted executives are riding through that sorriest piece of land, the stifling Florida wilderness, in a small aluminum fishing boat with an outboard motor. They wear crewcuts and white collared shirts with skinny black ties. Tall gum cypress trees tower over the visitors like gray skeletons, their ragged, mossy branches clawing at the water's surface. The rank scent of bougainvillea gags them.

In the middle of this primordial swamp, this rotten bog of pine trunks, dead vines, and mosquito eggs, the executives break for lunch at the driest hummock they can find. The local guides chuckle at the city boys. Who would want this land? It's untameable. Everybody knows it. Hungry alligators hunt at dusk. Wild panthers prowl at night. The bay head's dark waters, stained chocolate brown with tannic acid, are home to deadly water moccasins.

The guides tell the Disney boys all this, and the Disney boys listen. The locals may not know much about dental hygiene, but they *are* swamp rats—grim leatherfaces who tap trees for turpentine, who grind up sugar cane, who still refer to Orlando as "the settlement".

Back in town, one local official admits to the group that Bay Lake, which lay at the heart of the proposed property, is the "the worst terrain in the area."

Back the motel on their final night, lotioning the chigger

bites on their necks, the executives agreed to tell Walt the truth.

This is the devil's territory.

Which they do. But their irrepressible boss disagrees. *He wants that real estate.* And so he decides to check it out himself.

Uncle Walt merrily flies to Florida, rents a caravan of Land Rovers, and secretly tours the parcel himself.

Bureaucrats, he thinks, *always clipping people's wings.*

Within minutes he confirms his own decision. The swamp is habitable. It's merely a matter of drainage.

When he returns to California, things get moving fast. Real estate agents are quietly dispatched; a fake corporation is set up in Miami for the express purpose of purchasing this land. The studio even routes any mail traveling from California headquarters to the Miami address through Kansas City.

There is good reason for these extreme precautions. If word leaks that Walt Disney—the *man himself*—is interested … asking prices will multiply twentyfold.

The smoke screen wis successful. Before anybody realizes what is happening, Walt purchases 27,500 acres of land for an average price of 180 dollars per acre.

Anony-mouse-ly.

This gets Florida's rumor mill turning in 1964. The unknown buyer, the "mystery industry", is the subject of endless hours of speculation. The locals can't chew on the question enough.

Rumors reach a fever pitch at the Osceola Intercounty Barbecue. Folks toss possible buyers' names into the air like confetti. Lockheed, Boeing, McDonnell Aircraft, Douglas Aircraft, Ford Motor Company, Rockefeller, Swiss bankers. The government is going to build a migrant camp. Some even suggest Howard Hughes, the eccentric Texas billionaire.

A few mention Walt Disney, but they are quickly

reminded that he had categorically denied all interest the year before, while visiting Cape Canaveral.

Jock Lowery, the taciturn, sallow-cheeked owner of Jock's Corner, a small country store located on the fringe of the major land deals, finds himself in a key position to discover the identity of the mysterious buyers. A group of strange men wearing black suits frequently enter his store and buy cold Coca-Colas while touring the area. They usually take this opportunity to pick old Jock's brain for information.

"Awful lot of nosey people comin' in here askin' questions," he complains to friends. It's suggested that maybe the next time the men popped in, *he* should put the shine on *them*. Ask where *they* hailed from. After all, lots of folks in the community would like to know.

So Jock Lowery does exactly that.

To his surprise, one of the black-suited businessmen reveals that the group is visiting from California.

twenty-three

. . .

IT WAS MID-AFTERNOON, and the Cravings had stopped on the shoulder of a two-lane blacktop road. They were deep in cracker country. The sun was white-hot and blinding as it reflected off the bleached gravel at the shoulder of the road. The hot air crinkled and cooked above the asphalt.

Sharpy had pulled over after Grandpa Frederick had demanded it, claiming to hear a tiny screeching somewhere in the engine. Now the old man's sleeves were rolled up, and he was bent over underneath the open hood, probing the engine.

Sharpy stood behind his father, hands on hips. "Dad?"

"What?" said Grandpa.

"Can you let me help?"

"No, I'll handle this."

"I want to do *some*thing."

"You won't be able to fix anything in here," the old man said. "You have to be a computer programmer to do anything with these new cars."

"You don't know anything about computers."

"I know more than you."

Frustrated, Sharpy picked up a stick and chucked it into

the thin, green, piney woods that lined either side of the road. It bounced off a tree trunk and dropped into the soft dirt.

They had lifted Grandma Maya out of the minivan and sat her on a folding chair in the shade of a tall cabbage palm, near the edge of the canopy. Vivian had chosen to suffer the heat apart from the Cravings, and was several yards down the road, combing her daughter's hair.

Meanwhile, D.L. watched Tim step through the centipede grass. He picked up an old, rusted harmonica, lost for years in the dirt, and put it into his mouth.

"Did you wash that?" D.L. asked.

"I washed that," he said.

"Liar," she said. "Bring it over here." She scrubbed off the dirt from the mouthpiece, poured water onto it from her plastic bottle, and handed it back to her brother. He blew some chords.

"Oh Lord, he's a natural!" Grandma shouted. "Hoo boy!"

"Tim's really good with music," D.L. said.

"That boy's a blessing to this family." Her grandmother rocked back and forth, as though she were trying to catch hold of an ecstasy. "He's touched by God. He showed me the bear."

D.L. scooted forward on her log. "What bear?"

But Grandma Maya's mind had flitted off to one of the thousand other places that a senile mind visits in an hour. "Do you hear that whirring? The chiggers must be in the trees."

The harmonica was suddenly silenced. Tim had dropped the instrument into his pocket and zipped it shut.

"Why don't you keep playing, Tim?"

"Broken," he said.

"What's broken? The harmonica or you?"

Instantly D.L. regretted her comment. You couldn't joke with her brother because he didn't understand humor. It got worse. Tim clutched himself and repeated the insult:

"Tim is broken. Broken broken broken. Tim is broken. Broken broken—"

Quickly she stood up and hugged her brother. He quieted down. "Where's Travel Sheep?" she said. "Isn't he getting hot inside the car?"

Travel Sheep was a small stuffed sheep that Tim'd possessed since he was an infant. It used to be white, but years of use had stained it as yellow as tobacco smokers' teeth. He brought the discolored plush toy whenever he traveled, and he would scream like the damned if it was taken from him.

"Tim?"

He lurched sideways. "Travel Sheep can't feel changes in temperature because he's not a real sheep."

So much for patronizing. There was no denying the clear matter-of-factness in his voice. D.L. had seen these moments of total lucidity before. But they were always short-lived.

twenty-four

. . .

AN HOUR PASSED.

A pair of jaybirds came up from out of nowhere, whirling and shrieking, and disappeared into a clump of fetterbushes.

D.L. was asleep against her grandmother's leg. Tim was gazing into the immaculate blue sky. The lazy, distant drone of an airplane floated down somewhere from the south. A hawk soared high above them on the wind currents. Down the road, a crane with skinny orange legs was high stepping through wiregrass. The loamy smell of decaying palm fronds crawled out from the undergrowth.

And then, like the sound of a chainsaw in a chapel, came Grandpa Frederick's voice:

"I *knew* it! It's the *fan* belt. I can *see* it! But we have to get *under* it. We need a jack. Get me the jack, Sharpy."

The old man was still buried up to the elbows in the guts of the minivan. Grumbling, Sharpy went around to the trunk and humped out the suitcases and opened the spare tire compartment. Inside, there was a tire, but nothing else.

"Doesn't have one," he shouted.

"That's impossible," Grandpa Frederick said. "All cars

come with jacks." He stood up and wiped his brow, glaring at his son.

Sharpy felt that old familiar prick of parental disapproval. "This one doesn't. It probably got stolen by some other driver and the rental company never noticed."

"Let me see."

"Trust me."

The old man hiked around to the trunk. "Huh," he said. "Will you look at that? There's no jack."

Sharpy tried to be patient. "I just told you that."

"Hm."

"Do we really have to fix this now? Can't we wait until we get to the hotel?"

"It could get worse."

"It's a squeaky fan belt, Dad. We'll survive."

Grandpa Frederick wiped his face on a rag. "You can't just let your problems build, son. Ignoring them won't set them straight."

Sharpy decided to make peace. "I know what to do. We call Triple-A. They'll send us a jack."

Grandpa shook his head. "That won't be necessary."

"Why not?"

"Getting a truck out here"—he glanced around at the piney nowhereness—"that's eighty dollars at least. We'll do it ourselves."

Sharpy tossed down his cap. "You just said that everything is done by computer. How can we do this by ourselves?"

"We'll find a way." The old man stood alone in the blacktopped road, his lips locked stubbornly. "You can't rely on other people, son. You've got to fight the next guy to make sure you get your piece. That's the way the world works."

Sharpy had had it up to his eyeballs with Grandpa Frederick. He left the old man in the road and paced the shoulder instead, swinging his arms in violent circles, cracking his knuckles. Frederick Craving hadn't mellowed with age, like most people do. He was still the inflexible, intolerant, thick-skulled, pigheaded man that he had been since time immemorial—and he showed no signs of loosening up.

The jaybirds whirled over the minivan again, screaming, and flew into the foliage. Sharpy picked up a rock and chucked it towards them.

"Dad, *don't!*" said D.L.

"Why not?"

"They're *nice* birds."

"I didn't really mean it," he said. "Besides, I knew it wouldn't hit them. I'm a terrible throw."

She seemed to accept this.

"I guess we won't be fixing the belt today," said Grandpa. He dropped the hood with a heavy thump. "Everybody back in the car. Time to go."

Sharpy whistled down the road towards his mistress and her daughter. He made a come-over motion with his hand. As they drew closer, he could see that Vivian was steaming mad.

"What's the matter?"

"Don't you *ever* call me like that again."

"I'm sorry—"

"I'm not a dog. I'm a woman. Show me some respect." Her eyes showed that she had been flung back to something in the past. "I'm a woman. I *deserve* respect."

"It smells bad," Brittany complained, wrinkling her nose.

"The smell's inside the van," said D.L.

"We'll investigate it later," said Sharpy. He glanced around the empty landscape. "We need to find our way out of this place."

twenty-five

· · ·

SHARPY STARTED THE ENGINE. Grandpa Frederick sat stiffly in the passenger seat, as though he was physically pained by the fact that someone else was controlling the automobile.

They drove onwards, and soon the tropical forests shrank back, and an enormous citrus orchard engulfed the road. Orange trees with dark green leaves waved in the hot breeze. In the back seat, Tim—

(seventeen eighteen nineteen twenty DITCH one two)

—counted irrigation ditches between the rows.

The orange groves gave way to broad, flat meadows filled with sawgrass and grazing cattle. Then they crossed a short bridge, underneath which ran the waterway once called the Kissimmee River. A state maintenance vehicle was parked on the flattened grass at the side of the canal.

"I know where we are," said Grandpa happily.

"You must've seen something engineered," said Grandma, "I can hear it in your voice."

"Yessiree, there's my baby," Grandpa said, looking down at the artificial watercourse. "How ya doin', sweetums?" He turned to his granddaughter. "D.L., do you see that box canal?"

"Yeah," she said.

"That canal put the clothes on your father's back when he was a child."

Sharpy knew all about the canal. Grandpa Frederick had worked as a project coordinator in the U.S. Army Corps of Engineers. He had been stationed in Florida for several years as a young engineer, which accounted for his swift return in his retirement.

In the early 1950s, the Kissimmee River had been a pristine waterway, meandering south through lazy oxbows for over ninety miles before emptying into Lake Okeechobee. It had been an earthly paradise for thousands of fishermen, the jewel of central Florida.

But the marshy wetlands on either side of the river were owned by cattle ranchers, whose cows were routinely swept away by flood waters every autumn. Politically, cattle interests were expanding, so the ranchers banded together and lobbied the United States Congress for flood control—even though they had *voluntarily* settled upon flood plain marshes that lay underwater six months of the year.

Congress responded favorably, and the U.S. Army Corps of Engineers was assigned the task. They would impose plane geometry upon chaotic earth.

Years later, the result was Canal C-38, a fifty-two-mile superditch, a straight edge drawn upon nature's imperfections. The waterway's rate of flow skyrocketed; the surrounding flood plain marshes were reduced to one-third their original area; and without the marshes, eutrophication accelerated in Lake Okeechobee.

There were protests from the environmentally minded, but they were brushed off. A military spokesman maintained that "those silly butterfly chasers and self-serving politicians can't stand in the way of progress." Then he hastened to correct himself, stating that the Corps was "the nation's leading conservationist group" because "we have conserved the earth by molding it to suit man."

But those were just words. The Kissimmee River had been changed forever.

And Grandpa Frederick had helped do it.

twenty-six

• • •

THE SNUB-NOSED MINIVAN flew further down the two-lane road. D.L. was holding her grandmother's folded metal wheelchair against her legs, which bruised her shins whenever the van jiggled over a bump.

On the back bench, Tim was playing Connect Four with Brittany, who was gnawing on the plastic pieces. Vivian, too distracted to notice her daughter's misplaced hunger, watched the exotic landscape blurring by.

"What are you looking at?" asked D.L.

"Purses," said Vivian.

D.L. only saw scrubland. "Where do you see purses?"

"In my mind. I'm picturing the rack at Saks." She heaved a vulnerable sigh; her fingernail traced a design on the glass.

"You can make purses out of alligator skin," said D.L.

"Alligators?" said Grandma. "Here? We've got to—"

"Not here, ma," said Sharpy.

The old lady was still alarmed. "Oh, they're here, all right. One bit my nurse Rosie in the ankle while she was getting the mail last year. But she swatted him away."

"I want an alligator, Mommy," said Brittany. "I want an alligator! I want an—"

Tim jumped into the conversation: "The National Center for Animal Control advises that you should run in a zig-zag fashion when being pursued by an alligator."

"That's interesting, Snooker," said Sharpy.

"Such a blessed child," said Grandma.

Tim made a weird keening sound and beat himself in the head.

Brittany kicked the back of Grandpa Frederick's seat with her tiny shoes. "I want an alligator! *I ... want ... an ... alligator!* I WANT AN ALLIGATOR! I WANT—"

She was pitching an authentic temper tantrum. Grandpa Frederick twisted in his seat. "Vivian, you know how to raise a child, don't you?"

She was already stroking and soothing the little girl. "Yes, and I don't need any child-rearing advice from you, Rambo."

Alarmed, Sharpy swiftly interposed himself. "Have I told you what I'm going to do with our inheritance money?" he said. "I'm gonna build a big gazebo in the backyard. With a bird feeder. One of those kinds that the squirrels can't get inside. Then I'm gonna buy a BMW." He caught himself. "Well, maybe just a lease. That would be more affordable."

"That's foolish, son," said Grandpa.

"How come?"

"Invest the money. Save for the future." He balled his fist. "You've got to get yours before the next guy does."

"You're always talking about the *next guy*," Sharpy said. "Who is this next guy? Where does he live? Can I meet him someday?"

With such bitching, squabbling, kvetching, and kibitzing, none of the Craving clan had noticed that the sky had grown bizarrely dark.

Splat.

A large black insect squashed itself against the windshield. White yellow black smeared together.

"What is that?" Vivian said.

"It looks like a flying tarantula," said D.L.

"A *dead* flying tarantula," Vivian corrected. And then:

Splat splat splat.

Three more bug carcasses.

Sharpy fumbled for the windshield wipers. Then he spotted something ahead. It was dark and buzzing—and it was enormous.

"What's that cloud?" he asked.

"That's no cloud," said Grandpa.

The insect pest descended with full force. Within seconds, the windshield was completely coated in dark yellowish intestines. Through the air-conditioning vents floated a dastardly stink. Outside, a cloud of black stinkbugs slanted through the air above the fields.

"Jesus," said Sharpy. The wipers made a steady crunching sound as they smeared the carcasses into a paste. He angled his head, trying to peer through the small patch of clear glass.

"Mommy," Brittany whimpered, burying her face in her mother's side.

"Does anybody know what this is?" Vivian hissed.

"It's a warning," Grandma Maya said.

"Ma, please," said Sharpy, trying to peer through the windshield.

"You don't wanna believe, that's your business," Grandma said. "But we're getting the ten plagues. It's tellin' us something. It's a warning sent from God. We're being told to do something about ourselves." A strange light shone in her eye.

On the back bench, Tim's eyes followed one bug as it minced along the glass. He quietly unlatched the window—

(*come in*)

—and cracked it open.

Sharpy heard the rushing air behind him. He looked in the rearview, he shouted: "Tim, close that window!"

The warning came too late. Vivian watched as the black

insect crawled from the outside edge of the windowpane, horribly, onto the molded plastic interior ledge of the minivan.

Brittany screamed higher than any whistle. The insect lifted into the air; Vivian swung wildly with one of her four-hundred-dollar flats. Then it disappeared into Grandma Maya's nest of hair.

The kids gasped. The old woman hadn't noticed. Vivian looked at D.L. for one breathless moment—how to tell Grandma? Thankfully, they were spared the trouble as the intruder rose horribly out of the hair and floated into the front seat—

—where it was smashed against the dashboard by a rolled-up magazine. The carcass was swept into a coffee mug. Grandpa Frederick held up the weapon so the family could see.

"*Fortune* magazine," he said. "Money talks."

twenty-seven

. . .

THE MINIVAN, encrusted with hundreds of gooey, yellowish-black insect carcasses, stopped at a flashing yellow stoplight. It was a lonely, rural intersection. An abandoned gas station stood forlornly with a faded phone number painted on the sign. Long ago, this place had desperately dreamed of becoming a town, but the dream had withered and died on the vine.

"Where are we?" said Vivian.

"Hicksaw Crossing," said Sharpy, studying the map.

It was four o'clock, the hour for headaches, and the shadows were starting to slant and lengthen. Sharpy knew that the travelers' tempers were going to worsen very soon.

Through the filthy windshield Sharpy spotted Hicksaw's lone restaurant, the Wagon Wheel Cafe. He decided to cut off the objections. "What if we get some cold drinks in there?"

"That old juke joint?" Grandpa said.

"Is that okay?"

"It's *fine*," said D.L. "Let's get *out*. I'm sick of being in this car."

Sharpy wheeled the minivan around into the parking lot. A gang of brown, speckled roosters with red plumage scattered across the dirty yard as the mud puddles splattered beneath the tires.

He parked the car. The Cravings were facing the butt-end of the restaurant. A silver oil tank squatted like a heavy baked potato in the spindly grass. There was a white clapboard outhouse with an actual crescent moon painted on the door. D.L. had only seen that in cartoons. A small pen of rusted chicken-wire fencing held a few underfed chickens.

"I'm not going in that place," Vivian said.

"Suit yourself," said Grandpa. "Come on, kids."

Everyone piled out of the car, including a reluctant Vivian. Soon all seven travelers were trudging across the gravelly lot, kicking up plumes of white dust.

"Hi there," shouted the waitress as they entered.

"Hi," said Sharpy.

"How you folks doin'?"

He took off his cap. "I don't know. We drove through a hell of a lot of insects a few miles back."

"Oh, them's just lovebugs," the woman said. "Won't hurt nothin'."

The screen door banged shut. The Wagon Wheel Cafe was empty. The Cravings fell into a large circular vinyl booth as the waitress came around the counter, wiping her hands on her shorts. "Boy, how many a you are there? Tell me ya'll aint gonna be stayin in our motel out back?"

They angled their heads. They saw a row of tiny, rundown, one-story bungalows that appeared to have been abandoned for decades.

"No, we are *not*," said Vivian, touching her eyelashes delicately.

"Good thing, cause we dont allow no more'n five to a bed!" The waitress threw her head back and issued a hoarse, braying laugh that echoed through the empty room.

D.L. looked at the donkeyish woman. She was probably the same age as Vivian, but the cultural gulf between them was immense. This woman was wearing a greasy yellow t-shirt bearing the Hicksaw Wagon Wheel Cafe logo, a pair of black Lycra biking shorts with pink piping down the sides, and four-dollar transparent plastic flip-flops. Her potbelly pushed against the t-shirt and loose cellulite hung from her arms like sheets of pimply gelatin.

"It's hot in here," said D.L. "Could we open another window?"

"We don't have no more windows," the waitress said, "but we can bring ya an axe."

"The thing to do is forget about the heat," said Grandpa Frederick impatiently. "Everyone makes it worse by talking about it."

"That bear's gonna get me," Grandma Maya said. "It could get anybody."

"What bear?" said D.L.

"Ask him," the old woman said, nodding towards Tim.

"Don't pay your grandmother any attention," Grandpa said. "We'd like to see your menu."

The waitress didn't blink. "Hot dog hamburger cheeseburger gatorburger fries chili fries," she said. "You just saw it." Then she guffawed again.

Grandpa ignored the humor and reasserted himself. "This gang seems pretty hungry, so it's a cheeseburger for everyone —on me!" He spread his arms out in a selfless Christlike pose. His eyes searched out approval from his family.

But Vivian shook her head and crossed her legs underneath the table. "I don't care for anything, thank you."

Grandpa waved off the comment. "Just put one in front of her," he ordered the waitress. "I'm sure she'll pick at it."

"Gator burger," said Tim.

"Yeah, hon, you want one?"

"I want a gator burger too," Brittany whined.

Vivian shook her head. "That is *not* an option."

"One gator burger for Tim," said Grandpa, "and six cheeseburgers for the rest."

D.L. looked around the kitschy cafe. It belonged in a circus. There was a wooden box in the corner that said *Mongoose Will Bite (Hands Off!)* and which rattled wildly. The walls were covered in walnut veneer. The jukebox played some lazy Conway Twitty.

The waitress brought the plates to the table. She dropped the last cheeseburger in front of Vivian. "I left the calories in the kitchen. Ain't that thoughtful?"

Vivian forced a polite smile.

The travelers dug in. Everybody except Vivian contented themselves with the act of chewing and swallowing.

"How is everything?" the waitress said, returning to the table and standing with her hands on her hips. She looked at Vivian directly. "You aint eatin? I tole ya I left the calories in the kitchen."

Vivian politely explained that she was on a strict vegetarian diet.

"All right, I'll believe ya *this* time. Y'all headed to the parks?"

"Yeah," said Sharpy. "How do you get there from here?"

The waitress stuffed a pencil into her hair. "You know what money smells like?"

The screen door banged, and a lanky celery stalk of a man slowly seated himself at the bar. It was a Hicksaw feller, a local. He made a long, sad, hissing sound like air escaping from a dead tire. When he flipped off his black nylon baseball cap and wiped his forehead, D.L. could see the words Local 416 tattooed on his hand.

"Where's T.J. been?" the waitress said, rounding the counter.

"Hell if I know," the celery stalk said. "End of month maybe. Shippin."

"Oh yeah," said the waitress. She handed him a single can of Miller Lite with the six-pack ring still attached.

"How's that gator burger, Snooker?" said Sharpy.

Tim didn't answer.

"Let me taste it," D.L. said, reaching towards his plate.

"D.L.," Vivian said, "young women may *wear* alligator, but they don't *eat* it."

Sharpy glanced at his mistress. Vivian sat there in her terrific taupe blouse. Her thick dark hair fell down the sides of her face, a few strands tamped down to her temples by perspiration. Somehow she looked so . . . constant. No matter what environment—from the jungles of the Amazon to the penthouses of Manhattan—she knew herself. She was always a *sophisticate*. Always would be.

A bark outside, and D.L. saw a mangy hound standing at the screen door of the cafe.

"Is that y'all's dog?" the waitress asked from behind the bar counter. "Cause if it is, she kin come in here but she caint go in the back. Orlie don't like no dogs in his kitchen."

"She's not ours," Sharpy said.

"Well are ya comin' in or not," the woman said to the animal, holding the door open. The hound looked inside uneasily, then turned and ran away.

"Stupid dog," she said. Behind the bar, she suddenly whirled around: "Hey, did you guys notice our beautiful ceiling?"

When the Cravings lifted their eyes—a fanged plastic bat suddenly dropped from the ceiling and bounced in the air above their table. Brittany let fly another eardrum-cracking, high-pitched scream.

Irritated, D.L. threw down her fork. "Will you stop *doing* that? *God*! You've done that a *hundred times* already!"

"Oh, relax," said Vivian. "She's just a girl."

"So?"

"I don't blow up when *Tim* acts like an idiot, do I?"

"Give it a week."

The waitress interrupted the squabble. "Scared ya, didnt I?" She pointed to the plastic bats rigged up above every table in the cafe. They were all controlled by strings that ran along the ceiling and down behind the bar.

Grandpa Frederick admired the mechanics of the rigging. "How've you got those wires arranged back there? By table number?"

"Never mind him," Sharpy said. "I'd really like to know how to get to Orlando first."

"What do you mean, never mind me?" said Grandpa.

The waitress knew her directions. "Jus' take the turnpike south," she said. "That's 'bout four-five miles down the road. Cost ya probly seven dollars." Then she added: "Y'all look like you kin afford it though."

Soon, Grandpa Frederick paid the bill and the family left the restaurant.

After the screen door slammed shut, the waitress went over to the empty table and began loading the plates and glasses into a grubby black bus tub. She picked up Vivian's untouched hamburger. "Vegetarian my ass. She's tryin to lose weight she don't even got."

The celery stalk grimly lifted his beer can to his lips. "You can set the plate here if you want."

twenty-eight

. . .

OUTSIDE, the Craving clan was approaching their minivan when Grandma wrinkled her nose. "Something smells rotten," she said.

"I think it's the bugs," said Sharpy.

"It is *disgusting*, whatever it is," said Vivian.

"I don't think it's the bugs," said D.L. "It smells more like rotten meat." She sniffed the dead crusted bug carcasses. "I think it's inside the car."

"Time to find out," said Sharpy. "Let's get funky." He covered his nose in his shirt and lifted the minivan's hatch-back trunk. Immediately he leaped backwards as the stench of rotten meat billowed out from the interior.

"Whooee," said Grandpa. "Who left a sandwich under-neath the seats?"

"Not me," said Brittany.

Grandpa stuffed tissue paper into his nostrils and helped Sharpy removed the luggage from the trunk. Piece by piece, they set it down in the dusty parking lot.

Finally Grandpa lifted up the two black kitchen bags. "Here's the culprit. Why are you carrying live garbage, son?"

"That's not garbage," Sharpy said. "That's Tim's luggage."

"This is garbage."

"No, Dad—that's Tim's suitcase."

"Do you have a nose in that face of yours?" asked Grandpa. He shook the bags at his son. "Smell it! This is garbage!"

"Nope."

The old man lost patience and turned to his grandson. "Tim, open those bags."

"He won't do it," said D.L., breathing through her hat.

"Stop coddling your brother," barked the old man. "Tim, open those bags." But the autistic boy stared into the endless stupid blue sky. "We'll stand here all day until you do."

Nobody moved. D.L. realized that her family was veering dangerously close towards total paralysis. She decided to step into the breach. "I'll do it," she said.

Before anyone could object, she inhaled deeply, held her breath, and untied the first bag. Inside was white underwear. Her brother had packed about twenty pairs of his Fruit of the Loom tighty-whities. Where was his other clothing? More importantly, where was that smell?

That left the other bag.

She turned away and exhaled—then inhaled and dove into the second bag. She scanned the contents. There, thankfully, were Tim's shirts and shorts. She wasn't about to shop with her brother for a new summer wardrobe. She plunged her hand further into the bag, her face averted from the opening, rummaging deeper and deeper. Then she felt something slimy.

Warm.

Squishy.

As the other Cravings watched, D.L. lifted a package of raw chicken parts out of the bag, the type you buy at the supermarket, with the yellow foam platter and plastic shrink wrap and USDA approval stickers. Everybody in the family took two steps back as she held the rancid package aloft. Sour yellow poultry juices were dripping onto the dirt.

"Timothy," Sharpy said, turning slowly, "why did you pack raw chicken parts with your clothing?"

But the autistic boy was already lurching across the dusty parking lot away from the family.

"You can take care of this, son," Grandpa ordered.

Sharpy scowled. "Thank you for your permission."

D.L. tossed the chicken into a pockmarked dumpster behind the cafe, then joined her father in hot pursuit. They followed Tim across the road and cornered him inside the clapboard outhouse.

It was darkened except for slats of light that shone through the wooden walls. There was single flat wooden plank with a single toilet hole. Tim was trying to climb into the hole. He'd already gotten one leg in. His hands were stimming.

Quickly they hauled him out of the toilet hole, pulled him outside, and brushed him off with a towel. He didn't resist. He'd gone rubbery limp except for his fluttering hands.

"Snooker, don't think I'm angry," Sharpy said, "but why on earth did you pack goddamn raw chicken in your luggage?"

Tim stimmed more feverishly. His eyes were unfocused.

"Why?"

The boy hummed a snatch of a melody to himself.

Sharpy stared at him. "You're a lunatic," he snapped.

"Dad, don't say that," D.L. said.

Sharpy bowed his head. "I'm sorry, son."

Tim suddenly went rigid. He said: "Stressed-out chicken populations that lack fresh air tend to peck each other more intensely. This has led the poultry industry to institute a practice known as debeaking."

As the boy continued reciting facts about chicken processing, Sharpy's face sagged. The boy seemed to recede from his very eyes. He slumped onto the ground, crosslegged. "Twelve years, and I don't under*stand* him," Sharpy moaned. "Do you under*stand* him?"

D.L. was just as stumped. She knew that Tim had been fascinated with poultry for several months last year and had consumed many books on the process of chicken rendering. But what possessed him to carry raw chicken parts on a long car trip to sunny Florida, where the meat would be sure to spoil, was beyond her. Obsession, added to an utter lack of common sense, equaled uncommon weirdness.

This weirdness, however, was the hazard of living with an autistic person.

They walked back to the minivan. The vehicle's doors and windows were flung open to the sinking sun. Vivian was rapidly lighting matches, extinguishing them between her fingers, and flinging them into the backseat.

"We need to find the hotel," she said.

"I agree," said Sharpy.

"What did he say?"

He looked at her curiously. "He started reciting information about chicken farms. It was the strangest thing I've seen him do in a long time."

"He's hopeless," she said.

She lit a cigarette with one of the matches. Her face was arrogantly lifted upwards. Then she turned her head. Sharpy was watching her with a pained expression so open, so vulnerable, that it took her breath away.

"Please don't say things like that," he said.

Startled, Vivian eyed him while he finished repacking the luggage. A moment later, she reluctantly climbed inside the vehicle. When everyone was on board, Sharpy turned back onto the road and accelerated towards the turnpike.

Towards Orlando.

twenty-nine

· · ·

JOCK LOWERY'S NEWS—THAT the mysterious buyers hailed from California—shoots through central Florida like a greyhound. It reaches the ears of an Orlando Sentinel reporter named Emily Bavar. For several months, Bavar had suspected that Walt Disney is pulling a world-class piece of wool over Floridians' eyes.

She decides to put the question to him directly.

In early October of 1965, Bavar flies to Los Angeles, to the Disney studio on Hyperion Boulevard, for an exclusive interview with the famous animator. Why he was allowing the *téte-à-téte*, she has no idea. All she knows is that she is trying to get him to admit his role in the real estate upheaval.

The writer Vernon Scott once said of Walt Disney: "I've always thought that of all the successful producers and studio heads, Walt was the most interesting. He was a creative artist who was forced to become a businessman. Those other guys were businessmen who invaded the arts."

And so it is the height of irony that by 1965, Disney has become the best businessman of the group. He is the only chief of production in Hollywood who still holds complete financial control of his own company. He answers not to the bankers, not to the shareholders, not to the board of directors . . . but to *himself alone*.

The last remaining mogul in Hollywood.

When Bavar arrives, Walt's first secretary, Dolores Voight Scott, greets her warmly. A second secretary, Tommie Wilck—whom Walt calls "the Secretary of the Interior"—sits typing on the other side of the anteroom. And soon, here in the glamorous city, with mythical palms framed in the windows, the backwoods journalist is ushered into the holiest of holies, the *sanctum sanctorum*.

Walt Disney is perched on the edge of his desk, seeming very much like the friendly uncle who'd spoken warmly from millions of televisions every Sunday night a few years earlier. Now, he is chatting with a spit-shined nuclear family whose mother had won a call-in radio contest. The family looks as though it had stepped out from one of his own well-scrubbed television programs. He tousles the hair of the family's young boys. The parents beam two-hundred-megawatt smiles. Their children are being . . . *touched by Uncle Walt*! This is the American equivalent of embracing the pope, of kissing the bones of St. Francis. It's more than a blessing. It's familial cud. They will regurgitate the memory and chew it over and over, at every holiday gathering, for the rest of their lives.

He poses for a picture, and then Dolores ushers the family out of the office. They radiate holiness, golden *nimbi* circling their heads.

Uncle Walt turns to the journalist.

"Emily?" he says, offering his hand. "How ya doin'? Sit down over there on the couch." The journalist sits obediently and studied the plush office. Plaques and awards hang all over the olive-drab walls, including an honorary degree from Yale. There is a vivid painting of a submarine entangled with a giant squid hung prominently.

And there is a bronze paperweight statue of The Varmint —the original animator's term for the famous rodent—on his desk. By this point, Emily knows, Walt has started to feel frustated by his squeaky-clean corporate symbol. ("I'm trapped with the mouse," he once complained. "He's on a pedestal. I get letters if he does something wrong.")

The world's most famous animator turns to his next visitor. "Like some tomato juice?" he asks.

"Sure," she says.

Uncle Walt pours her a glass, then clutches his shoulder as he carries it over to the journalist. "My arthritis is flaring up," he says. "But Hazel'll take care of that at five. I swear that that woman knows more goddamned secrets about me than anybody else."

The woman is Hazel George, an attractive physical therapist who visits him after every workday. In a small room adjacent to his office, Uncle Walt climbs into a traction harness to stretch his neck. He blabbers away while her expert hands massage his old polo injury and applies hot compresses to the body that had been abused by years of tireless overworking.

Hazel's proximity to Uncle Walt stirs up plenty of gossip inside the studio. Rumors skitter through the hallways like roaches, rumors about the hidden nature of their relationship. Those in the upper echelons, however, know that Walt is faithful to his wife. He is, after all, a famous prude. He can't abide dirty jokes or sex talk. In fact, his only known concessions to the seedy underbelly of humanity are a childish delight in turds and—according to his animators—a penchant for characters with exaggerated *derrieres*.

"You're a woman," Uncle Walt says.

"Yes, I am."

"I was normal as a boy," he says, "but girls bored me. They still do. Their interests are just different. In Marceline there was one dame who—"

She interrupts him. "Mister Disney."

"Call me Walt."

"Thank you." She decides to state it bluntly. "Walt, I'm

here because someone has bought a lot of land in central Florida. Do you know anything about this?"

Uncle Walt, sitting behind his desk now, laughs. He pulls an unfiltered cigarette from his case. "Whoever bought that land will surely announce it in time."

She repeats the question.

Uncle Walt hedges again. "Well, you certainly hear a lot of rumors," he says. He sucks his front teeth and looks out the window, across the studio lot. The cigarette burns to a nub between his fingers. "You know, I've heard that *I've* bought it. Can you believe that?"

"Yes."

His eyebrow lifts, and a mischievous twinkle shines in his eye. "I'm sure you know, Miss Bavar, that I couldn't confirm any purchase, *if it were indeed a fact*, without consulting my advisors first."

"There are many people who think that the mystery buyer, *whoever it may be*, is planning to build an amusement park in central Florida," she says.

"Florida is completely unacceptable as a site for an amusement park," Uncle Walt replies, smiling. He is clearly enjoying the joust. "It's too humid, too oppressive in the summer months—that's when the families would come. And too wet—those regular afternoon rains would hurt attendance. Plus there aren't enough workers in Orlando to support a theme park anyways. I'd have to import them from elsewhere. And then build housing for them? No, Florida is out of the question."

Uncle Walt spins around in his swivel office chair. He casually flips a pen into the air.

"Of course," he says, "all of these problems could be overcome."

———

Emily Bavar returns from California convinced that Walt Disney is the man behind the land purchases.

She writes a lengthy piece in the *Orlando Sentinel* magazine proclaiming her opinion. It's a gutsy move, the kind that could end careers, but she is vindicated.

Four days after the article's publication, Florida Governor Haydon Burns admits at a municipalities convention that Walt Disney is indeed the mystery buyer. The official announcement is made in the Egyptian Room of the Cherry Plaza Hotel at two o'clock in the afternoon.

It is November 15, 1965.

Known forever afterwards as D-Day.

The standing-room-only gathering of guests is personally invited by Governor Burns. Uncle Walt, his entourage, and the governor arrive by private plane from Tallahassee. The men sit at a folding table on stage. A hand-stenciled posterboard reading *FLORIDA WELCOMES WALT DISNEY* hangs on the curtain behind them.

At the end of the conference, Uncle Walt poses for the photographers in front of an easel bearing a map of Florida. He points to Orlando with a long, thin wooden switch. He looks as chipper and avuncular as ever.

One year later, he is dead.

But it doesn't matter. The wheels are set in motion.

Land switches hands one day, then switches again the next. Donald Henry sells 180 acres to Norwood Gay for $360,000. Norwood immediately sells the same parcel to the North-South Development Corporation for $450,000.

The blood is in the water. The closer to Disney property your land is situated, the higher the price you demand. Even if all you own is a tiny scrap of shit-gullied, mosquito-infested, malarial swampland.

In 1971, a citrus farmer walks into his grove at seven-thirty in the morning to find a businessman in a dark suit and briefcase sitting underneath one of his trees, casually eating an orange. "Nice fruit!" the stranger says cheerfully. "And a nice orchard too! How much you want for it?"

The citrus farmer narrows his eyes and reaches for his shotgun. "Hey there—no need to get sore!" the stranger shouts. "I'll give ya three for it!"

He means three *million*, of course, and soon the citrus farmer gets out too. Even good old Jock Lowery sells his seven and a half acres, general store included, and scrambles for higher ground—which, in Florida, usually means a matter of inches.

There is no guilt. The local residents, generations removed from their spit-fired, gator-wrestling grandfathers, those mad hatters of yore, don't feel the same primal attachment to the bogs. Sure, there is the occasional protest at a zoning commission meeting, the hick who hitches his thumbs in his overalls and who mumbles something about carpetbaggers in a Karo syrup accent so thick that the commissioners have to lean forward over their microphones and cup their ears just to understand it.

But overall, almost nobody objects. Because nearly anybody with any pull is getting rich, from Senator Irlo Bronson himself down to the lowliest boiled peanut vendor.

It is an economic miracle.

And when the dust finally settles, the park begins to be built.

thirty

· · ·

THE DAY WAS ENDING, and the palm trees lined the edges of freeway ramps, their quilled leaves splayed against the indigo-blue sky. The red sun squatted on the rim of the horizon like a tired wrestler.

The minivan barreled across the darkening land.

On the back bench, Tim was arranging falling blocks on a handheld video game system. The liquid crystal display screen glowed pale grayish yellow against the dark interior. Brittany, who had fallen asleep against her mother's side, woke up whining at every deceleration.

D.L. was trying to read *Cosmopolitan* in the dimming light but finally closed its pages. She didn't know why she tried to read that magazine. The lead article detailed twelve ways to have better orgasms. Last month, the lead article had detailed fifteen ways to *give* better orgasms. Both of which were totally useless to a fifteen-year-old girl who hadn't yet dunked the doughnut, so to speak. The beanstalk models just made things even worse. She couldn't bear to look at them.

In the front seat, Grandpa Frederick crossed his arms and tipped his chin into the air. "Hope you've found us a swell place, son. Your mother isn't staying in any dump."

Sharpy said, "The Hotel Crown Palace is nice, Dad. All the guidebooks recommended it."

"Which guidebooks?"

"Fodor's."

The old man grunted. "Haven't heard of him."

They turned onto Route 192 in Kissimmee, known as The Strip for theme park pilgrims. It was one of Florida's all-time unsightliest thoroughfares. A long assortment of strip malls, Route 192 boasted the loudest and tackiest denim galleries, swimsuit shops, t-shirt emporiums, discount outlet malls, travel counters, fast food restaurants, novelty warehouses, souvenir kiosks, helicopter rides, Go-Kart tracks, laser tag arenas, alligator parks, dinner theaters, cut-rate car rental lots, and bargain motels in the entire state. They leeched off the tourists, day and night.

Around a bend shone a fifteen-story hotel, painted a bright flamingo pink. The landscaping was immaculate. Bright floodlights sent criss-crosses up the front façade as if it were the site of a Hollywood premiere. A well-dressed pair of valets stood at the ready under the portico.

The sign read *Hotel Crown Palace*.

"See! There!" said Sharpy. "I told you it would be nice!"

Grandpa Frederick's nostrils flared but he remained silent.

Sharpy stabbed the console with his finger. "Can't you just admit when I'm right? Can't you?"

The old man said nothing.

Sharpy huffed loudly. "At least I know Vivian can appreciate it." He turned towards his mistress in the backseat. "Doesn't it look classy, Vivian?"

"It looks okay," she allowed.

Brittany was popping in her seat now. "I want to go in there!"

"You will, honey," said Vivian.

The Cravings' minivan turned into the black

macadamized driveway, passed between two green tennis courts, and stopped beneath the lighted *porte-cochere*.

A tall elderly black gentleman with salt-and-pepper hair smiled and approached the arrivals. He wore purple epaulets with gold fringe and pulled a chrome cart with forest green carpeting.

"Welcome to the Hotel Crown Palace!" he said in a deep baritone. He opened Grandpa's door, then the sliding door. "Looks like you folks come a long way! Yes sir! Just pop the trunk, and we'll get you set up straight away."

"We don't need any help," Grandpa said.

"Let him help with the luggage, Frederick," Grandma said, "and you help with me."

"That's telling him!" the bellman said. "I see you're my kind of people already! My name's Carleton, welcome again. All *right*." He began unloading the trunk.

"Wait," Sharpy said. He carefully withdrew the ceramic urn from the top of the luggage.

Then Carleton saw Vivian. "Oh ho *ho*," the bellman said. He took her hand and helped her out of the minivan—then kissed the back of it without saying a word.

"Why *thank* you!" she said.

"It's always my pleasure to welcome beautiful women to my hotel," Carleton said gallantly. Suddenly he looked stricken. "What you want to do that for?"

"Do what?"

"I saw you sizin' me up like a side of ham. Don't you know I'm too old for you, woman?" He honked his nose into his handkerchief, eyeing her strangely. *Vuh vuhhhhhhh.*

The others laughed, but Vivian played it straight. "Not necessarily," she said.

Carleton looked her dead in the eye. "Do you know how long I've been walkin' this here green earth?"

She played along. "How long?"

"I don't know. I done forgot. I'm older than the dirt behind your pretty ears."

"Can I guess how old you are?"

"Can't nobody stop you from guessing."

She glanced him up and down. "You're sixty-four."

"I am *ninety-seven years old*," the bellman barked. He jerked a thumb at Grandpa Frederick. "That man there got a *long* way to go to catch up with ole Carleton."

"You're not *ninety-seven*!" Brittany screamed.

"And how do you know?" he said, bending down, jabbing the little girl's chest with his wrinkled forefinger.

"If you were ninety-seven years old, you couldn't lift this luggage," D.L. said.

"If you sold your soul to the devil you could," he said. "I done that too. Left me free to enjoy myself."

"That man's surrounded by lots of colors," said Grandma Maya. She was sitting in her wheelchair, gazing at him with her head cocked sideways.

"I've had lots of experiences," said the bellman. "You heard of the Tuskegee Airmen?"

"No," the old lady said.

"She hasn't heard too much of anything lately," said Grandpa.

"I heard *that*, you horse's ass," Grandma shot back.

"Well, I was one of them," the bellman boasted. He was stacking their luggage on the bellcart.

"That so?" Grandpa said, impressed. "I'm an old military man myself."

But Carleton wasn't finished spinning his story. "An' after the military I graduated with my doctorate from Howard University. That's a school in the District of Columbia for my people."

"Really? In what field?" asked Grandpa.

Carleton paused. "Engineering."

Grandpa brightened up. "Is that so? I'm an engineer myself. Which firm did you work for?"

Carleton waved off the question. "Oh, I didn't stay in it. I got into the insurance game. Saw the opportunity. Got some nice scratch from it too." He looked up ironically. "That means *money*, for you folks who don't know."

"If you're so rich, then why are you working here?" said D.L.

Carleton laughed as though he'd expected that question. "Just because I like helpin' nice people like you. No matter where you's from, I can talk to you. Atlanta, New York, Egypt, Mars. Don't matter. Where you folks from?"

"Indiana," said D.L.

"Hooboy! We just had a *real* nice family from Indiana here last week," the bellman said a little too quickly. He had finished stacking the cart and was now using a handsized broom-and-dustpan to collect the trash strewn about the interior.

Sharpy was impressed. "They really know hospitality down here," he whispered to his father.

"He's trying to make money, son," whispered Grandpa. "If you were working for tips, you'd be thorough too."

"But he said that he was rich," D.L. whispered.

"He's lying," said Grandpa.

"Front desk is right in there, folks," Carleton said, sweat streaming down his face, pointing straight through the double doors. "See the valet for your parking. I'll bring your luggage in two shakes of a gator tail."

thirty-one

· · ·

THE CRAVINGS ENTERED the cavernous lobby. It was decorated entirely in pinks and taupes. A collection of chintz sofas and low rosewood coffee tables were sprinkled through the waiting area.

"Does this pass muster?" he asked Vivian.

"It's okay," she said.

"Admit it, honey. This is a *nice* hotel," he said.

"I hate that."

"Nice hotels?"

"That word *honey*." She made an ugly face. "It makes us sound like a chubby married couple."

Sharpy thought of the engagement ring stowed inside his luggage, and a rising panic began to flood his vestibular system.

"Welcome to the Hotel Crown Palace," said a front desk clerk. She was a Latina of indeterminate age—could be twenty, could be forty, could be sixty. It was hard to tell with some women. She was known to the rest of the hotel staff as the Baby Cow. After all, she *did* have a rounded belly and thin legs and two thin udders, and she *did* stand in one place without moving all day, and she *did* chew on her gum as though she were ruminating an invisible piece of cud. And she *did* possess the uncreased agelessness of a face that comprehended almost nothing of what goes on in front of it.

"Checking in," Sharpy said.

"And your last name, sir." *An' you las' name, ser.*

"Craving."

The Baby Cow typed at her keyboard with only her forefingers. She looked like a child prodding a plate of vegetables. "Stephen?" He nodded. "Did you have a good trip?" *Di joo ha'e a good treep?*

Sharpy decided that he didn't need to reveal the sordid business of the will. "We're just looking forward to going to the parks."

"Smoking or no smoking," she said. *Sah-mokin o no sah-mokin.*

"Non-smoking," he replied.

"We'd like smoking," Vivian interrupted. "And could we have rooms as high as possible please?"

The Baby Cow studied the screen with her finger for a full thirty seconds. It felt longer than an eternity plus a drink. Her jaw slowly worked its cud. Grandpa Frederick shifted impatiently.

Finally she spoke. "Right now you have a standard room. The upgrade cost thirty dollars extra—" *Rai na-ow, joo ha' a standar' room. De upgray' cos' tirtee do'ars ess-tra—*

"Wait a second," Vivian said. "Did you say we only have one room?"

"Yes."

"We're going to need two rooms."

"No, we only need one," Sharpy said. "We'll just get a couple of rollaways."

"He's right," Grandpa Frederick agreed.

"Stephen!" said Vivian. "*Look* at your mother! She needs her own *bed!*"

"I think Vivian's right," offered D.L.

Grandpa whirled on his granddaughter: "Stay out of this." D.L. stamped off to the other side of the lobby, where she sulked on a couch.

"One room," Sharpy said to the clerk.

Vivian was apoplectic. "I am not sharing a bathroom with six other goddamn people, Stephen!" She turned to the clerk. "We'll have two rooms."

The Baby Cow looked to Sharpy. He seemed deeply distraught. Finally, he nodded. Grandpa Frederick made a spitting sound like *pffft*. Sharpy turned his back on his father. He couldn't face the codger's disapproval. Grandma touched his hand.

Meanwhile, Tim was hopping awkwardly along the patterned terrazzo floor—

(*The salmon lines are not allowed, the turquoise lines are allowed. The salmon lines are not allowed*)

—on alternating stripes. When he reached the pamphlet kiosk near the wall, he tapped the point of the obelisk. Then he blinked three times and tapped his left thigh. He wheeled around—

(*The salmon lines are allowed, the turquoise line are not*)

—and hopped back the other way.

Finally the Baby Cow finished the new booking. She presented a registration card to Sharpy. The rate said $169 per night. "How would you like to pay for the rooms, sir?"

"Credit card," Sharpy said, fumbling for his wallet. She took the card and typed in his number. Then she waited while the authorization zipped through. An indignant beep sounded from the terminal. "I'm sorry, but your credit card is declined. Do you have another?" *Joo credi' car' is dee-cline. Do joo ha' a-no-der?*

Sharpy owned three credit cards. He didn't know how many charges were sitting on any of them because his secretary always handled the bills. In fact, he hadn't looked at a statement in years. All he knew was that none of them were

American Express and that he was supposed to have about forty thousand dollars of credit total. How much of that was available, he couldn't say. It had always been enough.

He gave the clerk a second card. There was another indignant beep. "This one is declined too." *Dees one ees dee-cline too.*

"I don't know what's wrong," he said.

"Sharpy," Grandpa Frederick scolded. "Haven't you got better control over yourself than that?"

"It's not my fault," he protested. He looked for Vivian, but she had wandered off. She seemed to become very scarce whenever he was making financial transactions.

"Of course it's your fault," said Grandpa. "They're your cards."

"I've got one more."

The third credit card was finally authorized for $2114.90.

"Why don't you do like I told you and pay cash for everything," Grandpa said. "In 1940 I worked a second job scrubbing floors at the local gymnasium at night to pay for my first car. I bought my first house in 1947 for exactly ninety-two hundred dollars. Paid cash for both." His father stood stiffly, his right arm behind his back, his left hand gripping the other wrist—as though keeping his own hand from taking for something it didn't need.

"It's just easier this way," Sharpy said.

The clerk made the electronic keys and dinged the bell. Carleton trundled over with the bellcart, stacked high with their luggage. "Hey-ho, which room you all goin' to?"

"1410 and 1411," Sharpy said.

"Hoo boy, are you lucky!" he said. "Those are the finest rooms in the hotel. I'll meet you up there."

thirty-two

. . .

THE CRAVINGS ENTERED the luxurious glass-walled elevator and rose swiftly into the darkness. D.L. pressed her nose against the glass and gaped.

The nighttime vista that unfolded beneath the hotel was astounding. A long ribbon of garish neon lighting stretched away in both directions; far away, at the west end, she could see tiny fireworks exploding. That was probably Disney World.

"Isn't that pretty," Grandma Maya said. "Isn't it, Tim?"

Tim wasn't looking out the window. He was looking at the row of buttons—

(*lobby one two three four five six seven eight nine ten eleven twelve fourteen fifteen*)

—and rocking back and forth on his heels, highly agitated.

"What's wrong, Snooker?" D.L. asked.

"Thirteen," he said.

"We can't take Tim on the elevators again," she announced.

"Why not?" said Vivian.

"There's no thirteenth floor."

"Why should that bother him?" Vivian said.

"It just does. He likes things to be in order."

"Then he can take the stairs," said Grandpa Frederick. "It's good exercise. Gets him off the couch and away from that television."

D.L. realized that Grandpa didn't have a beggar's clue about his grandson's behavior. Tim had never watched a minute of television in his life. In fact, she thought, life would be much, much easier if he did.

"Thirteenth floors are unlucky," Grandma said. "I wouldn't stay on them."

Grandpa looked at his wife with infinite sadness, as though he were watching a drug addict stick another needle into her trackmarked arm.

"She's not the only one," Vivian said. "Hotels have always been superstitious."

"That's right," Grandma Maya said. "They never forget the bad things that happen inside of them."

The doors slid open, and the family traipsed tiredly down the fourteenth-floor hallway, beneath the electric flambeaux mounted on the walls just above the passable wainscoting. The corridor smelled like the carpet had been sewn from burnt tobacco leaves.

At room 1410, Sharpy pulled the plastic keycard from his packet, slipped it into the lock, then quickly pulled it out. A red light flashed.

"Take it out more quickly," said Vivian.

"Be quiet," Grandpa Frederick said.

"You'd die before you listened to anything a woman told you," snapped Vivian.

"Start turning a few honest pennies, and I'll listen to anything you say."

"It's better than pinching them until they bleed."

"You," the old man said, "are a wasteful woman."

"And you are a philistine."

The old man looked at her, wounded. "Just because

you've got a whole dictionary in your head doesn't make you any better a person."

Sharpy hadn't noticed the friction between his father and mistress. He'd been too busy trying to get the simple keycard to work. They were tricky, he knew, could even be erased by storing them next to a credit card in your wallet. Finally, the green light appeared. The door swung open, and the family pushed inside.

Carleton pulled up behind them. "Where should I drop the bags, sir?"

"On that woman's foot," shouted Grandpa.

"Oh, don't you make me laugh right now," the bellman said, laughing. "I ain't in the mood to laugh."

The hotel room had been decorated by someone with the limited imagination of a church secretary. There were two double beds with mauve bedspreads of Avora polyester; a small fold-out turquoise couch impressed with a damask pattern; a writing desk; a blonde-wood armoire with a television inside; and a nightstand beneath two wall-mounted reading lamps. The wallpaper was the texture of shredded wheat.

Vivian examined the bronze swag holders above the sliding glass door and shook her head. She fingered the faux-satin drapes. Finally she turned to the bed and touched the mattress with her fingertips. Then she frowned and wiped her hands on a small handkerchief that she pulled from her purse.

"It's dirty in here," she said.

"This is the cleanest hotel room I've ever seen," Sharpy said.

"We're obviously not standing in the same room," she replied. "There are more stains on that bedspread than I care to count."

"You're not being fair."

She ignored him. "This place should be condemned and

burned."

She stood in the middle of the room with her arms folded, turning in a circle. Sharpy saw that he wasn't going to win this one. Something in Vivian had an aversion to hotel rooms. They would just never be clean or classy enough.

He was saved by Grandpa Frederick, who entered pushing Grandma in her wheelchair.

"Yep, same as ours," he said approvingly, looking around. "Did you find the safe yet?" The old man knelt down at the armoire. Beneath the television set, there was a small beige electronic safe; its hinged door featured raised scrollwork. "You just punch your four-digit code in here," said Grandpa, pointing to the electronic panel, "and these thick metal prongs lock the door into place."

"Wow," said Sharpy. "Nobody's breaking into that thing."

"If they know the code, they can."

Sharpy snorted.

"Don't laugh," said Grandpa Frederick. "The next guy's always gunning for you. He'll take everything you've got."

Alarmed, Sharpy suddenly slapped the back of his pants, where his wallet resided. "I almost forgot. I've got to call my credit card companies. It looks like I may need some plastic surgery."

His laughter at his own joke subsided when nobody else joined in. Neither did anybody notice when Vivian slipped out of the room.

Sharpy dialed the toll-free number, punched his sixteen-digit Mastercard account number into the telephone, and chose from a series of options. Finally he reached an operator.

D.L. watched her father's jaw grow slack as he wrote down the amounts of the purchases and the stores at which they were made. "Thirteen hundred dollars at Talbot's … forty-five hundred at Saks Fifth Avenue … nine hundred sixty at Les Enfants …" Finally his pencil stopped writing. "That's all within the last ten days? I see. Can you tell me my available credit?" D.L. watched her father clutch the edge of the nightstand. Then he wrote down a figure, thanked the operator weakly, and hung up.

He dialed more numbers and repeated this with two other companies. When he hung up for the third time, he flopped backwards on the bedspread.

"How much do you have available, son?" Grandpa Frederick said.

"Not much."

"How much?"

Sharpy wished that all of them would just leave him alone. If he only had some time alone—to himself—he could think of a solution.

"How much?"

His father was a dog with a bone. "About thirteen hundred dollars," Sharpy said.

"Out of how much?"

"Forty thousand."

"It was Vivian," Grandpa Frederick said. His fist pounded into his open hand. "Where did that woman go?"

"I'll find her," Sharpy said.

thirty-three

. . .

SHARPY STORMED into the hallway and down to the elevator. He tapped his foot impatiently until the doors opened and he stepped into the lobby. His black-haired mistress was conferring with Carleton next to a chiffonier.

The bellman saw the furious look in Sharpy's eyes, the murderous set to his cheekbones, and quickly excused himself. Vivian was smiling as he approached. "I think I've changed my mind about this hotel," she said. "Carleton was just telling me about the *wonderful* amenities."

"Thirty-four thousand dollars," Sharpy said. He roughly pushed her in the shoulder. "You've spent thirty-four thousand dollars in *four months*."

Vivian maintained her wonderful smile but stepped backwards. "Why, Stephen, I just assumed you were allowing me *carte blanche*."

"I wasn't."

"That's fine," she said quickly. "I'll return some of the items."

"You'd better."

She suddenly looked deflated. "I hope Deborah isn't too upset."

"Who's Deborah," Sharpy said.

"Our personal shopper." It was no longer enough, for those in the nosebleed section of the income tax brackets—or those who aspired to join it—to merely *buy* expensive items from a department store. You had to have the possible items brought to *you*, in the form of a personal shopper who catered to your latest whims. Representatives from major upscale department stores could be seen trudging into the homes of their most profligate customers every day of the week, dragging bags filled with the latest Moschino dresses for girls, or Magil *fresco di lana* pants for boys, or tiny battery-powered Jaguars, or whatever the mothers were in the mood to indulge their children in that morning.

"She might be, but that's too bad for her. What did you buy?"

"Clothing for Brittany. Plus a Steiff stuffed bear that will look absolutely *ethereal* under the Christmas tree this winter."

"How much was that?"

Vivian shrugged her shoulders. "I never look at the prices."

"Give me those credit cards," he said.

"What?"

"Give them to me," he said.

"Hold on," she said. Vivian commenced a half-hearted rummage through her handbag. Sharpy grew impatient and snatched the bag from her. Vivian snatched it back. "Be patient! I'll give you the cards myself."

She finally produced the cards and handed them over. Sharpy grasped them in his hand. He savored the sweet taste of power. At last, he would control his own pocketbook again.

Once the plastic was in his hand, however, Vivian suddenly went sweeter than peach cobbler. She looked up into his eyes. Her hand went around his neck and up into the back of his thinning blonde hair. "Now, sweetie, listen," she said.

"No," he said.

"I know you have it in your heart to forgive me," she purred. Her other hand was curling around the cards. "I promise to be a good little girl." The very lineaments on her face were turning somehow younger, more girlish. She looked up with round, innocent eyes. "I'm sorry for being a bad girl." Then, in a seductive whisper: "Though I can still be a bad girl, if you want."

Sharpy felt the flutter of her eyelashes upon his neck, her warm breath in his ear, her perfume blooming in his nostrils like a thousand jonquils. Her fingers gripped the edge of the credit cards … and were gently tugging them out of his grasp. He felt himself beginning to knuckle under. Why not let Vivian do anything she wanted? After all, women with her particular skills didn't come around too often. What was the harm, if it meant keeping her? Let her spend … and spend … and spend …

Boom. The figure of Grandpa Frederick stood between them, in all his paternal sternness.

"I followed you from the elevator." The old man snatched the credit cards himself. "These," he declared, holding them in front of Vivian's face, "are not to be used by anyone except my son."

Sharpy was embarrassed. "Dad, I can handle my own affairs without your help."

"Is that why she had one hand in your pants while the other was tugging them out of your hand?" his father scolded. Then he turned to his son's mistress. "I will *not* tolerate you plunging my son into debt."

Vivian's eyes looked resentfully into the old man's face, then flicked towards the credit cards. Still, she didn't say anything. Grandpa Frederick quickly walked to the front desk and returned with a pair of scissors.

"Cut them up, Sharpy," he ordered. "Right in front of her."

"Maybe after we discussed this a bit."

"Do it now."

"Just a minute, Dad—"

Without a word, Grandpa Frederick immediately cut the three credit cards in half and dumped the shards into a garbage can.

"You're a bastard," Vivian said.

"I can't believe you just did that," Sharpy said.

"You both needed to be taught a lesson," the old man replied. He returned to the elevator with the stiff, correct gait that he alone possessed the correct recipe for a life well-lived.

thirty-four

. . .

LATER THAT NIGHT, after tempers had cooled, the Craving clan prepared for bed. The original plan had been for Grandma Maya and Grandpa Frederick to sleep in one room, and the other five to sleep in the other. But Vivian insisted that it would be more comfortable to split four-and-three, so D.L. found herself sharing a foldout bed with her brother—who was already asleep—in her grandparents' room.

In her wheelchair, Grandma Maya was wearing her frilly pink nightgown. She was watching a dating program on television with wide, innocent eyes. D.L. tried not to look at her grandmother's body underneath the thin garment. Everything seemed to be in the wrong place. Breasts drooped low. Shoulders were hunched high. Legs were bowed inwards. She looked like a bloodhound.

D.L. tucked the blanket around her sleeping brother, then opened her suitcase on the rack and took out a fresh t-shirt and plaid flannel pajama bottoms. Then she went into the bathroom. It was handicapped: the toilet was lifted extra high, with strong bars on either side. The floor of the shower was flush with the floor of the bathroom so that Grandma could roll herself into the shower stall and rinse with the detachable nozzle.

D.L. entered the bathroom and locked the door. She stripped naked and stood in front of the full-length mirror. She couldn't believe how lumpy she looked. Those hips—what could she do about them? Shave off an inch of pelvic bone on either side? The phrase *violin deformity* welled up from someplace deep inside. Since when was it a deformity to have birthing hips? It was her natural shape.

Through the door: "Everything all right in there?" It was Grandpa Frederick.

"I'm combing my hair," D.L. said.

She changed into her pajamas. Then she brushed her teeth and spit the froth into the pineapple-shaped sink, watching it dribble down the side of the high-resin basin, until the electronic brain magically sensed its presence, and a jet of water washed the spittle down the drain.

When she came out of the bathroom, the television volume had been lowered, and her grandmother had been moved to her bed. A single reading lamp cast a circle of yellow light on the other side of the room.

Grandpa Frederick, wearing only a wifebeater unershirt and his Sansabelt slacks, had turned off the big white lamp. He was placing the contents of his pockets on the desk. His wallet. His watch on top of the wallet. His coins inside the watchband's circle. The same ritual he'd been performing for seventy-two years.

"Is that what you wear to bed?" he said.

"What's wrong with what I'm wearing?"

Grandpa looked away, embarrassed to have criticized her nightwear. "Nothing. It's fine." He sighed, as if he was feeling his age for the very first time.

D.L. sat down on her bed. "Are we going to Disney World tomorrow?"

Grandpa nodded. "Your father is buying the tickets right now."

"I'm exhausted."

"Then you'd better grab some sleep, because we've got a six o'clock wake-up call."

D.L. wasn't thinking about what time she was expected to wake up. In fact, she barely even noticed the thick rollout bar protruding into her lower back, or that it felt like laying across a balance beam. Her drowsy mind had only one need: to fall into a deep, wonderful slumber, worlds away from the stresses of her broken family that was struggling to put itself together again.

thirty-five

. . .

IN 1966, construction of the Vacation Kingdom begins.

Major General William Everett "Joe" Potter is placed in charge of the operations. He boasts a stunning amount of experience. A former military man, he'd planned the Normandy invasion, directed flood control on the Missouri River, and served as governor of the Panama Canal Zone. Most recently, he had been second-in-command of the New York World's Fair.

In short, he is nobody to be trifled with.

First, General Potter orders the mucky bay head to be dredged and expanded. The black bottom is scraped clean; sparkling white sand is exposed. Earthhaulers push the sugar sand up onto the sides of the lake, and *kazaam*—an instant beach. The deodorization, of course, is complete. Not one sprig of elodea, not one twig of hydrilla, not one shoot of hyacinth, not one ounce of algae, ever grows in those waters again.

The lake is rechristened the Seven Seas Lagoon and stocked with seventy thousand fingerling bass.

Then General Potter calls in even more of the earthhaulers. Five more of these monstrous machines move more than eight million cubic yards of dirt. Much of the earth is dumped on top of a maze of hallways. Once buried, these service tunnels earn fame as the Utilidors—and become the envy of city planners everywhere.

And there are the cement mixers, the bundles of piping, the stacks of sheet metal, the slim cranes that poke holes in the clouds, the bulldozers that leave criss-crossed tracks in the mud, the yellow balloons that float above the site.

Throughout all this construction toil the day laborers.

Thousands strong, these shirtless men lift weighty hunks of sod onto their backs. Carry long metal tubes across their sunburned shoulders. They lean on their shovels, their eyes squinting into the sun.

The local newspaper steers a wide editorial path around these itinerants, comparing them to the hippies and their troubling protests. Of course, the day laborers don't give two drips of runny crap about the peace movement. No, the day laborers just follow the work, and wherever the work goes, they go too, and nobody remembers their passing.

Then General Potter orders that eighty-seven hundred acres of muck be reserved for a wetlands basin. For quality control, he creates the Reedy Creek Improvement District, an intricate fifty-five-mile-long canal system that threads its way throughout the area. He installs a protective dike around the property, interspersed with twenty-two double-ballasted automatic float gates of French design that refuse water of poor quality. It is all very ecological and forward-looking.

(Eventually, a Disney satellite is even parked in permanent orbit above the earth. It uses radio telemetry to monitor water flow and water quality in central Florida.)

Next, General Potter orders the elimination of all pests. There are many ways to do this. Canals are kept flowing briskly. Gator holes are excavated, which insures the survival of fish, which prey on mosquitoes. A team of Disney entomologists even monitors the movement of insects for up to twelve miles outside the park. If these methods fail, the bug brigade enters, and the ULV (ultra-low volume) truck unit sprays a formula of Malathion or Dibrom.

And the shipments begin to arrive, of course, the shipments of thousands of items manufactured off property. Prestressed concrete beams from Washington. Gas turbines from Toronto. Boilers from Houston. Skyway cables from Switzerland. Chillers arrive from Syracuse, wigs from Guatemala, watercraft from St. Petersburg, golden carousels from New Jersey, narrow-gauge steam locomotives from the Yucatan. A special shipment of one hundred and sixty scale-sized Grand Prix cars arrives from California.

Sometimes the work is surreal. A day laborer stands before of a mound of wet cement, holding a handful of small pebbles. He throws the pebbles against the mound until they stick. He is creating simulated coral rock for an underwater submarine ride.

And the changes occur outside the park too, dark changes in the backwater town of Orlando. Crime skyrockets. Car theft, robbery, fraud do too. Wherever the money-earners lead, the money-stealers follow. Two sides of the same coin.

And the reasons for this crime—the reasons are on the roads, the transient families who flood central Florida, looking towards The Varmint with baleful eyes for steady work. They don't know that Florida natives will receive first consideration in hiring, especially the young, the well-groomed, the good-looking.

Ultimately, almost none of the transients find work at the new park. There are forty thousand applicants for five thousand positions.

But things are stirring here, so the wandering families, for once, stick around. The Salvation Army owns a transient lodge on South Hughey Street downtown. The homeless double and triple up in single rooms. Children sleep on tiled floors. There are a few jobs open, gas station attendants or ditch diggers, but most turn instead to purse-snatching. The local court system is jammed beyond capacity. Many defendants happily see their cases dropped because the court can't meet the requirements of a speedy trial.

The commander of the Orlando Salvation Army Corps is frustrated. He complains on television, on radio, arguing that these itinerant families need more beds, more money, more attention. There is foul dust floating in Disney's wake, he says.

Until one of The Varmint's representatives knocks on his door and quietly asks him to please refrain from making these requests. Please be discreet, the representative says—after all, there are *fortunes* at stake.

For this is big business. The Disney corporation eventually invests nearly four hundred million dollars into the mammoth project.

By 1970, the public relations department has already shifted into high gear. A nineteen-year-old brunette named Debbie Dane, a former Tangerine Bowl queen, becomes the official face of the new park. Wearing short pleated skirts, she travels on a yearlong publicity junket, visiting with mayors at city halls, presenting them with plaques, taking questions at hotel conference rooms. She always wears The Varmint on her wristwatch. The serious face of an Eastern Airlines sales representative, her sponsor, always looms over her shoulder.

———

Opening Day is October 1, 1971. To commemorate this historic event, the Disney corporation decides to memorialize one family, a single nuclear family unit to represent their ideal visitors.

The lucky winners are handpicked that very morning from the ecstatic crowd singing at the gates of the theme park.

Their name: the Windsor family, a group of lemon-blond Nordic types from nearby Lakeland, Florida.

The Windsors are tossed into an antique fire engine and paraded down Main Street, flanked by a line of tour guides, with The Varmint serving as their driver. The dependable Debbie Dane also accompanies them, waving happily to the crowd, succumbing more than once to great gobs of happy tears. "I feel like I've known you all my life!" the spokeswoman gushes.

There is an official ceremony in front of the fiberglass castle. A Dixieland brass band cheerily plays "Hot Time in the Old Town Tonight". Furry characters race around a stage performing cartwheels. When the Varmint hands the First Family the key to the city, Mr. Windsor remarks to a reporter that this is "better than my Tuesday night poker game." Park officials exchange worried glances.

What the officials don't know is that the Windsors had arrived the night before in the family Volkswagen, which was packed with food and bedding. They had spent the night sleeping behind an Orlando gas station, slapping at mosquitoes, and shooing off police officers who had shined their flashlights into the car. That morning, frustrated by the traffic backup on the freeway, the father had swung that Volkswagen out onto the shoulder and blown past the entire snarling lineup at sixty miles an hour.

The irony couldn't be thicker. The First Family to enter the Magic Kingdom are *line jumpers*.

Not that anyone notices such minor hiccups. On the contrary, they're overwhelmed with joy.

In fact, the first pilgrims return from the vacation kingdom completely *awestruck*. They bring back tales of incredible magical occurrences, and soon the popular folktales begin forming, swirling in the misty reaches of mass consciousness.

The first pilgrims tell stories of a wilderness that had transformed itself, overnight, into a beautiful garden oasis.

They tell of white beaches and sparkling moonlit lagoons. They describe a futuristic bullet train that silently whooshes through a hotel lobby.

Impossible, say the listeners.

All true, say the tellers.

They tell more stories, stories of bears that strum banjoes, presidents that are brought back to life, and birds that wise-crack from enchanted perches.

Soon the tales grow bigger, wilder. They say that all cripples who pass through its gates are magically cured of their lameness. They say that strangers can meet each other in the park, fall in love, and marry—all within a single day.

There are even rumors that the founder of this marvelous city had not, in fact, died. They whisper that his body is laying *frozen* inside a mysterious cryogenic chamber, and that he will someday be resurrected, and that he will then return to save the people from themselves.

They talk wonderingly, achingly, of a pedestrian city where people smile at one another.

Where there is no competition, no crime.

No pain, no suffering.

A place ... where dreams really do come true.

thirty-six

. . .

THE HEAT in his eyeballs woke him up.

It happened like this every morning. Curtis Marshall wanted sleep. He *needed* sleep. He *coveted* sleep. But the heat always seeped into his head, like a hot broth poured into his nasal cavities, and it gradually leaked into his eyesockets until he awoke with the liquid of his eyeballs almost at a rolling boil.

It was summer in central Florida, and Curtis Marshall was one of the unlucky few who didn't have air conditioning in his apartment.

He stretched his arms and yawned. The broth was still simmering. His fingers gently massaged his eyelids.

Curtis shifted his weight slightly. He could feel a rogue bedspring digging into the tender part of his back. This was his first night on a puke-colored queen mattress that, underneath the fitted sheet, had been stained with a constellation of mysterious red blotches. Underneath that was the boxspring. Both had been purchased yesterday, for ten dollars a piece, from a consignment center tucked away in a dirty corner of a dirty strip mall nine blocks away. The store had been a very shady enterprise. The owner's eyes had darted around each other like a pair of fighting fish. The items had been strictly Garage Sale Chic—outdated vacuum cleaners, dusty cassette decks, unsteady halogen lamps, and tri-tiered end tables that wouldn't release their sticky residue no matter how many times anybody scrubbed them.

Getting the mattresses home had been even more of a chore. Curtis hadn't had the thirty dollars for delivery, and he hadn't known anybody who owned a truck or van or SUV, so he'd just rolled his sleeves up and *pushed* the motherhulking thing home, nine sweaty blocks, end over end. It must've weighed a buck twenty. Then he'd walked back and done the same with the boxspring.

This was Orlando. You helped yourself.

Now both mattress and boxspring were resting upon the bare carpet of his floor. The consignment store had been selling bed frames for fifteen dollars each, but Curtis had decided that that was fifteen dollars better spent elsewhere. Of course, this had meant persuading a certain other person that better slumber could be achieved *without* a frame. That people in some Asian countries actually chose to sleep with their mattresses flush on the floor.

Next to him lay that certain other person. Her name was Lucinda, and her chest gently rose and fell. A black corona of hair was flung across her pillow. His hand crept around the small part of her waist and felt the small bump on her lower abdomen.

Baby, he thought, *we can survive this.*

She was five months already. She had been holding two full time jobs: one as a bank clerk, the other as a babysitter for touron families. He'd been working scads of overtime too. All to save up six thousand dollars to pay for the delivery.

It wasn't going to be enough.

Curtis smiled at Lucinda's sleeping body. *She* never felt hot broth cooking in her eyeballs, that was for sure. She could sleep through anything: a fire alarm, an earthquake, a third-grade orchestra concert. Curtis leaned forward to kiss her cheek, then thought better. It might wake her, and with a sixteen-hour workday ahead, she needed all the rest she could get.

Curtis struggled to his feet. His studio apartment was nearly empty: bare plaster walls, bare bathroom, bare kitchen. On the carpet, there was a rectangular patch of darker carpet.

Yesterday, a team of three men from a nearby furniture rental center had entered the apartment wearing identical blue twilled cotton polo shirts and, without a word, had removed the couch, chair, bed, coffee table, and television set.

The reason was simple: Curtis had defaulted on the payment.

Though he'd lost his furniture, he'd been sure to keep his dignity. He'd offered the repo men cans of store-brand lemon-lime soda when they arrived. He'd asked politely if people ever gave them a hard time and received only a grunt in response. He'd even held the door open as they lugged the furniture out.

Afterwards, he'd made the trip to the consignment center for the new mattress.

Now the only big-ticket item left in the apartment was his prized 1974 Gibson Les Paul electric guitar. It stood in an elegant stand under the window, its famous brown-red-and-orange sunburst design glinting richly in the morning sunlight. Next to it sat a classic Marshall amplifier. The whole setup had been inherited from his dearly beloved Uncle Phil, gone almost five years now. Curtis could only strum three basic chords, maybe copy a lick or two cribbed from Clapton, but he'd discovered that a good amplifier could hide a hell of a lot, musically speaking. Best of all, playing it made him feel closer to his uncle.

He crossed the empty floor, entered the bathroom, and looked at himself in the mirror. Six feet nothing, square-shoul-dered, possessor of a *ricka-chicka-chicka* washboard stomach,

Curtis could easily have been a runway model, given another chance, another life.

In this life, however, he was living with a pregnant girl-friend in a shitty four-hundred square foot studio apartment near the butt-end of Orange Blossom Trail. The road's name was deceiving, with its connotations of a lovely, meandering, citrus-scented path. Nothing could be further from the truth. It was a seven-lane behemoth that screamed through the middle of the city. It had an especially unmerciful reputation among pedestrians.

Curtis scowled as he scrubbed his face. There was no point in showering. Judging from the temperature already, he was going to sizzle at work. He chose a plain pair of athletic shorts and an even plainer t-shirt from a small pile in the top shelf of his closet. He stuffed another set of clothes into an athletic bag, followed by a thermos and some salt tablets.

In the kitchen he quietly stuck two pieces of bread into the toaster—a three-dollar thrift shop purchase—and buttered them. He wished that they had some jelly, but the refrigerator was empty except for a shriveled mango, two bags of flour tortillas, and a six-pack of tamarind-flavored soda that Lucinda loved.

He peeked into the main room as he chewed his toast. She was still asleep. Curtis felt his lips quiver. The imminent arrival had really changed their relationship. Beforehand, he and Lucinda had been lovers—dancing at a moment's notice, sneaking into hotels to swim in their pools, rollerblading around Lake Eola on Sundays.

That was then.

Now they were two strangers who shared water and elec-tricity as they battled for their financial lives.

Curtis changed his mind. He leaned over and kissed the slumbering woman gently on the cheek. Then he picked up his duffel bag and headed out for work.

thirty-seven

. . .

ON HIS FRONT STOOP, Curtis noticed a document tacked onto his door with a piece of duct tape. The heading bore the imprint and crest of the apartment manager. His stomach sank to his shoes.

He knew what it was.

He removed the notice and scanned it: *"official notice … legal procedures … vacate premises immediately …"*

An eviction.

He'd received two earlier warnings. This was his final notice. His eyes skipped to the bottom of the paper. He would be forced to leave the apartment *unless* he could scrounge together nine hundred dollars by five o'clock tonight.

Curtis sank down the wall. They couldn't afford an eviction. They couldn't afford to stay, either. There was $148.22 in his bank account. Lucinda had about the same in hers. The monthly rent was $450. They were already one month behind, and Herb, the property manager, was demanding both months at once. It was completely unwinnable. They simply did not have $900.

We can survive this, he thought. *We just have to endure.*

He pushed himself up the wall. He straightened his t-shirt. He would talk to Herb before going to work. Herb would understand. Herb was a man of the people.

Curtis' apartment complex was a Floridian stucco night-mare—four hundred units in thirteen yellow boxy stucco apartment buildings, surrounded by a high orange stucco wall. It was called the Palms at Lake Katalpa, even though nobody could remember there ever having been either a single cabbage palm or a lake of any name there. It was owned by the Lessermann family. They were modern-day slumlords, through and through. They managed nearly every low-rent apartment property in the south side area, all of which had been built within the last ten years. And they were merciless. If you were evicted from one of their properties, you were barred from all of them, which left pretty much nowhere in greater Orlando to lease.

Nobody wanted *that* to happen.

Curtis walked along the parking lot. Ahead, shining like a freshly blackened eye, sat his close-to-pulp automobile, a gray 1987 Honda Civic. It had pitifully thin little wheels and a wheezy four-cylinder engine and rust bubbles that were popping out of the paint like sores on a dying dog. The front right fender had already been crushed in a collision caused by an old lady turning left into the setting sun. *Anything* could finish off this vehicle. It was like the poor shivering sucker poised on the trap door above the water tank at the carnival, shuddering with every fastball that bounces off the cage. All it would take is one good toss, and *ka-pow*, bullseye, *sploosh*—to the bottom it would sink.

"What's up, *amigo*?" a voice said.

Curtis turned. On the porch of the next building, a rotund Latin man wearing only green athletic shorts, a red visor, and two sleeves of menacing tattoos was lounging in an over-stuffed rocker. Tongues of yellow foam were popping out of the seat cushions as though devils lived inside the seat. He looked at Curtis through deep purple pouches hanging from his eyes.

"Not much," Curtis said. "It's going to be hot today."

"Every day is hot here."

Behind him, three guys carried the slump-shouldered looks of eternal sidekicks. When one grinned, Curtis saw that his teeth were sharpened like hyenas'.

Their interest in him was surprising. The Puerto Ricans who dominated the complex had never, not once, acknowledged the white boy, the *guero*, not even when they were falling off their porches drunk on Bacardi. Truth be told, Curtis was shocked to hear one of them speak English. He only ever heard them speak Spanish.

"Is that your car?" the man asked.

"Yeah," Curtis said.

"I can fix it for you," the *puertoriqueño* said, stretching out casually. "Only eighty dollars."

Curtis looked at the car. The man was pointing at the damage to the Civic's fender. Embarrassed, Curtis shuffled and kicked the ground.

"Well, this isn't a good time."

The man's eyes flicked down to the eviction notice in Curtis' hand. His eyes widened momentarily. Then they flicked away. "That's too bad. Cuz you have to do it today."

"Why today?"

"I only have the tools for one day."

"Really?"

The *puertoriqueño* nodded. The sidekicks shifted their weight and nudged things with the toes of their sneakers. They were hiding their smiles and looking anywhere except at Curtis, in the way that weak people avoid helping someone who is being scammed right before their eyes.

But the leader's eyes were calm and knowledgeable, even

as the knuckles of his right hand reached across and rubbed his left cheek. He knew how to create urgency, Curtis thought, could do it better than most legit salesmen. In a different life, he might be hawking pharmaceuticals to wealthy hospital doctors. Instead he was swatting lizards on the front porch of a slummy Orlando apartment and putting the squeeze on his neighbors.

"I'll be okay," Curtis said.

"If you need someplace to stay," the man said, glancing at Curtis' eviction notice again, "my brother and his wife and their baby, they can go over to my cousin's."

The men were sniggering at him now. Curtis tilted his head. It felt like there was some joke being played on him that he couldn't understand.

The front door to the apartment cracked open. He saw half of a woman's plump face looking out at him. She wore purple eyeshadow and had high, thin, arched eyebrows. The *puertoriqueño* spoke to her quickly in Spanish. The woman's fingers rubbed her belly and shut the door.

Curtis nodded to the crowd, slipped into his car. "Have a good day," the guy shouted.

Curtis started his car and sped through the complex. The cups and wrappers and assorted junk strewn across the Civic's floor rolled across his feet. At least the engine still worked— all ninety-one horses of it. He tried not to imagine what would happen if something essential needed replacing. A mechanic had warned him a few months ago that he might need a new alternator. That would cost almost three hundred dollars, without labor.

He pulled up to the property management office. It was closed. A stencil on the glass door read *Office Hours: 8 to 5, Monday to Friday.*

His watch read seven-thirty. Curtis simply couldn't wait until eight o'clock. He needed to get to work. He would have to call Herb from there.

Cursing softly, he folded up the final eviction notice and stuffed it into his bag. The day couldn't have begun any worse. He turned the wheel and the battered nose of his Civic swung creakily toward the I-4 freeway, towards his workplace.

Towards Disney World.

thirty-eight

. . .

AT EIGHT O'CLOCK that same morning, the seven Cravings were gathered around a table in the hotel's Veranda Café.

The remains of starches and pork products—pancakes, waffles, cereal, toast, bacon, sausages, salted ham—lay battered on their plates.

Nobody spoke; besides the inevitable food coma, it wasn't even eight o'clock yet. Only Brittany showed the remotest glimmer of life as she tried to push a forkful of syrupy pancake into her mother's mouth. Vivian grimaced and pushed it away. She hadn't eaten any breakfast. She never did.

Tim yawned. Grandma sat quietly in her wheelchair.

Sharpy rubbed the crusties out of the inner corners of his eyes. Part of him wished that his ex-wife were here today. She *was*—in a sense. He looked at the urn placed decorously on its own chair beside him. Suddenly he pictured his wife sitting in that same seat, in the full bloom of health, cutting Tim's food, chatting with D.L. about her upcoming Halloween costume, kissing him on the cheek. In that instant, Sharpy knew that the past could never be past. She was still influencing the family. The Cravings wouldn't be on this vacation—wouldn't be anything, *period*—without her.

Which reminded him of the photograph.

He felt a primitive thrill race up his tailbone and spread through his shoulder blades. One photograph: one million dollars. They were edging nearer and nearer. He suddenly felt very anxious and his eyes glanced around for the waitress.

Instead, they fell upon his father. Grandpa Frederick's fingers were twisting a napkin into a tiny knot.

"Dad?"

"Yes."

"What's the matter? You look different."

"I have something to say."

Sharpy felt his stomach drop into his shoes. This was serious. His father never usually prefaced things. He was too direct for that.

Grandpa Frederick straightened up as though he were addressing a conference room of colleagues. "This is a very important day for everybody in this family. I thought that my contribution would be to create a guide to the park."

"Did you buy a book?" said Vivian.

"No. I made one."

Grandpa Frederick dropped a document onto the table. D.L. picked up the document, weighed its heft in her hands.

"What is it again?" she said.

Her grandfather vibrated with impatience. "It's our *schedule*. A minute-by-minute schematic outline of our day at the park."

As D.L. flipped through its thirty-four pages, she saw that her grandfather had factored in every variable the family could possibly experience. He had included projected wait times, lunch breaks, bathroom stops, walking distances, estimated dizziness recovery time, wheelchair accessibility. It was frightening. Grandpa Frederick's decades of scheduling military engineering projects had been focused with laser-like precision upon this single purpose.

It was a monument in the history of overly controlled personalities.Meanwhile, Vivian scanned the document over D.L.'s shoulder. "How very thoughtful, Frederick," she said.

"Thank you," Grandpa replied stiffly. "What do you think, son?"

"I think you put a lot of effort into this, Dad."

"I'd recommend that we follow it today."

"Maybe a little."

When Sharpy lifted his head, Grandpa Frederick seemed crestfallen. Sharpy quickly followed up. "I mean, there's some really good advice in here. I really like the part about always choosing left when faced with a"—he read it out loud—"*binary progression model.*"

"What's that?" asked D.L.

"It's an engineer's way of saying that you have a choice of going either left or right," said Vivian.

"Correct," said Grandpa Frederick. "Given a fork in the line, a majority of humans naturally veer right. Choosing left will shave forty percent off your wait time."

Sharpy motioned for the check. His silence spoke volumes. Grandpa tapped his fingers against the tabletop. "You won't consider using it?"

Sharpy mulled over the reasons to abandon the conversation. One, this was a vacation, not an occasion for fighting. Two, he was never worried about maximizing his time. That was for the purpose-driven, and Sharpy was poles apart from his father on *that* score. Three, there was zero chance that he would do anything his father ordered. It was really that simple. Now that he was grown, he refused to bend to that enormous will, no matter how much sense his father's suggestion made.

"No," said Sharpy, "this is my vacation. My family. Not yours." He handed the document back to his father.

The pages hung in the air. Grandpa just looked at it. Grandma Maya intuitively took her husband's hand.

When it came out, the old man's voice was dry and scratchy. He choked out a barely audible word: "Fine." Then he left the table and walked out of the café, out of sight.

Sharpy withdrew the schedule. "What's the matter with him?"

"His feelings are hurt," said Grandma sadly. "Don't you care that you hurt your father's feelings?"

Sharpy lifted his palms up. "He never cared when he hurt mine."

Suddenly he brightened up.

"So is everybody ready for a fun day?"

thirty-nine

. . .

CURTIS MARSHALL WORKED in the character department at Walt Disney World.

Every day, he climbed inside a character costume—known as a "suit"—and entertained children by dancing, hugging, or signing autograph books. He was classified by the Disney corporation as a CT, which meant Casual Temporary, which meant that he was guaranteed a temporary part time job until the end of the summer, when the crowds thinned.

He was being paid six dollars and forty cents an hour.

Curtis followed the long, curving roads towards the hidden employee parking area. Before his death, Uncle Walt had planned long, curving roads because he didn't want any traffic lights on his utopian Florida property. Traffic lights evoked unpleasant memories of imperfect reality.

At the checkpoint, Curtis pointed at the yellow pass on his windshield to the guard, got the nod, and parked on the margins of a gargantuan employee lot. Leaving his car, Curtis threaded his way through the automobiles towards the back fence, towards the navy blue Crown Victoria that he knew would be parked there.

That was Manny's car.

Manny Vargas was a fellow "cast member" (Disneyspeak for employee) in the character department. Though most people assumed he was native tough-talking Italian New Yorker, he actually was a Dominican who'd emigrated to New York as an infant and spent years in Washington Heights as a short-order cook—with emphasis on the word "short". Manny maxed out at four feet eleven inches.

The only thing anybody knew about Manny was that he was homeless. He slept in the back seat of his decade-old Crown Victoria. He showered in the locker rooms after his shift. He ate nothing but take-out food—and he'd been living this way for almost four months. Of course, owning a coppish-looking car had its own peculiar benefits. He could park overnight pretty much anywhere and not get hassled by anybody, least of all the five-oh.

Curtis knew more than he wanted about the tiny man's abysmal situation. Manny had poured the horrendous sob story onto Curtis one beery night, then dragged him outside to the Crown Vic for proof. It would have been unbelievable otherwise. He was truly in a tough fix.

The crux of the problem was that Manny was under orders by Osceola County to pay four hundred dollars every month in child support to his ex-wife. This expense had proven so overwhelming—given that Manny's income was as miniscule as his stature—that he'd jettisoned his apartment. Curtis saw the logic in this decision. After all, Manny couldn't cheat his baby daughter out of her support money; he couldn't live without transportation to work either.

At one time, such a life seemed impossibly harsh.

Now, Curtis reflected, he was edging closer to joining Manny.

He knocked on the roof of the Crown Victoria, as was his customary morning ritual. In the back seat, windows rolled down, on a white sheet spread across the upholstery, the tiny man was already awake. It was impossible to sleep past sunrise, especially during August when the car's interior started cooking within seconds of being struck by the sun's first ray.

"Good morning," said Curtis.

"It's a *great* morning!" Manny said. He was shoveling forkfuls of leftover fried rice into his mouth from a white Styrofoam container. "I've seen lots worse mornings than this."

"That's the attitude," Curtis said.

Manny emerged from the backseat and stretched his tiny frame. He performed a few jumping jacks, deep knee bends, and sun salutations. Then he locked his car and slung his duffel bag over his shoulder. "Ready?" he said.

"Ready," said Curtis.

Together, the two workers started towards the employee shuttle stop.

"What's new with you?" said Manny.

"You don't wanna know."

"Go ahead. Nothin' to be embarrassed about. Christ, lookit me."

Curtis sighed. "I got an eviction notice this morning."

"First one's nothing, man. They hand those out like pennants atta ballpark."

"This is the final notice."

"Oh." Manny thought about it. "You gotta be strong, Curtis. You gotta stay in the black. With a baby on the way—"

"Believe me, I know."

A note of hysteria crept into Manny's voice and he swung his arms wildly back-and-forth. "You *gotta* stay positive, Curtis. For both of us."

"Let's *please* talk about something else."

Manny walked in silence for a moment. Then: "Did you hear about Sarah?"

Curtis perked up his ears. Sarah was a friend. "No."

"Oh man," Manny said, shaking his head as they boarded

the shuttle with a mob of other cast members. "Yesterday some Brazilian stabbed her in the belly with a fork."

Far from a type of genital waxing, a "Brazilian" was backstage lingo for a disruptive guest. It derived from the observation that a large number of obnoxious visitors seem to be from Brazil.

"A plastic fork is nothing," said Curtis. "That happens to me almost every day."

"No, this was a *metal* fork," said Manny.

"Oh."

"Somebody stole it from one of the buffet breakfasts. It went through the suit and punctured her lung. The kid must've swung harder than Sosa. You got no idea. She's in the hospital now. You know what else? The kid's *parents* were talking about a lawsuit." Manny shook his head disappointedly.

"Which suit was she in?" asked Curtis.

Manny lifted his head; a tense expression appeared on his face. "The big one," he said.

That meant The Varmint. That also meant that she had already been fired. The management was very, very strict about maintaining proper decorum inside the characters—most especially The Varmint. If you were in The Varmint, no matter what fiendish Torquemada-like tortures the guests committed upon you, even if they squirted lighter fluid onto your suit's synthetic black rodent fur and attempted to set you on fire—which had happened, more than once—*you could not retaliate*. You were the public face of Disney.

They boarded the purple shuttle bus, flashed their ID cards at the driver, and chose two seats together. "How are *you* holding together?" Curtis asked.

"Aw, you know," the little man said. "Scrapin' together a little bank for my own place. Not much longer now. Not much longer."

"Hey Minnie!" a voice shouted, "did you roll up the

window on your bed this morning?" There was rough laughter from a gang of workers wearing khaki horticulture uniforms.

The little man turned around, exasperated. His voice was small and crumpled like piece of tissue paper. "My name is Manny," he shouted at them. "Not Minnie. *Manny*."

"Okay, Minnie." More rough laughter.

"Go to hell," Manny said. He turned forward, lip quivering, and wiped the corner of his eye. "These people, Curtis … they don't care. Nobody cares about anything except the mouse." Curtis knew what he was feeling.

The shuttle pulled up to the main Utilidors entrance, below the land of fantasy, and the two men stepped off the shuttle into the bright sun. Hordes of ride engineers, concession workers, greeters, super greeters, characters, makeup artists, custodians, maintenance men, security officers, wardrobe personnel, and other support staff swarmed cheerily into the opening of the fifteen-foot-high tunnel.

"What's the high this afternoon?" asked Manny.

Curtis checked the information board. "Ninety-seven," he answered. "Hoo boy." They both knew that spelled trouble. The suits became crockpots under the tropical sun and in the unbearable humidity. Once someone had taped a digital thermometer inside a bear suit and recorded a temperature of one hundred and twenty-one degrees.

"I forgot my water bottle," Manny said.

"I've got an extra in my locker," replied Curtis.

forty

. . .

THEY ENTERED THE UTILIDORS, beneath the liquid nitrogen pipes and assorted conduits. The dark gray cement beneath their feet was spotless. A sour-faced girl dressed like Cinderella was leaning against a yellow maintenance vehicle in her bloomers, smoking a cigarette. A stiff ventilating breeze blew from behind them, pushing them forward.

Then there was a loud rattling, and all conversation halted as something like a tornado whooshed quickly through the pipes above their heads. That was the AVAC, a Swedish-designed garbage collection system that operated on an automatic vacuum (hence the acronym). There are seventeen yellow AVAC cans located in various restricted areas; the submarine-looking devices suck garbage at speeds of sixty miles an hour to a large hopper at the central compacting plant. The organic waste is trucked to a landfill off property, where it's converted into compost and sold as Mickey Muck.

Curtis and Manny passed the wardrobe department, the cosmetology room, staff kitchens, the employee cafeteria, the fire prevention center, and a hallway stocked with hurricane provisions. Curtis saw bags of Fuller's dirt, a very fine hypoallergenic, waiting to be scattered inside the ghostly mansion. In another hallway lay tanks of Rosco, a solvent that is mixed with water to create eerie mist effects.

An electric-powered maintenance vehicle shished quietly past them. No gasoline-powered vehicles are allowed in the tunnels, except for the armored Brinks truck that arrives every morning to collect huge bags of cash from Cash Control. The drivers don't know if the bags are filled with dollars or scrap paper.

They found the time clock and punched in using their ID badges. Easy-listening music floated down from the ceiling.

"Looks like next week's schedule is up," Curtis said, scanning the wall.

"How many hours we got?" Manny wondered anxiously.

"You've got twenty-two."

Manny's face fell. "What about you?"

"Only eighteen," Curtis said glumly.

They both fell silent. Curtis and Manny had been assigned over sixty hours a week during the summer, giving them the weekly take-home income, after taxes, of about three hundred and sixty dollars. With those kinds of hours, they'd felt like kings. Now it was late August, however, the crowds were already thinning, and there was incredible jockeying afoot as the CTs tried to secure themselves permanent status before the fall season.

Curtis knew how tough to was get permanent status inside the parks; supervisors usually only hire seasonal workers. He'd heard that this practice could be traced back to a deadly twenty-two-day strike in October 1984 that ended when the walk-outs agreed to a loss of benefits for future hires. That, apparently, was the beginning of the end: Disney was converted from a permanent full-time staff to a collection of demoralized part-timers.

"Hey boys," said a theatrical voice, "good news."

Curtis and Manny turned around. It was Tremont Williams, a flamboyant black man who also worked in the character department. He was a tremendous dancer who usually did the stage shows and the three o'clock parade dressed as a tiger. Curtis and Manny were mere chumps by comparison. They just stood inside furry suits signing autograph books.

"Scotty made me permanent," Tremont said. "Don't you love it?"

"Yeah, he also told everybody how much he loved those Belgian chocolates you sent him," Manny said.

Tremont wasn't offended. Everyone knew that he reveled in his reputation as a shameless kiss-up. This was the season of open brownnosing. CTs were giving their supervisors candy, flowers, clothes, you name it, all in a desperate attempt to secure themselves permanent positions.

"Y'all can take a lesson from me," Tremont said. "You've got to *work* that promotion. Nobody round here gonna give you nothin' without you gamin' for it."

Curtis and Manny ignored him. They entered the character locker room, commonly known as the "zoo". There were character heads and suits scattered everywhere: decapitated bears, beasts, dwarves, donkeys, ducks, dogs, chipmunks, crickets, mice, and more.

Curtis spotted Sammy Lucrash changing further down the bench and felt a pang of jealousy sizzle through his innards. Lucrash was a legend. He had become a millionaire by the age of thirty-four by selling life insurance in Texas but decided that he wanted to pursue a more fulfilling career. So Lucrash had retired, hung it all up, and gotten himself hired here, at Walt Disney World, first as a popcorn vendor, now as a character. His salary was just one dollar a year. Curtis tried not to think about the things he could do with just one of those unused paychecks.

Next to Lucrash was an uncomfortable-looking blonde man with a conservative business haircut changing into a Harvard College t-shirt.

"See that guy over there?" Manny whispered.

"Yeah."

"He's from *up there*." The little guy gestured with his finger extended heavenward.

He meant from above the glass ceiling. This was routine for the character department. New executives were sometimes sent down to work as characters for a couple of weeks; this supposedly infused the Ivy League elite with the spirit of The Varmint.

"He looks like it," said Curtis.

"He's been complaining," said Manny, who started mocking him. "You know: 'The suits itch, it's too hot, the kids are rude.'"

"One of those," said Curtis. "You want to really torture him?"

"Sure."

"We'll *talk* to him."

Manny scratched his head. "How's that gonna bug him?"

"Oh, it'll drive him up the wall to have to chat with guys like us. You can see how arrogant he is. Watch."

Curtis casually sidled over between the benches and approached the man. "Hey there."

The man attempted to ignore him, but a quick sideways glance betrayed his pretense. Curtis stepped a little closer.

"Hi there. I notice you've got a Harvard shirt."

"I most certainly do," the man said.

"Did you go there?"

The man rolled his eyes. "Yes, I *attended* the Harvard Business School."

"Wow. That's really something."

Harvard shot him a look of contempt. "Thank you."

"How did you get into that school?"

The man didn't crack a smile. "By being born into the right family."

"Really?" Curtis liked playing dumb when it suited his needs.

"Yes," said Harvard. Then his chin tipped up. "Being born into a culture of entrepreneurship rather than a culture of labor really, in the end, determines one's place in society. It keeps one out of"—he looked up at the rafters disgustedly—"places like this."

Curtis Marshall wasn't fazed. These executives came down every few weeks all spouting the same attitude. Of course, he didn't like working in the zoo either, but he had the good sense not to pollute the air with that toxic jabber.

Curtis shrugged. "Hope you enjoy your time down here with guys like us." Then he stuck his hand out.

Harvard looked at the large hand. He seemed to be unsure of exactly what to do in such a situation. Even a handshake had to be calculated.

So Curtis slapped him on the back and returned to his locker.

"Told ya," he said.

"You were right," said Manny.

forty-one

. . .

THE NEXT STEP IN CURTIS' morning ritual was always the same: He picked up his suit from the rack.

This morning, he'd been assigned the strange, lanky, doglike creature with long ears. The one with a dented stovepipe hat, pullover turtleneck, and poor man's vest. Curtis always thought this character was vaguely reminiscent of a down-at-heels Depression-era scrabbler. He didn't mind playing this character. It was better than playing one of the dwarves, which he was ineligible for because of his height, but which was Manny's usual assignment. Most workers hoped that all seven of those miniature cretins would be taken out of circulation. This had happened before. A pair of violent twins with round bellies, the ones popularized by Alice in Wonderland, had once been retired from the park for several years, reportedly because one park official thought they looked like they had Down Syndrome.

Curtis winced as he sniffed the inside of his head. It reeked of Lysol, the heads' customary cleaning solvent. The disinfectant always turned his eyes bloodshot for hours after work. He wouldn't complain, though. At least it had been cleaned. There were plenty of horror stories about costumes that had gone unwashed for months.

A bleary-eyed guy stopped by with a cup of coffee and mumbled good morning. Then he began helping Curtis with the costume. This was the "lead": someone less than a supervisor but more than a mere character. The lead escorted the character into the park and served as a human accompaniment to answer children's questions.

Finally Curtis broke the ice. "Could be better. Thanks for asking."

The lead frowned. "Whatsa matter?"

"They dropped my hours."

"So what? You're with the college program, right?"

Curtis felt a stab of anxiety. He *wasn't* with the college program. He'd never even *been* to college.

"I'm not a college student," Curtis said.

"You're not?" The lead seemed shocked. "How old are you?"

"Twenty-five."

The lead looked like he'd just woken up to find himself pounding a baby seal with a mallet. "Sorry, dude, I didn't— you just look so young, and, I don't know, I just assumed." He shrugged, then stuck his hand into his pocket and pulled out a handful of salt tablets and offered Curtis some. Curtis swallowed four right away, then placed the rest in his locker. They were to replenish the salts he would lose throughout the course of the day.

The lead was looking at his watch. "It's almost showtime. You're gonna have some fun today."

"Why?"

"Three troops of Boy Scouts."

"You're kidding me."

The lead shook his head. "Wish I was, man."

Curtis cursed under his breath. Boy Scouts were the scourges of the character department. Even veterans would turn tail and run hell-bent-for-leather at the sight of those olive-green shirts and red neckerchiefs. The awful thing about the Boy Scouts—what made them even more abusive than most teenagers—is that they were almost always unsupervised. There was, at most, one adult chaperone for every twelve or fifteen boys.

He strapped on his shin guards to protect his legs from juvenile kicks, then pulled up the costume's pants and strapped on his size twenty-four shoes.

"You got everything you need?" the lead asked.

"Yeah, thanks."

"Curtis, work with me here." The lead was smiling quizzically at him. "Don't you want anything else?"

He tilted his head. "I don't think so. Why?"

"Nothing to put a little extra spring in your step?"

It wasn't the first time Curtis had heard such an offer. But he was determined not to get caught up in an amphetamine habit. It was well-known that certain characters shot or snorted speed before work, especially during the summer, when there were so many double shifts to cover. Getting waxed made you perform better inside the suit—it helped you work longer, and it inspired zanier, more cartoonish movement. Except for drivers, mechanics, and hazardous waste managers, nobody was ever drug tested.

Curtis said, "Not today."

"No problem. Just let me know whenever—"

"Thanks."

"It's always here. Whenever you're ready just—"

"Let's go."

"After you." The lead bowed courteously.

They left the locker room and walked down the corridor to a service elevator, Curtis carrying his head underneath his arm, giant shoes clopping on the painted cement. They shuffled through one dingy service corridor after another until finally they came to a black curtain.

They both stopped. Curtis stretched his leg muscles. The lead played with the stovepipe hat.

"Give me that," Curtis said.

"Relax," the lead said.

"Look, I'm not in the mood to goof around today." He popped some gum into his mouth and chewed proudly. "It hurts knowin' I'm gonna be fired."

"Calm down, you're jumping the gun," the lead replied. "Besides, you find a wallet today and I'll look the other way. Swear to God." In character, Curtis liked to sit down next to women and rifle through their purses. It made good comedy. The leads were always urging him to push the prank as far as possible and steal the women's money.

"I can't tell if you're joking," said Curtis.

"Scout's honor, I'll cover for you," the lead said, holding up two fingers.

"You think I trust Scouts?"

"Okay, on *my* honor."

"You'd rat me out."

The lead shrugged. "Maybe you ought to just quit."

"Maybe I will," Curtis said. "We can't trust *anybody* here. People get fired for tasting an hors d'oeuvre."

"Let's go," the lead said, "it's time."

Curtis rose, lifted his mesh-and-rubber head, and dropped it on top of his body. The lead took a final look at his appearance, adjusted his floppy ears, and then gave him a thumbs-up.

Together they stepped onstage.

forty-two

. . .

AS THE DIGITAL readout on the dashboard turned to nine o'clock, the Cravings' minivan was inching down Route 182, boxed in by automobiles on all sides. Every car on the highway was aiming for the same place.

The gates of the magic kingdom.

D.L. peered into the other cars. She could see the other pilgrims' families in the windows. Their faces looked just like her family's faces: doddering old faces, grim middle-aged faces, hyperactive little faces. Sometimes she caught a reflection of her own teenage face, anguished and tortured.

At the Disney property line, where public transformed to private, the roads widened, the traffic opened, and everything got somehow better. The sky grew somehow bluer, the grass swayed blissfully, animals pranced happily, and the world became a spinning daisy.

The Cravings' minivan rolled down the road, and the family members looked out the window with starry asterisks shining in their eyes. Soon they came to a wide pink-and-purple medieval arch spanning the way. The minivan crept to a stop next to one of fourteen tollbooths.

Gripping a safety handle with one hand, the attendant

leaned out of the booth and said, "That'll be six dollars please."

"Six dollars for what?" said Sharpy.

"Parking."

Sharpy turned to his father. "Do you have six dollars, Dad?"

Grandpa Frederick groaned like he'd just been asked to donate a kidney. He reached for his wallet—then lowered his head towards Sharpy's lap and craned his face up, so he could see the attendant, and said, "It's not like you people don't have enough space out here."

The attendant pretended not to hear him.

"Six dollars. Whew," said the old man. He rooted through his wallet, lifting out ID cards and health insurance cards.

In his rearview mirror, Sharpy saw the drivers behind him drumming impatient thumbs upon their steering wheels. "Dad, people are waiting."

"I'm trying to find exact change."

"Never mind," Sharpy said, reaching for his own wallet, "I'll take care of it."

"No, son—"

"Yes, Dad." Sharpy quickly forked over six dollars to the attendant. "See? It's done."

Relieved, Grandpa Frederick gave up the charade and snapped his wallet shut. "I didn't have change anyways," he said. The old man made a sucking sound with his teeth and pounded his thighs twice with his fists.

A series of cast members wearing yellow pinnies directed the minivan into a parking space. They were in the middle of a sun-baked expanse of black asphalt. Everywhere were the sounds of doors sliding open and children emerging like butterflies from their cocoons.

Sharpy stepped out and cracked his neck. He was wearing a white t-shirt that read *Florida!*, tan shorts, and new white Reeboks. He caught Vivian staringat him.

"What?"

"Are those new sunglasses?" she said.

On his nose he had just fitted a pair of Oakley knock-off wraparound sunglasses with florescent green arms and a florescent green spec cord that trailed around his neck. He'd purchased them last night at the hotel sundries counter.

"You bet. How do they look? Tell me the truth." He spread his arms out and a stupid grin appeared on his face.

"Ridiculous," said Vivian, looking away.

"Of course they look ridiculous," he said. "How else would I embarrass my daughter?"

But D.L. wasn't paying attention to her father's eyewear. "I have a question," she said.

"Try me," said Sharpy.

"How are we going to get Grandma on the tram?"

"We'll just lift her up," said Grandpa Frederick, unfolding the old woman's wheelchair. "No problem."

"Are you sure it's that easy?" D.L. said.

"Sure I'm sure." Her grandfather waved the schedule at her. "Remember? I *researched*. Unlike some other members of this family."

Meanwhile, Vivian was rummaging through the trunk, preparing Brittany's day bag—a can of applesauce, a water bottle, two store-bought plastic-wrapped sandwiches, cheese-and-crackers, a chocolate bar, suntan lotion, aspirin, safety pins, an extra t-shirt.

"I have to pee," her daughter said.

"Not here," snapped Vivian.

Too late. Brittany crouched next to the tire. A thin rivulet of yellow urine had begun trickling onto the hard ground and was pooling near her feet.

"*Brittany*!!" she said. "*Are you a young lady*??"

"Yes."

"That's not what young ladies do!"

D.L. watched Vivian vainly trying to clean up the puddle

on the cement. At least the little girl hadn't been totally femi-
nized yet—not like her mother had been. Vivian had dressed
provocatively even for this amusement park. She was
wearing a pair of expensively tailored denim overall shorts
with nothing but a orange lacy brassiere underneath. D.L.
was both repulsed and jealous of the full, expensive breasts
that swelled inside their hammock like a pair of saline
zeppelins.

"We need to get going or we're going to miss the tram,"
Grandpa Frederick announced. The other pilgrims were
running across the lot towards the row of yellow cement
poles which marked the boundary of the tram lane.

"There's no hurry, Dad," said Sharpy. "Why do we have to
be first?"

"I don't want us to get left behind," said Grandpa stiffly,
looking at his wristwatch. "Hurry up, son."

"I'm *coming*," Sharpy shouted. "How old do you think I
am, Dad?"

"I know how old you are—"

"I'm *forty-two years* old!"

"Can't tell from the way you're dawdling," he said.

D.L. waited for the sideshow bickering to die down—but
it never did, not while Grandma was placed in her wheelchair, not while she applied Tim's sunscreen, not while the
entire troupe traipsed towards the tram car station.

This was how they lived.

She felt nauseated.

forty-three

. . .

"FOLKS, how ya doin, and welcome to Disney World's very magical kingdom. For the safety and courtesy of everybody on the tram, please no smoking. Please remember folks, you're parked in Minnie 25. Write it down, memorize it, tell it to yourselves, tell it to each other, tell it to your children, tell it to your children's children, burn it into your forehead, but do not forget Minnie 25. I won't be here later to remind you, I'll be gone home. Please duck your head and watch your step."

(*Sir, you can go back to the car and drive grandma up front so she don't have to get on board. Go on, I'll radio ahead you need a handicapped space. Well, no, I'm not tellin you what to do. Of course it's up to you. Okay, bring her on board then, I don't care one way or the other. I'm just tryin to help.*)

"Children to the inside, adults to the outside, please collapse all strollers. There is another tram behind us, there will be no further boarding, no further boarding please, no further boarding, okay just ignore what I'm saying ma'am, no further boarding, no further boarding. There'll be another tram in four hours, ha ha ha. And we're off.

"Welcome to Walt Disney World Florida, the land where genies are funny, hunchbacks are adorable, and beasts become ballroom dancers. My name is Huey and your driver's name is Bud, we will be taking the next curve at approximately four miles per hour."

(*What's your question, sir? No, nobody allowed to ride back here but cast members. What'd you ask? Sure I studied for this job. I studied a long time. Oh yeah. You gotta know psychology. And comedy. Keep 'em laughing, insult Disney, insult them, insult their kids. They eat it up, trust me. Hold on a minute.*)

"Please, folks, those of you exiting to the left please watch that tram coming from the opposite direction, it weighs twenty-four tons and will not stop for you, it has the right-of-way. I don't want you leaving the park with that … *run-down* feeling. Ba-dump. And we're off."

(*These trams? These tootsies got brakes on every car. Sorta like driving a big dog train. Top speed? Fifteen miles an hour. Well, it's a Caterpillar engine. But we got some mad power under that hood. Put it this way, if a barge ever sunk in the lagoon, these pups would pull it out.*)

"Please watch your heads as you exit. The lady mouse on the left, the lady mouse on the left, the last planet in the solar system on the right."

(*Hey, you might wanta hang onto your grandma. Last year I saw an old bag fly off her seat at this turn and smack her head right into a pole. She wasn't no pile of feathers neither.*)

"And here we are at the transportation center, folks. Please collect all personal belongings before exiting the tram to your right. Please watch your head, folks, and if you bump your head, then please watch your language. There are free shuttles to the other parks throughout the day, and I strongly urge you to take them as you will not find very much that is free here at Walt Disney World Florida."

forty-four

. . .

AS THE REST of the family helped Grandma off the tram and unfolded her wheelchair, D.L. sat on the edge of a treepot next to Brittany, who was already tucked into her stroller. The tiny blonde moppet was pitching a hissy fit, her stubby legs kicking, tiny fists clenched. Her face was contorted into a devilishly red mask of agony.

This girl needed to be taught a lesson.

Impassively, D.L. extended her foot and pushed the stroller. She watched the tyke roll backwards towards the curb.

But Vivian caught the rolling stroller. She hadn't noticed the push. "Let's color-code you," she said to her daughter, wrapping a piece of orange tape around the handle of the stroller. "We wouldn't want anyone to steal my baby treasure."

"That would be a tragedy," said D.L.

"Just wait until you have a daughter," said Vivian. "You might not be so quick to judge her."

"Can I interrupt?" said Sharpy. He handed his D.L. a folded bill. "I have a promise to keep. Fifty dollars."

He'd sworn to give her spending money inside the park.

D.L. accepted it and managed a smile. Her grandfather was looking at her oddly.

"Fifty dollars?" said Grandpa Frederick.

"Yes," said Sharpy.

"I never saw fifty dollars until I was twenty-one years old working the cash register at my father's feed store."

"It's a different world now," said Sharpy. "Fifty bucks doesn't go as far as it used to."

The old man snuffled. "How do you expect to control your children, giving them money like that?"

"I'll put it in the bank, Grandpa," said D.L.

"You shouldn't have it at all," he said.

The Cravings stepped onto the monorail, rode around the lagoon, then exited at the formal entrance to the amusement park. An ecstatic crowd of families and couples was already milling about in front of the black wrought iron gates, singing along to the greatest hits that sounded from stereo speakers hidden in the trees.

It was *Egeria*, it was Lourdes, it was Fatima, it was Mecca —it was every pilgrimage site in the history of gods and men.

Then there was a mad rush as the gates opened, the crowd heaved like an enormous belch, and the Cravings were pushed through the gates and plunged beneath the train station before emerging onto Main Street with the rest of the throng. The street was lined with idealized gingerbread Victorian shops. The soft ringing of bicycle horns. The deep grooves of the trolley tracks. The smell of cinnamon.

This was how America once looked and sounded and smelled.

Somewhere.

At the far end of the street sat the huge fiberglass castle, its turrets and spires leaping upwards into the clear blue sky. The castle uses a sneaky effect known as "forced perspective" to simulate height: its proportions grow smaller as it gets higher. Nonetheless, it was beautiful—so lovely, in fact, that hundreds of families were jostling each other in the plaza below, each striving to get The Photo at the same time.

"There are too many people," D.L. said.

"I know," said Sharpy.

"We need that picture," Grandpa said tensely.

"It's too crowded, Dad," said Sharpy, irritated, "and we won't be able to get a good shot. You know what else?" He felt around his pants. "I think I forgot the camera."

"You can buy one over there," said D.L. "It looks like an oldtime photo shop."

As they crossed the street, D.L. noticed that her brother was—

(*down, one two three four, laser too close, down, one two three*)

—scampering on all fours. Trying to crawl underneath the path of other families' photographs.

They entered the oldtime photo shop. A cast member dressed like a nineteenth-century store clerk, in suspenders and straw hat, welcomed them. An old-timey box camera was pointed at a pair of stools in front of a screened background.

"Where are your cameras?" Sharpy asked.

"We don't sell any, sir."

"What *do* you sell here?"

"Personalized period photographs. Care to take one?" The clerk pulled down a succession of different background screens. "We've got Old West, Valley Forge, an afternoon picnic. You name it."

"That sounds fun," said Vivian. "Let's make a period picture, Stephen." She turned back to the photographer. "What kind of costumes do you have?"

The photographer blew air out of his lips. "What are you looking for? We've got coal miners, aristocrats, railroad switchmen, drum-and-fife corps—"

"This is silly," Grandpa Frederick scoffed, watching the couple arrange themselves before the camera. "Isn't it, Maya?"

There was no answer. In her wheelchair, Grandma Maya had fallen asleep.

"Why don't you wait outside with her?" said Sharpy.

"I'm going to wait outside with her," said Grandpa Frederick. "This photo is costing us time. We're already behind schedule."

The door closed behind him. The couple eventually chose a saloon theme, with Sharpy wearing a bowler hat and a handlebar moustache and holding a tumbler of plastic beer. Vivian was dressed like a prostitute, a frilly white blouse revealing her plunging neckline.

"Smile and say mouse cheese," the photographer said from underneath the historically accurate black cloth. Sharpy beamed and held a fistful of nineteenth-century cash. Vivian held a kissing pose on his cheek. A light bulb popped uselessly.

"Excellent," said the photographer. "It turned out well." The sepia-tinged photograph of a prostitute kissing her drunken john appeared on a video screen.

"I'm getting out of these clothes," said Sharpy. He went back into the dressing room and closed the door. Vivian and the photographer were alone in the shop.

"That dress looks good on you," said the photographer.

"Was that a compliment or an insult?"

"Depends on how you want to interpret it."

Vivian gave him a stony stare, and didn't speak again until she had left the shop.

forty-five

. . .

UNFORTUNATELY, there were now even *more* tourists milling about for The Photo. To get a clean, unobstructed, and —most important—legally acceptable shot of the fiberglass castle, Sharpy and Grandpa agreed that they would wait until people stopped pouring through the gates.

That left the morning wide open.

The Cravings explored the park, like so many millions of others had before them. They clambered inside the giant treehouse with polyethylene leaves. They rode the thunderous mountain railroad between the weathered, ochre buttes made of lathe stretched over rebar. They boarded the jungle cruise and laughed at the roaring plastic hippos.

By noon, they had stopped to rest on a pair of benches. Vivian purchased a carton of rich European ice cream for her daughter.

"Come here, Brittany," she said.

The little girl, wearing a pointy pink princess hat with flowing pink gauze trailing down her back, skipped over. Vivian commanded her to open her mouth, then decorously placed a piece of ice cream on the little girl's tongue.

"Do you like how that tastes?" asked Vivian.

"Mm-hm," said her daughter.

"That's the very best ice cream money can buy."

"It tastes good."

"That's right, honey. I would do *anything* to make sure you get only the best."

Brittany wrinkled her nose and made a funny face. "Would you kill somebody?"

Vivian froze. Her eyes searched her daughter's face. "If there was no other way," she finally said, "then yes I would."

Meanwhile, Grandma Maya had persevered through the morning. Though not entirely lucid, she was awake and aware despite the heat: a considerable victory. Her eyes followed a pair of sparrows fighting over a french fry on the ground.

"Those are pretty birds," she said.

"Yes, they are," said D.L.

"Are they real?" the old lady asked.

The park's conflation of real and imaginary had confused the old woman. D.L. decided to test her grandmother: "No, they're mechanical birds."

To D.L.'s surprise, Grandma Maya *believed* it. "Isn't that something," the old lady said, shaking her head in amazement. Then she pointed with an unsteady finger to a small lagoon nearby. "What about that? Is that real water?"

D.L. found herself lying again. "No, Grandma, that's cellophane tape with hairdryers blowing underneath."

"Oh." The old lady seemed satisfied with those answers. Then she twisted around in her seat to look at D.L. directly. "That's a pretty shirt you've got on."

D.L. managed a weak smile. It was a green spaghetti-strap number with a hippy-dippy blue flower across the chest. She was also wearing flared jeans, shell-toed sneakers, and a khaki kangol cap. Still, she felt like the lowliest cockroach on the planet for deceiving her own grandmother—*her own grandmother*—for absolutely no reason at all. What was wrong with her?

"Thanks," she muttered.

The old woman sighed. Her body shifted by itself in the wheelchair. "You know something?

"What?"

"I miss having sex."

D.L. felt her gag reflex seize her throat. A small bolus of vomit worked its way up her esophagus. Grandma Maya continued, oblivious.

"Your grandfather never really liked doing that. I used to pull all sorts of tricks to get him interested. I'd take him to go see sexy movies, you know. But whenever I'd try to touch his leg in the dark, he'd always push my hand away."

"Anybody have to go to the bathroom?" asked Sharpy.

"Yes!" shouted D.L.

"I'm timing you," said Grandpa, looking at his wrist-watch. "You've got five minutes." His granddaughter ran across the pavement to the restroom.

"What should we do next?" Sharpy took the map from his father and looked over the attractions. "Let's ask Brittany what she wants to do."

"I want to eat ice cream," the little girl said.

"You're already doing that," said Sharpy. "What about after you finish?"

"We should take that picture," Grandpa said.

"We will."

Grandpa watched the queue at a lunch stand; tourists were lined fifteen deep. He whistled to himself. "Boy, that's doing a brisk business. What do you think is the sales per square foot? A thousand?"

"At least," Sharpy agreed.

"Prices are high too," the old man said. His voice betrayed his admiration. "They really know how to squeeze the bucks out of you here."

Brittany tugged at her mother's overalls. "Mommy," she said, "I want some of those." She was pointing at the pairs of Varmint ears displayed in a cartoonish window of various Varmint collectibles.

"Brittany's ready to go shopping," Vivian announced.

"I'm not," said Sharpy.

Vivian was applying lipstick in the reflection of her sunglasses. "Well," she said, "maybe you could just lend me your credit card. I swear to be a good girl."

"Haven't you made enough purchases?" he said.

She suddenly whirled on him. The niceties scattered like birds from a tree. "My daughter wants a pair of *mouse ears*. Is that honestly too much to ask at Disney F'ing World?"

She'd chosen her issue well. Sharpy couldn't deny the mouse ears to a child. Sharpy produced the plastic from his wallet and handed it to her with great ceremony.

"Thank you," she said, pecking his cheek.

"You be careful with that," Grandpa warned her.

"Oh, Frederick," Vivian said sarcastically, "can't you see that I've learned my lesson?"

Grandpa Frederick stood up. "I think I'll accompany you anyways."

She struggled for a response; her hand worked itself a hundred different ways. Then: "That would be wonderful."

The mistress sweetly took the old man's arm and guided him into the souvenir shop.

forty-six

. . .

NOW THERE WERE three family members left, but only two were conscious. Grandma Maya's chin had drooped into her chest.

Sharpy removed the ceramic urn from the carrying bag. It weighed as much as an illustrated hardcover Bible and had caused the bag's strap to bite into his shoulder. It was, he thought, a too-literal symbol of the weight upon his soul. But he was toting it around without a complaint. He was performing his penance. He was knitting his family together again.

Tim spotted the object with his peripheral vision and lurched over. He took the urn from his father—

(*Vivian is splurchasing Soo Vin Ears*)

—and traced the scrollwork with his index finger.

"Careful, Snooker," warned Sharpy. "You know what's in that urn."

Tim didn't respond.

"Tell me what's in that urn, Snooker."

"Brown scarf," Tim replied.

Sharpy felt his spirits suddenly plummet. Here was proof:

Tim didn't know that his mother was dead. Autism was devastating, even heart-wrenching, in the way that it casually reduced traditional relationships to object fetishes. A mother could selflessly dedicate twelve years of her life to her autistic son, and "brown scarf" would be the only way that he would remember her after death.

Sharpy watched his son bobble the urn in his left hand as the index finger of his right hand compulsively traced every curlicue in the design.

"Snooker, give me that," he said. The boy's finger traced madly but he refused to release the ceramic. His father tried to take it, but Tim twisted away—

(*haven't finished*)

—and scooted further down the bench.

"Snooker, give me that goddamn urn before you do something stupid." Sharpy stood up and stormed angrily towards the boy. Tim leapt up from the bench and—

(*haven't finished*)

—raced out into the milling crowd, cradling the precious cargo in the crook of his left arm. Enraged, Sharpy darted behind him and yanked his elbow.

The urn dropped to the ground.

It cracked wide open.

Sharpy staggered backwards, howling. His wife's ashes had spilled onto the asphalt, the filthy ground, to be ground beneath hundreds of strangers' shoes! Goddamn his son to goddamned damnation!

Sharpy sprang left and right, windmilling his arms, trying to create space around the small heap. "Everybody back up!" he shouted to the passersby. "Please back up!"

He may as well have tried to shout down a cattle drive. Somebody's rubber-toed sneaker inadvertently kicked the pile. Immediately Sharpy dropped down and tried to protect her. She was spreading! He was losing her! He threw his arms around the fine powder, the earthly remains of his first and only wife.

"Snooker, go find help!" he said. "*Go!*" He knew the command was useless before the words had left his mouth. His son stood there in his peculiar crooked manner, a beatific smile on his face. He was in a far distant galaxy.

For several embarrassing seconds Sharpy maintained the protective crouch, helpless, until a blue-shirted cast member approached him. "Can I help you, sir?"

"This is my wife," he said.

"Your wife's what?"

"This is my wife," he said. "Her *ashes.*"

The cast member's eyes widened. Then he lifted his Motorola to his face and barked a series of incomprehensible numbers and acronyms.

A moment later, a sweeper arrived with a brand-new broom and dustpan, probably deemed suitable for the sweeping up of remains of loved ones. The sweeper also had a thermos bottle stamped with the ubiquitous Varmint.

Sharpy snatched the broom and swept the fine powder into the dustpan. Then he gingerly emptied it into the Thermos bottle. He tried to pull out the plastic straw, but it had been welded into the lid. It would do for the moment. He stowed the bottle in his backpack and set about collecting the shards of the urn.

When he looked up, the cast members were watching him with baleful eyes. "We're sorry," one said.

"Thank you," he replied.

Sharpy found his son hanging off the back of a bench. His first impulse was to clobber him. But that was neither fatherly nor humane. Instead, Sharpy swallowed his pride, reached out, and hugged the boy to his chest.

"I love you," he said.

There was no response. There was nothing beneath the skin. What had he honestly expected?

He released Tim, disappointed. And when the remainder of the Craving family trickled back to join him, he said nothing about the accident.

forty-seven

. . .

THE HEAT SHIMMERED over the fantasyland, rippling in caloric waves. The families swarmed like summer insects, licking ice cream cones, adults yelling for children to slow down.

Inside his costume, Curtis Marshall assumed his goofy persona. In character, he was expected to be clumsy, silly, and lovable. It wasn't difficult; he could imitate just about any type of physical movement. Curtis was comfortable with his body in the way of professional athletes and actors.

It was this quality that had won him the job at the character audition four months earlier. In a huge dance hall, there had been three hundred people competing for twenty spots. He'd received a piece of masking tape with a number; then he'd taken off his shoes for a Polaroid snapshot in front of a height chart. Then the entire assemblage, thirty at a time, had learned a sixteen-step jazz dance in front of a long mirror. Curtis had mastered it easily. Four hours later, Curtis had finally been called into the auditioning room without a clue in the world about what he would be expected to do next. "Pretend to paint a fence," the judges had told him. Curtis had instantly brightened up. He could do that! He'd mimicked opening an imaginary paint can, mixing the can, getting his foot stuck in the can, pulling the can off his foot, turning the can upside down over his head, getting coated by paint, wiping paint off his face.

One stonefaced judge had giggled.

A minute later, they'd given him the job.

And now, on this sweltering day, four disillusioning months later, he was wearily moving through the magical kingdom, signing small children's autograph books, posing for pictures. He resorted to all his usual tricks. He pretended to trip over invisible wires. He worked a Michael Jackson spin. He jumped and landed on one knee with his arms spread out. Children especially seemed to like it when he put on the special walk, an elbows-out bouncy strut with a lot of roll in the shoulders.

Inside the head, there was only one ventilation hole, and no way to touch one's face. As the heat grew, sweat trickled down Curtis' face in agonizing rivulets. Wearing one of these heads was a very peculiar sort of torture, he thought. Like slathering someone's feet with honey while standing him on an anthill.

Near the end of his forty minutes onstage, he was performing in front of the entrance to the skyway cable ride when he encountered a mean-looking family moving with an aggressive swagger. They were thick-shouldered, squinty-browed people, and even through the ventilation hole he could spot the perverted glint in their eyes. They meant trouble. Short of climbing over a bench, however, Curtis had no escape route.

Eyeing him evilly, the family's youngest boy yanked on the lead's hand. "How does he breathe?"

"The same way a dog breathes," the lead sid.

"I mean the person inside," the boy said.

"That's not a person. That's a dog."

"Hey there, champ," the father said, sticking out his hand

to Curtis, "put 'er there." Curtis put his hand out, then pulled it away. He put his other hand up to his mouth and shook his head up and down: a pantomime laughing at his own simple-minded practical joke.

The father wasn't amused. "Smartass." He turned to his son. "Son, go punch the bastard. Go on. I'll take your picture. Give 'im a good whack."

The little boy ran directly towards Curtis' knees with a vicious grin on his mug. Curtis deftly stepped aside, grabbed the boy's arm, and led him a few steps away. The father had crouched to shoot a photo; now he was standing up, a vexed look spreading across his face like spilled beer.

Curtis crouched down next to the boy. "I'm your special friend, Jeffrey," he said. "Did you know that?" He knew that his voice could be clearly heard through the ventilation shaft. He didn't have voice clearance, but this rule could be quietly broken on *very* special occasion—especially during his last week.

The boy was enraptured. "You are?"

"I'm your special friend, and no one can hear me but you."

"Okay."

"You're the *only* one who can hear me. Are you listening?"

"Yes."

Curtis paused. "Your parents don't love you."

"Yes they *do*," the boy said.

"No they don't," Curtis whispered. "Only *I* love you. Stay with me at Disney World forever."

"Come on, Jeffrey," his mother shouted. "Say goodbye to your friend."

Curtis squeezed the boy's arm. "Don't go, Jeffrey. Stay here with me."

Jeffrey faced his parents. "I want to stay here," he shouted.

"Come *here*, Jeffrey," his mother said.

"But he *told* me to stay here!"

"Jeffrey, don't be an idiot," his father shouted. "That's an animal. He *can't talk*."

"Remember, Jeffrey, you're the only one who can hear me," Curtis whispered.

"He can *too* talk!" Jeffrey cried. "He says I'm the only who can hear him!"

Curtis finally released the boy, and the dark family moved on. The lead smiled: *I know you broke no-vocalization*. Curtis lifted his palms up and shrugged.

forty-eight

. . .

HOURS LATER, Curtis strutted near a concession stand. He was surrounded by a gang of small children. He heard the whining voices; he saw the crowns of messy hair; he felt the tiny fists assaulting his legs and butt.

This wasn't uncommon. Curtis knew several nonviolent methods of calming aggressive children. One way was to accidentally step on their toes; another was to accidentally bat them across the face with an exuberant elbow. The best method, however, was to squeeze them like a python. Curtis liked to wrap his arms around their heads and hug them hard enough to pop their brains out of their skullcaps. That usually left even the wildest children blinking and stumbling.

This time, he didn't need to resort to those measures, because the lead suddenly intervened.

"Hey, guess what, kids!" the lead said, looking at his wristwatch. "They just told me that it's time for the goofiest dog on earth to go have lunch before the three o'clock parade. Say goodbye!"

The children all cheered, and Curtis waved goodbye animatedly. He couldn't wait for the break. His lungs were burning, his thighs already felt quivery and rubbery from all the high-stepping—and there were still six more of these performances today. At the same time, he felt nervous. This was probably the most enjoyable work he had ever done, period, in his short life upon this earth. It was pure playfulness. What other job allowed you to be so physically and creatively *free*? He thought about it. Maybe he *should* play the suck-up game. Maybe he *should* buy the gifts, pucker up and crawl towards his supervisor's ass. He could get permanent status ... maybe even some benefits ... a little stability in his life. *That* would be heavenly. Suddenly a career in the character department wasn't looking so terrible.

The lead stopped. "Look over there."

Curtis swung his mesh-and-rubber head around. Through the ventilation hole, he saw two dwarves being brutally mobbed by a Boy Scout troop. There were at least thirteen pre-adolescent boys going apeshit around the two characters, kicking them, clubbing them, brutalizing them. The dwarves were standing there with as much dignity as they could muster, like martyrs, their arms crossed in front of their chests —the agreed-upon signal that the cast member is in serious trouble. Most visitors see it just before their favorite character either vomits through the ventilation shaft or pitches forward facefirst on the ground.

"Where's security?" Curtis said.

"I'll find out," the lead replied. "And stop talking. Someone's going to hear you."

"I have to help them," said Curtis.

"You're in character."

"I don't care."

"Go backstage!"

But the lead might as well have been talking to a sheet of drywall. Curtis was extremely loyal to those close to him—his greatest strength and weakness—and he was constitutionally incapable of allowing his fellow characters to suffer such abuse.

The Scouts had pushed one of the dwarves backwards over a low fence. Some were raining kicks upon the inert form; some were blowing cigarette smoke and pouring soft drinks into the suit's ventilation shaft. Curtis was infuriated. That could asphyxiate the cast member inside. Plus, the Scouts obviously hadn't considered the possibility that there were usually *girls* inside the dwarf suits.

What the hell, why not. After all, it was his last week. He had nothing to lose.

Punching his plush fists together, Curtis broke into an energetic trot and arrived at the scene just as several Scouts succeeded in wrestling the second dwarf to the ground. One was trying to pull his shoes off his feet. Another was sitting on top of the character's chest, mercilessly bashing his rubber face. There was a huge indentation in his nose that was getting deeper with every punch. Curtis could tell the person inside the suit was struggling for help. A small voice was shouting.

It was Manny's voice.

Fire and fury hazed Curtis' eyes. His chest swelled as he approached the smallest of the Scouts, the one pounding Manny's latex nose. The little miscreant didn't see him until it was too late. Curtis grabbed the boy by the knotted neckerchief and hauled him to his feet.

"Stop!" the Boy Scout screamed.

But Curtis felt possessed. Curtis lifted him high in the air with both hands and carried him over to a trash can.

The Scout twisted and panicked: "Don't, oh please, no, oh God—"

His pleas rang on deaf ears as Curtis stuffed the boy head-first into the can. His pair of legs were straight up in the air like a pair of swizzle sticks in a drink.

The other Scouts stood stock still. They'd been struck totally dumb. They'd just seen one of their gentlest childhood icons flat-out kicking ass. Suddenly one of the Scouts roared—

"Get 'im!"

—and they turned *en masse* upon Curtis. Twelve preadolescent bodies slammed into him, knocking him backwards. He could feel their small yet surprisingly strong fists landing all over his body. Someone was yanking on one of his ears.

"Hey, goofy, how'd ya like this!" one screamed. He felt diabolical fingers scrabbling at his neck, tugging on his tall stovepipe hat, twisting his enormous head—

And suddenly Curtis suddenly found himself blinking in the daylight. Sunshine was everywhere. The unthinkable had occurred.

They'd ripped off his head.

The little furies were stopped right in their tracks. The sight of Curtis' human face—*he looks like us*—calmed the youth.

Curtis looked around worriedly. Touron families had started to congregate; even worse, some were snapping pictures. He was violating the most sacred rule in the character department:

Never be seen without your head onstage.

His fate was sealed, etched in concrete. Curtis would be fired. But he was twenty miles past caring about anything so prosaic. First and foremost, his dignity needed repair.

"You little dickheads," he said. "Why do you think you can beat the hell out of a Disney character? We're real people! Are you too dumb to understand that? Or are you trying to earn your asshole badges? Huh?"

He stared at each of the boys, but they couldn't look meet his eyes. Disgusted, feeling very much like a middle-school teacher, Curtis snatched the head from where it had fallen on the ground. Then he kneeled beside the fallen dwarf.

"Manny?" he said.

From inside the dented head, a small, wounded voice replied: "Curtis?"

"Let's get you backstage."

"I think they broke something."

"We'll find out in a minute." He crouched and scooped up the dwarf in his arms. The dwarf's head bobbed and angled weirdly. Curtis realized that Manny was trying to look at him.

"Curtis, where's your head?" said Manny.

"They ripped it off."

The dwarf's molded face seemed to somehow absorb the news. Then Manny's voice said: "I guess this is your last day then."

"Yeah."

"Mine too," said Manny. "Let's go."

Curtis lifted his small, injured friend in his arms and slowly carried him towards the nearest exit.

forty-nine

. . .

AFTER THE LATE afternoon sun threw their shadows slantwise, after the cotton candy had stickied their fingers, after the rides had shaken their innards and the inane songs had frayed their nerves—Sharpy made the decision.

It was finally time for The Picture.

The seven travellers headed back towards Main Street, the *axis mundi*. Sharpy entered a photo shop and emerged carrying two rolls of film—he wasn't taking any chances— and a package of batteries. He loaded the batteries and the film into his trusted Nikon 35mm, which had recorded the family history for over a decade. He'd been meaning to buy a digital camera—everybody at his workplace raved about them—but in honor of his wife, he'd decided to take the film on one last trip before converting to the future.

"Dad," said D.L.

"What?" Sharpy replied.

"Don't you at least want to get a disposable camera?"

"Why?"

"In case something happens to that one."

"This camera is very dependable," he said. "Your mother and I have used it for years."

"And those little throw-away ones are made in Japan," added Grandpa Frederick, as if that explained everything. D.L. rolled her eyes and followed silently.

Sharpy led the family into the small plaza beneath the fiberglass castle—the holiest of holies, the *sanctum sanctorum* —and arranged its sunburnt members in a rough semicircle. Above them, the silver edifice leapt skyward, glassy and imminent, like something glimpsed in a dream.

"Everybody smile and say *money*," D.L. said.

"That's tacky," said Vivian.

"It was a joke."

"It doesn't matter. Nobody with money talks about it." Vivian wore an anxious, serious look on her face as she brushed invisible lint from the tops of her overalls. She was facing the camera squarely and seemed to be on her very best behavior.

Sharpy loaded the new batteries and the roll of Kodak film into the camera. He snapped a couple of practice shots, then looked at the photo counter. It read "3". All systems were go. He loved this camera.

He lifted the camera to his face. Vivian had patted her cheeks and applied some last-minute lipstick. Brittany thrust her little belly forward beneath her denim halter top. Grandpa Frederick cleared his throat and stood rigidly erect, hands clasped behind him. In her wheelchair, Grandma Maya stared at her toes while her curled, dry tongue pressed against her lips.

"Snooker, look over here," said Sharpy. Tim was staring off to the side, banging his wrists together. "Snooker?"

D.L. gently turned her brother's head towards their father, but she couldn't turn his eyeballs. He wouldn't look at the camera.

"He's frightened of it," said D.L.

"Still?" said Sharpy. "He's almost a teenager!"

"Let him be," said Grandma Maya. "He's blessed."

"What about you, son?" said Grandpa. "You have to be in the picture too."

Sharpy felt irritated. He *did* have to be in the picture. How could he have forgotten? Even worse—why did his father always have to be so *right*? They would have to find a surrogate shooter. Sharpy scanned the milling tourons and spotted a plump, trashy woman smoking an unfiltered Marlboro nearby. She had no children in sight.

Quickly he approached her with his most solicitous smile. "Excuse me," he asked, "but do you think you could take our picture?"

The woman shrugged. "Why the hell not."

He handed her the Nikon. "Just press this button here."

The woman accepted the camera. Sharpy quickly ran to Vivian's side and threw his arm around her shoulders, beaming with happiness. *Just a few seconds away! A million smackers! Money money money money ... money!*

"Which button was it?"

"The one on the right."

"Which one?"

Sharpy grew irritated. "It's the one that says—"

"Never mind, I found it."

The Cravings showed their tensest smiles as the woman crouched down and snapped a picture. "There's one," she said. Then she snapped another. "There's two." She stood up and brought the camera back to Sharpy.

"No!" said Sharpy, his hands spinning a frantic circle. "Keep going! Use it all up!"

The woman blanched. "The whole roll?"

"It's worth a lot of money," Grandpa said.

"A million dollars!" shouted Brittany.

The woman's eyes gauged the family and saw that the girl was telling was the truth. "Well, hope you give me some of it. I spent two thousand dollars on this sparrowfart trip."

The Cravings posed motionless for several minutes as the

woman took photos from every conceivable different angle: left, *click*, right, *click*, on her knees, *click*, above her head, *click*. Five, ten, fifteen, twenty pictures. Finally, her finger pressed the button once more—

There was no click.

"That's it," the woman announced.

The family fell apart with seven sighs of relief. Sharpy lifted his arms into the air like a prizefighter at the end of a bruising bout. Adrenaline flooded his bloodstream. His chest ballooned with pride. Success! The vacation was a success! His family was a success! *He* was a success! The gauntlet had been thrown—and he'd picked it up and flung it right back! Flung it back in the face of that sanctimonious attorney and those prim, desiccated sisters! He felt his cheeks hardening from the grin that was plastered his face. What was that movement? He looked down. His feet—dancing! Herky-jerky in the street! Giddy with excitement!

Sharpy wasn't the only one in an infectiously happy mood. Grandpa Frederick was walking up to strangers and pumping hands like a politician congratulating the winners of a watermelon-growing contest. Grandma Maya's lower lip trembled happily and her weak arms extended towards Sharpy for a hug. His children appeared at his sides and he squeezed them tightly. Vivian seized the back of his head and planted a deep, luscious kiss on his lips.

"Congratulations," she said, "you're a rich man."

"Don't I know it!"

When they pulled apart, it was to the sound of cheering. A small crowd of touron families had gathered. Some of the parents were smiling and clapping. "Your family is *so happy*!" shouted a teary mother. "What's your secret?"

Sharpy knew he had lipstick smeared across his face, but he didn't care. "Money," he said. "We've finally got *money*."

fifty

. . .

THE CRAVINGS LEFT the plaza and moved down Main Street towards the exit gates. Sharpy bounced along, slapping his hands together cheerily, even breaking out into lusty songs from his childhood that he barely remembered knowing.

Grandpa Frederick looked at him sternly, and said, "Get a hold of yourself, son. You're not acting appropriately."

"But I'm happy!" Sharpy shouted. "This isn't the time for" —he lowered his voice in mock-sobriety—"prayer and reflection. This is the time to celebrate!" He watched Vivian's eyes light up. She wrapped an arm around his waist happily.

D.L. followed behind them. She'd never seen her father this unhinged, and it disturbed her in the way that any wild behavior from authority figures disturbs young people who are still unsure of their own hearts. Plus, she was concerned about her brother. She could see Tim's eyes flicking towards the camera in her father's pocket.

"What's up, Snooker?" she said.

"Vivian."

D.L. pointed to their father. "That's not Vivian."

"Want to picture Vivian," he said.

"With what?"

Tim darted ahead and snuck his hand into the pocket of his father's shorts. Sharpy whirled around with his fists up. "Whoa there!" Then he saw the culprit, laughed, and tousled Tim's head. "Thought I was getting pickpocketed! What do you want, Snooker?"

Tim pointed toward the camera.

"The camera? Do you want the camera?"

"Want to picture Vivian."

"Well, there you go," Sharpy said, handing him the Nikon 35 mm. "Just be careful."

Tim fell back and turned the device in his hands, pressing the shutter button. Then he held it against his face.

"You'll take a picture of your nose that way," said D.L. "Here, like this." She turned the camera around so the shutter faced outwards. "Now look through this hole and press this button." Tim obeyed.

"No click," said Tim. "There's supposed to be a click."

"That's because we used all the pictures."

"Used all the pictures."

"And now Dad has to put in a new roll of film."

The Cravings had passed underneath the railroad station and were pushing through the turnstiles now, officially leaving the park. D.L. entered the turnstiles ahead of her brother. The stainless steel bar pressed against the small paunch of her belly, and for a moment she panicked as she imagined that she wouldn't be able to fit through the narrow threshold.

Outside the gate, she turned and waited. He passed through the turnstile with odd grace. She also noticed that he was fiddling with the side of the camera.

"The button's on top," she said.

That's when she realized that he wasn't pressing the button. He was trying to open the casing.

"Stop that, Snooker!" she said. "Don't touch the—"

It was too late.

In the space of a single breath, he had popped open the casing ... and yanked the entire length of film from the camera. The useless strip of celluloid dangled down by his knees. D.L. stopped, her arms hanging equally limply at her side.

The entire roll had been exposed to the daylight. Now the oxidization had slowly begun.

The pictures were ruined.

Even worse: the entire family had passed through the turnstiles.

"Dad?" said D.L.

"What is it now?" He was chatting with a park attendant.

Sharpy turned and saw the boy. He saw the exposed film dangling from the camera. His nostrils flared like those of an enraged horse. An eerie silent rage descended upon his face. The family suddenly became eerily quiet.

"Timothy ... Weller ... Craving," he said.

"He didn't mean to do it," said D.L.

"Wait right here," said Sharpy. He went back to the gate, exchanged a few words with the attendant, then stormed back. "Goddamnit!"

"What did he say?" said Grandpa Frederick.

"No readmittance!"

"No!" Grandpa Frederick staggered backwards, holding a forearm to his forehead.

D.L. couldn't believe the melodrama. Her father and grandfather were overacting, like mourners on a *telenovella*. Sure, this was a blow, but not quite the disaster that was being portrayed. They could come back the next day, she thought.

Sharpy, however, wasn't even remotely finished blowing off his anger. He turned to his son. "Did you hear that, Snooker? We can't get back inside! We're *screwed*! God*dam*mit!"

"It's not his fault," D.L. said.

"When is something going to *be* his goddamned fault?" her father shouted. He punched the air. "Do you realize what we have to do now? We have to *come back* and *take the picture all over again*!"

"So what?"

"That's going to cost us seven more tickets," Grandpa Frederick said.

The teenage girl stood her ground. "So what?"

"They're fifty dollars each."

"But we're getting a *million dollars*!" said D.L. "What's the big deal?"

"What's the *big deal*?" shouted her father. "What's the *big deal*? The *big deal* is..." His eyes and lips and hands searched for an answer, but it never came. That was the heart of it, right there. D.L. had discovered the quicksand of cheapness, hoarding, and greed that had ensnared the two eldest generations of the Craving family.

Simmering like a lobster in a kettle, Sharpy suddenly snatched Tim by the ear. The helpless boy began to giggle. His father was stupefied by this response. He stared at his son for a moment with an inexplicable expression. *He's an idiot*, Sharpy thought. *He'll never be anything but an idiot*.

Then a film of red clouded Sharpy's vision, and he watched himself shove the boy down, with both hands, a tremendous push to the chest. Tim's gangly ninety-five pounds bounced lightly on the asphalt.

Breathing heavily, Sharpy watched his son struggling to flip over, his legs paddling frantically in the air, in what a specialist might have described as total ataxic disorder. To the average person, the boy was just wriggling like a cockroach on its back.

"Look," said Sharpy. "He can't even stand up. It's pathetic. He can't stand up, he can't answer questions"—here his voice broke—"he couldn't even cry at his mother's funeral."

Nobody moved. Grandpa Frederick stood by with a reserved look on his face, unwilling to interfere. But Grandma leaned forward in her wheelchair and tightened the muscles of her face into a hard rictus of concern.

"I said don't bother that boy," she said. "He's special. He's *touched*."

But Sharpy was in another place. "The kid doesn't even goddamn cry when his mother's laying right there in the casket," he said. "What kind of person doesn't cry seeing his mother in a casket? Does that make any *sense*? She loved him! She was the most selfless person in the world! And he didn't even cry!"

His audience shifted uneasily and studied their shoelaces. Other tourons streamed past them, unmindful of the dreadful oration. Then D.L. finally summoned her courage.

"Dad—" she said.

"What?"

"Shut up."

Taken aback, he did just that. His daughter knelt down and lifted her brother to his knees. She dusted off his clothing and dabbed a tissue onto his skinned knee. A circle of blood immediately showed through the paper.

Sharpy felt ashamed. There was D.L. again, picking up his slack. Fifteen going on forty. Then he felt a pain in his jaw and realized that he'd been clenching his teeth. His dentist said teeth-grinding could cause massive orthodontic damage and warned him, at the very least, to wear a night guard. That was another order he'd failed to execute.

Just like the one posed by his wife.

His shoulders slumped under the mantle of family leadership. Grandpa stepped forward and caught Sharpy by the arm.

"We'll come back," the old man whispered.

"It seems so simple," said Sharpy. "Doesn't it? Go on vacation. Take a picture."

"You already got the picture," Grandpa urged. "You'll get it again."

With that, the old engineer turned to the group and assumed his can-do authoritarian voice: "Don't worry, everybody. We'll come back. Maybe even tomorrow. What do you think about that, little one?" He pointed a friendly finger at little Brittany. "Would you like to come back again tomorrow for even more fun?"

The little girl squinted her little facial features into the sun. "I want to go home," she said.

The child spoke for everybody. Sweaty, with aching arches and troubled hearts, the sad travelers turned and trudged towards the parking lot, towards the darkness climbing up the eastern edges of the sky.

Sharpy yanked the remainder of the useless film out of the camera and slam-dunked it into a trash can. Trudging behind the others, he covered his eyes with his smudged palms. There were hundreds of voices screaming inside the cavern of his skull—upset voices, sympathetic voices, agonized voices, even furiously violent ones. Which one should he listen to? How should he behave? He didn't have any answers —except one.

Next time, he would get that picture.

fifty-one

· · ·

CURTIS SAT in the parking lot of a discount outlet strip mall, the engine of his Civic puttering. He was far away from the magic kingdom, which no longer seemed quite so magical. The ecstasy of rescuing Manny had melted from his eyes, and he was coming to the concrete realization that he had just cost himself his job. It always hurt Curtis to be fired, even from a piddling place such as the character department.

Even worse, on a pay phone—he had ended his forty-dollar-a-month mobile phone plan when Lucinda announced her pregnancy—he'd just endured a harangue from Herb, his apartment complex manager. The tiny Vietnamese tyrant been emphatic that Curtis was going to lose his apartment if he didn't get nine hundred dollars by this evening. That rigid little mandarin wouldn't budge a minute.

Curtis faced up to the hard reality: He needed a loan. But where to turn? His parents had split up when he was only two. His mother was barely making her payments back home in Georgia, where she worked as an RN and supported her new boyfriend, Dale, who suffered from premature arthritis so severe that he could only work two days a week. Curtis thought of his dad, who was rumored to be living somewhere in California, but nobody'd heard from him in over a decade. Nobody else in the outer wings of the Marshall family even had so much as two coppers to spare. They were hillbilly people who were so poor that they had practically turned to subsistence farming.

That left Lucinda's parents. Hitting them up for money was impossible. They were living in El Paso and didn't approve of anything she did, least of all getting knocked up by a penniless *gabacho* in Florida. Which is why she and Curtis hadn't told them about the baby yet. No, that inferno would best be saved for another time.

Mentally, he went through a list of relatives, friends, acquaintances, co-workers … and came up with zilch.

There was nothing and nobody he could depend on.

With one exception. The last refuge of the truly desperate.

The car-title loan company sat in the corner of the parking lot. It was housed in a former fast-food restaurant, probably a Taco Bell, judging from the tall parabolic windows that decorated the front and sides. The drive-through window was still extant but boarded up.

Instead of quick enchiladas, however, the building was serving quick cash, money in the form of loans guaranteed by car titles. Credit unions were all but invisible these days, and to the denizens of the growing underclass, a weekly paycheck often wasn't enough.

Curtis tentatively pushed open the front door of the company and peered inside. He was shocked. He'd been halfway expecting a dark backroom populated by goombas with two o'clock shadows and a jar of severed fingers.

Instead, he was surprised to find a bright, yellow-and-orange establishment that shone like a freshly cleaned McDonald's. The floor glowed with the brisk smell of disinfectant. The clean windows sparkled. Plastic counters along the walls offered pens on beaded strings and a pleasing array of forms. *Fill us out*, they seemed to be saying, *we can help you*.

A potted palm decorated one corner. What used to be the taco counter had been elevated and converted into the customer service desk. A thick wall of Plexiglass was dropped from the ceiling.

Near the door a thin, paint-speckled grasshopper of a man stood writing. He wore a painter's white shirt, carpenter's pants, and tan Timberlands that seemed about six sizes too big for his skinny calves. His little pink tongue flicked out to the corner of his mouth as his callused fingers slowly filled out a form. Others waited quietly—a toddler trying to untie his mother's shoe, a gangbanger with a tattoo across his face, a businessman trying his damnedest not to be noticed.

Curtis hung his head and tweedled his baseball cap between his fingers. He felt the same embarrassment. Shuffling in here, hat in hand, the stench of addiction and dysfunction everywhere ... he felt embarrassed in a place that reeked of such Depression-era beggary. Who would've thought that he, Curtis Marshall, would ever have sunk to this level? He had some intelligence. He had a good mother. He even had white skin, for Christ's sake—which, like it or not, was *something* of an advantage. Why wasn't he on the winning end of the rope?

It had to be college. Until recently he couldn't have admitted this to himself. But now the evidence couldn't be ignored any longer. Curtis didn't have a degree, had never even enrolled. And now he was going nowhere. The high-paying manufacturing jobs at the carpet factories, the ones that his daddy and his daddy's daddy had held ... those jobs had been dragged out behind the woodshed, hacked apart, and sent to distant lands.

Today, men like Curtis Marshall had two choices: service jobs or unemployment.

The damnable thing was that Curtis had *wanted* to go to college. He'd been something of a local tennis champion in high school, with a blistering serve, quick reflexes, and tireless quadriceps. There were plenty of decent universities that would've dumped bags of cash at his gifted feet. But the college admissions gauntlet had been so intimidating, with its eight-part application forms, that he'd left everything in the hands of his guidance counselor—who'd promptly forgotten about him. Months later, Curtis discovered that he had missed the deadlines for every major college or university athletic scholarship. Panicked, he'd sent groveling letters to local schools—University of Georgia, Georgia State, Auburn, Emory—but they'd all shrugged him off. So he'd decided to apply again the next academic year ... but life's distractions had somehow grown. His mother had gotten sick, the house had needed maintenance, his girlfriend had needed attention ...

Sooner than expected, the years had slipped by. Now where was he? Age twenty-five, begging for money from a car title loan company, the last refuge of the friendless and indebted.

Disgusted with himself, Curtis pulled a paper number from the dispenser.

fifty-two

. . .

HALF AN HOUR LATER, the clerk called the number 42. Curtis looked down at the green ticket in his hand.

That was his number.

He stood up and sauntered as casually as possible towards the Plexiglass. He could feel the eyes of the other people boring into his back.

The clerk was an attractive young black woman. Her burnished orange hair was pulled back into a tight ponytail. Her cheeks shone with exotic oils. Her lime green polyester shirt tightly cradled her plump upper arms.

"Welcome to Ampax Car Title Loans," she said pleasantly. Her voice came out of a speaker embedded in the Plexiglass. "How are you today?"

Curtis leaned forward so that his lips were almost touching the metallic speaker.

"Not so hot," he said.

She held up her palm and shook her head. "Don't lean so close, baby. I can hear you fine."

"Sorry," Curtis said, leaning back.

"What can we do for you today?"

She knew damn well what she could do for him today.

Curtis couldn't bring himself to say it. He hemmed and hawed. He shuffled his feet. He coughed a little. The clerk suppressed a small smile.

"How can we help you?" she asked again.

"I need a loan," he finally stammered.

The clerk studied Curtis. This one looked different. He had good clothes, good skin, good teeth, even good grammar. Yes, this one seemed respectable—even somewhat attractive. She thought about the others she'd seen that morning, the heroin abusers, the gamblers who'd lost their skins at the craps table. This sweetheart didn't seem to have any of those problems.

"May I have your car title please?" she asked.

Curtis nodded. He felt inside his jacket, producing a sheaf of carefully folded papers. He unpeeled the car title with trembling fingers and pushed it into the scooped-out aluminum tray. He also had a W-2 form, a recent paycheck stub, last year's tax return—all the financial evidence he might need to prove his credit history.

The clerk immediately set about typing his information into the computer. "I also need your driver's license."

Curtis shoved it underneath the Plexiglass. His eyes watched her as she typed. He felt the foul sweat of desperation popping out all over his skin. What did he expect to gain from this woman besides money? Some kind of sign that his life would soon straighten out?

She turned to him. "Mister Marshall, this car title indicates that you drive a 1987 Honda Civic. Is that correct?"

He winced as the words hit the air. She made his beloved Civic seem so small, so pathetic, so worthless. He glanced at the other supplicants behind him. If they were listening, they didn't show it.

"That's right," he said. "How much will you be able to loan me?"

She ignored the question. "And what's the mileage?"

He played coy. "Well, I'd have to check."

"Can you estimate?" she said. Her almond eyes fixed upon him with eerie detachment.

He scratched his cheek. He knew the mileage, but should he tell her the truth? Would it affect his loan? Would they even *give* him a loan?

He chose to be upright. "It's got about a hundred and twenty thousand miles."

She returned to the computer without batting an eyelash. Her fingertips flew across the keyboard. He leaned his midsection against the countertop.

Finally she looked up again. "Based on your motor vehicle equity, we're willing to offer you a line of credit. Congratulations."

Curtis cocked his head. Shouldn't she have asked for more documentation? It seemed a little too easy. "Don't you want to see my proof of employment?" he said.

"No," the clerk said, "that won't be necessary."

"My credit history?"

"No," she said.

"Not even a credit check?"

She leaned forward. "Stop asking questions. I am trying to help you."

Curtis heaved an audible sigh of relief. He felt completely validated. This woman was ready to *believe* in him, in his manhood ... no questions asked. He felt something leap near his pubic bone, something primal. Suddenly the clerk felt extraordinarily attractive to him. But he ignored his urges and concentrated on the task at hand.

"You are a godsend," he said. "Can I get at least nine hundred dollars?"

She consulted her computer. "Based on the wholesale value of your automobile, we're willing to extend you a loan of one thousand five hundred dollars."

He lifted his arms to the ceiling. A choked cry of relief escaped his throat as he sank to his knees. Hosanna!

In their chairs, the other debtors lifted their eyebrows. This man must be in serious trouble.

Curtis turned back to the clerk. She looked him straight in the eye and said, "Before we go any further, I'm going to need a key."

Still giddy, Curtis was a little slow to respond. "A key?"

"To the collateral," she answered coolly.

"You want a key *now*?" Curtis said. Why was she demanding the keys so soon? He was going to pay off the loan as quickly as possible. He was responsible. But she didn't know that.

"The key," she said.

He fished around inside his duffel bag. He pulled out the Honda's spare key, which was rusted and dirty, and pushed it into the aluminum scoop beneath the security glass. He always carried it with him; preparedness was one of his virtues. The clerk took it and labeled it with a paper tag.

Then the printer in her workspace spat out a multipage pink form. She made a quick series of Xs on the blanks. She pushed the form towards him in the scoop. He saw the words "loan agreement" at the top.

"Sign here and here and here and here," she said, "and initial here and here and here and here."

Curtis remembered his mother telling him to never sign a contract until he'd read it thoroughly. He began to look over the terms.

The clerk shifted slightly. "Please sign and initial," she ordered.

"Hold on," he said. His eyes scanned the contract. He was looking for the terms of agreement. There: it said thirty days.

There was a loud knocking sound. He realized that the clerk was actually pounding on the Plexiglass with the bottom of her fist. She stabbed toward the contract with a burgundy fingernail studded with tiny sequins. "Sir," she said, "there's nine people waiting on you."

He looked behind him. The other debtors didn't seem particularly upset. And this was the most important part of the process. Her sudden pushiness made him feel suspicious.

He turned back to the clerk with an eagle's eye. "This loan says that I have to repay within thirty days. Is there any way I can get more time?"

She rolled her eyes in annoyance. "Yes, you can file for an *extension*."

"And what about the interest rate?" he said. "Where is that?"

"It's there," the clerk said. She had swiveled around in her chair, so that her back faced him. She was putting on makeup in a mirror. This was an extremely weird thing to do at the moment.

Curtis looked down the page. Near the bottom, inside a box, was the number 271. What did that mean? He looked more closely.

Above the number was a small percentage sign. *Above* the number? Curtis' heart skipped a beat. Was that the *APR*? He looked at it again. It *was* the APR! Annual percentage rate of two hundred and seventy one percent! At that rate, his loan was going to accrue almost twenty-five percent every four weeks—almost four hundred dollars a month!

His breath caught in his throat. It was flat-out usury! Even worse, this predator hadn't wanted him to see the APR, so she'd *moved* the percentage sign above the number—just to *confuse* him.

He looked up, and immediately saw that the clerk's face had changed expression. She was softer, more innocent, more girlish.

"It's gonna be the same no matter where you go," she said. "You might as well do it with us."

Curtis bowed his head. She was right. These car title loans, payday loans, pawnshop loans—such bottom-feeder lenders didn't have to pretend to be honorable. They fleeced people, plain and simple. Curtis lifted his head wearily. It didn't matter. He wouldn't let a single month accrue. He'd get a new job tomorrow, a better job. He and Lucinda would be back on their feet in two weeks.

"Okay," he said. He signed and initialed the contract. A few minutes later, when the clerk shoved him fifteen hundred dollars in cash, Curtis Marshall signed and initialed for that too.

fifty-three

. . .

AS CURTIS PULLED into his apartment complex, the possibilities of life filled his head. He had lost his job, but it didn't matter. He was keeping the home. He would paint the walls a beautiful rose. He would sand and refinish their modest Queen Anne kitchen table. Then he would build a bassinet.

He pulled into his customary spot. He noticed the curtain in his living room flutter. That was unusual. Lucinda wasn't supposed to be home. Unless she'd left the door open, there was no way the wind could move the curtain. He thought he glimpsed a small movement ... a flash of blue denim and white cotton t-shirt. Was he imagining it?

Curtis threw the gearshift into park. Leaping out, he slammed the Civic's door. It bounced open, so he slammed it again. It bounced open again. Exasperated, he carefully lifted the door up and pushed it into place until it clicked.

Then he bolted across the dirt yard, then into the front door and up the stairs—

There, at the end of the hall—

His apartment door was open. Curtis scratched his

temple, confused. What was wrong with Lucinda? She never forgot to close the door.

As he drew closer, however, he realized the problem was much worse. *The door was completely missing!* Gone! Nothing but a rectangular aperture and a trio of broken hinges!

Curtis stepped inside his apartment—and stopped dead in his tracks.

Inside his apartment were his four neighbors, the *puertoriqueños*, smack in the middle of ransacking his home. One was holding a heap of clothing across his arm. Another was emptying the contents of Curtis' bathroom medicine cabinet into a pillowcase. Two more were struggling to lift his mattress.

"What the hell are you doing?" Curtis said.

The men holding his mattress instantly dropped it and bolted for the door. Curtis spread his arms across the doorframe, but the pair shot beneath them. The third man barrelled out of the kitchen window, busted through the screen, and sprinted across the grass.

The fourth thief dashed directly toward Curtis, as if sheer velocity might overcome him. But Curtis readied himself in a classic scrimmage line stance and—

Boom—they collided. The *puertoriqueño* fell onto the ground clutching his left clavicle. Curtis hoped it was broken.

With no time to spare, he dashed outside. The other thieves were already disappearing around the corner. He chased them for a few hundred yards, to the far end of the complex, but they were too far ahead. He'd never catch them in this late-afternoon heat. It'd been too rough a day.

Chest heaving, he returned to his unit. The floor where the clavicle-broken man had been was empty. That was no surprise.

Curtis wearily looked through what remained of his apartment. They had stolen almost everything—the kitchen table, the chairs, towels, shirts, and pants. Even his shoes were gone. How mortifying! The ultimate disgrace, to have your shoes taken from you, like a junkie in a park! Curtis scanned the room quizzically. There was something else missing.

The guitar. His precious sunburst Gibson Les Paul. Curtis rushed over to the space on the floor where his precious instrument had once stood. The Marshall amp was gone too. They'd even lifted the five-dollar stand.

He started to punch the wall but stopped himself before committing horrific damage to his knuckles. He forced himself to think. Who would've stolen the door? Who would've first broken into his apartment … and *then* removed the *door*? It made absolutely no sense.

He suddenly stopped. Maybe the door had already been removed. Maybe this had been an opportunity theft.

He heard footsteps echoing in the hallway. A voice shouted, "Mister Marshall!"

It was Herb, the property manager. The little man was glaring at him, every stringy muscle tensed. He stood in the doorway with his fingers interlaced behind his back and smirking condescension on his face.

"Did you do this?" Curtis said.

The manager looked down at his feet and rocked on his heels. He was relishing the encounter. "Did I do what?"

"Did you take my door?" Curtis said.

"It's not your door," the manager replied, stabbing a finger at Curtis. "It's *my* door."

So it was true. The Lessermann management group had literally removed the door from its hinges. This was their way of telling evictees that the time was up. How barbaric! Curtis thought back to the way that the *puertorriqueño*'s eyes had lit up when he'd spotted the eviction notice in Curtis' hand that morning. He'd already known what was coming! He and his boys had been licking their chops!

"You can't do that," Curtis said evenly.

"Yes, we can," said Herb. "It's in your rental agreement."

He produced a document from his pocket which Curtis vaguely recognized.

Curtis took the document and studied it. Herb was right. There, waiting in the thickets of verbiage like a crouching lion, sat an agreement to allow the removal of "any piece of property as a warning to potential evictees." Curtis hadn't read the rental agreement since signing it. He'd always assumed that he'd never have to worry about such a situation.

"My neighbors stole everything," Curtis said. "They took clothes, shoes, furniture, even my guitar. What do you plan to do about that?"

"We can help you file a police report," Herb said, shrugging, "but we're not liable for any losses that come about because of this warning measure. It says there."

Curtis felt the tears welling up in his eyes, but he steeled himself. He placed his hands on his hips. "You didn't have to do this," he said. "I *have* your nine hundred dollars. I was about to pay you. See?" He flashed the envelope of cash. The Vietnamese man looked surprised; then his eyes flashed with greed. Curtis suspected that nobody in this complex had ever been able to successfully fight off an eviction. "But I'm not going to give it to you," he said.

Herb's face contorted. "Why not?"

Curtis walked up close to him. He enunciated very carefully: "*Because you didn't show me any respect.*" With that, Curtis placed the rental agreement upon Herb's face—and shoved the little tyrant backwards into the hallway.

The manager stumbled but recovered his footing. He saw Curtis towering above him, in the doorway. "This is going to kill your credit," Herb said. "You won't be able to get a house. Or car."

"That's hardly possible anyways."

Herb wilted. Curtis was a suicide bomber. You can't point a gun at somebody's head if there's already one there.

Herb straightened up. He rolled his shoulders like a boxer, stretched his jaw. "You have to leave by tomorrow morning."

"I'll be gone before then."

The manager looked like he was searching for a way to challenge that statement. Then he brushed dust off his shirt and shrugged.

"Okey-dokey," he said.

The manager spun around on his heel and walked out. Curtis mechanically reached out to close the door, but his hand pawed at empty air.

Then he shut his eyes and thunked his forehead against the plaster wall. There was no way he could *ever* live under the thumb of someone willing to casually dismantle his home. It just couldn't be done. He'd rather face the unknown than submit to such a reptile.

Curtis sighed loudly and began to gather his remaining property into a garbage bag.

fifty-four

· · ·

THE SWIMMING POOL at the Hotel Crown Palace had officially opened at seven o'clock in the morning, but few families were there that early. By ten o'clock, however, its chlorinated water was wracked by the splashing and thrashing of children.

Which explains why, as Vivian, Brittany, and D.L. stepped into the flagstone pool area, there wasn't a single empty chaise lounge chair. Instead, a panorama of two or three hundred fat carcasses was arranged upon the terrace. D.L. felt grossed out by the sight of so much fatty flesh baking in the sun. She decided that the terrace was a grill for human meat patties.

It was the Hamburger Platter.

The sizzling flesh on the stones. The horizontal straps on the deck chairs searing a grill pattern into the touron backsides.

"Can you believe this?" said Vivian.

"We're going to have to sit in the woodchips," said D.L.

Vivian sent the girl a disgusted sidelong glance.

"Mommy, watch me," shouted Brittany. The little girl's feet stumped loudly on the pavement as she sped towards the pool. They had strapped inflatable swimmies to her arms, an inner tube around her belly, and reptilian-looking hologram goggles on her face. Plus, Vivian was carrying a large stylish black bag containing every variety of aquatic toy known to the modern world—face masks, splash bombs, dive rings, foam noodles, paddle pumpers, pool floats, whistling footballs.

Beside her, D.L. was attired in a blue one-piece swimsuit with sarong. It had taken a massive act of willpower to pull its stretchy straps over her shoulders. She'd held her back to the mirror, never daring to look at the pinched-up fat that was no doubt rippling across her belly and thighs.

Though the family had made half-hearted plans to return to the park for a second attempt at The Picture, it wasn't to be. This morning they'd all woken up grouchy, dispirited, and irritable from yesterday's disappointment. Nobody had needed much convincing to lounge around the hotel.

D.L. surveyed the Hamburger Platter with her hand over her eyes.

"I'm sure if we stand here long enough," said Vivian, "something will open up."

"How do you know?"

"I have a feeling."

Vivian felt confident because she was staging her Grand Entrance. No doubt she'd done this many times before. D.L. looked at her. She *was* beautiful. Dressed in a wide-brimmed straw hat, black Lolita-style sunglasses, and black wrap, she posed regally at the edge of the meat patties. Her skin shone in the bleaching sunlight.

"Do you need a place to sit?" a man's voice said.

It was an ugly middle-aged man in a nearby deck chair. He had big ears with thick fleshy lobes and a flattened little prole's nose with little wiry hairs sprouting out of it. He was wearing nothing but a silver Speedo swimsuit and a white baseball cap. There was an ostentatiously thick gold chain around his sunburnt neck and chest. D.L. noticed that he was trying to suck in his hefty gut, which curved outwards like the skin of a wiener ready to pop.

"Why, in fact we *do*," said Vivian.

"Here, have both seats, my wife's gone to town," he said. The stout man hoisted himself out of the seat with an undisguised grunt.

"You're a prince among men," replied Vivian. "It's *so* crowded here. I don't know how *anybody* can find a place to sit."

The man made no attempt to hide his admiration for Vivian's figure. "Do you lovely ladies need anything to drink?" he said. "Margarita? A Shirley Temple for the little girl?"

"I'll take a strawberry daiquiri," said Vivian, "and a Coca-Cola for my daughter over there. Let me give you some money."

She made a show of moving toward her purse. He lifted a pudgy palm in protest. "Your name is crime," the man said. Vivian tilted her head like a dog hearing something it doesn't understand. Then he delivered the punchline: "Crime doesn't pay." The man's moustache crinkled happily.

Vivian mustered a polite smile. "That was very witty."

The gentleman attempted a deep courtly bow, which, besides offering an unobstructed view of his bald spot, did unflattering things to the size and shape of his belly.

"Don't go anywhere, you lovelies," he said. "I'll be right back." He disappeared towards the snack bungalow.

After he disappeared, Vivian shook D.L.'s arm. "Did you see the gold around his neck?" she said. "He's swimming in a lot more than just chlorine."

"He's gross," D.L. replied. She stepped over to the second deck chair and plopped herself down unceremoniously. She became aware that Vivian was staring at her. "What's wrong?"

"That's not how a lady sits down," Vivian said.

"Why not?"

"You straddled the chair between your legs and then just dropped your ass. It was crude. That's the way *men* sit down."

D.L. was taken aback. "How am I supposed to do it?"

"Like this." Vivian stood and walked a few paces away. Every pair of male eyes was fixed upon her. In fact, the question of what tantalizing delights lay underneath her black wrap had hung inside the pituitary gland of every red-blooded male at the pool from the moment she entered the Hamburger Platter. They had girded their loins for her inevitable striptease—and now it was happening.

Vivian didn't disappoint. She dropped her black wrap with a flourish, revealing a black-and-white polka-dotted bikini with a bandeau top and French-cut bottom. D.L. imagined a collective orgasmic groan from the male assemblage. Then Vivian returned to the chair.

"Step one, approach the chair from the side. Step two, turn and lower yourself *delicately*." She lowered her shapely rear end to the seat. "Step three, which is optional, is to toss your hair." She threw her head backwards; her mane of glossy black hair arced across the blue sky and bounced against her shoulder blades. "That's purely for attention. Step four, lift your legs, remembering to point your toes. And step five, pivot ninety degrees on your tush, then lower your legs and settle back." She demonstrated.

"That's a lot of work," said D.L.

"That's what separates the women from the girls. Every move is calculated."

D.L. felt outclassed. She'd never thought that much about the simple act of sitting down in a deck chair.

"Don't worry," said Vivian. She began smearing citrus-scented lotion onto her arms and legs. "You'll learn. Just remember that it's the little things. Like this lotion, for instance. What am I *not* doing?"

D.L. studied her. As Vivian spread the butter upon the rounded tops of her breasts, her face was lifted upwards.

"You're not looking at yourself."

"Exactly," said Vivian. "Never look down when you're applying lotion to your chest."

"Why?"

"Because it makes you frown. Look at that woman." She nodded towards a heavy matron whose chin fat was plumped up as she tried to peer at her own cleavage. "See? Through body language, she's already told everyone at the pool that she's unattractive."

"She's gross anyways," said D.L.

"She's married," said Vivian, as though the words were synonymous.

D.L. let her eyes slide off the matron and across the terrace. The hotel had sculpted the area into a remarkably accurate imitation of a tropical oasis. The pool was a bright azure and shaped like a large kidney. A deafening waterfall plunged over an overhanging ledge into the deep end, under which several courageous bathers were getting their skulls pounded like veal. To one side of the pool stood an artificially decrepit snack shack; to the other was a beach-style hair-wrap booth. The entire terrace was bounded by thick ropes threaded through wooden stanchions.

"I don't get it," said D.L. "Why do I have to use sex appeal?"

"Because."

"Because why? Why can't I just be myself?"

Vivian looked at the girl over the top of her sunglasses. "There are very few women in this world who can achieve things in a straightforward fashion. Those women are what we call 'honorary men'. They have special privileges. The rest of us—you and me—have to use our charms."

"My mother always told me that women could do whatever they wanted," the teenager said.

"Your mother was right," Vivian agreed. "But she never told you that you need sexiness to do so." Vivian reached into her purse and took out a breath mint. "For women like us, it's not enough to be competent. We must also dazzle and glitter. Feminism didn't change that."

D.L. turned onto her belly and slumped face first onto her deck chair. Everything she had been taught was a lie. She stared sullenly through the plastic slats at a pink magazine subscription card that had fallen from a fashion magazine. It had sealed itself to the wet pavement, its pink dye beginning to leak around the edges.

The squeeching sound of wet flip-flops on the pavement announced Brittany's return. "Mommy," she whined, "that boy pushed me." She was pointing to a hyperactive little blonde torpedo in a baggy bathing suit whizzing around the pool with a handheld water cannon.

"Stay away from Mommy," said Vivian, holding up her hand. "You're soaking wet."

"But he *pushed* me!" the little girl yelled.

"Then push him *back*!"

The little girl pouted and stamped her feet. Then the storm cloud passed, and she dashed back to the pool, all squeals and curls again.

"I thought you were teaching her to be a lady," said D.L.

Vivian shook her head. "What's more important is that she learns to stand up for herself—the sooner the better. Lord knows I did."

"Here you are, ladies," said the portly man. He had returned with a tray of drinks.

"You are such a dear," said Vivian, touching the frosty red daiquiri with her fingertips. She jumped with an exaggeratedly feminine shock. "Oh, it's cold!"

"Do you want me to get a warmer glass?"

"No, that's okay."

She nearly spilled the drink trying to get it onto the side table. D.L. couldn't believe the transformation she was witnessing. Vivian had become a perfect piece of giggling, tittering, bouffant-haired, bubble-gum-snapping helplessness.

"So, do you have a name?"

"Robert." He stuck out his fleshy hand.

"Vivian Talon," she said, shaking it. She gave another feminine jump. "Oh! Your hand is so *calloused*."

"I'm a plumber," he said proudly. "Makin' thirty-nine dollars an hour. Can't believe it myself. Never thought I'd have this much dough."

"Then we shouldn't bother to repay you, Robert."

"Well, you can by coming up to my room."

Vivian blinked at the forcefulness of the come-on. "You're a very aggressive man," she said.

"My wife's leaving to visit her cousins tonight. I got a big empty suite and nothin' to fill it."

"Thank you for the invitation, Robert," the vixen said. "Take care."

"It's up to you," he said, grinning.

Vivian pulled a paperback novel from her pool bag and pretended to begin reading. He remained crouching next to her chair. D.L. turned her back and covered her face. Didn't the plumber realize that he was embarrassing himself?

"I'm in 802," he said. "You can let me know anytime."

The words were swallowed by the silence. Vivian continued reading. There was a horrendously awkward moment until the plumber's brain, clouded as it was through the thick smear of lotion and sweat, understood that his invitation had been snubbed. At last the plumber shuffled off, carrying his dignity under his arm like a wounded sheep. D.L. watched him go—his shapeless trapezii, his blubbery waist, his tiny concave buttocks. He tossed his towel into the bin and disappeared into the hotel lobby.

"Is he gone?" said Vivian.

"Yep."

Vivian closed the book with a sigh of relief. "I was afraid he wasn't going to catch on."

"Why didn't you just say that you had a boyfriend?"

"Because I was increasing my perceived value," she said. "Every woman knows how to do it." She lay back. "You have to make them fail. Then, next time they'll try even harder."

D.L. felt a shiver in her shoulder blades. Was this what you needed to do to be a good woman?

"Is that how you captured my dad?"

Vivian stiffened and her eyes swam away worriedly. "Your father's a sweet man."

"I think he's going to ask you to marry him," D.L. said.

There was no answer. The raven-haired predator was staring into the blue sky, her muscles tensed, not daring to breathe.

fifty-five

. . .

LATER IN THE AFTERNOON, after Brittany had been thoroughly waterlogged, the three females adjourned to the beach-style hair wrap stand on the opposite side of the Hamburger Platter. The worker, an overweight, perspiring blonde woman, was slumped on a tall wooden stool underneath a broad striped umbrella. A wooden cart behind her displayed several spools of brightly colored string.

"Hi there," said Vivian. "How much do you charge?"

"Dollar an inch," the woman replied. She was of indeterminate age with flat, ironed hair.

"That's fine," said Vivian. "Go pick your colors, Brittany."

The little girl ran to the cart. "I want pink . . . and yellow . . . and blue . . . and orange . . ."

"Pink and yellow," said Vivian.

The woman slid off the stool and unwound the colored strings from the spool. "How many inches?" she said.

"How many do you want, baby?"

"I want some," said Brittany.

"I can tell," she said. "How many do you want?"

"Lots of inches."

"Give her ten," said Vivian.

The woman hoisted Brittany onto the stool and began braiding the wrap into a hank of hair behind the girl's ear.

"You're a pretty one," she said as her fingers worked. "Has anyone told you that you look just like your mother?"

"She resembles her father," said Vivian.

"He must be gorgeous. Can I see him from here?" The woman craned her head towards the pool.

D.L. listened closely. She knew that Vivian always avoided the question of Brittany's father.

"He's actually not in Florida," Vivian replied, then switched the subject. She seemed oddly solicitous. "What about you? Do you have any kids?"

"Two boys, four and two," the woman said.

"Had enough yet?"

"Oh yeah. Let me tell you—"

As the women chatted, D.L. found herself on the outside of the conversation. She felt herself starting to panic. Why? She was losing Vivian's attention. Though she was hostile towards her father's mistress, D.L. paradoxically *needed* the older woman—something needed an older female, something buried deep in her psyche. She was vaguely aware that she had lost something when her mother had died, in the way that you are aware of a dull throbbing in your head. Now it had come roaring back like a migraine. She desperately scrabbled for a way to interrupt.

D.L. touched Vivian's shoulder. "Guess what, Vivian? Did you know I've got sixth-row seats to see the O-Town Boys next month?"

"Ew," Brittany said, scrunching up her face.

"Those guys are ugly," said the hair-wrap woman.

But Vivian seemed excited. "Really? That one with the dark hair is a gorgeous piece of steak. Mm hm."

"You mean Richard?" asked D.L.

"Oh yes. Just give me fifteen minutes in a room with him."

"Vivian!" she said. "He's, like, seventeen!"

"And loaded," said Vivian.

"That's right," the woman said. She helped Brittany down. "Who's next?"

"Me," said D.L., hopping on the stool. "Turquoise and yellow. Ten inches."

"Are you paying for this?" said Vivian, tapping her foot. D.L. stared back at her challengingly. There were smiles on both their faces.

"I thought you were."

"We're going to spend thirty dollars by the time I leave here."

"So?"

"Your father won't be pleased."

"I didn't think that was a problem."

There seemed to be nothing for Vivian to say to that. The woman twined the wrap into a hank of hair behind D.L.'s right ear. As the tropical sun cooked the white pavement outside the shadow cast by the umbrella, the teenager watched Vivian pull a breath mint from her cleavage.

"Why do you eat those so much?" said D.L.

She stretched comfortably. "You couldn't handle why."

"Yes I could."

Vivian suddenly became aggressive. "Let's talk about *you* instead, shall we? Let's talk about your weight problem. How would you like to do that?"

D.L. instantly plunged her chin into her cleavage. She'd unleashed the tigress now. She prayed that the conversation wouldn't go a syllable further.

But that was not to be. Vivian had begun to prowl around the stool, pointing her toes with each step. "What do you like to eat, D.L.?"

The teenage girl pulled her sarong over the fatty midsection and said nothing.

"Oh, really? You don't eat anything?"

Head down, D.L. focused her eyes upon the cart's caster.

Couldn't Vivian just drop the subject? She was sorry to have ever asked about the stupid mints.

But Vivian was like a hyena circling a wounded wildebeest; she wasn't going to be scared off the kill. "I bet you shovel big plates of pasta down your throat, don't you? And then a half-gallon of ice cream right before bedtime. Don't you?" She inched closer. "*Don't you?*"

D.L. nodded. She felt her eyes brimming with tears. Vivian was dead on. She had become a glutton since her mother's death. In the darkest moments of the night, unable to sleep, wracked with pain and loss and disconsolation … she'd been tiptoeing downstairs, gorging on butter creams, snickerdoodles, coconut cake—Lord did she love coconut—anything that would spike her blood sugar. Her father hadn't noticed. But Vivian had known it all with her frighteningly strong woman's intuition.

Vivian drew even closer. "Do you want to know a secret?"

D.L. nodded but kept her eyes on the caster.

Vivian lowered her voice: "*I eat like that too.*"

Through the teary film on her eyes, D.L. glanced at Vivian's terrific figure. That claim was ludicrous. The woman didn't eat. She had barely swallowed a Tootsie Roll since the start of their vacation.

The teenager finally met Vivian's eyes: "How?"

"I throw it up."

D.L. felt her mouth fall open. The hair-wrap woman's fingers stopped braiding for a second, then continued. Vivian had admitted this horrendous disease without an ounce of sorrow or embarrassment. She could talk about it the way you describe Raisin Bran.

"It's nothing to be ashamed of," Vivian said. "I've been doing it for years. Standing before you is a full-blown active bulimic." She stood and posed heroically in a weightlifter's stance. She was a German Romantic sculpture, an *uberfrau* with popping biceps and flat abdominals and superhuman breasts.

"I didn't know," said D.L.

"Nobody does. The breath mints kill the smell."

"Of what?"

"Stomach acid." She touched D.L.'s shoulder. "You could do it too."

D.L. felt a weird scrambling in her tummy. There was no way she could start a lifetime of vomiting. Her esophagus was one-way.

"I don't think so."

"Why not?"

"It's dishonest. It's like cheating—the easy way to skinniness."

The fury in Vivian's eyes sent D.L.'s gaze down to the caster again. "*Easy?*" she hissed. "It's *not* easy, D.L. You have to be *committed*. You have to *want* to be beautiful with your entire mind. You have to be *dedicated* to the goal of achieving a perfect body, no matter what the cost. It has to be an *obsession*. Most people don't know anything about real obsessions. Most people don't *care* about anything enough."

"It's just not for me," said D.L.

Vivian sighed. "I guess I understand. *Your* mother never pushed you to be beautiful. Not the way *mine* did. You never had birthday parties without any cake or ice cream. You were never grounded for outgrowing a pair of shorts. And you won't"—Vivian struggled to control her quavering voice— "you won't ever fuck medical interns for the hypothyroid medication that keeps you thin, either."

The beach-wrap lady suddenly dropped the twine and wiped her hands. "I'm finished," she said.

Vivian tossed a credit card at the lady. "I'm not ashamed. It's a part of me. It's always been there. And if this is the least of my troubles, then I count myself blessed." She picked up her towel. "Bring me the card when she's done. I'll be on the lounge chair."

The mistress headed back towards the pool. D.L. turned to the beach-wrap lady. "I'm sorry she was a bitch."

"Oh, it don't matter," the lady sighed, swiping the card. "I seen all types here."

"I think she's going to marry my father."

The lady handed the credit card back. "Then you better tell him to use this thing to buy some running shoes. He's gonna need 'em."

fifty-six

. . .

IN THE HEAT of that same afternoon, Grandma Maya and Grandpa Frederick had drawn the curtains across the window of their room.

The old couple sat in silence in opposite chairs. A chintzy overhead light cast a pall upon their faces. The room somehow already stank of a day-old ploughman's lunch. It was probably because of the stale heat blowing at maximum power out of the room's thermostat—a suffocating practice which, over the years, Grandpa had learned to tolerate. There was, after all, a rational explanation: Maya had poor blood circulation.

Lately, however, nothing seemed to be able to warm her. He watched her pull a pink knitted cardigan tightly around her hunched shoulders.

He returned to absorbing the television news. Every day for decades he had cast his gimlet eye towards the idiot box and weighed and wrapped the news reports like parcels of meat. Sitting in judgment upon the world. It was how he maintained an iron grip upon reality.

It was a point of pride.

He imagined that Grandma sat in awe of his powers of

reason. Sure, she read Sydney Omarr horoscopes in the newspaper, she claimed to have these ludicrous intuitions about people ... but he just knew that she had always, deep down, admired the fact that he was an *engineer*. You couldn't do better than to have that square of framed parchment over your desk. He was part of a select group of men who had successfully gone the distance. That is to say, he and his brethren had eliminated the need for *feelings*—those intrusive, inefficient emotions that hampered the rest of the human race. That prevented bridges from being built, planes from being piloted, concrete from being poured.

The proof of this superiority was sitting right there on top of the credenza: his little black book. It looked like the kind of thing that would be filled with lipstick-stained napkins and women's phone numbers. Not even remotely. Frederick used it to record his purchases at the end of every day. *Thirty-five cents for a newspaper ... two dollars and seventeen cents for half gallon of milk ... five dollars and ten cents for film developing ...* He kept hundreds of such ledgers moldering in a cardboard box in a storage unit. He liked having a history of his spending.

The weather forecaster was talking about an approaching hurricane. Grandpa watched the Doppler radar sweeping in its circle. There was certainly a horrific swirl forming out in the Caribbean, he thought, but the chances of landfall were small. These things were like drunks stumbling out of a bar, lurching from one side of the Caribbean to the other. Besides, the Cravings were in Orlando, which was fifty miles safely inland. The real battering always took place on the coasts.

Grandma moaned quietly. Grandpa's thumb pressed mute on the remote control.

"What's the matter?" he said.

She shuffled her slippers under the table. "My feet."

"Do you need your Epsom salts bath?"

She nodded. Grandma Maya was convinced that Epsom

salts helped with her edema, which had affected her so badly that her ankles had swollen to resemble an elephant's. Grandpa Frederick had tried to rationally explain that elevating her feet was the proper treatment (along with compression stockings), but Grandma had insisted on salty foot baths, once a day. Since it calmed her, he allowed it.

"I'll call room service," he said. His finger dialed 7 on the phone and he held it to his ear. "This is Frederick Craving. We need some Epsom salts." He listened to the response and stiffened. "Epsom salts. I'm giving my wife a foot bath." He sighed and he hunched over the cradle. "Then tell me where I can purchase some. The store in the lobby? Thank you." He dropped the receiver on its cradle.

"I knew they wouldn't have any," Grandma said.

"Yeah," he said.

"This whole trip was a bad idea. It's coming to no good."

He rubbed his hands together, preparing for action. "Just sit tight, Maya. Everything is under control. I'm going to take care of you." He paused. His jaw worked feverishly. He couldn't think of what he was about to say next.

Grandma turned up a saucerish eye. She looked like a squid. "I'll call Sharpy if there are any problems."

Frederick's jaw jutted out. "Good. That's what I was about to say."

"I know."

"I'll be back shortly."

At the door, he doublechecked his pockets. Eyeglasses, check. Wallet, check. Black book, check. Maya cleared her throat. "Frederick?"

He turned back. "Yes?"

"Thank you," she said.

In the elevator, he straightened his few remaining wisps of hair in the mirror. How had she known what he was going to say next? He had a world-class brain, trained at Princeton and Cornell. His thoughts had always flown light years ahead of

—*oh, just admit it!*—the rest of humanity. But he couldn't maintain it forever. Maybe the inevitable deceleration had finally begun. Maybe the circulation problems that were lowering his wife's temperature were also slowing the speed of his thought. But that particular string of analysis invited all types of nagging questions about *death* … such an imprecise, nebulous subject …

The doors shushed open. As he stepped into the cavernous lobby, Grandpa felt a rush of importance. His chest swelled; his knobby legs suddenly felt stronger. Retired? He'd *never* retired. Didn't matter how old he was. He wasn't going to be one of those chicken-legged doddering mouth breathers with black rayon socks hitched up to their knees who puttered uselessly in the garden on Monday mornings. Not on your life! He had *purpose*.

Which, right now, was to find Epsom salts. Even if they were only a topical relief, these bath salts helped ease his wife's final … years? Months? Days? Nobody knew how much longer Grandma Maya had on this side of the grass. She was a gift basket of assorted maladies. He felt impatience rising within him like a black tide. Why did she have to become so *old*? She was slowing him down.

He realized that his fists were clenched. This impatience, his horrible trademark … it had to be stopped. He *willed* himself to feel sympathy.

Grandpa Frederick strode across the pineapple-patterned lobby carpet with strict precision. At the front desk, a line of check-ins were trading plastic credit cards for plastic room cards at this overpriced hotel. Of course it was overpriced. That was undeniable; all hotels were. But how many of these bums had tried to get a better deal? How many knew what a rack rate was? Or even a basic Triple-A discount? Some people called him cheap. He called it smart.

In the sundries shop, Frederick found the Epsom salts sandwiched between Dr. Scholl's pads and the hydrogen peroxide. He lifted the sixteen-ounce bag and read the price tag. It cost four dollars and thirty-nine cents. That was a dollar and twenty cents more than it cost back at the retirement home. The skin on either side of his neck flushed. The audacity! The temerity! The unmitigated *gall*! The least they could do was offer a bag of salt at an affordable price. He was being *gouged* by this *state*, with its hotel taxes, its car rental taxes, its restaurant taxes—not to mention the ludicrous eight percent sales tax. Living here was like being slowly pecked to death by ducks.

He paid the cashier without a word and marched out of the store.

With his new purchase gripped tightly in his palm, the old man nodded as tourons actually *stepped aside* for him. The way it should be! His every muscle fiber, every ganglia, every mitochondria—all of it commanded people's respect. *This* was why Indianapolis' top engineering firm had scooped him straight out of grad school five decades ago. *This* was why he'd powered up through its executive ranks: entry level, associate, manager, project manager, and finally vice-president. He'd never earned a corner office, but it hadn't been his fault—the firm's office building had been circular. The invention of some mad avant-garde German architect with ideas about flattening hierarchy. Grandpa Frederick's stubborn jaw protruded another inch. That was ludicrous. People *needed* hierarchy.

Then a young woman's voice interrupted his reverie.

"Excuse me, sir? You look like you want to save some money."

fifty-seven

. . .

HE TURNED.

A young girl, not more than nineteen, was perched on a stool behind a low desk. She was wearing a nametag on a red polo shirt and was waving happily in his direction. Something glittery in her hair caught his eye. He peered closer. It was a butterfly. She was wearing a *sparkly butterfly hairclip*. And she was waving *him* over like some silly little galpal? With that *thing* in her hair? He felt the irritability pumping into his bloodstream.

Grandpa Frederick turned on his heel and approached her. "Why are you wearing that in your hair?"

The girl was unfazed. "Can I ask *you* a question first?" she replied. Then she snapped her bubble gum loudly between her tongue and the roof of her mouth.

Frederick stood there, stricken. She hadn't even noticed the tone of his voice. Over the years, that same voice had reduced brilliant engineers to blubbering piles of crewcuts and slide rules. But this girl ... she wasn't even fazed! What was *wrong* with her?

He mustered his patience. "Okay."

"How much money are you spending on tickets to the parks?" she asked.

Grandpa Frederick's breath literally caught in his throat. He drew himself up to his full height. "Funny you should ask that. We're spending far too much."

"I know, right? The tickets cost *so much* now."

"Ninety dollars and fifty-three cents each," he replied.

"Ten years ago they were only forty-eight dollars."

"It's outpacing inflation," he said angrily. "They've really got us over a barrel. Just outrageous."

"Totally," she agreed.

Grandpa Frederick felt more comfortable now. This young girl was on the same page. She knew his pain. He felt his rage redirected towards some larger, more nameless injustice.

The girl snapped her bubble gum. "What would you say if I said that you could get two free tickets to the theme parks?"

Frederick perked up. "I'd say that my family would definitely appreciate that."

She pushed a laminated informational brochure across the desk. It featured a perfectly landscaped condominium perched on a perfectly landscaped blue inland lake. Across the top were the words "Florida Jewels Timeshare Condominium—Make Your Vacation Last a Lifetime!"

He gave her the stinkeye. "What's the catch?"

The girl laughed delightfully. "There's no catch! You tour the resort tomorrow, and we give you two free theme park tickets."

"Somebody's going to try to sell me something."

The girl shrugged.

"Right?"

"It's mostly an informational tour."

Grandpa Frederick looked at her pensively. She was offering him one hundred and twenty-four dollars. Sharpy and Vivian had blown a lot of cash. This could begin to repair the damage, put them on the right path. Should he do it?

Of course he should. He would sign up the entire family for that kind of money. It didn't matter if nobody wanted to go. They'd ignored his meticulously written itinerary, then blew the picture. Yes, tomorrow was the day Frederick Craving would reassert himself. He would teach his wayward son the meaning of resource management.

"Okay," he said. "Let's do it."

The girl clapped. She reached under the desk and slid a pink form across the table. "Just fill in your name, your home address, and your annual income."

Frederick gripped the pen. "Why income?"

"You must earn at least twenty-five thousand dollars per year to be eligible."

Frederick laughed as his pen scratched across the paper. "If anybody in my family earned less than twenty-five thousand dollars a year, I'd disown him." He shook his head sadly from side-to-side. How pathetic, how underprepared, how ill-equipped would you have to be to sink so far down the economic ladder?

Then he felt the eyes upon him. It was the girl. She was looking squarely at him and a sliver of pain was visible behind her dark eyes. His stomach dropped as he realized his gaffe. *She* didn't make twenty-five thousand a year. She was probably earning seven dollars an hour, plus a fraction of commission. And now he had just revealed himself to be enormously old—a geezer, a relic, out of touch, unaware.

"So what about you?" he said, stammering. "Do you like this job?"

"I guess it's okay," she said, returning to her chipper self. "They let me talk on the phone, so, you know."

He searched for a reply. There wasn't any. How did a retired military engineer with a reputation for slave-driving punctuality *talk* to a teenage service worker with a sparkly butterfly hairclip in her hair? The short answer: He didn't.

The old man was spared further embarrassment when the

girl handed him the official invitation to the resort. "Just arrive anytime after eight-thirty tomorrow morning," she said, "and you'll be all set. There's a map on the back."

"Thank you."

"Have a great day tomorrow at the Florida Jewels!" She waved happily again. She seemed to have totally forgotten his comment.

As soon as he was out of sight, Grandpa Frederick breathed a sigh of relief. The way he'd pulled the conversation out of the toilet proved that he wasn't completely socially retarded. His ego gradually reinflated. His critics were wrong, wrong, wrong. He *did* have communication skills that didn't involve directing, dominating, and scheduling. He *could* feel emotional attachments to people.

The old man walked back to the elevators, bag of salt in one hand, swatting the invitation against his thigh with the other. They were going to visit a timeshare condo tomorrow.

No questions asked.

fifty-eight

. . .

THAT EVENING, as twilight settled across the land, D.L. was stretched on her foldaway bed with a book in her hand. It was a Miss Bitch young adult novel, fourth in the series.

Like the first three, this book was another variation on the same glamorous theme: an impossibly beautiful sixteen-year-old girl from an impossibly ritzy East Coast family is faced with the impossibly perfect decision of either enrolling on scholarship at Yale or signing a Versace modeling contract. The character was also confused about a boy, who was obligatory and handsome.

D.L. threw the book against the wall.

She couldn't even *begin* to relate.

Her father and Vivian had gone out for a romantic dinner. It must've been fancy because her father had ironed his best collar shirt. D.L., on the other hand, had been given the job of babysitting Tim, Brittany, and even Grandma Maya. Grandpa Frederick had announced that he was going to investigate the new road construction on the boulevard and wouldn't return until nine o'clock.

Tim lay next to her immersed in a coloring book. He was very meticulous about his coloring. Using one of Brittany's crayons, the burnt umber, he was methodically filling every space—

(A A A A A A)

—marked by the letter A. He went through the whole book this way until he'd finished that letter. Then he'd choose a different color and begin the Bs.

Next to her brother lay the tyrannical tot. She was coloring freehand pictures. D.L. peeked over. Brittany had drawn a picture of a white princess riding a white unicorn with a long pink tulle streamer trailing off the point of her pink peaked princess hat. How appropriate.

In the corner of the room, Grandma Maya was dozing in the upholstered club chair, purse on her lap. As though she were going to suddenly stand up and walk off to some glamorous party.

Suddenly the eyes slitted open; the old, crooked tongue wetted its lips; and the voice croaked: "D.L."

"Yeah?"

"Can you do my hair?"

"Right now?"

"It's Tuesday."

"So?"

"I always go to the salon on Tuesday."

D.L. didn't really want to touch her hair, but she also couldn't refuse such a sentimental request. What Grandma Maya really seemed to need was some attention.

That's how, a few minutes later, D.L. found herself washing, drying, and then brushing the old woman's tresses, which were surprisingly thick. She noticed Grandma's eyes watching her in the mirror.

"You're such a pretty young lady," said the old woman.

D.L.'s face lit up into ten different shades of red. "Not really."

"The boys must be getting very interested in you."

"They don't like me."

"That's not true."

"Yes it *is*."

In the mirror, Grandma stared directly at her granddaughter. D.L. paused, her fingers entwined in the hair. The old lady was staring … and staring … tilting her head, this way and that. It was creepy and unnerving. D.L. knew about her grandmother's ability to see through people and read their most closely guarded secrets. This was feeling like one of those moments.

"What are you doing, Grandma?"

"You're still a virgin," the old woman said.

D.L. dropped the brush in surprise. Of course it was true. But how had she known? Granted, there was a fifty-fifty chance, acey-deucy, and D.L. knew that her personality didn't exactly strike people as that of a nymphomaniac. But why did Grandma have to *go* there?

The elderly woman was still studying her. "I hope I didn't embarrass you, dear."

"Kind of."

"How far *have* you gone with a boy?"

This will never end, D.L. thought. What did Grandma want to hear? That her granddaughter hadn't gone *any*where with a boy—not a bedroom, not the woods, not a car, not even the movies? Oh, she'd heard all about the other girls' shenanigans, about their lipstick parties and their train parties and their whatever parties. She'd heard *all* about it. She just wasn't part of it. Was her grandmother just trying to live vicariously?

"Do we have to talk about this?" she said.

"No—"

"I mean, I don't ask you about *your* sex life."

The old woman dropped her head. Suddenly D.L. felt ashamed of herself. She'd crossed some kind of line.

"I'm sorry," she said.

"I should've expected as much," said Grandma Maya with

sadness tingeing her voice. "No young girl wants to be stuck doing the hair of some depressing old woman in a wheelchair." She managed a rueful smile. "But look on the bright side."

"What's that?"

A sparkle glimmered in Grandma's aged, yellow eyes. "At least I don't talk constantly about the old days."

"That's true."

"The other ladies at the home go on and on. It gets *so* tiresome."

D.L. smiled. Then the smile turned into amazement as the old woman's other hand fumbled inside her purse and pulled out a few wadded-up bills and shoved the money into D.L.'s hand. "Please take them," she said.

"But Grandma—"

"It's all I have right now. Go downstairs and enjoy yourself."

Taking the money, D.L. felt the tears welling up in her eyes. She hadn't really known her grandmother, not since Grandpa had taken her out of Indiana for her health. Her long trip down the slippery slide of senile dementia wasn't helping the bonding process either. They had largely become strangers to each other—which is why the gesture was all the more touching.

"What about you?"

"Don't think about me," Grandma said. She lifted her trembling arms above her head and pulled her thin tresses into a ponytail. "I'm not worth it."

"Grandma—"

The old woman shooed her away. "Go. Have fun. Be a girl."

D.L. obeyed the old woman and dutifully reached for her shoes.

fifty-nine

. . .

THE WINDFALL AMOUNTED to seven dollars. D.L. decided to drag her two young charges to the video arcade. Not that spending all night playing first-person shooter games with a brother who dwelt on the far fringes of the obsessive-compulsive spectrum was in any way attractive. There was basically nothing else they could do, since Brittany was too small for sports and they were all sick of swimming.

The video arcade was housed in a former laundry room that was buried in an obscure corridor on the mezzanine level of the hotel. D.L. could hear it before she saw it—a deafening mélange of roars, shouts, screeches, squeals, smashes, crashes, crunches, curses, collisions, explosions, and a million other varieties of simulated mayhem.

Shuffling down the hall, she felt the heavy weight of ten dollars in quarters she'd gotten from the front desk banging against her thigh. She looked down at her cargo pants. She hated the way they clung to her figure and highlighted her disgusting bulges. People who complimented her couldn't *really* see her. Look at her thighs! Who would want a set of hocks that huge, that hammy? Or a jelly belly that gelatinous? Her grandmother had touched the sorest string in her soul:

she, D.L. Craving, was utterly *unlovable*. It was the truth! She was going to be boyfriendless forever. Not that there was much to choose from in Indiana. The strapping, stupid farmhands back home, with their 4-H mentality and blunted conversation, were beyond unappealing. Lately, out of desperation, she'd begun buying fashion magazines and ripping out pictures of androgynous looking male models and taping them on her bedroom closet. She felt a weird, indescribable longing when she looked at the photos. It wasn't for love, it wasn't for sex, but for … what? Companionship? Maturity? She couldn't put it into words. She would just know it when she felt it.

"I hate this place," she said to no one.

"I want to play the Barbie game!" wailed Brittany.

"You *would*," D.L. said.

They stopped in the doorway. Thirty different video games fought for her attention: auto racing, sharpshooting, boxing, hand-to-hand combat, you name it.

Tim lurched in his awkward, off-balance gait—

(*mode recycle*)

—towards a racing game featuring a red Kawasaki motorcycle. D.L. hoisted him onto the seat. She closed his fingers around the handles. It felt as though his soul were somewhere far, far away.

She dropped fifty cents into the illuminated red slot. Onscreen, the engines thundered, the checkered flag dropped, and the road moved slowly forward. A green GO!!!! popped onto the screen.

"Accelerate!" said D.L., turning his wrist. The road sped up and the little digital spectators blurred. When she released his wrist, the speedometer dropped. The taillights of the competitors irised out.

She looked at Tim's eyes. They were cast sideways. She sighed in frustration. It wasn't that he didn't know how to play the game. He could master any activity he wanted. The problem was that he didn't know there even *was* a game. This is the way it was. This is the way it would *always* be—for days, weeks, months, years, decades to come. He would always be circling Neptune, always wearing a tinfoil hat, always acting spacey.

D.L. ground her teeth and clenched her fists. Why *her*? Why had *she* been born into such a spectacularly bizarre family? With this handicapped brother? With this incompetent father? With this departed mother?

"Hit the gas," she said. "*Punch* it. Go. *Go.*"

Then she felt an unfamiliar anger blaze inside of her. She watched her hand turning Tim's wrist so savagely and holding it so tightly that the whites of her knuckles showed.

The motorcycle lurched forward, and the sound of cheering spectators *hurrah*-ed again from the speakers in the console. Tim still wasn't watching. She clutched the back of his hair with her palm—it was fine and soft, like a newborn's —and twisted his face toward the screen.

"Watch the road!" she ordered him. "You can't play the game unless you watch where you're going!"

But he still wasn't watching. She saw his glassy eyes focused on the beige plaster wall behind the machine. Why was she even doing this? Then she felt a thick, warm wetness dribble onto the back of her hand. Oh God. Tim had *drooled* on her. That was the last straw. What an ungrateful little—she hesitated ... should she think it? ... oh why not—what an ungrateful little *retard*! Here she was, sacrificing her entire evening to keep him entertained, a cruise ship director, and he couldn't even keep his own *saliva* inside his own freaking *mouth*!

A boy's voice behind her suddenly said: "Can I get next game?"

The voice was relaxed, carefree, a barefoot stroll down a dusky orange-pink beach.

It was a glass of iced tea and a shoulder massage after a hard day.

It sent shivers down her body.

She turned. The voice belonged to a boy, about her age, his handsome broad face highlighted by a pair of green eyes, and a preened hairstyle that spiked up on the left side of his face and cascaded foppishly down the right. It kind of made his head look like a seismograph reading, but it was still cute. Beneath that he was wearing a loose black t-shirt with sleeves scissored near the shoulder. They showed off his raw-boned adolescent musculature. A black belt studded with silver squares cinched his jeans, whose leg fronts had been artificially faded.

"Yeah," D.L. said.

He peered around at Tim. "Is that your brother?"

"Yeah."

"No offense, but he's not even lookin' at the road."

"He's autistic," D.L. said.

The strange boy bobbed his head as though agreeing with an invisible voice. "There's some of those in a special wing at my school. I see them sometimes. Autistic." He rolled the word around on his tongue like a candy, sucking the meaning from it, then shrugged. The subject ended.

D.L. felt her breath quicken and her eyes widen. *He's comfortable with my brother!* Who was this effortlessly empathetic stranger? She tried to compose herself. She needed to stay calm, she needed to stay in control—and most of all she needed to quiet the enormous attraction that had bellyflopped between them and was barking like a sea lion.

"Where do you go to school?"

"Brandywine."

"Where's that?"

"Why don't you guess?" he said. A glimmer of mischief sparkled in his eye.

Her heart hammered against her chest. She couldn't let herself be cornered like this.

She nodded towards his jeans instead. "Did you dye those yourself?"

"My friend did it for me."

"Your friend's pretty good."

His demeanor changed. "Actually, I did it."

"Liar."

"I did. Look." His finger pointed to a swatch of fabric near his boot-cut cuff. There was a conspicuous streak of white. "That's where I tested the peroxide." Then he pointed towards the rough whiskering on his lap. "And right here I used a cheese grater."

Tim rocked back and forth in his motorcycle seat. The screen read Game Over.

"Someone else wants to play, Snooker," said D.L. She helped Tim climb off the seat.

"You can only watch on one condition," the boy said.

"What's that?"

"Don't look at my butt."

D.L. scrunched her nose. "Don't worry. Nobody wants to see your butt."

"They should. It's juicy like a peach." He slapped it and grinned at her as he climbed onto the machine.

"Oh, you think you are so *clever*," she said.

"Hey, can I have fifty cents?"

She emitted a short, sharp laugh like a donkey braying. It surprised her as much as it surprised him. She clamped a hand over her mouth.

"What's so funny?" he asked.

"You said *have*. Most people say *borrow*."

He sighed exasperatedly. "*Okay*. Can I *borrow* fifty cents?"

She reached into the side pocket of her cargo pants and drew a couple of quarters from the roll. Why not? It wasn't *her* money. She could fling it around a little.

"No, you can *have* fifty cents," she said, holding the coins out in her palm, "since we probably won't see each other again."

He didn't even look at it. "Could you drop it into the slot for me? I can't reach it from here."

This was outrageous. She was trying to lend him money, at *his* request, and he wouldn't touch it! Treating her like the housekeeper! True, the coin slot was slightly out of his reach, but still … the cockiness! The most unbelievable thing was that—she shuddered as happy tingles raced through her belly —she actually *liked* it! She *enjoyed* taking orders from this perfect stranger!

She dropped the coins into the slot and stepped back.

"There," she said.

"Thanks," he said. He immediately hopped off the motor-cycle game and sauntered towards the door as if it were the most natural thing in the world to be doing just then. What was *wrong* with him? Was he leaving? Her foot curled vulner-ably underneath her.

"Where the hell are you going?" she said.

"Oh, I don't know."

"But I thought you wanted to play the game."

"Nah." He smiled. "I just wanted to see if you would pay for it." He was completely serious.

A smile curled around D.L.'s lip. She'd been played like a violin! Jerked like a Jamaican! Alone among teenagers, this boy knew the secret to successful flirtation, which is to *tease*, maturely but mercilessly. Mock their shoes, grimace at the sight of their hair, push snot-filled Kleenexes into their hands —whatever it takes.

"What am I supposed to do now?" she said.

"Your brother can play again."

"You're a jerk," she said.

He shrugged. "You just don't know me yet. See you around."

D.L. panicked. She wanted to get to know him, but he was poised to leave. What should she say? Should she offer to play against him? Should she suggest meeting him at the pool? No, that would require her bathing suit and exposure of massive thighs. Should she tell him her room number? She was aware that that carried all sorts of adult implications. He might think she was alone. He might suddenly have *expectations*. But she wasn't ready for sex! Not unless she was in love, and she wasn't in love with this *player* …

Was she?

It didn't matter. He wasn't even sticking around for an answer. He flashed a charming grin—

—and vanished through the door. The room vibrated as though someone had swung a mallet at a gong. D.L. leaned against the motorcycle, dazed. Her fingers lightly touched her abdomen.

Who *was* this Arcade Boy?

sixty

. . .

THE MINIVAN WAS STOPPED on a darkened two-lane road in the furthest reaches of exurban Orlando.

Behind the wheel, Sharpy's left hand toyed with the knee of his pleated khakis that he'd bought for thirty-five dollars off a pile at a department store. He was also wearing his best Geoffrey Beene polo shirt; it featured tiny tan, black, and white braids and was ringed by a tan collar. In Indiana, this shirt was *de rigueur* for a man of a certain age and class. It was this sense of propriety that had always kept Sharpy afloat.

Beside him, Vivian was cloaked completely in black—jacket, blouse, skirt, and boots. Her legs were crossed tightly and her tar-pit eyes were black holes which bore straight through the windshield. She was sitting very still, except for occasionally pushing back a tuft of carefully sprayed hair that had been disturbed by the balmy breeze gusting through Sharpy's open window.

The clouds had tumbled in low and dense that afternoon; a voice on the minivan's radio was warning about a low-pressure system that threatened wind, rain, and hurricane conditions upon the Florida coast. But Sharpy wasn't really listening. His eyes were fixed on the ghastly orange glow that lit up the clouds.

That was their destination: the Orlando StreetPulse entertainment complex. It was a brand-new promenade offering NASCAR bars, rainforest restaurants, medieval shows, plush theaters, bric-a-brac tourist shops, and tchotchke palaces. The thing crouched between the brackish inland lakes and palmetto prairies like a duchess in a brocade dress squatting in a muddy garden to pee.

Of course, there was nothing "street" about the StreetPulse. That little moniker was a fabrication, the product of corporate real estate development group that had waved its magic wand and transformed this pathetic loblolly patch of *tierra cienega* into a mammoth, moneyed nightlife machine.

The road was dark because there were no streetlights. There were no streetlights because the speed of its construction had caught the county sitting on its hands. The county hadn't even been able to expand its roads.

Which explains why Sharpy's minivan was cooking in a mile-long backup of red brakelights. The cars snaked into a rutted, woefully short left-turn lane that in turn shunted drivers into a six-story, state-of-the-art parking garage … a turn that had once led into somebody's peaceful rangeland …

Sharpy's fingers traced the outline of a square on his pants again. He *must* stop doing that. It was drawing attention to his pocket—and, inside, the box that contained the fabulous ring. This was *the* night, of course, the Big Popper, the Bended Knee. He was going to atone for the lousy seventeen years earlier. The memory made him shiver horribly. It'd been at the Dairy Queen, of all places, at the freaking *DQ*, at a red picnic table, over a pair of soft serve cones, with cars whizzing by… At least Felicia had been a good sport. Thank God she'd been too young to know any better.

Fingers! He quickly clasped the steering wheel and cleared his throat.

The movement caught Vivian's eye. She tilted her head, like an owl spotting a mouse. What had possessed him today? All afternoon Sharpy had been making jerky, fidgety movements. Plus the oversolicitousness. He'd fetched her mai tais, massaged her toes, feigned an interest in her *W* magazine. He'd even opened the minivan's passenger door for her—a gesture that had pretty much disappeared since the invention of those black keyless entry fobs that swing from everybody's keychain. Now he wouldn't even tell her where he was taking her. There was no doubt that *some*thing was brewing. He *never* paid this kind of attention to her.

"Are you going to tell me where we're going?" she asked.

"Maybe."

"Is it a restaurant?"

"Do you want to know?"

She pouted a little. "Maybe."

"It's called Under the Sea."

Vivian stiffened. "Is that a *seafood* restaurant?"

Why had she stated it like that? So accusingly? Sharpy rooted through the file drawers in his mind when ... of course! The heat of panic suddenly bloomed in his cheeks: *Vivian didn't eat fish!* She'd suffered poisoning from a piece of halibut when she was young and hadn't touched seafood since. Shit! It wasn't *his* fault that he'd forgotten! How was he supposed to have remembered? Up until now, she had only been his mistress. He hadn't had to know her likes or dislikes. He had just given her the plastic.

"I think so," he stammered, then added quickly: "But I'm sure they've got other things on the menu."

"Did you make sure?"

God, she was pinning him to the wall. This was hardly the best way to build up to a marriage proposal.

"No, I didn't," he admitted, "but it came very highly recommended."

"By who?"

Jesus, he thought, only every information hotline, booth, kiosk, website, concierge, clerk, bellhop, ticket taker, and janitorial staffer in the city—that's who. The StreetPulse was the talk of tourist Orlando.

"Oh, you know," he said, "people."

"Was it a bellhop or concierge?"

"I don't remember. Why?"

"They get *paid* to recommend certain places. It's called a kickback."

"I know what it's called," he said testily, "but this is a special place. The chef opened La Fleur in Chicago, you know."

That did it. Vivian's immaculately waxed eyebrows raised, and a small approving sound escaping from her throat. She was impressed.

Never mind that it was a total lie. La Fleur didn't even exist. Sharpy'd seen the name on a perfume advertisement in one of her fashion magazines.

That it was a lie didn't matter. He had won the battle.

sixty-one

. . .

THE MAIN DRAW at Under the Sea was not the food, but the aquarium. It was a gargantuan tank, one hundred and eighty thousand gallons of blue salt water, and it literally encompassed the diners, climbing the walls, spanning the ceiling, reaching down between tables in twisted blue pillars like the stumpy legs of dinosaurs.

The fish on the menu were ordinary—trout, salmon, orange roughy—but their cousins in the tank were far more glamorous: abalone, adders, moray eels, sting rays, tiger sharks, and more. In the mornings, a team of three marine biologists monitored and cleaned the tank.

But they were gone by the time the first guests were seated for lunch, and Sharpy marveled at the ambience as they opened their menus. Alongside their table ran the glass wall of the tank. Small dogfish darted in and out of coral reefs; a rockfish swam stupid circles near his head.

"What are you going to order?" Vivian asked.

He hadn't even glanced at the choices. He'd been too preoccupied by that square bulge in his pocket. When would he do it? How would he introduce the subject? He should've planned it out!

He glanced up at Vivian. She was coldly beautiful tonight. Her skin glowed tubercular blue in the aquarium's reflection. The silver pendant necklace hung against her breast like a sliver of ice.

"Stephen?" she said.

"I haven't decided yet. What about you?"

"Probably just a salad."

"I told you they'd have more than just seafood."

"You were right," she said, as though it pained her to admit that.

The waitress took their order and brought their drinks, and Vivian lifted her glass of chardonnay.

"To the Cravings," she said. "To making your family whole again." They clinked glasses. "I can't *imagine* ever doing what you're doing. My mother would've had two nervous breakdowns before we got to Chattanooga."

"Thank you," he said. He felt that it was about time his effort was recognized.

"Do you know what I like best about our relationship?" she asked.

"What?"

"I like how it isn't about money." Vivian had somehow become more feminine. Her shoulders had become narrower, her lips smaller.

"That's true," Sharpy said, not wanting to disagree right now.

"I mean, when we started dating, I *knew* you had money," she said. "But we're so much deeper now. I feel like we're really connecting." She reached across the table. Her hand felt cold and tiny and dead. "Finding someone like you is every girl's dream." Her black eyes looked deeply into his and her front teeth bit down on her lower lip.

Sharpy's chest swelled with pride. He still had *it*! The mojo, the pheremones, that invisible but undeniably right stuff that causes women to swoon! Seventeen years of marriage had *not* wrung it out of him!

"Can I ask you a question?" she said.

Sharpy winced slightly. What would she ask? This vacation had revealed to her all of the family's embarrassments. She'd looked into every moldering crevice, sniffed every proverbial pair of dirty underpants. What more did she need to ask?

"Sure," he replied.

She tried to suppress a smile. "What's in your pocket?"

His face quickly bloomed crimson. She *had* noticed! Why had he been fidgeting so much with it! Now what would he do? Well … he would lie! He wasn't going to let her usurp this evening! His heart sped up. *Thump thump—*

"Just my wallet," he said. "Why?"

Vivian had suddenly grown very large in her seat. Her eyes were the barrels of two pistols aiming for his forehead. He felt his deodorant suddenly expire.

"You were playing with something in your pocket all the way over here," she said. "I was wondering what it was."

"What do you *think* is in my pocket?" It sounded more accusing than he'd meant it to. His heart was now beating like a frightened rabbit's. *Thump thump—*

"I don't have a clue," she said innocently.

"Guess." *Thump thump—*

"I don't want to guess. I want you to tell me."

"No, I want you to guess." *Thump thump thump thump—*

"This is immature," Vivian said. "Why can't we be grownups tonight?" She sat back, disgusted.

Now. The time was right. He'd wrestled control of the evening back into his own grubby fingers.

"What if I told you"—*thumpthumpthumpthump*—"that there was a ring in my pocket?" He felt his heart slow down at last. He'd finally hacked up the hairball that had been choking him.

Vivian didn't flinch. She held his eyes very carefully. Then they flickered down beneath the table, toward his pocket.

"I don't believe you," she said.

"Why not?"

"You've never talked about it."

"But I've been *thinking* about it."

"Show me."

"What would you say if I showed you?"

Her face remained carefully composed, but her chest had begun to rise and fall more quickly. "Why don't you show me and find out?" she said.

She had thrown the gauntlet now. There was no turning back. He slid his hand into his pocket and grasped the velvet box.

Should he kneel? No, that was too clichéd. Even worse, it was demeaning. He needed to keep the high ground. He *must* show Vivian that he was a man, and that there would be no more yipping free-for-alls with his Visa Platinum at Neiman's or Barney's or anywhere else.

On the tablecloth he gently placed the velvet box. He squared it just so. Then he folded his hands and watched Vivian. Her eyebrows lifted approvingly. She stroked the purple velvet with a single finger. Then she curiously pulled the box towards her, opened the hatch, and her eyes went wide. From the box she lifted a massive engagement ring: a platinum double-row pave setting with a three-carat marquise cut stone. That's what the jeweler had told him it was. Sharpy himself didn't understand that type of lingo. The jeweler had pretty much picked it for him.

Vivian slipped the ring onto her finger. It caught the light and threw tiny bits of rainbows everywhere.

Her face was aglow. "It's amazing!" Then: "How much did you spend on it?"

"Don't worry about it."

"Tell me! I want to know!"

Sharpy shook his head. How could he tell her that he had taken out a seventeen-thousand-dollar loan to afford it? He couldn't.

"It *doesn't matter*. What matters is this." He clasped both her hands. "Will you marry me?"

sixty-two

. . .

VIVIAN PAUSED. The ring suddenly shone blueish cold. She opened her mouth, then closed it, then opened it again. She looked profoundly confused. Then she stowed the ring back in its carriage and closed the lid. "We have to talk about a few things first," she said.

Not exactly what he wanted! But what else did he expect? He'd always known that she was a pragmatist—a cold-blooded one, some might even say. A romantic would've flung her quivering arms around his neck and stained the shoulder of his shirt with great sobbing streaks of tears. Not Vivian. It felt like she was negotiating an auto workers' contract.

"Like what?"

"Brittany."

"I'll be happy to have Brittany around. She's a lovely girl."

Vivian sneered. "Oh, come on. You can't give her everything she needs." She tilted her head backwards and drained the chardonnay down her throat. "You probably think I spoil her. I don't." She thought twice about this. "Well, not *too* much. It's mostly her nature."

"We can work it out."

"What about Tim? Do you expect me to care for *him*?"

She spat out the final word with surprising viciousness. Sharpy was taken aback. He hadn't even realized Tim might be an issue. There were no surprises with his son. What you saw was what you got. Tim had always been *dependably* strange.

"Everybody in the house has to help Snooker," he said. "Me, D.L.—"

"I like D.L.," Vivian said. She sounded like a child pointing to her favorite flavor at an ice cream shop. "She's strong. She doesn't need anybody."

"I know she likes you too," he said. It was another lie. How many times had D.L. complained that she didn't trust the new raven-haired mistress in his life? Sharpy always brushed off these complaints. D.L. would be leaving for the greener pastures of some university in a couple of years.

"And where will I live?"

"With me."

"Where will that be?"

Sharpy played dumb. He knew exactly what she was asking. The reason his extramarital liaisons with Vivian had been so successful for so long was because she lived in Chicago. She adored the city. It was urbane, sophisticated, the architectural centerpiece of the nation, packed with people who loved fine art and read the latest books and ordered *foie gras*. It had *class*. And if Chicago was a cashmere sweater, then Indianapolis was a polyester windbreaker. *His* city had tractor repairmen, football coaches, and livestock pens. Truth be told, Sharpy preferred the Windy City too, but his job, his friends, and his history were in the land of Hoosiers.

"I know how important Chicago is to you," he said with the utmost tact, "but it has to be Indianapolis. For now."

Vivian said nothing. Under the table, however, her hands twisted the edge of the cotton tablecloth into a small damp knot. Sharpy knew that she was struggling with the decision —and that pragmatism would always win out.

Finally she released it and broke out into a winning smile. "That's okay," she said. "I like Indianapolis."

"I'm glad to hear you say that."

Her eyes widened. "Everyone is so into sports! It's so healthy!" There was a note of hysteria in her voice.

"Then it won't be a problem!" he said. "Is there anything else I should know about?" He was in full alpha-male mode now.

Vivian calmed down. She was considering. Her nose twitched like a panther's. "I don't think so," she said.

There followed an awkward silence. Sharpy leaned forward on the edge of his seat. Vivian leaned backwards in hers, arms crossed.

"So are you waiting for an answer?" she said.

"It would be nice."

"Okay."

"Okay what?"

She leaned forward and her lips enunciated the words very carefully. "I will marry you, Stephen Craving." Her arms remained crossed.

Sharpy felt a rush of pure, distilled ecstasy swelling his heart. *She said yes!* So what if her body language was saying "I'd rather dig an ice pick into my toenails"? *She said she wanted to marry him!* This was about more than just a new wife; this was about a new *life*. All that bad karma ... vanished! His thoughts raced feverishly. He would snap the million-dollar picture tomorrow. Then he would thrust it into the face of that prickish, arrogant lawyer the nanosecond they got home. With any luck, Sharpy would receive the inheritance inside of a month. And then what? *Anything!* The world would be at his feet! He could invest in a start-up! One of those new media Internet streaming wireless global superconnected something or others. He didn't understand any of it, but no matter. He'd find some wangdoodle fresh out of Stanford who did, and then he'd fund the kid all the way to Valhalla. All those VCs were getting rich, rich, rich. Yes, entrepreneurship was the way. He was *meant* for it … self-motivated … tireless … an American success story …

He leapt to his feet, which felt incredibly light in their Rockports. He extended his hand to Vivian. Reluctantly, with the faintest tinge of a smile, she stood up.

He embraced her. He felt the heartfelt declaration stirring in his chest. "I love you," he said, "and I want to spend the rest of my life with you."

"I love you too," she muttered.

"No matter what?"

She hesitated. "What do you mean?"

"I'm thinking about a pre-nuptial."

Vivian stiffened in his embrace. Her eyes suddenly flashed with distrust. Sharpy knew that uttering this word was dangerous and off-putting. It had planted distrust into marriages across the nation.

"Why would you want one of those?" she said.

"It's not personal."

"It's not?"

He tried to explain. "See, I would want this regardless. It doesn't really matter who the woman is." Vivian's eyebrows crinkled disapprovingly. What was wrong? He was trying to explain something *rationally*. Why did he feel like he was digging himself into a hole? He continued: "I could be marrying the most"—he almost said *sweetest*—"helpless, dependent woman in the world"—why didn't he *stop talking*? —"and I would still want her to sign one."

"That makes sense," she said.

"It's not negotiable."

"Of course not."

"It's just something I have to do to protect me."

"I understand." But Vivian had frozen over again. With a

gust of frosty air, the ice queen had reappeared in her majestic glory. Even worse, he'd blown the most supposedly romantic moment of both their lives by jabbering on about how she was no different from any other woman. He lowered his head. He *had* been digging a hole, and now it was so deep he could hang pictures on its walls.

He felt her hand touch his wrist. He lifted his head and found her staring deeply into his eyes.

"It's *okay*, Stephen," she said.

"I'm an idiot."

"No, you aren't."

"You really deserve better than me."

His new fianceé stamped her foot. "Christ! Stop *whining*, Stephen!" Her voice cracked his ears like a whip. Then she whispered: "I already *have* a pussy. I don't need another."

Her crass words rang in his ears. This caused the alpha-male running dog, the marauding instinct, to rear up on its hind legs again.

"I want you," he said.

"Really?" she said.

"I want you *right now*."

Vivian's soul seemed to be somewhere else, even as he stood up, grabbed the back of her hair, and pushed her lips onto his. And as they stood there, liplocked in the middle of the restaurant, the sound of clapping filled the restaurant and rang in their ears.

Sharpy pulled away. The other diners were applauding! He smiled broadly and spun around Vivian for the crowd. A rigid plastic smile was painted on her face.

They were engaged.

sixty-three

· · ·

THE WINDSOR KNOT on his tie was giving Reedy Lawler a real problem. He'd successfully gotten the piece of fabric around his neck, but somehow he couldn't make his fingers work properly. With the muddy ground heaving underneath his feet, who could? He felt like a silver ball rolling around a tilting wooden maze.

He was standing in the off-site employee parking lot of the Florida Jewels timeshare condominium resort, and the sky was a gorgeous deep navy blue, it being barely quarter to seven in the morning. A warm breeze tickled his cheeks.

Lawler was a timeshare condo salesperson.

As such, he was forced to park his car in this unpaved stretch of dirt every morning and wait in the balmy blackness for a shuttle to transport him to the resort sales pavilion, which was over a mile away. All the sales reps considered this the height of indignity. There were reps making sixty, eighty, even *one hundred* thousand dollars per year who were still parking their Infinitis and BMWs in the dirt. There always grumbling in the afternoons when they returned to find the layer of brown dust that had invariably settled upon their gleaming machines. Some washed their cars every afternoon.

But Lawler didn't have to worry about his car this morning. The reason was that he couldn't remember where he'd left it the previous night. What the hell had he been doing? He rubbed his eyes with his knuckles and tried to recall. Nothing was firing; his synapses were a jumbled mess. Last night was a brownish, sweet-smelling haze of blonde hair and bottomless pint glasses. He vaguely recalled a four o'clock happy hour at the Alehouse, a favorite haunt of his party-boy extended-adolescence crowd.

He squinted. Ah—now it was coming back.

He'd met Goldie, a buddy who moonlighted as a manager of mid-sized hotels, and a couple of gorgeous young tourists, Tina and Jennifer, who looked like models with their black Stretchlon clubbing pants and bareback pink tube tops and sparkles around their eye sockets. The girls had ordered chili fries and eaten them with their fingers and giggled. Then he and Goldie had ditched the girls—or had it been the other way around?— and met up instead with the Rincón brothers, a couple of *boricuas* who owned a successful auto detailing shop on the south side. Together the quartet had splashed through a night of debauchery at Rachel's, a fancy strip club with a famously delicious buffet on early Sunday mornings, and since the brothers were tight with the owner they would be good for the bill. That's where he'd met up with Bianca and Carmine, two dancers who were technically off-duty but who loved slamming shots with the boozy patrons anyways because there was so much cash being tossed around. If you made sixty grand a year, and if you were at all physically attractive, you could count on getting at least one good fuck out of them, Lawler knew, even though that was against the official house rules. Lawler didn't make that kind of bank, not even close, but the ladies never seemed to mind. He remembered that their shells of bleached platinum blonde hair had shone brilliantly under the flashing lights, and that they were small the way strippers usually were, the waists feeling tiny under his hands as they twisted the night away …

Everything after that, however, was blackness. He'd woken up in the backseat of a taxi with the driver misting him with a water bottle.

Lawler continued fumbling with his necktie, then finally abandoned the enterprise and stuffed the thing into his pocket. He was still wearing yesterday's suit, a nice black Italian ensemble with four buttons and a handkerchief permanently stitched into the breast pocket. It was dashing, except for the slept-in wrinkles.

Lawler felt angry with himself. It was high time, he thought, to end this madness. Starting right now, from this very nanosecond, there would be *no more* partying on work nights. He would absolutely *stop* going out.

It wasn't the first time he'd said this.

Suddenly the earth gave another tremendous heave underneath Lawler's feet, and he clutched a nearby cement stanchion for support. There was no doubt about it: He was still drunk. One good strong cup of coffee from the pavilion was all he needed. Then the dark cranial clouds would disappear, and he'd be ready for the sales line.

A pair of headlights swung around and pulled up alongside the woozy salesman. It was the shuttle bus. A long billboard along the side read *Florida Jewels Timeshare Condominiums—Make Your Vacation Last a Lifetime!*

He staggered up the steps, gripping the handrails. On the seats there were already twenty other sales reps, immaculately dressed in business attire, their artificially whitened teeth shining under the overhead track lights. They stared as he stumbled down the aisle, clutching his attaché case to his chest.

"Looks like someone had a good night," said someone.

"Oh yeah," he said.

"Going to deeding today, Reedy?" said another.

"You bet," he mumbled. "Ready to rock 'n' roll."

"We're all going to deeding today," a third voice said cheerfully. "Everybody's going."

"Taylor went yesterday."

"What'd he sell?"

"One week Flex Plan."

"That's his third this month."

"When you're good, you're good."

Lawler crashed down onto an unoccupied seat. "Going to deeding" was shorthand for a sale. The salesmen were just trying to keep up their morale with this kind of talk, since selling timeshare is so torturously difficult. At Florida Jewels, an average closing rate was twelve percent, a good closing rate was anything over fifteen, and twenty meant that you were a Top Gun. Therefore, even the best sales reps were rejected by four out of every five families that they toured.

It was brutal, and everyone did his best to stay positive. They slapped each other on the shoulders, gave words of encouragement, and smiled constantly. On the other hand, if anyone showed even the smallest hint of pessimism, criticism, or general gloominess, that person was avoided like a cholera victim. That person would Bring You Down. So Reedy Lawler always tried to join in the general buoyancy.

Every day, nearly one hundred and fifty families toured the Florida Jewels timeshare resort. These families didn't come out of curiosity. They were lured by the guarantee of two free theme park tickets. Over the decades, timeshare developers had discovered that this technique yielded much greater sales volume than print or television advertising.

The bus shuddered and rocked, and Lawler felt a great tsunami of nausea roll through his gut. He leaned forward and buried his head at his knees. He *really* needed a sale. The rent on his apartment was due on Saturday.

The shuttle bus carried the salespeople onto the 110-acre

resort, located on a sprawling piece of property circling half of the lovely Lake Sarandon. The pond was unswimmable because of the gators that lurked there. To the snowbirds, however, it promised a freaking paradise, with fourteen six-story condominium towers circling its banks. Rumor said that the site cost nearly two hundred million dollars.

Lawler felt the shuttle bus jerk to a stop, and he pulled himself to his feet. They'd arrived at the sales pavilion, a vast stucco welcome center with Spanish tile roof and leaded glass windows whose front walk was studded with magnolia trees and shrubbery that had been snipped with surgical precision. It had all been designed to wow the winter birds, to tempt the tourons.

To suggest that they weren't vacationing as well as other people were.

sixty-four

· · ·

LAWLER and the other sales reps poured out of the bus and presented their ID numbers to a girl at the registration desk. He walked down the main corridor towards the breakfast room, a long, low space filled with hundreds of beige tables and patterned chairs. Along one side of the room was a huge picture window, through which the crystal blue waters of the lake were displayed like a Venetian mural. This is where the morning meeting was about to begin.

The sales staff had developed their own little rigid caste system which expressed itself in the way that they seated themselves during this meeting. The Top Guns, the twenty-percenters, always gathered nearest the front, and the solid fifteen percenters were right behind them. Behind both of them were the members of the Spanish line, who toured the thousands of South American families who visited Orlando every year; behind them sat the British line. The newest reps were shunted to the back of the room. Nobody liked to be seen mixing with those poor souls, for the simple reason that most would only tour a few weeks before they were terminated. Lawler thought of them as Fruit Flies. Classes of twenty-five or thirty Fruit Flies were routinely trained and then fired as the management searched for the single hardy sales rep who might actually go the distance. The distance itself always turned out to be short anyways—the average lifespan of a timeshare salesperson was about four months. It was a punishing profession, even to those talented enough to be earning ten thousand dollars a month.

Lawler itched his neck nervously. It had been five months for him, and his closing rate had been steadily dropping. He knew that his string would soon be plucked.

"Goooooooood morning Florida Jewels!" shouted the general manager from the front of the room into a wireless microphone. "Are my representatives awake? Chipper? READY TO GO TO DEEDING?!?!" The sales reps cheered with barbarian lust, the primal greed-for-gold. It made Lawler's headache even worse. He clapped feebly before swallowing another mouthful of hot coffee.

"Yesterday was an outstanding day!" the manager announced, waving a ream of printouts. "As a group you closed at . . . *twenty-four point two percent*! Give yourselves a hand!" The assemblage hooted and hollered.

"You can't believe anything you hear in these meetings," a man in the next chair remarked cynically. The man's name was Cranston. "We only closed eleven point seven."

"Yeah," said Lawler.

"It's all horse pucky," Cranston muttered. He was one of the poisonous ones, someone who would Bring You Down, and had been excommunicated long ago. He spent most of his time moping around the sales pavilion alone with a black crinkled expression on his face.

"Just remember," the manager was saying, "that we must sell it *now*, sell it *today*! Create that sense of *urgency*! Stay positive! Lower the relationship tension and increase the task tension! Now let's go out there and *make some money*!"

There was a final burst of applause, and the meeting broke. Lawler had already stood up and was yawning—when he noticed the general manager beckoning at him. He instantly froze. Didn't dare to blink. There was no mistaking it: The manager wanted *him*. Lawler was petrified. The Florida Jewels was very hierarchical, not the kind of place where the big boys chummed around with their minions.

Lawler plastered a smile on his face as he approached the boss. "Yes sir?"

"Lawler," the manager said, "your numbers are in the basement." His callused finger followed a line of numbers on his clipboard. "Ten point three."

He wasn't wasting any time. Lawler'd never imagined that this was how it would end. He wouldn't even be allowed the dignity of being escorted inside an office before being fired. They were going to decapitate him right here in public, before his peers. He dropped his head.

"I'm sorry, sir."

"I'm giving you one week to get to deeding," the manager said. "Otherwise—" He jerked a thumb over his shoulder.

Lawler lifted his head. A reprieve!

"You bet!" he said. "I'm going to deeding, you watch."

"I hope so," the manager said. He narrowed his eyes. "Where's your tie?"

Lawler pulled it out of his pocket. "Right here, sir." His useless fingers made a desperate show of putting it around his neck.

The manager left, brushing the lapels of his own sportcoat, as though cleansing himself of the miserable dust that the poor under-twelve-percenter carried with him.

Lawler felt a dark shape draw up stealthily alongside him. It was Cranston. "What'd he say?" he whispered.

"I've got one week," said Lawler.

Cranston sucked his teeth loudly. "You got a plan B?"

"No. Mind your own business."

"Hey, I'm just bein' realistic."

The sound of a bell rang across the room—the signal that

the line had officially opened and that the tours would now begin. Lawler headed into the bathroom. At the sink, he caught a glimpse of his reflection in the mirror. He was a young, skinny, moderately handsome twenty-six-year-old, with a head of receding hairline and watery but luminescent green eyes. Or they *would* be luminescent, if they weren't currently couched inside the sagging gray-blue flesh of his pouches. He washed his face and dried it with a paper towel.

He stepped back into the hallway and spotted an Up Girl dashing through the crowd. In her hand was a greensheet. Her face was scanning the faces of the salespeople. When her pupils landed on Lawler, her wide mouth broke into a grin. Her index finger pointed at him.

Lawler's entire spirit collapsed. Why *now*? Why couldn't they have waited? He needed a few minutes to recover ... steady his equilibrium . . . have a cig on the porch . . . play a hand of poker with the boys. The general manager must've pushed him up in the rotation. Now he'd have to slip into Sales Guy character—be charming, play with kids, ply the snake oil, and pray for the best.

He took the greensheet from the Up Girl, who scampered away without a word. He looked down at the information.

The name at the top of the page said Craving. He scanned the information. Seven family members ... Indiana ... family income ... what? Lawler rubbed his eyes and read the income line again.

One million dollars?

This guy was either an outrageous liar—or a possible sale.

Lawler suddenly felt a hell of a lot better.

sixty-five

. . .

THE CRAVINGS TUMBLED out of the minivan and spilled onto the grass of the Florida Jewels timeshare resort.

Grandpa carefully unfolded Grandma's wheelchair. "Remember, these people are trying to sell us real estate. Under *no circumstances* are we going to buy anything. This family has *no use* for a timeshare condo." He straightened himself. "Are we all agreed? Vivian?"

She was craning her body to apply lipstick in the minivan's passenger-side rearview mirror. "I hear you, Frederick."

"Sharpy?"

"Yes, Dad," he said. Sharpy nudged a clod of dirt with the toe of his sandal. He really did agree. He had zero intention of buying real estate in Florida. But he was feeling sullen for a different reason. Last night, he'd returned to the hotel sky-high, breathless, dancing on the ceiling. He'd been ready to show off Vivian's expensive ring, the way it splattered its expensive rainbows across the walls.

But his family couldn't have been less enthused. Grandma Maya, Brittany, and Tim had been asleep. D.L. had muttered something before turning back over in her bed to face the wall. Even Grandpa Frederick ignored the news; instead, he'd delivered a long leture about taking advantage of two free Disney tickets and the value of thrift. Sharpy agreed to trot along just to put an end to the old man's yammering.

So here they were, dawdling on the well-appointed lawn of this expensive timeshare resort, all to save a hundred bucks —instead of snapping the photo that would bring them a million.

"Isn't this lovely," said Grandma Maya, looking around the property. "We should stay here, Frederick."

The old man snorted. "Anyone who falls in love with Florida Jewels has got sand in their shoes. I've read all about this place. The developer's in debt up to his nostrils."

"You brought us here," said Vivian.

"Not to buy," the old man said. "Remember, we're *not* buying. Hear me, son?"

"Loud and clear, Dad," said Sharpy.

Inside the sales pavilion, Grandpa Frederick registered at the counter in the foyer while D.L. absorbed the lobby. The lobby looked like a spread in one of those vacation magazines published solely to flatter the rich—wicker credenzas, oxblood leather chairs with clawed pedestal legs, bright tropical paintings. She was craning her head to admire the expensively coffered wood ceiling when she heard a voice.

"The Craving family from Indiana?" The Cravings wheeled around. The voice belonged to a young man in a rumpled suit striding confidently across the pile carpet. "I'm Reedy Lawler, your sales representative. It's a pleasure to meet you ... Mr. Craving?" He stuck out his hand towards Sharpy.

Sharpy smiled back. This little shad didn't look so dangerous. Not high-pressure at all. Brushing him off at the end wouldn't be too difficult. He felt himself letting down his guard. His hands unclenched themselves; his shoulders relaxed.

Grandpa Frederick regarded the sales rep with a frosty eyeball. "You're quite a young Turk," he said. "Just how old are you, son?"

"Twenty-six, sir."

"You look younger."

"Well, I won't let my old age and experience affect our relationship."

Grandpa snorted. "Stole that one from Reagan."

Lawler shrugged. "He had the best writers."

"Got a real estate license?"

Lawler was taken aback at the invasive question. He looked at Grandpa Frederick. The old man was wearing some kind of godawful chintzy slate-blue polyester pants. His sparse white hair was bending crazily across the top of his pink scalp like windblown prairie grass. There was a hawk-like, merciless look to his face.

"Of course," Lawler said. "I'm an expert in my field."

"Good closing rate?"

Lawler tried not to roll his eyes. You especially didn't ask salespeople about their sales numbers.

"Don't you worry about me," he said. Then he offered a gleaming Pepsodent smile: "Just worry about having a good time in Orlando! Are you happy to be on vacation?"

To his left, a sudden movement caught his eye. It was a woman with black hair. She was wearing an expensive cream-colored sleeveless top and perfectly applied makeup. She was lethally attractive.

"This is my fiancée, Vivian Talon," said Sharpy.

"A pleasure," she said as Lawler shook her hand. It was perfectly formed and ice cold despite the heat outside.

Lawler crouched down to Brittany. "Aren't you beautiful?" he said. "What's your name?"

"I want Golden Grahams," replied Brittany.

"You're in the right place, because we've got a big bowl of them waiting for you right down that hall," said Lawler. "You know, that's a pretty dress you're wearing, Miss Golden Graham."

"Yeah," she said.

"But I think it's missing something."

"What?"

"This." From the inside pocket of his suit, Lawler pulled out a small sticker with a picture of The Varmint. Brittany squealed like a giddy little piglet and clapped her hands. He peeled the sticker from the backing and pressed it gently onto the fabric of her shirt. "How do you like that?"

"Say thank you, Brittany," said Vivian.

"Thank you," the little girl said.

Grandpa Frederick was growing impatient. "Reedy, what the hell are you doing?"

"Getting to know your granddaughter, sir."

The old man snorted. "That's *not* my granddaughter. Listen, we're on a pretty tight schedule. They said this presentation would take an hour and a half. We don't want to hear any sales spiel." He tapped his wristwatch. "Ninety minutes. Starting now."

"Don't you worry," Lawler said. He grinned and snapped his fingers. "I'm one of the quickest reps here. We're gonna be movin' and groovin'."

Grandpa Frederick grumbled as Lawler led the family down the long corridor. D.L. noticed that the walls were lined with framed photographs. In each one, the same crusty old man was posing with a different luminary—Magic Johnson, Donald Trump, Mick Jagger, four different presidents.

"Who is this guy in all the pictures?" asked D.L.

"That's our billionaire developer, David Wrangle."

"He must be quite an influential man," said Grandpa Frederick.

"He likes younger women," noted Vivian, inspecting one photograph. "Here's his new twenty-five-year-old wife."

"Mr. Wrangle is off the market," said Lawler. "She was Miss Florida."

"No one is ever off the market," said Vivian.

sixty-six

. . .

THE CRAVING FAMILY gathered around a square table, grazing on plates laden with muffins, bagels, cereal, instant scrambled eggs, and fruit salad. They drank watery red fruit punch out of styrofoam cups. Brittany had attached herself to Lawler's side like a barnacle to the hull of a ship.

"Look at that," said Vivian. "You're her first crush."

Brittany waved a sausage in her tiny fist. "Dog poop."

Lawler decided not to pay any more attention to the little girl. It would make him look trifling. Plus, it was clear that most of the family despised her. But Lawler's sense of intuition had been pinging like a sonar detector. He sensed something lurking below the surface of this group. He figured it had something to do with the mother.

He turned to the teenage girl because she seemed the most helpful. In a low voice, he said, "If you don't mind me asking, where is your mother?"

But he hadn't lowered his voice enough. The rest of the table had heard him.

Grandpa Frederick turned squarely to Lawler. "Young man, we don't have time to explain the—"

Sharpy interrupted him. "No, Dad, we have to talk about it." He quickly explained the conditions of the will to Lawler.

After he'd finished, Lawler casually said, "I'm very sorry about your loss. I'm sure that inheriting a big pot is no consolation." Inwardly, however, he was leaping with exultation. This family did have money! That greensheet had been no lie! It was easy to make families *want* to buy timeshare, but their *ability* to buy it was a totally different matter. This was a sale! He could smell it! The Cravings were wallowing like pigs in their filthy lucre! He was *going to deeding*!

Still, playing suave, he tamped down the excitement in his voice.

"Let me explain how I'm going to proceed today," he said calmly. "First I'm going to tell you about this company and this timeshare program. Then I'm going to take you on a tour of our beautiful condos. After that, I'll show you the price."

He dove into his well-rehearsed, natural-sounding sales pitch, and soon even Grandpa Frederick had leaned forward to examine the materials that Lawler had produced from his attaché case.

"Stephen, how many weeks per year does your family vacation?"

"One," Sharpy replied.

"Do you usually stay in a hotel?"

"Yes."

"How much do you pay, on average, for that hotel room each night?"

Sharpy lifted his palms up. "I don't know. About a hundred and fifty dollars?"

Lawler produced a small calculator from his pocket, flipped over his information sheet, and drew some numbers on the back. "Seven nights times one hundred and fifty dollars." He circled the number $1000. "So you normally spend about a thousand dollars on hotel rooms for each week of vacation." He multiplied that number times ten: $10,000. "Over the next ten years, that's ten thousand dollars." He multiplied it by thirty: $30,000. "Over the next thirty years, thirty thousand dollars." Then he paused, as though he had just thought of something. "You know, something's still missing from that figure. Do you know what it is?"

Grandpa Frederick instantly said, "Inflation."

Lawler was stunned. Hardly anybody thought about the devastating cost of inflation, but this hawk was no turkey. "Absolutely right, sir. Do you know how much Motel Six cost thirty years ago? Six dollars per night. What does it cost today?" He looked at Vivian.

"Don't look at me," she said. "I would never stay there."

"Thirty dollars," said Grandpa Frederick.

"So inflation has increased fivefold over the last thirty years. Let's assume the same rate over the next thirty years. Your thirty thousand dollars suddenly becomes . . ."

He wrote down $150,000, circled it, and turned the paper around so that the family could read it. He loved this part of the presentation. He could see the shock creeping into the faces of the adults. No one *ever* thought about the compounded future cost of hotel rooms.

"One hundred and fifty thousand dollars," he said again, "just for *one week* in a cramped hotel room over the next thirty years."

Lawler knew that he'd hooked them when Grandpa Frederick slammed a fist onto the table. "You'd better be prepared to back this up with some hard figures."

"He just did," said Vivian.

"Those were hypothetical!"

"They looked real to me."

Grandpa Frederick sputtered. "Don't tell me that you're listening to this garbage?"

"You signed us up, asshole," said Vivian. She turned to Lawler.

"Reedy, keep talking."

sixty-seven

. . .

AFTER BREAKFAST HAD FINISHED, Lawler drove the family across the resort on a superstretch golf cart. Behind the wheel, Lawler, with coffee in one hand, casually pointed out the amenities: water sports on the dock, seven heated swimming pools, volleyball courts, state-of-the-art health spa, children's magic show on Thursdays.

"Tell me," said Grandpa Frederick, "just how many of these units have you sold, Lawler?"

"Oh, I can't remember," he replied. "I just sold a family yesterday on vacation from Illinois."

"Liar," said Grandpa.

"Scouts' honor," said Lawler, smiling.

"More importantly, how much does all this *cost*?" said Grandpa.

"I'll show you the price at the end."

He pulled up at the front of a long spread of salmon-painted condos. "Notice the concrete block construction," Lawler said. "It's inexpensive and perfect for Florida. Fireproof, termite-proof, and hurricane-proof."

The Cravings followed him towards the front door of the model condo. Lawler paused, then dramatically flung open the door. Not even the grimmest, most pickle-hearted killjoy could deny that the condo was beautiful. Decorated in mauve and turquoise, the living areas opened onto a patio with a stunning lakefront view. As the family scattered to explore the rooms, Lawler threw superlatives into the air like confetti.

"The greatest vacation innovation of the twentieth century," he said, inspecting his fingernail. "Simply fantastic."

"There's a jacuzzi tub in the master bedroom," shouted Vivian, "and a bottle of champagne!" Brittany bounced on the king-sized bed, squealing.

"I could spend some quality time on that leather easy chair," said Sharpy. "Lemme take a test run. Hold my bag, Dad." He tossed his backpack at Grandpa Frederick, then crashed ass-first onto the chair.

"What do you think, Frederick?" asked Grandma Maya.

"This is good tile," Grandpa Frederick admitted, looking down at the floor and stamping it with his heel. "The construction is solid. What about you, Maya?"

"I smell cookies," Grandma Maya said, sniffing the air. A doughy scent had begun drifting across the room.

"You've got a good nose," said Lawler. "Around this corner you will find your fully-equipped kitchen, with everything you could possibly need—except this delightful woman."

A chubby, apple-cheeked woman in an apron had just pulled a baking sheet of chocolate chip cookies from the oven. "Would anybody like a cookie?" the baker asked, offering the tray. A motherly smile spread warmly across her face as Sharpy chewed one of her creations.

"I don't know why you're showing us this part of the condo," said Vivian. "I don't even want to look at the kitchen when I'm on vacation."

"I bet you don't look at it at home either," said Grandpa.

Lawler swiftly cut them off. "Actually," he said, "the American Automobile Association recently conducted a study showing that on vacation, the typical family of four spends a hundred dollars a day on food. *A hundred dollars*. You all know how much a theme-park hamburger costs. Just imagine how much *money you could save*"—he looked at Grandpa—"by eating breakfast and packing lunches here in your own condo."

"A heck of a lot," the old man said.

D.L. stood near the door, arms crossed, touching nothing. She was appalled by the fakeness of the entire morning. Lawler, the breakfast buffet, this old spinster baking cookies —all of it was transparently staged. Most of all, she felt ashamed that her father was now literally eating up this Skinnerian sales technique.

Sharpy, meanwhile, was peering around the condo. "Where's Tim?"

"In the bathroom," D.L. replied.

"What's he doing?"

"I don't care."

Sharpy looked at his daughter and his brow creased. "Something wrong? Got a mosquito under your bra?"

D.L. shrugged and averted her eyes.

"He's your brother. You're supposed to look after your brother."

"I don't care," she said again.

Sharpy himself entered the bathroom. Tim was standing in the shower, stimming, his hands fluttering intensely. "Snooker, stop whatever you're doing and come out. We're getting ready to leave."

Meanwhile, as Lawler explained the annual maintenance fee, Grandpa Frederick stood half-listening and running his tongue around his lips. He was parched. He opened the backpack that Sharpy had given him.

Inside was a squeeze bottle.

With the Varmint stamped on the outside.

Grandpa Frederick screwed open the top and peered inside. The bottle was filled with a fine white powder.

Koolaid mix, he thought. His son did have foresight, after all—enough to see that the family would need a flavored drink.

"Tell me your honest opinion, sir," said Lawler. "Do you like this place?"

The old man went to the kitchen sink and patiently filled the squeeze bottle with water. "I do, Reedy. I promised that I wouldn't, but it's truly a sensible, economical method of vacationing." He screwed on the cap and shook it. The water turned whitish-gray.

"That doesn't look like any Koolaid that I know," said Lawler.

"It must be one of those new flavors."

"Are you sure that's Koolaid?"

"Of course it is."

"I wouldn't drink it."

Grandpa Frederick ignored the warning. He lifted the bottle to his lips and squeezed the liquid into his mouth. Immediately he spat the stuff into the sink.

Sharpy heard the violent explosion and returned with Tim from the bathroom. He saw the disgusted look on his father's face. He saw the squeeze bottle with the Varmint stamped on the outside. He saw the milky liquid spattered inside the stainless steel basin.

"Tell me you didn't fill that bottle with water," he said.

"Whatever that is, it isn't Koolaid," Grandpa Frederick declared. He spat again, coughed, and wiped his mouth on his sleeve.

"That's my wife's ashes," Sharpy said. "The urn broke yesterday."

Grandpa Frederick stood motionless, as his mind tried to process the enormous awkwardness of what had just transpired. Nobody in the room so much as twitched a single muscle fiber.

Except Lawler, who turned away and buried his face in his hands.

This sale was *lost*.

sixty-eight

. . .

THE HOPELAND WAS A LOW-INCOME, extended-stay apartment-motel on the south side of the city.

It was a long, beige stucco complex, with four wings thrown around a central courtyard, which featured a majestically dead brown palm tree and a dry cement fountain. Crinkled leaves gathered in the corners of the plaza.

Its clientele being not very reliable, the Hopeland's management refused to take reservations. As a result, there was always a ragged line of stragglers underneath the concrete portico each morning, waiting for the office to open.

Which is exactly where Curtis found himself at ten minutes before eight. He was crouched on his New Balance sneakers, watching the red sun rise through the tips of the palm fronds on the other side of the road, smoking an unfiltered cigarette. He tasted the tobacco numbing the tip of his tongue. Why had he started this wretched habit again? He couldn't afford it. They made his throat and lungs ache. The few shirts he had left already reeked of stale tobacco. And of course there was the health of the Imminent Arrival to worry about. Their child was going to be facing a big enough handicap the ways things were currently headed. It didn't need to be handed a pair of compromised lungs too.

Curtis stubbed out the cigarette on the pavement, then crushed it beneath the tread of his rubber sole. He'd heard about this place from Manny and a few other characters who'd used its services. They'd called it the No-Hopeland. He didn't understand why. On the surface, it seemed promising. For one hundred and forty dollars a week you could have a room with a kitchen and HBO. He hadn't even had basic cable at his apartment.

But the parking lot looked awful. The cracks in the pavement were choked with unruly brown weeds. A row of cement stanchions flecked with long-faded red paint stood like a battalion of forgotten sentinels. Broken parking blocks lay snapped in half, their truss rods rusting in the corrosive air.

Nobody had given a cold bucket of piss about this place for a very long time.

Curtis' eyes lighted upon the sole bright spot in this wasteland: his Civic. Inside, Lucinda lay sleeping in the passenger seat. She had reacted to the cataclysm of the previous day surprisingly well. She'd even helped to stuff their meager belongings into black plastic trash bags and trundle them down to the car. It wasn't at all fair to her. His heart ached that they had to be so uprooted during this time.

They'd spent most of the night parked in a Wal-Mart parking lot. It was perfectly legal to sleep there. In fact, it was the retailer's national policy, one that most city-dwellers were completely ignorant of, to allow RVs to camp in Wal-Mart parking lots overnight. Sometimes, in the mornings, the blue-smocked employees even passed out free coffee and bear claws to the occupants.

Curtis hadn't known if the same courtesy was extended to cars, but, in any event, nobody'd bothered them last night. He'd tossed and turned restlessly in the driver's seat, which, even when reclined, couldn't prevent the steering wheel from pressing into his lap.

The No-Hopeland. Curtis thought about it. Inside Manny's snappy nickname, he admitted, there hid a kernel of truth. Curtis looked at his fellow hopeful boarders. They seemed about as unhappy as human beings could be. There was a sunburned cracker fast asleep with his reddish-blonde head tilted back against the wall, prolonged snores escaping his rounded mouth. To his left, a sketchy young kid twisted knots in a dirty plastic six-pack ring. His eyes defied anybody to look at him. To his right, a hefty blonde woman sat cross-legged with six inches of droopy, spotted cleavage in the middle of a riot of clearance-rack pastel polyester.

All these creatures had reached the last station on the track of deterioration.

And now he, Curtis Marshall, had joined them.

A thin shadow fell across him. Curtis looked up and saw a rangy, twitchy black man. He wore no shirt and shot-to-hell cargo pants with one leg rolled up to the knee. He carried himself with a peculiar roll in his left hip, as if his ball-and-socket joint were grinding into powder, and his face carried a look of manic desperation.

"Help a brother out?" he asked, holding a filthy Arby's cup out.

"I've got barely enough for myself," said Curtis. It was the truth; he needed every cent of the fifteen hundred dollars in his duffle bag.

"You got some jack," the drifter said. "Clutchin' 'at bag like that. I kin smell it." He shook his cup again, and a few pathetic coins rattled inside.

Curtis stared him down. "I got fired from my job and evicted from my apartment yesterday. My girlfriend is five months pregnant. I have *nothing* to give you."

His candor was completely lost on the drifter, who rattled the cup again. This time, Curtis lifted his hand and slowly pushed the cup aside. The drifter moved on down the line. "Help a brother out..."

Curtis couldn't really fault the drifter for such a hard sell.

After all, he was edging perilously close to the same existence.

sixty-nine

· · ·

SOMETHING SCRAPED INSIDE THE OFFICE.

The plastic digital watch on Curtis' wrist said five after eight. A heavyset black woman with a ten-inch-high sculpted ziggurat of orange hair was unlocking the office door from the inside. She flipped the sign from CLOSED to OPEN. Then she pushed the door open and stepped outside. Using a newspaper to shield her eyes from the sun, she turned and surveyed the people under the portico.

"We only got seven rooms opening today," she said. "Y'all are gonna have to organize yourselves. Cut some deals or somethin."

And then she was gone. Curtis had been warned that this might happen, that space was very limited. Now there were thirty people vying for seven rooms. Things would soon be ugly.

That was okay. He was young and agile.

Quick as a shot, Curtis leapt to his feet and slipped inside the door, ahead of the others. Let the others fight it out. He *needed* this room.

A bell attached announced his arrival. The office was already suffocatingly hot. Ziggurat Head had assumed her position behind the wood-paneled counter, spectacles on her nose, rifling through a file bulging with registration cards. Where was the computer? Of *course* there wouldn't be a computer. This was basically a welfare hotel.

He stood silently before her, waiting. Then Ziggurat Head produced an empty card. Without looking at him, she said, "Your name."

"Curtis Marshall."

"What can I do for you, Mr. Marshall?"

"I need three nights," Curtis said.

"We only do weeks."

"Okay, one week."

She placed a card on the counter. Her lack of eye contact, her plastered scowl, the way she removed any indication of personality from the interchange—all of these mannerisms told Curtis that she had encountered some truly chilling shit in this very office. "Fill this out."

Curtis paused. "Is it non-smoking?"

"No."

"I need non-smoking. My girlfriend is pregnant."

Ziggurat Head said nothing but pulled a different registration card. She was sensitive after all.

The bell tinkled as the others had poured inside. Curtis hadn't dare turn around. He didn't need to. He could hear the muffled grunts and mumbled curses. He could feel the caged heat from too many bodies as two, three, four, five, six, seven, eight, nine, ten people lined up behind him. He could smell the ugliness of the mob.

Ziggurat Head leaned across the counter and aimed a stinkeye towards the crowd. "All y'all got to straighten out right now! Ain't nobody getting no rooms without some *organization* up in here." Then she held her glare with the practiced intensity possessed by drill sergeants, parole officers, and inner-city high school teachers.

The scraping and shuffling quieted down. Curtis listened quietly. *One more minute* ... and he was homefree.

"That's one hundred fifty-three forty with tax," she said.

Curtis glanced backwards. The tortured faces were watching him. Reluctantly, he unzipped his duffle bag. Inside lay fifteen hundred dollars, all in twenties, from the title loan. He gingerly peeled off eight of the bills, careful to keep the rest of the giant wad hidden, and laid the cash on the counter.

Behind him, the rangy drifter craned his neck and hopped up and down, trying to see inside the duffle bag. "He got money!" he shouted. "Ay! He got scratch!"

That caused other ears to perk up. A man of about fifty tilted his neck to study Curtis. A young plump woman adjusted her shirt and licked her lips. Two gangbangers watched him peripherally through their hooded eyes.

Curtis quickly zipped up his bag, swung it around, and clutched it against his belly. "I have almost nothing," he said.

It didn't work. He could still feel the stares on his neck. There was a pack of wolves at his back. He drummed his fingers and tightened his lips and pressed himself against the counter, nearer to Ziggurat Head, the only safety he sensed.

At last Ziggurat Head pushed his change across the counter and handed him an electronic key card. "You're in one seventeen, baby. Laundry and ice in Building B. Curfew ten o'clock."

Curtis thanked her. He turned into the scrum, head tucked down, hugging his backpack tight. His shoulders brushed the others but he paid no attention.

"What the—"

"Watch your damn self—"

"You git me an extra bed, one seventeen—"

At last there was only one person remaining between him and the door: the drifter. He was mad-dogging Curtis with the type of intensity that only street people can execute.

"Whyn't you help a brother out?" he demanded.

"Don't do this," replied Curtis.

"You gots plenty of dough. Whyn't you help a—"

Curtis tried to move around him, but the drifter quickly stepped to the side. His mad-dog stare never wavered.

So this was how it was, Curtis thought. He plunged into his pocket and brought out the six dollars and sixty cents in change. He picked up the drifter's hand and put the change into it.

"Will this make you happy?" he said.

The drifter smirked. "If you can gimme six, you can gimme twenny."

This was pointless. Curtis liked to give people the benefit of the doubt, but this guy was a leech. He sucked people dry. And every second Curtis pursued this kangaroo conversation, he drew more attention to the suspicious bag hanging at his side.

Drawing a deep breath, he pushed his arm out like a battering ram and surged past the drifter, knocking his skinny frame backwards against the wall. The door slammed shut behind him.

It was full morning now, and the ground was starting to cook under the sun's brutal blows. Running across the parking lot, oblivious to the shouts behind him, Curtis held his breath until he reached Lucinda.

seventy

. . .

CURTIS PARKED the Civic on the other side of the complex. In the passenger seat, Lucinda slumbered heavily. He gently shook her knee. She didn't stir.

He cracked the window, then slipped out of the car and quietly closed the door. No sense in waking her. He would inspect the room, then carry up their belongings. She needed the rest.

Marching up to the building, Curtis entered the main hallway, a naturally-ventilated corridor made of cement blocks which made a perfect square around the four units. Through the spaces between the blocks he peered into the central courtyard. Saw the dead palm. The dried-up fountain.

He felt another prickling feeling upon his neck. He whirled around. A fluttering movement caught his eye. Was that a curtain? Across the courtyard, behind the cement blocks. No, that was no curtain. Those were *eyes* watching him! He was being monitored! Somebody was waiting!

He skittered along the corridor to room 117, hugging the bag and creeping along the wall. He slipped the keycard into the lock and entered the room and bolted it behind him.

The room was a letdown. What had he expected—the Four Seasons? A double-sized mattress with a floral bedspread … tattered paisley curtains … stained carpet the color of baked mud. He smelled the air. It was stale. No ventilation. He went to the window. It was welded shut, like the glass window of an office tower. There would be no ventilation whatsoever.

He paused. Something was missing. What was it? The answer clocked him across the head like a frying pan: *The kitchen*! He wheeled around. Where was the full kitchen that was promised? Nothing in this room even hinted at food preparation. Panicking, he flung open the closet door, which rolled along its track with an awful screech.

Inside sat a single mini-refrigerator. On top of it rested a turd-brown microwave, with rotary dials, circa 1987. He opened the refrigerator door and stuck his hand inside. It was warm. Of *course* it would be warm. Why on *earth* would management have plugged it in? He crawled onto his hands and knees and found the plug behind the unit. It was missing a prong. Of *course* it would be missing a prong. Why on earth would management require a working plug on the refrigerator?

He started to curse but caught himself. This wasn't the time to succumb to negativity. He needed to power through this crisis. He would rely on his wits. He would fashion a new plug, somehow. And he would still have the three-dollar bottle of sparkling grape juice (purchased at the Wal-Mart the previous night) waiting for Lucinda in a bucket of ice when she awakened. It would be a beautiful gesture. They needed these gestures to keep their dignity. She could use the ice to rub on her pregnant abdomen.

Ziggurat Head had said there was an ice machine in Building B. That would be the first order of business. He found the ice bucket on the shelf in the closet and washed it out in the bathroom sink. Pausing in the doorway, he remembered his duffle bag thrown onto the bed and quickly slung it around his shoulders.

He would keep that money on his person.

No matter what.

The heavy door clicked shut behind him. Curtis moved briskly down the cement-block corridor. His light shirt clung to the small of his back. An inverted U of perspiration traced the bottom of his ribcage. People wage endless arguments about whether it was the heat or the humidity. Curtis felt that, beyond a certain point, those arguments were meaningless. A hundred and five degrees was unbearable no matter *how* it was measured.

He found the ice machine humming inside an alcove. A padlock was looped through the steel handle. A nearby sign read, "Ice Machine Key In Office".

Curtis moodily sucked his teeth. The office was on the other side of the complex. This was supposed to have been a quick trip down the corridor. Now it was turning into a hike. He wasn't scared of going back; most of that mob had probably dispersed by now.

The quickest way to the office was to cut diagonally across the bare courtyard. He zipped through an opening and streaked across the square, staying as low as possible. It wasn't low enough. The brutal subtropical sun was still clubbing Curtis upon the head. His vision reeled. The cement of the courtyard had been bleached like a bone in the desert. The fountain's vivid maroon and cerulean blue tiles popped out against its blinding whiteness.

Then he felt that familiar prickling on his neck. His eyeballs instinctively scanned the courtyard again. He couldn't see anybody. Still, he couldn't ignore the instincts of his million-year-old lizard brain. Somewhere, he was being watched.

He increased his pace and quickly found the main office again. True enough, the crowd had disappeared, and now

Ziggurat Head was folding raggedy white terrycloth towels and dropping them into a bin. A lit cigarette drooped from the corner of her lip.

"Yeah," she said.

"I need the key to the ice machine," Curtis said.

"Which room are you in?"

"One seventeen."

She looked up suddenly, as if that number had been a magic password. "Them boys give you trouble yet?" Before he could answer: "If they do, then you jus' do what you gotta do. I'on't say nuthin'." Her eyes leveled with him.

"What boys?" Curtis said.

"Don't you mind," she said. She threw him a foot-long piece of wood with a key attached to the end. "Bring that key back or I got to charge you."

Curtis strode into the courtyard again. He held his chest thrust out. His ears, eyes, and nose quivered in hyper-alertness.

Thunk. He whirled at the tiny sound. A brown frond had dropped from the dead palm to the pavement. The paranoia was stressing him. He felt like a wire coat hanger had been jammed through his shoulders. And then—

Patter patter patter patter.

He whirled again. It was unmistakably the sound of running feet. Then he heard a muffled whoop. He whirled again.

He stood dead center in the middle of the courtyard. Clutching his duffel bag.

Watching and listening.

Nothing moved.

The only sound was a spigot's *drip-drip-drip*.

He suddenly ran across the rest of the courtyard to where an arrow directed him into the alcove with the ice machine.

Time was of the essence. Curtis quickly used the key to undo the padlock and open the aluminum panel. There it lay:

a glorious bed of ice cubes. Cold air blasted his face. The humming of the machine's cooling system drowned out all other noise. A metallic scoop rested on the bed of ice cubes. He reached for it and quickly scooped the crunchy cold cubes into his bucket—

—when his knees suddenly folded and gave way. His armpits caught on the lip of the ice machine. Its sharp metal edge bit into his sensitive skin of his underarms. What was wrong with him? Why weren't his legs working?

Then a smashing pain arrived, on the back of his neck, and Curtis experienced a something entirely new: The sensation of his body falling all the way onto the floor, and his body flopping onto its back, and his skull thudding on the concrete.

Through woozy vision, he saw the four faces. They wore baseball caps turned a rakish forty-five degrees to the side. Two also wore handkerchiefs around their skulls. Curtis blinked twice and squinted. They were *kids*. The smooth faces, the concave pubescent chests. Couldn't be older than thirteen.

One waved a crowbar. That must've been what did it. First the backs of his knees, then the back of the head. He tried to lift his arms but they had gone numb. This must be what boxers felt as they lay fallen on the mat.

One-two. Down for the count.

The kids were laughing and whooping and arguing and pushing each other. He studied the squiggles of the particulate ceiling tiles above his head as he struggled to roll over, lift his arms, stand up. But his body—his athletic physique, his best and only tool—had been rendered completely useless.

Then he felt his torso being lifted up and his duffle bag being tugged off his shoulder. Curtis hazily remembered the money hidden inside. They would *never* take his money. He gritted his teeth and clutched the its handle with his left hand as if he were a diver hanging onto his airhose in the midst of a shark attack. With ferocious effort he tried to sit up, and must've succeeded, because he immediately felt several swift pulses on his ribcage—those would be kicks—before sinking back down. The fingers of his right hand clawed uselessly at the air. He was losing consciousness.

Somebody's sneaker stepped on his left inner arm, and stayed there, and a few seconds later the resulting density of blood in his forearm and wrist caused his hand to finally open. He watched the backpack being slipped out of his grasp.

Oh God.

He screamed in agony as he saw the kids unzipping it on the floor, only a few feet away. The goddamned delinquents! Why didn't they take it out of sight ... like *civilized* thugs! Why torture him like this? He turned his head again. They'd found the wad of money, were peeling off the bills, waving them around, high-stepping. They were high fiving each other, clapping hearty hands across each other's backs. Curtis felt the vomit building in his stomach and rising up his esophagus.

Then two black walls began to close off either side of his vision. Curtis really was losing consciousness. Through the darkening fuzz, he saw one of the boys snatch the wad of money from another and sprint for the door. Then he saw somebody tackle the boy near the door, and then there was a flurry of hands and feet as the plunderer was punished for stealing more than his share...

The room faded to black.

seventy-one

. . .

WHEN CURTIS OPENED HIS EYES, he was still laying
on the floor next to the humming ice machine. A puddle of
yellow vomit decorated the floor and the side of his cheek. He
silently thanked God that he'd landed with his head turned
sideways. Choking on your own vomit was the tragic death
of choice for rock stars—but was just silly to everyone else.

He propped himself up on one elbow. Shooting pains
knifed through his torso. This wouldn't be easy. He wiped the
vomit with his shirt sleeve and drew a deep breath. He
listened to a tiny wheezing somewhere in his bronchial tubes.

Next he dragged himself onto his knees and clung to the
still-humming ice machine for support. Winded, he nonetheless gathered himself and rose unsteadily to his feet.

He had triumphed. He was standing tall. He had his
dignity, but nothing else. The bag lay on the floor, upside
down. He could tell from its crumpled shape that it was
empty. Not only that, but nobody had witnessed the attack.
What could he do? Where could he turn?

In great pain, he picked up the bag, then the ice machine
key—he was warned to bring that back—and then placed one
foot in front of the other as he headed toward his only friend.

The walk to the front office took ten minutes. He gasped in pain. At last, Curtis staggered up to Ziggurat Head for the third time. She was painting her curled fingernails with the phone tucked under her ear: "You cain't listen to Allen an' them. Them fools ain't right. Nuh-uh, they don't know you. Girl, *no*—"

She stopped as soon as she saw Curtis. "I got to call you back." The receiver clattered on its hook.

"They got me," Curtis said.

Her eyes roved across his ripped shirt, his bruised face, his empty bag. "You see who it was?"

"Buncha kids. Four, I think."

She made an all-knowing *mm-hm* sound as though she'd expected this very incident. "Sit down there," she said. He lowered his body into a chair. He balanced his elbows uncomfortably upon the rusted aluminum arms. Something in his ribcage hurt incredibly.

Ziggurat Head dialed a phone number with the tip of her fingernail. The nail was two-toned, pink and white, and studded with tiny emeralds. "Alonso?" she said. "We got a problem. No, not later. Right *na-ow*."

The phone clattered in its nest. Then she picked it up again and dialed a different number. "So, what was we sayin'? Oh yeah, Gordon an' them. They ain't no good for you. I know his cousin Chenelle an' she said—"

Curtis peered around the desk. Ziggurat Head was filing her manicured nails, one leg casually folded under the other, the puckered surface of her thighs spilling everywhere like ricotta cheese. She swiched her sympathy on and off like a flashlight. Right now, not one ounce of concern could be wrung from this Gibraltar.

Here he was, a freshly battered guest, bleeding and moaning not ten feet away, and there was Ziggurat Head, chattering as if she were alone.

Soon Alonso entered the door. A stooped old Cuban

wearing a short-sleeved security guard uniform. His face was the color of a desiccated kidney bean.

"Security?" Curtis said. The old *cubañero* didn't nod. He wasn't even going to bother to go through the motions. He just fixed his cloudy eyeballs vacantly on Curtis' chin and let his shoulders slump.

"I was jumped," Curtis said.

"By who?" *Bi hoo.*

"A gang of boys."

Alonso shifted his weight from his right to his left foot. At last, a sign of consciousness.

"What color?" he asked. *Wha colur?*

"I don't know. They were thirteen, fourteen. It was in the room with the"—the room spun crazily and Curtis slumped against the armrest of a chair—"near the ice machine."

Alonso smacked his lips. Then his clipboard slapped once against his ass cheek. This was what passed for anxiety in his deadened limbs. "I know which boys this is," he finally announced. *Wheech boiys thees ees.* "They don't have no parents." *Dey doan haf no parents.*

Curtis absorbed this news. Judging from the security guard's indifference, the delinquents had probably bludgeoned plenty of other guests.

"Why are they here?" Curtis asked.

"The state leave them here," said Alonso. "They don't go to school or nothing."

Curtis cocked his ear. Could the state of Florida be *that* short of cash? Could it be so strapped for shelters that it would house juveniles in *welfare motels*?

"Please call the police," he said.

"We can't do nothing about them," Alonso said.

Suddenly Ziggurat Head piped up from behind the desk: "They paid through to December."

Curtis turned towards her. "You can't call the police because the boys are *paid through to December*?"

The security guard's eyes pled for mercy. In a flash, Curtis understood: The welfare hotel was on the Department of Social Service's gravy train. Alonso and Ziggurat Head had probably promised to supervise the little miscreants. They couldn't *afford* this kind of trouble.

He stood and smoothed his shirt: "Then I'll call them myself."

The security guard shrugged again. That's when Curtis knew his case was hopeless. Most likely, the little convicts had already rolled a bunch of motel residents. He could see how everything would play out. The cops would ask for confirmation of juveniles in residence; the office would deny everything. There would be eye contact, significant pauses, maybe a folded fifty … and his piddling complaint would wither away in a police file.

Curtis delicately sucked the inside of his cheek. It was all becoming too much. The firing … the eviction … the usurious loan … and now a robbery. He was feeling like a forgotten morsel of food being scorched beneath the stovetop burner of the world.

Another heavy pain ricocheted through the lower part of his left ribcage. He clutched the chairback until it subsided. When he came to, Ziggurat Head was checking out another scraggly guest. The security guard had disappeared.

Curtis Marshall would soldier on. He would *have* to. This was America at the dawn of the twenty-first century, and God helped those who helped themselves.

Folding his empty duffel bag, he staggered out the door, wincing at the pain.

He wouldn't look back.

seventy-two

· · ·

THE CRAVINGS WERE SUBDUED as they rode in Lawler's superstretch golf cart to the final sales building.

Grandpa Frederick hadn't uttered a single word since his horrific gaffe. He'd just stood by silently, like a drug store Indian, head bowed, as the family members frantically debated different theories for recovery of the mother. Should they strain the ashes with a superfine colander? Or should they let the water evaporate? That would take weeks, especially in the humid climate of central Florida. Nobody dared mention boiling the ashes dry, but if she'd already been cremated, did it really matter?

In the end, they'd decided to keep her in the squeeze bottle for the moment. But there was no denying that the accident had totally killed the sales high. Lawler was devastated about that. Usually he created emotional momentum on the tour, lifting the family's spirits higher and higher to the crest of a wave of euphoria that carries them all the way through to the final negotiation table.

But the incident of the mother's ashes had interrupted all that. Instead of reaching the pinnacle of unfulfilled desire, this group of travelers had sunken into a sullen gloom. There was no selling the Cravings. Not like this. Lawler smiled ruefully to himself. At the very least, he had a great war story to tell at the poker table. He decided to finish the tour as quickly as possible and hope to be assigned another family before the line closed.

In silence they arrived at the sales floor. Like the breakfast room, it consisted of a hundred or so tables. Unlike the breakfast room, there were no panoramic windows, no waterskiers slicing across the lake, no instant scrambled eggs, no music wafting overhead—in short, there was nothing to distract from the business of purchasing real estate.

It was all business.

Lawler chose a table and pulled out the chairs for the family. There was a reason for this courtesy: The chairs were bottom loaded with what felt like slabs of lead. You could barely move them. It was nearly impossible to get up from the negotiating table.

Even Lawler's attitude was changing. This was the hardest part for him. Up until this moment he was always the perfect tour guide, the raucous buddy you want to pound a beer with, the spit-shined charmer you'd love to see your daughter with. Now he was preparing to become the mercenary who demanded cold cash in return for the right to remain in this Edenic paradise.

"Can I get anybody anything to drink?" asked Lawler.

"Nope," said Grandpa Frederick, crossing his arms. "You can say or do anything you want, but we're walking out of here with our two tickets and *nothing else*."

Lawler wasn't intimidated by this blustering. He turned to Sharpy. "For you?"

"We don't have much time," said Sharpy.

"Just a quick coffee?"

Sharpy shrugged. "Okay."

Grandpa Frederick glared across the table. "We're not interested in *anything*."

The salesperson shouldered off towards the beverage cart along the sidewall. The Craving family found itself alone. Vivian touched Sharpy on the forearm lightly and lifted her sweet face to his.

"I think this place is wonderful," she purred.

"I agree."

"I especially love the hot tub."

"It *is* nice."

She became a little more insistent. "Brittany loves it here too. Can't you see her on that adorable little beach?"

"We're *not buying*, Vivian," said Grandpa Frederick, punching the table with the heel of his fist for emphasis. "No way."

"Can you say something else please?" she shot back. "I've heard you repeat yourself at least twenty times today."

"It's worth repeating. You both need to learn restraint."

Lawler returned with a tray bearing several Styrofoam cups of coffee and fruit punch. He took his seat and looked at Grandpa in the eyes. "Frederick, you said earlier that you liked this resort, that it was sensible and economical, and that you'd use a condo if you were to purchase today. Were you interested in the two-bedroom unit?"

"I never said any such thing," said Grandpa Frederick. "We'd like our tickets now."

A crestfallen look passed over Lawler's face. "Is there something I haven't explained?"

"It's just too expensive," said Grandpa Frederick. Lawler noticed the sweat beading on the old man's bare scalp. The fish was circling the hook.

"I haven't shown you the price yet, sir," he said.

"It doesn't matter."

"Would you buy a computer without looking at the price?"

"This is much more expensive."

"How do you know how much this costs?"

The old man was flustered. "Because I just do. Everybody does."

"Let me show you the prices. Okay?"

Without waiting for an answer, Lawler quickly pulled out a laminated sheet from his attaché case. The entire Craving family leaned forward and crowded around it as the salesperson pointed at the numbers with the tip of his fountain pen. "The price is $21,400. With the first-day discount, you get two thousand off. That's state law. So your price is actually $19,400. We require twenty-five percent down. Your financing is for ten years at 17 3/4 APR."

Lawler paused, watching the faces. Grandpa Frederick's lips had screwed themselves up into a tight knot. Suddenly an indignant sound burst out of him like air from a punctured tire. "Are you kidding? You must think we're a bunch of *rubes*! A percentage rate like that would chase anybody off!"

"What do you think?" said Lawler, turning to Sharpy.

"It does seem high," he said.

"But there's no problem with the price?"

"Not really."

Lawler's heart leapt through his chest. This Craving guy— the dad—he really *was* a rube! Here sat the only guest in the history of timeshare resorts who was actually prepared to pay the first price he'd been shown! Had Lawler resuscitated his sale? It would be worth at least two grand in his pocket. His salvation! Visions of tequila shots and lace brassieres danced through his head.

But the old man squashed his premature dreams. "My son," said Grandpa Frederick, "has as much business sense as a turnip." His eyes turned intense. "We're ready for your manager to lower the price."

Lawler's stomach sank to his feet. Of course the old man would put the kibosh on his son. This had been too good to be true.

"You could pay full down and avoid financing all together," he stammered, hoping to resurrect the sale on his own.

"Not at this price," said Grandpa. "Bring your manager over so we can get our tickets."

There was nothing Lawler could do. He'd been swept aside. He had to find a closing manager to salvage the deal.

"Absolutely. I'll be right back."

He pushed his chair back, left the table, and shuffled along the borders of the room. Sales managers came in more flavors than ice cream. There were old managers, young managers, white, black, Asian, Latin, male, female, aggressive, modest, charming, brutish, athletic, nerdish, just to name a few. He needed to select a closing manager who would complement the touring family … someone in whom the family would trust. And the most immediate indicator of trust was geography.

He knew exactly who to go to.

It had to be Andy Gushbottom.

seventy-three

. . .

A PORTLY MIDWESTERNER WHO used to be a contractor in the defense industry, Andy Gushbottom was a legendary closer. He was also a legendary actor. Everybody liked him, because he possessed the amazing ability to build trust and close the sale simultaneously. He knew the Cravings would take a shine to him.

Lawler found Gushbottom chatting on his cell in a corner.

"Andy," he said.

Upon hearing his name, the man cupped one hand over the mouthpiece and arched an eyebrow towards Lawler. He had a flattop crewcut that looked like a gopher-eaten lawn—thick and brown and disappearing in large clumps. A pair of reading glasses perched on the bridge of his nose.

"You got somethin'?" he said.

"Family of seven," Lawler said quickly. He had to be quick. Managers sniffed out sales the way record-company execs listened for melodies. "Money up the wazoo, but energy's low. Watch Gramps, he's the torpedo. A nosebleed might do it."

"Where they from?"

"Indiana."

"I'm from Chicago, that's close enough." Gushbottom uncupped his telephone. "Lemme call ya back, I got somethin' here."

Lawler lead Gushbottom back through the tables. He never ceased to marvel at the hundreds of families packed around the heavy marble-topped slabs, Styrofoam drinks in hand, lofting excuses into the air like sick little birds. *We don't have the time … My husband doesn't like to … We vacation differently every year …* All playing a polite game of thrust, parry, thrust, parry, with their salespeople.

Approaching the Cravings, Gushbottom suddenly seemed to transform. He hitched his waistband higher on his gut, flashed some charisma, and became everybody's oldest and best drinking buddy. He extended his hand to Sharpy. "Mr. Craving? Andy Gushbottom, great to meet you." Sharpy actually rose to his feet, the man exuded so much authority.

As they vigorously pumped hands, Gushbottom asked, "I looked at your sheet and noticed that you're an Indiana boy. That right?"

"Born and raised."

"I'm from Chicago myself. Used to go to Indianapolis for football clinics every summer."

"Really?" Sharpy said. "I went to a few of those. Down at the stadium."

Gushbottom ran the tip of his tongue around his dry lips. "I don't expect you'd remember me. Judging from your beautiful lady here"—he nodded to Vivian—"I've got at least a decade on you."

"You are a dear," Vivian said.

"Oh, my wife would be quick to correct you about that," he said. Everybody at the table chuckled, even Grandpa Frederick. Tapping his pencil, Gushbottom leaned forward and screwed up his face into a perfect mimicry of sympathy. "So I hear you don't like the price of our condos."

"That annual percentage rate is ridiculous," said Grandpa Frederick.

The manager looked Grandpa and Sharpy in the eyes. "If your family can wait two years to use your timeshare, we just received a trade-in this morning that we can sell for a discounted price. What do you think of this?" He wrote $9600 on a sales sheet, circled it, and turned it towards the family. "That's for everything. You'd own a piece of real estate in the world's most visited city."

Sharpy blanched. They'd cut the price *in half*. "That looks awfully nice," he said.

"Forget it, son," ordered Grandpa Frederick. "There'll be hidden fees."

"But it's still a great deal."

"You've got enough debt for two lifetimes. And you don't have that inheritance yet."

Sharpy waved his father away. "It's a lock."

"If it's a lock, then why don't you have the picture? Did you think Tim would ever rip out the film? Anything could happen." The old man shook his head. "Until the check is in hand, you're risking your future with every dollar of debt."

Sharpy looked at Gushbottom imploringly. "Can you hold this unit for a week?"

A saddened expression washed across Gushbottom's face. "I'm afraid not. This offer is good today only."

Sharpy exchanged a guilty glance with his father. Everything about him seemed to suddenly deflate. "I don't know."

But Gushbottom smelled green and wasn't going to be thrown off the scent. He leaned forward and thumped his elbows heavily on the table. "Mr. Craving, how much money do you make annually?"

"About seventy thousand," he said.

Gushbottom theatrically dropped his jaw. He tore the spectacles off his face and tossed them onto the table. "Seventy thousand dollars? Where the hell *is* all that dough?" he yelled. Everyone at the table suddenly tensed. "Do you mean to say that you just *piss away* seventy thousand dollars a year?"

"Of course not—"

"This is nine and a half thousand measly dollars! Chump change! You earn this in six weeks!"

Sharpy glanced quickly at Vivian. "We enjoyed your resort, but—"

"There ain't but nine butts at this table ... and one boob!" roared Gushbottom, jabbing a finger towards the hapless Sharpy. "Don't you care about your children's futures? Your lovely daughter? Your son? They can *inherit* this." He looked around the room conspiratorially, then lowered his voice. "I'm not supposed to say this, but *it's also a great investment.*"

Lawler knew that Gushbottom was treading on thin legal ice here. It's illegal to sell timeshare real estate as an investment without a securities license. Rumors about decoy families sent from the Securities Exchange Commission keep most reps toeing the line—except at desperate moments. Like this one.

"Don't listen to him, Sharpy," said Grandpa Frederick.

The manager whirled on the old man. "I didn't ask you *any*thing! Not *one goddamn thing*!" he roared. To everyone's surprise, Grandpa Frederick instantly clammed up. Lawler smiled inwardly. This family had mistaken Gusbottom for an average Joe. Nothing could be further from the truth! Hiding beneath the sales manager's straightforward John Deere exterior lay ... a *master thespian*. He was the Stella Adler of timeshare, the Brando of Orlando.

The only question was whether this nuclear sales tactic would work.

Sweating, Gushbottom turned his wrath back towards Sharpy. "How do you tolerate this guy? Huh? This exhausted carcass peering over your shoulder? If he were my father, I would've given him a few pieces of my mind." He sighed exaggeratedly. "How long are you going to allow your father to bully you, Stephen? When are you going to start making your *own* decisions?"

Sharpy's face flooded with color. This closing manager, who'd suddenly morphed into a titanic prick, was nonetheless ... absolutely *right*! Grandpa Frederick had to be resisted! Sharpy wasn't an adolescent—he was a full-grown man!

Digging into his khaki shorts, Sharpy produced his wallet. He threw a platinum Visa credit card onto the table.

"Charge it," he said.

seventy-four

. . .

LAWLER COULD BARELY CONTAIN his excitement. Gushbottom had saved the game at the bottom of the ninth! But the sale was far from over. Anything could happen, and Gushbottom must've known it too, because he stayed in character. "Charge *all* of it?"

"As much as you can."

The serious glint in Sharpy's eye said that he wasn't kidding. Gushbottom bowed theatrically. "I'll be right back with your contract."

As soon as the sales manager had left, a tense silence hovered over the table. Sharpy was wreathed in a cloud of self-satisfaction. Grandpa Frederick stared towards the distant windows. "I signed us up for this tour to save you money, son," he said.

Vivian was feeding Brittany a slice of chocolate cake. "Frederick, that manager was right. It's a great investment."

"You've made the right decision," Lawler said. His job, what was left of it at this point, was to keep them from kicking. "You just saved yourself over a hundred thousand dollars in future vacation costs."

Just then he saw Gushbottom returning from the credit

card station. The portly manager was nearly running between the tables, his prodigious belly twisting like a tribal chief's as he rounded each corner. This wasn't good.

Sharpy knew what was coming. Of *course* the card had been rejected. He couldn't charge a pair of tweezers on that account. But flinging around the platinum Visa sent an honest-to-God thrill down his spine. It just felt *good* to buck the old man. Grandpa Frederick and his hardscrabble, solemn-faced, train-jumping generation, the creaky old millionaires who still stole thirty-cent soaps from hotel rooms … they didn't understand how the world had changed. Nobody Sharpy knew was in desperate straits today. America just wasn't that poor anymore.

Was it?

A more pressing question loomed: Where *would* Sharpy get the money? He couldn't back out now. He needed to recover his dignity in the eyes of this sales manager.

"Mister Craving," Gushbottom said, wheezing, "your card has been denied. Do you have another you'd like to use?"

"No, I don't."

Gushbottom didn't miss a beat. "Would you like me to get you a loan application instead?"

"No, that won't be necessary," Sharpy said. "I'll pay in cash."

Gushbottom's nodded vigorously as though an invisible hand had grabbed the back of his neck and was shaking it. "That's even better. Tell me how we can work with you on that."

"You can let me make a phone call."

"Of course. We'll use an office upstairs."

Vivian snaked a braceleted arm into Sharpy's elbow, then kissed his cheek. "When he wants something, Stephen *makes it happen*."

———

Ten minutes later, Sharpy found himself in a private deeding office on the third floor of the sale pavilion. The walls were decorated with framed posters of idyllic tropical locales. He was sitting on the edge of a leather seat, a large telephone receiver tucked under his ear. The toes of his Reebok sneakers nervously tapped the tile.

On the other end of the line was his money manager, Sam Rothchild. They'd been working together for over a decade. Rothchild had not exactly welcomed the request for an emergency selling of shares but had agreed nonetheless to determine which stock could be sold most profitably. Sharpy could hear the *clickety-clack* of his fingertips on a keyboard.

"Twenty-eight and a quarter percent," the money manager said. "Not great, but okay."

"Can you wire it to me immediately?" asked Sharpy.

"That's not customary."

"But I need it now."

"It won't be any problem to dump, I assure you, but I … er, this company … we can't really assume the risk in the meantime."

"The meantime is what?" Sharpy said. "Three hours?"

Rothchild grumbled something.

Sharpy crouched over the phone and whispered urgently. "I'm about to inherit close to *a million dollars*. Most of that will be going into your hands. Do you really want to lose my account over a few hours' gap?"

There was a pause. Then Rothchild sighed. "Fine. Tell me where to transfer it."

"Western Union."

"Which one?"

Gushbottom helpfully offered an address on a business pad. Sharpy read it to his money manager.

"It'll be there by end of business," Rothchild said. "But Sharpy?"

"What?"

"We've known each other a long time—"

"Yes, we have."

"I have to ask. Do you really *need* to reach into your retirement account?"

"I wouldn't be doing it if I didn't need to."

Rothchild's voice sounded pained. "Do you have any idea how low your equity is, Stephen? This withdrawal is going to nearly close your account with us."

"Just wire the money, Sam."

Sharpy dropped the receiver into the cradle. Gushbottom was twirling a pair of worry balls.

"I'll have it by end of business," Sharpy said.

Gushbottom looked up at the ceiling. "My kindness is legendary, Mister Craving, but"—he searched for the most delicate possible phrasing—"we're going to need something to hold this unit until we receive full payment."

"Do you mean collateral?"

"That's right."

"But I'll have the money by five o'clock."

"You're going to leave this resort to get the money, correct?"

"Of course."

Gushbottom narrowed his eyes. "How do I know you'll come back? Why shouldn't I release this unit right now? We've got at least twenty other families downstairs who'll buy it immediately. Families with much better credit, I might add."

Sharpy briefly wondered why this guy was still playing tackle. Then he wondered how he could scrape together a deposit. He rifled through his wallet. "How much do you want? I have about sixty—"

Gushbottom smoothed his sleeves. "We need at least a couple grand."

Sharpy's eyes traveled around the ceiling. How could he

get *two thousand dollars*? He noticed the manager's eyes quickly flit towards Sharpy's left hand.

His wristwatch.

It was a Patek Phillipe. The pride of Switzerland, a fortieth birthday gift to himself. Sixteen thousand dollars of diamond, onyx, and brushed steel. It stood out in his staid Indiana neighborhood like Cinderella in a field of corn stalks.

Sharpy slowly released the clasp, slipped the wristwatch off his wrist, and laid it on the table. Gushbottom waited the perfect beat—this was, after all, a priceless *objet d'art*—before solemnly placing it in the drawer of his desk. He locked it carefully.

"Thank you for understanding," he said. "I'll see you in a few hours."

"Absolutely," said Sharpy.

Gushbottom tinkled the keys to the drawer. "Remember—we close at five o'clock."

———

Outside, in the parking lot, Sharpy hotfooted it towards the minivan, the rest of the Cravings following quickly.

"What's happening, son?" shouted Grandpa Frederick. He was pushing Grandma in the wheelchair.

"We're going to the Western Union in Ocala," he said.

"Why?"

"Because my money manager is wiring me some cash. We only have a few hours."

"Where is this money coming from?"

Impatience tramped across Sharpy's face. "It's none of your business, Dad."

But the old man was relentless. "You withdrew it from your retirement account, didn't you?"

"It's none of your *business*, Dad."

The old man *tsk-tsked*. "I hope there's still enough left for a tent and a sleeping bag someday. You're putting an awful lot on the line."

Sharpy whirled on his father. Grandpa Frederick saw the unmistakable rage in his son's clenched fists, the thick ropes bulging inside his neck. He quickly backed off. "Okay, son—it's your life."

"Goddamn right it is." Sharpy swiveled around, pivoted left, paused—then veered right. Then he stopped altogether.

"What's wrong?" said D.L.

"I forgot where we parked the car."

He stood marooned in the parking lot as a stiff, salty breeze began to blow.

seventy-five

. . .

THE DOOR HANDLE was supposed to be simple. Step one: pull it. Step two: door opens.

But not for someone like Curtis.

He sat trapped in the driver's seat of his Civic. His beloved but shitty car was a true detention chamber. Shreds of disintegrating foam drooped out of the fabric of the ceiling and tickled the top of his head like a patronizing uncle.

He was parked in the lot of Orlando General Hospital, a brutally modern complex with seven floors of anodized glass curtain-wall construction that reflected the dark palms outside and the gray, blustery sky overhead. Through the windshield he could see the automatic doors. He could see the red sign marked EMERGENCY. He could see the folded wheelchairs. He could see the admitting nurses helping patients into the lobby.

He could see *all* of this.

What he couldn't see was how in the blazes he was ever going to exert enough pressure with his left hand to pop open the door. Each time he tried, an excruciating pain seared across the left side of his chest like a chemical burn.

He made another attempt. For the forty-umpteenth time,

he reached across his body with his *right* hand. For the forti-eth-umpteenth time, he gritted his teeth as the pain over-whelmed his body. Finally he slumped back in his seat. He felt tears appearing in the corners of his eyes. He was willing to pay whatever the hospital wanted as long as they could make this pain go away.

The windshield rearview mirror had been knocked askew by his exertions. It was now tilted crazily so that it pointed down, into his backseat ... and there, upon the moldering gray cushions, sat his emergency umbrella. It was a broad one, the type favored by golfers and street vendors, with fat yellow-and-white stripes. He'd found it in an empty Utilidor one night long ago.

Now it gave him an idea: He would use the umbrella as a lever.

Curtis stretched out his right arm, felt for the edges of the umbrella, and dragged it unceremoniously into the front seat. Using his right hand, he carefully pried its tip into the door handle, then jiggered the contraption left and right.

The door swung open. A blast of wind blew his hair back-wards and caused a tornado of loose gas station receipts and fast-food wrappers to swirl around his head. There was a vertiginous feeling in the air, as though the weather was on the cusp of changing.

Like something was coming.

———

Curtis struggled up the front walk, wincing with each step. It was mid-afternoon, but the clouds blowing across the sun had cast a gray pall across the parking lot.

The admitting nurse was standing outside in his hospital blues, directing a couple of EMTs as they swiftly unfolded the legs of a gurney.

Curtis leaned against a brick pillar and waited. It didn't

take long for the nurse to notice him. "Can you walk?" the nurse said.

"I guess," Curtis said.

He jerked a thumb over his shoulder. "Admittance inside, man."

He'd expected a wheelchair at the very least. But instead he got a thumb and a gruff move-along-now command. There'd be no help from this quarter.

Breathing heavily, Curtis peeled himself off the wall and staggered onto the black ribbed automatic mat. The doors slid open.The people sitting nearest the door hunched over miserably as the humid, brackish wind swept across them.

Curtis stepped inside and blinked several times. He didn't have the slimmest idea of what to do next. In fact, this was his first visit to a hospital in almost twenty years. Even as a child, he'd always been the very picture of health. He'd never faced anything worse than an ear infection.

The waiting room was packed with narrow beige upholstered chairs with black plastic arms. The chairs were circled into ten small pods in which the patients all faced each other. Long stretches of berber carpet the color of a migraine headache lay everywhere, crossed by the high-traffic pathways, which were standard white tile.

A young nurse wearing her greens and a pair of white sneakers approached Curtis but made no eye contact. "Welcome to Orlando General. Fill out this form and return it to the desk." She thrust a clipboard into his hands.

"My left side hurts," he said.

"We'll look at you later."

"Can you look at me *first*?"

"After you fill out the form."

The nurse walked away. Curtis lowered himself onto a nearby chair and curled his aching torso around the document and began filling out its seven pages. *Name ... age ... allergies ... current medications... cause of sickness/injury ...* he wrote "fell from roof" … *insurance*. Blue Cross, no, Kaiser Permanente, no, Cobra, no, Medicare, no, Medicaid, no. He checked the box marked *uninsured*.

Then he hobbled over to join the line at the admittance station. There were only two nurses behind the desk. Curtis scanned the other patients in line. There were at least twenty-five people—young, old, mothers, fathers, sisters, brothers, a family of seven Latinos. In his pain, he felt vaguely annoyed. Why did Latin families always seem to go everywhere together as a unit? He'd once seen a family of nine Mexicans at the post office waiting to mail *one* envelope. Didn't they know how to do *any*thing by themselves?

Then he realized that he was succumbing to negativity. He closed his eyes and tried not to breathe too deeply.

———

An hour later, he was still aching. This time, however, he was at the ER front desk. His seat was warm from the butt heat of other patients.

The nurse, a matronly woman with a mass of gray curls and diamond-tipped eyes that could drill through sheetrock, was tapping his information into a keyboard.

"It says that you have a pain in your side," she said.

"My left side."

"You fell off a roof?"

"Yes."

She lifted an eyebrow. "Are you a roofer?"

"Yes."

"But it says here that you're unemployed."

"I'm paid under the table," he said.

"Are you here illegally?"

"No."

"On parole?"

"*No*."

"You don't have a permanent address."

"Not right now, but—"

"You don't have any insurance either."

He dropped his head. "No, I don't."

"Do you have a major credit card?"

"Yes."

"Don't worry," she said. "There's a place for you here." She smiled at him like a stern mother taking control of a wayward child; then she faced her computer monitor even more intently. A moment later she ripped a page from the printer, clipped it to his chart, and pointed towards the waiting room. "Have a seat and a doctor will see you shortly."

seventy-six

. . .

FOUR HOURS LATER, Curtis was still wondering what "shortly" meant. He was reclining in a chair, his lightweight windbreaker wadded into a tight roll between his left ribcage and the chair's arm. His cross-trainers were planted wide and his long legs were splayed apart. His head lolled sideways, propped up by his right hand. He was drifting in and out of sleep.

If he were still employed, this day would've cost him almost forty-two dollars so far: a small fortune. But that wasn't a problem anymore.

Why had he agreed to the hospital visit? Because Lucinda had insisted upon it. Simple as that. She'd clucked like a mother hen as soon as she'd spotted him limping down the hallway, past the strewn bottles and condom wrappers, in that rat's-nest No-Hopeland extended-stay motel. She'd daubed his cuts and abrasions with some homebrewed tincture that had felt like drips of battery acid. She'd hugged him and told him that she needed her man to be *healthy*, uninsured or not. Neither of them had the tiniest speck of a clue what this hospital visit would cost. To Curtis, it didn't particularly matter. He was in such dire straits that something terrible was happening to his mentality. He was starting to *embrace* his debt. In a perverse way, he looked *forward* to this hospital visit. He drooled over the idea of decimating his credit. One more bough to throw onto the bonfire of his future.

A blast of pain coursed through Curtis' body. In the uncomfortable chair, he struggled to an upright position, his face twisted into a grimace. The Tylenol was wearing off and he found himself getting grouchy. There was no way to get any decent sleep in this waiting room. Curtis was surrounded by misery. To his right, a gasping sunburned man with a face the color of a maraschino cherry breathed with one hand resting heavily on his wheeled oxygen tank. To his left, there was an even more marginal character wearing what seemed to be a green jerkin with knee breeches tucked into soft leather Robin Hood boots. His coarse reddish hair was marcelled down the back in High Trailer Park style.

How could you expect to be taken seriously wearing *knee breeches*?

Hack hack hack hack … The sound of a raspy cough drew his attention across the chairs. A chunky little girl clutching a pink vinyl purse sat cross-legged between her mother's thighs. There was a deep fissure running across her head like the crevice on a rotten cantaloupe. It looked as though she'd suffered a small explosion inside her skull. Periodically her head tilted back, her mouth caved open, and that awful noise rose up from her solar plexus like the bleats of a wounded walrus. *Hack hack hack hack hack hack* … Curtis could almost see the swollen pink uvula jerking around at the back of her throat.

Meanwhile, her mother's glassy eyes were fixed on the overhead television … *hack hack hack hack hack* … The daughter was leaning forward and barking into the air as though trying to dislodge a ribeye bone from her throat…. *hack hack hack hack hack* …

The mother noticed Curtis. "You keep starin' like that, it gone cost you," she said.

"Your daughter sounds pretty sick."

"She ain't sick. She just clearin' her throat."

"The doctors might think different."

She made a sound like *pffft*. "Doctor tell you a tummyache goin' be lung cancer if he could make a nickel from it."

The more Curtis looked at the daughter *hack hack hack hacking*, the more it occurred to him that she didn't have an emergency.

"Can I ask you a question?" he said to the mother.

"Yeah."

"Why did you bring your daughter here?" he said. "Why not go to a clinic?"

The woman looked at him as if he was the poorest, most ignorant son-of-a-bitch on the entire planet.

"Cause we already *been* to all the clinics. We can't go back to none of 'em till I pay up. This here hospital the only one in the goddamned state that ain't seen my daughter yet *and* don't need goddamned insurance neither."

Curtis felt his face flushing. "That's not fair."

"My daughter *ain't* sick," the woman said again, as if willpower and sheer repetition would make it true. "You hear me? *She ain't sick.*"

"You're her mother," he said. "You know best."

"Damn right I do. She ain't sick."

Curtis was saved by a nurse's voice on the intercom announcing *Marshall*. As he limped towards his examining room, the thought fell upon him, like a spadeful of dirt upon a coffin, that he was plummeting towards that same existence.

seventy-seven

· · ·

A PLUME of warm breath clouded a pane of glass.

Sharpy had pressed his face against the glass doors of the Florida Jewels Resort sales building. Through the beveled aperture he could see the empty selling room, its marble tables wiped clean, its heavy chairs arranged neatly for the next day's crowd.

He looked at his wrist, then remembered that he had given his wristwatch to Gushbottom. Through the glass, a clock on the wall read 5:35.

Not a single salesperson remained inside. Sharpy pounded on the door with the heel of his fist and waited. No response.

The lights were suddenly turned off.

Gushbottom had said five o'clock. Who could've known that he'd really meant it? Sharpy assumed there would be some leeway, some wiggle room, a little play in the wheel. Nope. This had been as firm as a court date—and he had missed it.

Sharpy punched his fist into his open palm. He hadn't been dawdling! He'd been rushing like a maniac! The problem was, it had taken over an hour to find the Western

Union because the only one in central Florida that had the reserves to dispense ten thousand biscuits on a moment's notice lay on the opposite side of the metropolitan area, out in the boonies, over an hour's drive away. Once he'd found the strip mall with the black-and-yellow storefront and filled out the forms, he'd plopped onto a bench with his family and watched small lizards crawl up and down the stucco until, a thousand miles away, Rothchild had finally transferred the money, and the clerk had signed over the neat little wad of green hundred-dollar bills banded with the Western Union logo.

By that time, everybody had become unbelievably cranky from the heat and the hunger, and lunch was badly needed—but Vivian had nixed all fast-food restaurants, even fast-casual franchises, and demanded a real sit-down place, with laminated menus that you hold in your *hands*, "something *refined* for Chrissake," she'd said, and not any of those chain sitdowns either, where the food is precooked at a regional processing plant four hundred miles away and microwaved onsite. And so they'd blazed the sun-dappled boulevards, between the high walls of the wealthy gated communities, going sometimes over a mile to find the next turnaround, until Vivian'd finally relented and allowed an Ethiopian restaurant. By the time they'd finished the chewy bread and turned back towards the resort, afternoon rush hour had begun, and they'd marinated in a three-mile-long broth of gasoline fumes provoked by an open sewer line, a single truck, and a row of plastic orange pylons.

Now it was five thirty-five. He'd lost Gushbottom's offer. The unfairness of the situation chafed at his psyche. He'd *tried* to be punctual. He *wanted* that timeshare unit. He had ten thousand dollars sizzling in his pocket to prove it.

He pulled on the door handle again. Still locked.

Would they really turn down ten thousand dollars if he came back tomorrow? Should he buy anything at all?

He looked at his reflection in the glass door. Stephen Craving was a middle-aged man with an empty savings account, a worthless stock portfolio, almost incomprehensible credit card debt, and an inch-deep retirement plan. And yet here he was, traipsing around central Florida trying to scrape together the dough for a hundred future vacations. Why?

Because he'd been led to believe that it was his right.

He gripped his head between his palms and squeezed. What had he been thinking? How had he allowed himself to get so sidetracked? To dredge the only puddle of liquid left in his possession?

There was almost a *million dollars* waiting for him. All he needed to do was to return to the Magic Kingdom, snap another picture, and keep the camera away from his clueless son. Why had he been putting it off? Laziness was one reason. Truth be told, fear was another. A million dollars was a double-edged sword. It could cost him friends. It could make him enemies. It could disrupt his life in hundreds of unforeseen ways.

Sharpy felt his interest in the resort draining from his body. Buying a timeshare property suddenly seemed about as important as brushing the hair on a crash-test dummy.

His next move was simple: He would redeposit the money into his retirement fund when he got back to Indiana.

It was the responsible thing to do.

He turned and shambled down the manicured path back towards the empty parking lot, where he'd parked the minivan diagonally across two spaces. His family was flung around the trim vehicle in a beautiful tableau—his son, daughter, parents, mistress. Their skin looked healthy and warm in the amber light. An Old Master couldn't have painted the scene any better.

Sharpy looked into his children's faces and felt warm fingers of love caress his heart. He saw their aching needs, the desires for better clothing, better cars, better *lives*... He was *failing* them, goddamnit. They were telling him to refocus his priorities, clinch the deal, swipe the million dollars.

"Is it closed?" D.L. said.

"Yep."

"Are we coming back tomorrow?"

"Nope."

Grandpa Frederick uncrossed his arms. "Good decision, son. That Gushbottom fellow talked a blue streak, but his type never comes through."

Sharpy felt a wave of good cheer course through his body. "I know that I haven't been as warm or as affectionate as I should be," he said. "That's going to change right now. Tonight, we're going to spend the evening together, doing something fun—as a family."

"Can we go to a movie?" said Brittany.

"You can see a movie at home, sweet pea," said Sharpy. "We're on vacation."

"Why can't she see a movie on vacation if she wants to?" said Vivian.

Sharpy threaded the conversational needle. "Because we're going to do something way better than a movie."

"What's that?" said D.L. skeptically.

"You'll see."

"You don't even know," she said.

Sharpy maintained the smile. "Yes, I do. And tomorrow we're going to go back to the Magic Kingdom to take that picture again."

"I don't feel good," said Grandma Maya.

"Mom, we'll get you to bed," he said. "That's our number one priority. Your health."

"You'll feel just fine after a good night's rest," said Grandpa Frederick. He put a reassuring hand on her forehead.

On the faraway hills, against the purple-gray sky, the grass bent sideways as the wind began to rise.

seventy-eight

. . .

THE MYSTERIOUS EVENING activity turned out to be shuffleboard. In most places, this was a game reserved for the mustiest of retirees. The official recreation of God's waiting room.

The Cravings, however, had a longstanding love for the game, at any age, and the tournament on the pool's terrace became heated and intense. Every member of the family played—even Grandma Maya, who couldn't bear to stay in her bed, not with irresistible visions of disks skittering across cement.

Sharpy was knocked out early. That was just as well. He was more interested in draining several highball glasses instead. At the poolside bar, he motioned to the bartender for another tequila sunrise. It was the fourth of those heavenly citrus concoctions, and now he was wobbling in a warm brown drunkenness that felt like floating in a bowl of warm maple syrup. He slouched contentedly on a stool and gazed at his family. His daughter, laughing with her grandfather. His fiancée, brushing her toddler's wet hair. His mother, twenty years restored to her bones.

Everything was just as his dearly departed wife had wished. *He'd made the family whole again.*

Boozily, he leaned against the side of the bar—and felt a strange lump against his thigh.

The ten thousand dollars.

He'd forgotten that it was still there. He needed to store it. But where? The safety deposit box at the front desk was not an option. Those things were Christmas gift boxes for corrupt hotel staffers everywhere. Who in their right mind would entrust their antique heirloom earrings to someone making seven-fifty an hour?

In the hotel room, however, there was a safe—with an electronic lock. Granted, housekeepers weren't any more trustworthy than front desk staff, but he'd hang the Do Not Disturb sign on the door.

Suddenly it became important to store the money now, at this moment, before he got any more wasted. Sharpy signaled the bartender to hold the drink, then lurched towards the elevators and went up to his room.

Inside, Sharpy discovered Tim sprawled on the queen-sized bed. When had he come up here? The boy was arranging crayons—

(*one red two two blue three three three green*)

—into an arcane pattern on the comforter.

"Why doncha come outside, Snooker?" he said. "It's the final game of the Craving Cup. Your sister said she wants you."

"Coloring," said Tim.

"Don't you need paper for that?"

In response, Tim thumped his legs on the bedspread. Through his tequila haze—or maybe because of it—Sharpy suddenly felt very close to his son. Could Tim have thumped his leg for the same reason a dog thumps its tail? To show happiness that his father was present? Did Tim want a man-to-man talk? Quality time?

In his inebriation, Sharpy decided that this *must* have been *exactly* what Tim had communicated. Male bonding at last! Drunken tears brimmed in the corners of the father's eyes. He tenderly lowered himself onto the edge of the queen-sized bed and placed his unsteady hand on Tim's shoulder. It felt cold. Tim always felt cold.

"How you doin', Snooker?"

The boy said nothing.

"Yeah, kiddo, me too." He gazed at the crayons. "I been thi'kin' 'bout what you 'n' I are gonna do with all 'is new moolah af'er we get home. Whadda you think we shoul' do?"

Silence.

"Sky's the limit, kiddo. New bike? Notepad computer?"

More crayon-arranging.

"Thi'k it over and' lemme know. But, hey, Snook'r?" He craned his head so he could peer at the boy's face. "These gifts? Our li'l secret. Don't tell your sist'r, 'kay?"

The boy hummed to himself.

Sharpy sensed that he had finally pierced Tim's indifference. All that bizarre behavior, the stimming, the rituals, the obsessions—he instantly felt that those were all just an act. His *real* son lay imprisoned somewhere inside. Yes, he had finally enjoyed a deep, soulful communion with the *true* Timothy Craving.

Hadn't he?

Sharpy stood up from the bed, lost his balance, and toppled clumsily to the floor. He barely felt the crash, or the carpet fibers pressed into his cheek. He now had the crazed determination of a drunk. He crawled across the carpet towards the armoire and opened the bottom cabinet. Inside lay the safe. It looked exactly like a microwave oven. Two metal prongs extruded from the open door.

Sharpy fished the envelope with the ten thousand dollars out of his pocket. He carefully laid the envelope inside the safe. His tongue touched the corner of his mouth, like a five-year-old in art class, as he squared the envelope just so, and tapped it lovingly.

Next, he tried to shut the door but the prongs were still extruded. So he turned to the digital keyboard. It required a four-digit code. He chose the number of his home street address because it was easy to remember: 7131. He entered the code, entered it again for verification—and finally the prongs retracted. He closed the door and entered the code a third time. Inside the door, he could hear the prongs extrude. An electronic beep told him that the safe was now secure.

He eyed the device. Was that all? He decided to double-check the number. Just for an extra precaution.

In the mounted mirror, Tim's eyes—

(*7131*)

—watched his father's fingers punch the keypad. The safe sprang open. Sharpy nodded with satisfaction. Then he closed the door again and Tim's peripheral vision—

(*7131*)

—noted the number again.

Sharpy pulled himself to his feet and immediately fell headlong into the dresser. The handles shook against the drawers. He picked himself up. "If you wan'a play shuffle-board, we're down by the pool."

Tim made no sound—

(*7131 7131 7131 7131*)

—except for the thumping of his leg. Sharpy stifled a burp and watched his son with the crayons. It didn't really matter if Tim played shuffleboard or not. The kid was happy. More importantly, *he* was happy.

Sharpy tousled his son's hair and turned towards the door. There was another tequila sunrise that needed his attention.

seventy-nine

. . .

A MATRONLY FEMALE nurse led Curtis into the examining room. It was small, sterile, and functional. A sheet of sanitary paper had been stretched over the vinyl examining table.

"Go ahead and remove your shirt, please," she said.

"Actually, I can't."

"Oh. Does it hurt?"

He nodded.

"I see. Lift your arms."

He didn't complain. She was a plump woman whose figure boasted a small waist and flared hips. He'd always liked birthing hips. That was how Lucinda was shaped, and images of his girlfriend went skipping through his mind— Lucinda laughing, Lucinda on her knees at the toilet in the morning, Lucinda's abdomen rounded and swollen with *his* child.

As the nurse folded his shirt, he hoisted himself onto the edge of the table and gritted his teeth. His ribcage exploded in pain.

The nurse handed him a gown. "Put this on. The doctor will be in shortly."

"I'll be here."

Curtis watched the door click shut. With great pain he lifted his shirt off his chest—why hadn't the nurse helped him?—and affixed the gown around his shoulders.

Then he waited.

He looked at the jars of sterile pads and tongue presses and the disinfectant by the sink. He listened to the tiny insectile humming of the overhead florescent light. What would the doctor say? Would he prescribe all kinds of expensive antibiotics? Surgeries? How could he—the unemployed, homeless, and injured Curtis Marshall—afford any of it? He fought the urge to grab his t-shirt and walk out the door. Such an act would be a blow to his body, but it would save his pride.

Then the door swung open, and it was too late. The doctor briskly entered the room, studying the charts on her clipboard. She was a middle-aged white woman with auburn hair pulled back into a business-like knot. Her flawless skin framed a pair of intense gray eyes behind her oval-shaped spectacles. A stethoscope hung around her neck and her white lab coat had been starched and ironed. She was pure American professionalism.

"Mr. Marshall?"

"That's me."

She hadn't looked at him yet. "It says here you fell off a roof and injured your side."

"Yeah."

"Let's see what happened." There were still no introductions. This doctor wasted not a second of precious time. She placed her stethoscope onto his chest. "Breathe in for me."

Curtis inhaled—and felt his chest crackle. His face squinched up; the small crow's feet at the sides of his eyes deepened.

She nodded in the reassuring way doctors do, as if to say, *Good, that's exactly the type of pain I expect from you.*

"Does that hurt?" she said.

"A little."

She circled behind him. "I'm going to touch you again. If this hurts, tell me."

When her fingertips met the skin on his left side of his chest, Curtis stifled a cry. Then he felt a small but distinct pressure which grew stronger and stronger. She was pressing down on the inside edge of his ribcage, under his pectoral muscle. The pain was intolerable.

Finally, he cried out; gasping for breath, he twisted away. The doctor circled around to his front again. She began making notes on the chart. She still hadn't looked at him directly.

"Are you ready for the bad news?"

"Okay."

"You probably have some broken ribs. Probably two false and one floating. I can't say until we do further testing."

The room was blinkering on and off. Curtis felt hot white dizzy flashes behind his eyes. "So what do we do now?"

"We take some x-rays to find out exactly which ones and how bad, and then…" She trailed off as she finally noticed her patient. He had buried his face in his hands. He was shaking it back and forth ever-so-slightly. Everything about him radiated a sense of noble failure.

She softened. "Ribs heal pretty easily, you know."

Curtis didn't look up. "I don't care."

"Excuse me?"

"I don't have health insurance."

The doctor looked at him neutrally.

"I don't have a job either, or a house. I'm living in an extended-stay welfare motel. My girlfriend is pregnant beyond belief. I took out a car title loan but the money got stolen by a bunch of juvies. They're the ones who did this, actually. So please don't tell me how lucky I am that ribs heal easily. I still had to come here today and no matter how small the procedure, your hospital is still going to screw me on the cost."

The doctor started to answer, but Curtis wasn't finished.

"Oh, I know all about it," he said. "You'll charge me three times as much as an insured patient for the same procedure. Why? Because insurance companies buy your medical services in bulk, and you give them deep discounts. Me, I get the full price. Yeah, I know all about how this country works. Now, why don't you shuffle me over to the x-ray lab and let's get this rape over with. "

He slid off the table and stood there defiantly, grimacing but nonetheless challenging the system.

The doctor bowed her head. This poor patient—what was his name?—she'd already forgotten, she saw so many ... Curtis, that was it ... this Curtis, he was truly heart-breaking. He knew the score, though. And he was asking all the right questions.

The doctor went to the counter and laid down her clip-board. Then she turned to Curtis.

"It's not three. It's seven."

"What?"

"We sometimes charge *seven* times as much for not having insurance. Depending on the procedure."

Curtis started to answer, but her hand stopped him:

"Here's the truth: There's nothing anybody can do for your broken ribs. I could put on a compression wrap, but extra-strength Tylenol works just as well. I could take x-rays, but all that will do is tell me exactly which ribs I *can't* treat. Your injury will heal itself. Get a full night's sleep for the next six weeks, no physical labor, and you'll be as good as new."

"You're very honest," said Curtis.

"So are you."

They stood there, doctor and patient, facing each other.

"Now what?"

"Now it's time for you to leave." She pointed at the door.

He narrowed his eyes. "I don't understand."

"I'm saying *you were never here*," the doctor said. "You skipped out before I got into the room. A case of nerves. I never saw you." She pressed her hand sideways to her mouth, as though hiding her words from the hospital administrators. "*It's free. Pro bono.*"

Curtis blinked in wonder. Could it be true? This licensed professional was holding open the door. She was letting him off the financial hook. Curtis almost dropped to his knees. This blessed woman ought to be canonized.

He wiped the saltiness from the corners of his eyes. "Do you know how much this means to me?"

She shrugged. "About two thousand dollars."

That set Curtis rocking back on his heels. "You don't even know me. This makes no sense."

"I see twenty patients a day," the doctor explained. "Most hard-luck cases deserve their hard luck, if you know what I mean." She shifted her weight and looked uncomfortable. "I can't say why. Maybe it's your noble face. But I just can't let one more decent person fall through the cracks."

He stuck his hand out. She shook it professionally, and he winced in pain.

"Is there anything I can do for you in return?" Curtis said.

"We've got a really good ob-gyn unit when your girlfriend comes due."

He looked up impishly. "You got any more free coupons over there?"

"No," she said, "but I could put in a good word."

"I'll think about it."

He hopped off the examining table. The doctor leaned against the wall with her clipboard pressed against her body.

"Good luck," she said. She turned to the sink and rearranged the jar of tongue depressors.

When she turned back, Curtis Marshall was gone.

eighty

. . .

THE CRAVINGS FILED into the famous theme park for the last time.

At the rear of the line came Grandpa Frederick, wheeling Grandma Maya through the extra-wide handicapped gate. She looked about ten minutes from being on the wrong side of a pallbearer's procession. Her skin hung like ghostly drapery from her arms. The whites of her eyes had turned the yellow of smoker's spittle. Her chapped lips were working themselves in little fishlike gasps and her chest barely moved.

But Sharpy hadn't noticed his mother. His eyes were fixed on some distant point far ahead, his back ramrod straight, and he walked with a strange, measured fixity of movement. The family was under his command. Rolling smoothly. He unzipped his knapsack to double-check his equipment. Inside lay his 35 mm Nikon, *another* 35 mm he'd picked up at a Wal-Mart, *and* a six-dollar disposable. Three cameras: no more risk. Not to mention seven different rolls of film and two packages of spare batteries. And this time, Tim wasn't going to be allowed within drooling distance of any of it.

"Who's ready for another fabulous day at the park?" he

said. "Kids, are you ready? Brittany?" He put his hand on her moppet head.

The little girl pouted and stamped her foot.

"What's the matter, sweetie?"

"I want one of *those*," she said, pointing towards a rack of spiral-shaped rainbow lollipops in a shop window.

"Of course," said Sharpy. He tucked a ten-dollar bill into her jumper. "Buy as many as you want."

Vivian cleared her throat significantly.

"I didn't forget," he said, handing her mother a crisp fifty. The night before, Vivian had declared that she didn't want to return to the Magic Kingdom. This fifty represented the deal that they'd struck. He was used to this type of arrangement.

Sharpy turned toward his daughter. "What about you, D.L.? What do you want to buy today?"

His daughter shrugged. What she *really* wanted was Arcade Boy. She'd lain awake the last two nights, dreaming about moonlit trysts in the pool, on the mezzanine, in the laundry room. The sound of his voice echoed everywhere. It haunted her, lured her, serenaded her, wrapped itself around her head like a fog. And she hadn't even found out his name. She imagined it was something exotic yet masculine. Like Stellan. Or Goddard.

But to her father, all she said was: "I don't want anything."

"Nothing at all?"

D.L. shook her head.

He rolled his eyes. Teenage girls were the bane of parents everywhere. Gloomy at theme parks and giggly at funerals.

"Most girls would kill for an opportunity like this," he said.

"Well, I'm not most girls."

"You certainly aren't."

She struck a sassy posture. "What's that supposed to mean?"

"Some girls who lose their mothers at your age draw closer to their fathers."

"Really?" she said sarcastically. The topic was too close, too painful to talk about in a straightforward way.

"Yep."

"Then maybe you haven't been the best father," she said.

"Maybe not," he said. "And maybe you haven't been the best daughter."

Part of Sharpy understood that he was treading dangerous emotional waters here. But that warm sensation of invincibility—he was about to earn *a million dollars*—made his every utterance feel right and true.

"Forget it," she said. She turned her adolescent back on him. Her black t-shirt was stretched across her twin shoulder blades, and her waist flared out nicely into a wide pair of hips. His daughter, the best and brightest of his family, already bore the look of a woman.

He swiveled towards Grandma Maya instead and assumed his brave face. This was a necessary defense—considering the death mask that lay stretched upon her bony skull. "You look fantastic, Mom!"

"I don't want to be here," the old woman said. Her fingers squeezed the edges of her raggedy purse tightly. "I feel slower than a turtle's ass."

"We've got to snap one little itty-bitty picture," said Sharpy, "and then we'll get you parked under some shade."

"Maybe you'd feel better with a tall soda pop," said Grandpa Frederick.

Outrage swelled in her eyes as she swiveled from her husband to her son. Her ethereal voice suddenly grew harsher. "I don't want shade and I don't want a soda pop! I want to go someplace where people *care* about me!"

"Now, Maya," Grandpa said. "I care for you."

"You're a liar."

"I've cared for you my whole life. That's a fact."

The old woman dismissed him with a wave of her hand. "You just wanted a pair of strong arms to cook your breakfast and scrub your underwear."

"Mom—"

Sharpy tried to hush his mother, but Grandma raged on, her glassy, limpid eyes bulging. "This family is full of phonies! I want to be with one person who isn't using me to get what they want!"

"Nobody's using you," said Sharpy.

"*You're* using me."

"No, Mom. We *love* you."

"If you loved me you'd take me home!"

Sharpy couldn't think of anything to say to that. He tried to touch her, but his mother twisted away. He looked to Grandpa Frederick. A pained expression appeared on the old man's face but he said nothing.

Then a chill passed through the crowds as a gray, billowing storm cloud blotted out the sun. The spires of the make-believe castle cast an eerie pall upon the people below.

"Time to get down to business, son," said Grandpa Frederick, looking anxiously at the sky.

"You bet," said Sharpy. "Let's take that picture."

"Dad," said D.L.

Sharpy ignored her. "So we get lined up right over by that bench."

She raised her voice. "Dad, something's wrong with Grandma."

He followed his daughter's gaze. The old woman had lurched over the side of her wheelchair.

Grandma Maya was unconscious.

eighty-one

. . .

QUICK AS A CHEETAH, Grandpa Frederick darted over and examined his wife. The old woman's dangling arm knocked feebly against the spokes of the wheelchair. Her eyes had rolled backwards in their sockets. Her breath was coming in short, fast, hyperventilations.

"Maya, can you hear me?" he said. "Maya?"

"Of course she can't hear you!" said Vivian. Her voice had grown unnaturally loud and a trio of unseemly creases forked across her forehead. "Look at her face!"

Grandma's tongue was lolling out of its mouth. Sharpy felt sickened watching it. Grandpa put his hand to her wrist and listened carefully. "I can't find her pulse," he said. "I can't feel her pulse. What do we do?" He looked around at his family. "*What do we do?*"

The family looked to Sharpy. Why should he have the answers? Every muscle in his body resisted movement. Just lifting his arm to wipe his forehead felt like pushing through a vat of syrup. True, he was sworn by blood to take care of Grandma. But this was *a million dollars*. He would never get this chance again. He *needed* that money ... had promised to buy nice things for his children ... for his fiancée ... for himself ...

"We have to take the picture," he said. "Everybody line up by the bench. Come on. Hurry up." His hands propelled his children towards the site. Grandpa wiped his palms on his pants. "I agree. Let's do this quickly, and then we'll get help for Maya."

D.L. gaped. They were going to take the picture with Grandma Maya *lolling* there! In the throes of death! Both her father and grandfather—total mercenaries!

Then she remembered the little bottle at the bottom in her backpack, the one that the director of the assisted-living home had given her. She whipped her blue Jansport off her shoulders. Dropping it at her feet, she quickly fished out the bottle of tablets, the word *Nitroglycerin* on the label.

"Wait!" she said. "I have something for her!"

D.L. twisted off the childproof cap and dumped a couple of the golden capsules into her palm. She darted to her grandmother's side and delicately placed them under the old woman's tongue. Then she closed her jaw and held it shut.

"D.L.!" said Grandpa. "This isn't the time for vitamins! Go line up for the picture."

"But this is nitroglycerin!"

"I don't care!"

"Your medication nurse gave them to me!"

The old man made a *pffft* sound. "That woman sorts pills by color. A pigeon could do her job."

"Wait—"

But Grandpa was having no more of it. Suddenly he gripped his granddaughter's arm with long, bony fingers and tried to pull her from the old woman. She twisted away. He reached for her again—

But the dust-up stopped right there. Grandma Maya suddenly made a sound like *huff-huff-huff*. They realized that she was catching her breath.

"See?" said D.L.

"I'll be damned," said Grandpa.

The old lady slowly straightened up in her chair, blinking as though she'd just woken up. Her pupils had expanded slightly. She reached into her mouth with trembling fingers and removed the now-shrunken tablets and peered at them, totally unaware of how these things, these alien pebbles, got stuffed into her mouth.

"Don't take them out," said D.L.

The old woman promptly dropped them on the ground. D.L. placed two new tablets into her wrinkled hand and guided them back into her mouth. "How do you feel?" she said.

"My ... chest hurts."

"It's time to get that picture," said Grandpa.

D.L. whirled with the impatience of a cougar. "Can we *forget* the picture? Grandma's having a heart attack!" She turned to her father. "Tell him, Dad?"

But Sharpy couldn't answer his daughter. There was a ringing in his ears and a dizzy, balloon-like sensation behind his forehead. The voices sounded tiny, as though they were shouted from a faroff mountain:

"Dad!"

"Hel-*lo*?"

"Sharpy! *Do* something!"

How odd. Why would anyone be yelling at him? The world was at peace. His vision blurred. An eagle's scream sounded across an empty canyon somewhere. He lifted his face to the cool, blue infinite sky.

D.L. watched her father slip into what looked to be a peyote trance. He was totally useless.

"Forget about him," said Grandpa. "He's always been like that in an emergency."

But then the professional Disney EMT squad arrived in their blue shirts, most likely alerted by bystanders. Wordlessly, the three men kneeled beside the ailing grandmother. One listened to her heart and checked her blood pressure, a second examined her eyes, and a third barked into his radio. In one fluid motion, the first gripped Grandma's wheelchair handles and began to push her in a stooped little shuffling run, like a Shanghai rickshaw driver, towards some unseen door.

Grandpa Frederick marched briskly behind them. An attendant strode with him, explaining park regulations, medical waivers, how things would proceed. D.L. followed, dragging Tim.

Grandpa noticed his granddaughter. "Where are you going?"

"I want to help," said D.L.

"No, that won't be necessary," said Grandpa.

"But I saved her!"

"You have to take care of your brother." Then he added: "And your father too."

The group of attendants accelerated and disappeared around a corner.

D.L. stopped in her tracks. First Grandpa Frederick had tried to keep her from using the nitroglycerin. Now, he had slammed another door into her face. Had she made a mistake by showing sympathy? Had she committed the cardinal sin of caring *too much*? D.L. felt a massive lump of resentment growing inside her belly. She had tried to care for her mother, without success. Now she had tried to care for her grandmother—and the proverbial door had been slammed in her face.

Her eyes grew a little darker. If this was the thanks that caregiving would earn her, then maybe she wouldn't care for anybody at all.

eighty-two

. . .

MEANWHILE, Sharpy felt himself descending from the delightful mental happy place. Then there was a tremendous jolt as his feet bumped into the cold hard earth.

His mother was gone.

"Wait," he cried to the attendants, "we still need to take the picture!"

He may as well have tried to catch the wind. The group pushing the wheelchair scampered on, Grandma Maya's white curls bouncing with every bump.

"That's my mother!" he shouted. "We still have to take a picture with my mother!"

It was too late. They disappeared behind the facade of a gingerbread Victorian house. Sharpy saw his words turn sickly gray on the air and die.

He had failed.

His mother, his suffering mother, had been crushed by some kind of heart attack, angina probably, and now she'd been spirited away into the bowels of this airy-fairy kingdom. And he'd stood there like an imbecile while it was happening. How could he have been so useless?

He stood in Main Street gazing around. All he could see

were details. The little cartoonish shutters painted bright orange. The white lace curtains pulled tightly over the storybook windows. That smell of piped-in cinnamon wafting up his nostrils. And everywhere the fellow porky pilgrims—gutbusters with fanny packs, blobbed thighs, and fluorescent green arms on their plastic sunglasses.

They all looked so damn *bovine*. His mood was worsening by the second.

Then he heard the click of a camera. It came from a sunburned father with two wide-eyed children clinging to his fatty, pasty thighs. He had his camera pressed to his face.

"What do you think you're doing?" said Sharpy.

The man looked confused. "Taking a picture."

"You can't take a picture of me. We're having a private family crisis."

"I didn't take a picture of you."

"What was that click?"

"I took a picture of the castle."

"Bullshit."

The father, a decent-seeming man, tacked the other way. "I'm sorry, I saw the problem with your mother. If there's anything I can do—"

Sharpy felt his blood boil. "My mother? Now you're bringing my *mother* into this?"

"Please, sir, if you would just settle down—"

"I'm not settling down—"

"Maybe you thought—"

"I don't *care* what you think I thought. You can't bring up my *mother*."

"I just wanted to help—"

"We don't need your help!"

"There's no need to get upset—"

"I'm not upset! I just don't want my family to be treated like goddamned animals in a zoo! We're a *family*! We're a *goddamned family*!"

Blinded by anger, fear, and desperation, Sharpy seized the rival father's shoulders and viciously shoved him backwards. The man's arms windmilled as he stumbled backwards into an antique streetlamp, then tumbled onto the asphalt.

The man's children ran to his side. Sharpy stood panting over his weaker rival. He felt alive, fully engaged! His biceps —gorged with blood! His heart—thrumming! Alpha dog *woof woof woof woof*—

"Why are you acting like such an animal, Stephen?" said Vivian. She was clasping Brittany to her chest.

"He took a picture of me."

"No he didn't."

"Yes he did."

"Even if he did, you are in *public*." Vivian lowered her voice and hissed through clenched teeth: "*People are looking at us.*"

She was right. A small crowd of tourists had now gathered like spectators at a cockfight. But there wouldn't be any more fighting. The fallen man had crawled to a bench where his wife was daubing his scraped arm with a moistened napkin.

"I'm sorry," said Sharpy. He felt the long slow *pffffffft* of machismo leaking out of his body. His hands dangled weakly by his sides.

"I'm going back to the hotel," Vivian said.

"Please stay with me. I need to find my mother."

"Brittany doesn't feel well."

"I need you."

Vivian fumbled for words. Her eyes were searching for something off in the distance. "Brittany really isn't feeling well."

"What's the problem?" The little girl's eyes were open. She was quiet but seemingly healthy.

"Diarrhea." Her face was totally neutral.

Well, Sharpy wasn't about to investigate that. "You have a key?"

"Of course. What are you going to do?"

He forced a smile. "Find out where they took my mother."

"Okay."

"Yeah."

They faced each other, emptied of words. "See you later," she said.

"I'll call you."

Vivian didn't hear him. She pivoted on her heel and weaved through the crowd towards the front gate. Like a tiger slinking through the underbrush in search of its next meal.

———

An hour later, Sharpy found D.L. sitting on a bench under a fake magnolia tree. Tim was crouched next to her, running his index finger—

(*ding dong it's the paperboy give him the money ding dong it's the paperboy give him the*)

—between the slats of the wooden bench.

Sharpy collapsed heavily next to them. "I found them at the infirmary. Grandma's doing better. She was already looking better when they loaded her onto the ambulance. Isn't that good news?"

D.L. swung her legs moodily. On her list of interests, talking to her father, exchanging *anything at all* with him, lay somewhere below cleaning her own sinus cavities with a pipecleaner.

"Did you really get those pills from the retirement home?"

She nodded.

He tilted his head oddly towards her. "What's going on with you?"

"Tim wants to go home," she said.

"I know."

"I think we should go home too."

Sharpy nixed the idea. "We'll wait a few days until Grandma gets better and try the picture one more time."

"I don't care about the picture."

Sharpy bunched up his lips tightly as though they were a cork stuffed into the mouth of an explosive bottle. He enunciated every word with barely contained anger. "Try not to think only about yourself, okay?"

D.L. shrugged. "Why does it matter if we take the picture or not? I'm going to get the inheritance anyways." There wasn't the faintest tinge of greed in her voice. There was only the cold sound of facts.

Sharpy had nothing to say to that. She was right. He could've bypassed the inheritance and allowed his daughter to receive it in ten years or so. Yes, this entire journey was his attempt to stick his fingers into his children's pie. Stephen Craving: guilty as charged. But did that make him a bad father?

"What would you like to do with the rest of the day?" he said.

She said nothing.

The billowing storm clouds were massing overhead. Nearby, an umbrella vendor opened his stand for business. Images of Arcade Boy danced inside D.L.'s head. A smile curled her lips. Anticipation curled her toes.

"I'd like to go back to the hotel," she said.

"Don't you want to ride the teacups?"

"I'm *fifteen*, Dad."

"What about the skyway?"

"We already did that."

"Yeah, but how often do you get to come to Disney World? Don't you want to make the most of it?"

"Not with you."

Ouch. Sharpy drummed his thumbs against his duffel bag. Her mood had passed through hormonal irritability and entered the dark land of outright hostility. "I always knew you'd turn out like this," he said. "I saw it in your eyes when you were a little girl."

Their relationship had dropped to a couple degrees north of absolute zero. D.L. too felt it calving apart like an ice floe. "I'll take Snooker back on the shuttle," she said. She jumped off the bench and helped Tim tie his shoes.

Sharpy watched her, his eyes moistening. Part of him was dimly aware that he was straddling a point of possible no return. But a larger part of him was exhausted. He hadn't expected this job of emotionally centering the family to be so *taxing*. He'd learned that it wasn't enough to simply be optimistic with his children. A clap on the shoulder, a hearty attagirl—those things worked best while standing on a grassy playing field with a whistle around your neck. But being the head of a family also meant *maintenance*—the long, grinding, endless business of emotionally recalibrating children, spouses, grandparents. Reminding them that they were loved, that they were necessary, that there was a place in this world for them.

Sharpy shuddered. For the first time in his life, he appreciated everything his wife had ever been. This role had come naturally to her. By contrast, here he was, age fortysomething, trying to learn this the same way he'd tried to learn salsa. But he'd given up on that impossible dance.

Was he giving up on this role?

Was he still going to try to fill his wife's shoes?

The answer was too apparent. Too painful. He shrugged it off and got to his feet. He brushed off his shirt. "D.L., you're old enough to make your own decisions."

"I know," she said.

"Don't stay up too late."

D.L. led her brother by the hand towards the exit. Sharpy watched his children leave, then wandered away.

In the opposite direction.

eighty-three

. . .

THEM POOR TOURIST BASTARDS. *They don't know how bad it's goin' to be.*

Folks see them high wispy clouds an' think sunny weather. Usually they'd be dead-right with that. But hurricanes ain't usual. I studied this shit after Andrew, see. It's low pressure air inneracting with hot water. An' that gulf ain't like the old days. Callin' it bath-water don't even do it justice.

Trailers. That's all northern folks seem to think about us. They seen the parks on the news during Andrew, crushed worser than pineapple. But normal houses got whupped jus' as bad. Stucco ain't nothin' but a pile a baked mud. Aluminum siding even worse. Slice your head off, come whipping through the air like helicopter blades. Don't even let's talk 'bout roofs. Nobody made one yet worth the sweat on a flea's forehead. Cee-ment blocks—now that's what you want. Uglier 'n' a bull's balls, but they stand up to that mother-humper like nothin' else.

Some say you got to board up the windows but not me. I say you got to leave open your windows. Ain't practical to shut the place up tight with all the pressure and wind and whatnot. You leave a sealed pot on a stove it bursts right? I say, let that motherhumper in. Let

375

him in. Tie down granny to her bed. Tape them kids together like hostages. Let him blow through. Things gonna git broke anyways.

Back when Andrew come through Rhonda saved my house, bless her dead soul. Once Rhonda laid down in the pasture, I knew it was a-gonna be bad. Heifers can tell. They know it better than the others. It's they stomachs. Some folks say it's when a cat sneezes but I don't put no stock in that. Cat's crafty. Livestock tells the truth. Too dumb to do anything but.

Yeah, I watched that storm wall chewin' up my paddock, all brown with the churned-up dirt. I was settin' right there on the porch. When I felt my insides go trembly I climbed down to the cellar an' sat it out with a couple drums a gasoline an' a Igloo cooler an' cribbage board. Nothin' worse than hearin' your house and home shredded right above your head and you's sittin' there cain't do a damn thing. Next day all my cattle was gone. Found eight a them down the road a ways. They was upside down in a ditch. Thirty-two hoofs to the sky. Never did find the others.

Forget about goin' near them hardware stores. They been sold out all summer, folks gearin' up. You know, people is people, they gone protect they own. I seen people nail plywood to they windows an' then neighbors come along an' strip it right off when they wasn't lookin'. Fistfights, robberies. An' all that's before the storm. Gets ten times worse after.

It's like I said. Them poor tourist bastards don't know how bad it's gonna be.

'Course, I don't neither, on account of Rhonda's bein' gone.

eighty-four

. . .

D.L. SAT with her brother on the shuttle bus.

As the shuttle bus pulled away from the park, she was trying to come to grips with the morning's events. Shoving her fingers into the octogenarian's mouth had been easy. She hadn't even realized that she'd done it until after the heart attack. Or was it only angina? They wouldn't know for a few more hours yet. D.L. sincerely hoped that Grandma Maya would live. She hated to see anybody die.

Now, however, the family picture was lost—*again*—and with it her dad's chances at her mom's fortune, which she still felt indifferent towards. Then her dad had assaulted someone else's dad. Then Vivian had whisked Brittany away with that limp excuse. Then her dad had been proven himself grossly insensitive to the entire story of D.L.'s existence.

D.L. recognized the elephant in the room. It couldn't be ignored any longer. This vacation wasn't working.

More importantly, this *family* wasn't working.

Urp.

The odd sound came from Tim, who was pressing his face against the glass. She ignored it.

Urp.

A prim young mother was seated next to her. She was a series of right angles—blouse perfectly composed, spine perfectly erect, hands perfectly folded.

Urp.

The mother finally turned with exaggerated politeness. "Excuse me," she said, "but do you think you could make your brother stop doing that?"

"No," said D.L.

"He seems *very* disturbed."

D.L. looked at the woman from her far-distant place. She could hardly believe the next words that escaped her lips. "Then don't pay him any attention. I don't."

———

Eventually the driver called out the name Hotel Crown Palace. The air-piston hissed, the door opened, and the two teenagers bounded down the rubber-mat steps.

As soon as her sneakers hit the ground outside the bus, D.L. winced. There was an ache in her left knee. She took another step: more pain. Every step was now a mild agony. She was stupefied. Only fifteen years young—and already arthritic!

What she didn't know was that, as the hurricane approached, the barometer was plummeting with the force of a bowling ball to the bottom of the Mariana Trench. She also didn't know that thousands of other people across the region were, at that *very* moment, feeling the same rattles in their teeth, bones, and bunions.

In the foreground, against the façade of the lobby, maintenance workers in yellow hardhats stood on Genie scissor lifts hammering sheets of plywood against the rectangular windows that towered over the revolving doors. Five more stacks of the chipped-wood slats were stacked at intervals down the length of the building.

D.L.'s hair blew wildly around her face. She uselessly pushed a hank of it behind her ear. She watched Tim pick a yellow marigold from a garden. Normally this would have earned him a useless lecture about respecting property. Not today. Why did she feel so devil-may-care?

Because, inside this hotel, there was a *boy*.

Arcade Boy.

He was could hold a mature conversation. Who also held the twin virtues of sweetness and cockiness. Oh yes—her crush was in full bloom. Let the hurricane blow down the walls of the hotel! She could suffer anything. Her spirits were skyrocketing just knowing that there was an inkling of a chance to see him again.

She knew exactly what she would do when that inevitably happened, too. She would dig her fingers into the pockets of his jeans, drag him to some darkened corridor, and let nature take its course. Not all the way—she still wasn't ready for anything like that—but there would be some hanky in her panky for once.

Excited, nervous, she seized Tim's hand and walked into the hotel.

———

The lobby was a honeycomb of activity. Guests criss-crossed the lobby in urgent flip-flops. Over a hundred people, baggage in hand, stood in a scraggly line to see a pair of extremely frazzled front desk agents. D.L. guessed that these were check-outs. She was wrong. They were check-*ins*, mostly residents of the low-lying coastal areas who fled inland during every hurricane to take shelter far from the wicked storm surge.

To her left, someone had tacked a handwritten sign on the gift shop door: *Out Of Umbrellas*. D.L. thought it seemed faintly ridiculous to buy one. What good was a thin piece of nylon against gale-force winds?

Then she felt a strong, warm hand on her shoulder. It was Carleton, sharp in his purple epaulets with gold twine piping.

"You lookin' for your momma?" he said.

"Sort of," D.L. said ironically.

"Where's the rest of the family this afternoon?"

"We split up."

"Y'all should be stickin' together. It's goin' get rough 'round here."

"Yeah."

"Hey, that high-born lady that's with y'all? The one with the nasty little girl?"

"Vivian?"

A gleam shone in his eye. "She ain't your momma, is she?"

"Definitely not."

"I knew it." He mugged. "She still with y'all?"

D.L. sensed something underneath his words. "I guess so. Why?"

"Mm hm," Carleton said. Then he slid into his next thought. "Hey, if the young feller here ain't too busy playing video games, why'n't both of you come down to the ball-room? We gonna be serving refreshments in a couple hours."

"Really?"

"Yeah, cookies, punch, you know. Take people's minds off the shitty weather."

She smiled at his casual use of profanity. "Maybe we'll come," she said.

"I'm a get you if you don't," he warned. "It's goin' get rough 'round here."

———

High above the lobby, in her room, Vivian was stuffing her daughter's clothing into a tiny pink suitcase. Pink tube tops, pink frilly shirts, pink undies, pink swimsuits, pink ruffled socks. She muttered under her breath as her arms worked quickly.

Brittany tugged at her pants leg. "Mommy I want—"

"I don't *care* what you want!" Vivian said. "Jesus! Don't I buy you anything other than pink?"

"Mommy I want—"

"Go sit in the chair and wait!" Vivian's arm hung in the air, pointing toward the corner. "Now!"

Slowly, Brittany squinched her face into a hateful rictus— her mouth wide open, the corners turned down. A horrible silence. Vivian knew all about this time delay. She had five seconds until the hollering struck, and it was going to be *loud*.

Vivian returned to packing. She zipped her daughter's suitcase shut. Worry creases darkened her forehead. Beads of perspiration sparkled along her hairline. She didn't know what sorry activity Sharpy was pursuing, and she didn't *want* to know. All she wanted was to get out, scram, flee, *vamoose*, before he returned.

She checked her wallet. Two hundred forty dollars.

The scream finally struck. Brittany bellowed like a demon being sprinkled with holy water. Vivian crossed into the bathroom and slammed the door. She would wait out the tantrum here, where the screams would be muffled.

In her inner sanctum, Vivian brushed her hair and applied her cherry-red lipstick. Then she gazed at herself in the mirror. She would never apologize for wanting only the best for her daughter. There was nothing wrong with demanding quality—was there?

The telephone rang loud and long. At last: the signal. Vivian quickly swept all of her makeup into a cosmetics bag with a single stroke of her arm, zipped the bag, and opened the door.

The screaming kept on, unabated. Brittany was pounding her little legs against the seat cushion. Her tiny fists were clenched. Her face had turned a bright crimson.

Vivian crossed the room. She lifted her nose into the air, picked up the phone, and plugged her other ear with a finger.

"Hello? Yes, it's me." Brittany was making conversation impossible. "I can't—yes, that's my daughter. Can you hold on one second?"

She set the phone on the table. She rummaged around inside her valet and fished out a roll of double-sided tape that she normally used for a couple of her more inviting tops. She stretched out a length and ripped it off. Then she stalked towards her daughter and planted it across the little girl's mouth. The screaming was suddenly muted.

"I'm sorry," she said, "but this is business."

She tossed her hair as she lifted the phone to her ear again. Her mouth widened into the magnificent smile of a huntress.

"We're ready when you are.

eighty-five

. . .

CURTIS JERKED AWAKE. Something had lifted his bed.

The problem: he wasn't in a bed.

It was almost ten o'clock at night, and he had been dozing behind the steering wheel of his tattered Civic. Just like Manny. He'd slid the seat bottom all the way back, so he could stretch his legs, and then he'd jacked the seat backwards until he was lying almost horizontal. His arms were crossed and his spare blanket—a frayed, faded Pendleton with oil stains from its history as a drop rag—was flung over his chest. A dirty slumberous cocoon.

The wind was howling, and his little Civic had been shuddering and wheezing and whistling and banging, and that had been just fine. He could sleep through that. But when the car had actually *tipped up* under the force of a vengeful gust, he'd started awake. It felt as though an adrenalized mother were lifting his vehicle to rescue her trapped infant.

The first thing Curtis did was gauge the condition of his ribs. His fingers cautiously probed his side beneath his t-shirt. The injury felt slightly less achy, but that was probably due to the eight Advils that he'd gulped two hours earlier. The upcoming job wasn't going to be easy.

Why was he here? There was a perfectly decent bed, a real one, with a lovely expectant girlfriend in it, waiting for him back at the No-Hopeland. Why was he sleeping in his car parked in a row of other cars on a one-way street in a no-name industrial district on the outskirts of downtown Orlando?

The answer could be found inside the loading garage at the end of the block. Inside its grimy maw, protected from the approaching storm, a bored security guard smoked a cigarette, watching the thin palm trees bend in the howling wind. This was the ass-end of the *Orlando Sentinel* building. Curtis was here because he was scheduled to deliver newspapers. For the last two months, he'd spent every Saturday night wheeling a dolly stacked with bundles of the Sunday paper through the hallways of local hotels. He didn't mind the night shift. It paid him nine dollars an hour—a fortune—and it paid in cash.

Now it was exactly ten o'clock, which meant that the presses were running and the first edition was going to be trundled up in about four minutes. Sure enough, he saw the security guard nod towards an unseen person inside, stub out his cigarette under his foot, and step out into the wind.

There was a line of cars parked ahead of Curtis, each with another delivery person sleeping behind its wheel. The security guard walked down the queue, his hand clamped onto his hat, rapping his baton on each window to wake up its occupant. One by one, the engines rumbled to life, and a row of red taillights lit up the night.

Curtis popped up his seat, started up his car, and waited. This was the most interesting part of the night. He was never assigned the same part of Orlando twice. Some nights they would send him towards Winter Haven; other nights towards Ocala; still others out near Daytona Beach. It all depended on the mood of the supervisor. On these nighttime runs, Curtis sometimes wished he could explore the sights and sounds and scents and flavors of his adopted state. He'd heard vague rumors about hot springs somewhere nearby where you could swim with real otters. He lost himself in a reverie.

The car in front of him started forward. Curtis drifted back from Otterland, into the hard reality of now, and followed into the loading garage. He parked alongside the long dock. A pallet of freshly-printed Sunday editions featured a pink paper with the name "CURTIS MARSHALL" scrawled on it in blue marker. Curtis exited his car and tore it off. On the back of the paper was a printout of his evening's delivery locations. He read quickly.

Shit.

They were sending him to Hotel Row, which was near the parks, almost to Kissimmee. The traffic would be unbearable, especially with the exodus of people in advance of the hurricane. Still, he was a fool to worry. By the time the storm reached this far inland—Orlando was a hundred miles from the west coast—it'd probably just be wind and rain. The worst this area would see would be some banged screen doors and blown-inside-out umbrellas.

The pallet was perched on the lip of the dock, about four feet above the floor. Curtis popped his trunk by pulling the little lever under the steering wheel on the left. The bigger problem now faced him. How was he going to get the papers inside the car? He couldn't lift those bundles, not with his ribcage. He couldn't just topple the pile either. That could take out the entire back end of his car.

He didn't dare ask any of the printers for help; they were too busy. And his supervisor—standing on the far side of the bay with a clipboard and surrounded by other delivery men —well, Curtis had barely spoken three sentences to the man in his entire life. He sure as hell didn't need to know about the injury. Maybe the security guard. Curtis headed unsteadily towards the fellow, but the guard casually turned his back and sauntered away.

Curtis felt his heart sink. There was no one to turn to.

"Curtis?" a voice said.

The voice was familiar. He turned—and saw Manny. Four-foot-ten Manny! Beaten-like-a-bowl-of-cake-batter Manny! After the brawl with the Boy Scouts, they'd been forced apart by Disney security, made to give statements independently of each other, unsure of how or when they might see each other again.

The little man's left arm was couched in a blue fabric sling. A couple of purple shiners decorated his eyes and reddened scrapes rouged his cheeks. His face wore the tired smile of a soul that has passed through many trials.

"They fixed me up in the infirmary," he said. "Then they fired me. Can you believe it?"

"At least you're walking," said Curtis.

"You bet I am," said Manny. "I'm a survivor. Me and the cockroaches."

They hugged each other as best as possible, Curtis careful not to touch his sling.

"I thought you'd be in the hospital," Curtis said.

"I couldn't afford it," said Manny.

"Me neither. I busted a couple ribs yesterday."

"How?"

"Got robbed and beaten."

A look of infinite sadness came across Manny's face. "This place," he finally said. "I can't ... I can't do it anymore. Not like this."

"Come on," Curtis said. "Look, you got a new job. Did Stevie set you up?"

Manny nodded. Stevie, a former character, had hooked up Curtis with this gig. Manny motioned towards his vehicle. "But with this arm, I don't know how I'm gonna get these papers in my car."

Curtis heaved a sigh of relief. "Me neither. We'll work together. How's that?"

"Pretty good, pal."

Knocking the pallet to the floor, the friends stooped down and together lifted each bundle into their respective trunks—Curtis with his right arm, Manny with his left.

When they finished, Curtis leaned against the dock and wiped the sweat off his face with his shirt sleeve. "But how are we're gonna get 'em out?"

Manny thought about it. "Are you going anywhere near Cocoa Beach?"

"Kissimmee."

"Oh." Manny looked crestfallen. "I thought we could work this together tonight."

"Hey, you wanna get breakfast at Sizzler in the morning?"

"Yeah. I'll call you."

"I'll call *you*."

"No, I'll call *you*."

"Wait a minute," said Curtis. "Neither of us has a phone."

Manny stopped for a beat. Then a small convulsive giggle grew inside of him, slowly at first, until it blossomed into an enormous convulsive laugh. It was contagious. Curtis felt it too, first chuckling, then soon guffawing. They leaned on each other, tears streaming down each other's cheeks. Why this reaction? The comment hadn't been that funny. Plus it was killing his broken ribs.

"You know something?" Manny said when they were finished, wiping a happy tear. "I think we've got some good stuff coming to us."

"You think so?" said Curtis.

"I do."

"God, I hope you're right."

"Good night, Curtis."

"You too, Manny."

They returned to their cars, each feeling a little stronger.

eighty-six

. . .

AT THE HOTEL CROWN PALACE, D.L. hadn't yet found the object of her desire. In fact, she hadn't even left the hotel room—the weather was too amazing.

She had scooted the room's armchair up to the edge of the window and was admiring the turbulent sky with her fingertips pressed against the Thermopane. From this fourteenth-floor vantage point, the landscape was as sublime as a Thomas Cole painting—if Cole had ever visited the tropics. The lush swamp canopy. Squashed and pummeled under the weight of the stormclouds. Blackness falling.

The panorama took her breath away. This looked like nothing D.L. had ever seen before.

Her father hadn't appeared or called. D.L. had knocked on the door of Vivian's room, with no response either. She didn't know where the daddy-eating vixen could have gone in the middle of a hurricane, especially with that knee-high brat in tow. Only Grandpa Frederick had phoned. Grandma was in critical condition and was going to be kept in the hospital for several days, until a stress test could be safely given. He was spending the night at her bedside. He had been brisk and businesslike, but there was a trembling tinge to his voice that told D.L. that things were not under control.

The teenager pulled a blanket around her shoulders. Her toes burrowed into her complimentary slippers.

"We're all alone," she said.

There was no response from her brother. She glanced over. Tim was laid out on the bed, flat on his back, clad in only his white Jockey briefs. His body was stiff. She could see a sliver of white through his slightly opened eyelids. His eyeballs had rolled back inside his head.

Waxy catalepsy.

That was its technical name. Most people would say he was "frozen". Sometimes Tim entered a state—no one knew why or how—in which his arms, legs, and back became perfectly rigid but pliable. You could pose his limbs as if he were a Gumby figurine. This state could last from six minutes to six hours, and he was always exhausted afterwards.

D.L. sighed. She had no patience for his physiological oddities *here*, in the middle of this freaking storm, with angry rain slashing the windows like a rapist. He shouldn't be allowed his weird indulgences right now.

There was a sudden loud rapping on the door. A little frightened, she padded across the carpet over to the peephole and peered out. Through it she could see Carleton. D.L. instantly felt happy.

Her happiness receded as she flung open the door. The bellman's face was taut and his eyes were rounded with fear. "Little Miss Craving," he said, "you'd better git yo'self downstairs to that ballroom."

"Why?"

"Cause we're evacuatin' all the rooms. It's gone be worse than we thought."

"It is?"

"You bet your little blue eyes." He leaned forward with a grin. "Plus there was some boy askin' about you down there."

She didn't move. But her stomach leapt; her jaw dropped.

He jerked a thumb over his shoulder. "Ballroom, now. I got better things to do than haul stubborn little girls out of they rooms."

Then he turned and walked to the next door, where she heard him rapping the exact same way. She heard him deliver the same warning: "Evacuatin' rooms ... gotta go ... ballroom ..."

She closed the door. Had that been Arcade Boy asking the staff about her? Or was Carleton so intuitive that he could sense her desperate loneliness? Had he guessed that she would've already chatted with some boy in the hotel? Was it just a ploy to get a tip?

She decided that Carleton couldn't be *that* manipulative. Arcade Boy must truly have been putting out his feelers. So to speak.

D.L. approached the window again. Carleton hadn't used the word *hurricane*, but maybe that was because he was trying to keep her calm. Intensely curious, she pressed her hands up to the window and peered into the distance.

What she saw set her knees trembling.

It wasn't quite dark yet ... but through the grayness, looming on the far western horizon, a churning blackness was tearing across the groves. It looked like a threshing machine, chewing up everything in its path.

D.L. felt panic race through her body. *That* was a hurricane —and it stretched from the roots of the trees to the roof of the sky.

A whimper slipped out of her mouth. Fear slithered its fingers around her body and squeezed like a lecherous stepfather. Should she do as Carleton had ordered? Of course she should. *He* would be there—Arcade Boy—if she were lucky. Her heart pattered like an excited rabbit's.

Her brother was the only stumbling block.

"Come on, Snooker," she said. "Snap out of it. We have to

go downstairs." She stripped out of her sweatpants and yanked on her most stylish jeans. She chose a red halter top, hoisted up her hair with a clip, and daubed just the barest line of mascara upon her eyelashes. She studied herself in the mirror. She looked natural but attractive. She was ready for action.

Her brother, however, was still lying on the bedspread in his underwear.

Still waxy. Still cataleptic.

D.L. stalked over to the bed and shook him fiercely. He felt lightweight, like a piece of balsa wood. "Look out there, Snooker! That's a *hurricane*! We have to *go*! We have to take *cover*! Like the tornado drills at home!"

No response.

"Tim!" She shoved her thumb and her forefinger into her mouth and wolf whistled. Their secret signal.

He didn't move.

This was inconceivable. He *never* ignored the secret signal. She raced through other options in her mind. She couldn't carry him downstairs, not even if she wanted to. What teenage girl wanted to be seen toting a freakishly stiff twelve-year-old boy wearing nothing but underwear? Into a crowded *ballroom*? That was a recipe for embarrassment. Especially if Arcade Boy were waiting. What were the other options? There *were* no other options—except the unthinkable.

She would leave him behind.

"Do you want to stay here?" she said. "Is that what you want?"

No response.

She backed away from the bed. The truth had been revealed. *She had done her best.* If Tim couldn't open his eyes, couldn't face the meteorological terror wheeling across the swamps, couldn't take the teensiest speck of responsibility for himself—then she couldn't be responsible for him either. The rules weren't any different for autistic people, were they?

She looked back at her brother as she opened the door. "I wish you were normal, Tim."

His arm was lifted grotesquely high into the air. Like a frozen wave goodbye.

D.L. left the hotel room and stiffened her lower lip. The door's tongue clicking shut in its latch sounded like a bomb exploding in her head.

eighty-seven

. . .

CURTIS GRIPPED the tattered steering wheel of his little Civic as he drove under the darkening sky.

He was bearing south on Route 535, towards the famous theme parks. He didn't know this road, because normally he took the freeway in this direction. But with the recommended evacuations for the coastal areas, half of southwest Florida had jammed the northbound I-4 so badly that state authorities had turned *both* sides of the freeway into northbound lanes, all the way to Orlando.

So he had been forced to follow the surface road instead. His was the only southbound vehicle, heading straight into the heart of the storm. Though his headlamps clawed at the darkness, he whistled happily. There was really nothing to worry about. The forecaster on the radio said that the hurricane—yes, they were using that word now—wouldn't really hit until three o'clock a.m., and he'd be safely back at the motel room by then, snug in his girlfriend's arms.

Even so, in the rare gap between the walls of the gated retirement communities, he glimpsed the horrific blackness in the west. It was approaching quickly. Fear cinched his stomach into a sack of bilious green worry, and he pushed down the accelerator a little further.

A sudden gust of wind picked up the right side of his car and buffeted it over into the opposite lane. Swearing, Curtis wrenched the wheel back to the right, and the car careened back onto the correct side of the road. He breathed relief. Thank God for all those newspapers in the trunk. That ballast had just saved him from spending the next four hours strapped into an overturned car with spinning wheels. Still, he was trembling. Was driving into an approaching hurricane really worth nine dollars an hour?

He was in no position to be turning down work. He consulted his assignment sheet again: Hotel Plaza Boulevard. A green sign announced that it was on the right, he cranked the wheel, and then the Civic was tearing down the leafy boulevard lined on either side by tall, mid-range hotels.

On his left, he caught sight of his first destination: the Hotel Crown Palace. Not even a blind man could miss it. Fifteen stories high and painted a bright, scandalous, flamingo pink. Curtis pulled up the driveway and parked under the *porte cochere*.

The area was deserted except for a single valet, who was hunched intensely over the phone. Curtis exited his car, grabbed hold of a bellman's cart, and began unloading the bundles onto it. This was torturous work for a young man with broken ribs: hoist the bundle onto the edge of the trunk, then tip it over onto the baize-carpeted cart and try to keep it from falling onto the concrete. When he'd loaded four bundles this way, he slammed his trunk closed and inched the cart towards the automatic doors. He was straining at the weight as if they were a stack of concrete blocks.

The lobby buzzed with excitement. Children darted across the floor, chasing one another, giddy in the expectation that Something Important Was Happening. They must not ever have experienced a real hurricane. Neither had Curtis, but he knew better than to welcome it. He'd heard horror stories about hurricane survivors dying from diarrhea. Or the "disaster specialists" who coaxed credit card numbers from shell-shocked homeowners. Some of the tragedies even verged on the surreal—ask the lady in Homestead who'd opened her car door to find three hundred gallons of water gushing onto her shoes.

This hotel, however, appeared to be under control. Polite staffers with grim smiles on their faces were positioned near the doors, directing everyone towards the ballrooms. Curtis nodded to them and headed towards the abandoned front desk. Sure enough, next to the bronze bell, whose ding attracted bellmen like stray dogs to dinner, he found the occupied rooms list, and the words *Orlando Sentinel* scrawled across the top. This hotel was *tight*. Even in the midst of this crisis, they remembered to print out a rooms list for the paperboy.

He dragged the cart to the elevator and rode it to the second floor. When the doors opened, he pulled out the stop button to hold the car. This was something he always did. Commandeering an elevator was his right. Besides, management wouldn't want guests riding a lift with this sweating, stinking delivery boy.

Curtis pulled the cart with his right hand while he consulted the list with his left. The hotel was almost half full: 193 of 402 rooms occupied. On this floor, he only had three rooms. Stopping before the first, he pulled a folding knife from his pocket and snipped the yellow plastic twine around the first bundle. The front-page headline announced HERE SHE COMES, with the predictable picture of a homeowner hammering boards onto his doublewide.

He lifted the issue—Sundays were extra heavy, with flyers and comics and special sale inserts that nobody read—and dropped it onto the floor in front of 205. It landed with a resounding *whump*. Then he repeated this for the other two rooms.

Then he returned to the elevator, depressed the stop button, and rode to the third floor. Repeat: find target room, drop paper, *whump*. Depress stop button, fourth floor. It was mindless scut work, but he enjoyed it.

For the first time that week, Curtis Marshall didn't have to think about his problems.

eighty-eight

· · ·

A SPRAY of water showered the side of Sharpy's head.

His eyes blinked open. He found himself slumped on a wooden countertop. A foot from his face, a shrunken pygmy head with brittle wisps of gray hair stood guard over a dish of salted peanuts.

"Bar's closed," said a female with a smoker's voice.

It was the bartender, a skinny, fiftyish woman with a figure like a misshapen pretzel. Her skin had the orange, leathery texture of a skin cancer patient. She was holding a dripping shot glass above his head. Slowly he pieced it together: The gristly barkeep had tossed water on him.

She began stacking chairs against the wall as Sharpy took stock of his surroundings. The sides of the bar were lined with some scratchy palm thatching that could slice skin. Surfboards and pictures of tiny bare atolls surrounded by blue ocean hung askew on the walls.

He seemed to be in a tiki bar. He squinted as he tried to remember the afternoon. After his parents and mistress and children had all abandoned him—that was the way he told it to himself—he'd stood in the middle of that idiotic theme park with its rodents and chipmunks and fairy tales and hopeless dreams ... and realized that his bullheadedness may very well just have cost him a million dollars. Why had he persisted in forcing Grandma beyond her physical limits? Why hadn't he listened to her? He'd screwed himself. If she passed on, the inheritance was gone. If she became permanently hospitalized, it was *still* gone. The self-loathing he'd felt at that moment was indescribable.

He'd decided to drown himself at the nearest bar. On the advice of a park attendant—a college guy who bashfully gave him a recommendation as though he'd been asked for his favorite pedicure salon—Sharpy'd beelined out of the Disney area towards this desolate stretch of road south of Kissimmee.

To this tiki shack.

It was supposed to be a locals' favorite. Sharpy had blazed a pair of trenches in the road to get to the place. He hadn't expected it to be open, considering the weather forecast. He had just needed the *promise* of a derangement of the senses. He had been surprised to find the battered screen-door propped open with a cement block and some crusty old alligators sipping light beers at the bar. He'd chosen hard stuff, mostly tequila, slammed shot after shot, groused with the alligators, and fallen asleep facefirst in the peanut shells.

Now it was nighttime, the hurricane was nearly upon them, and he was half-soused in an empty bar somewhere in rural Osceola County. He fell off his stool and wobbled to his feet.

"I need to get back to the hotel," he said.

She snorted. "I need new tits. Life's tough."

Sharpy tried again. "Can you tell me how to get back to the, um ..." He snapped his fingers, fumbling for the name ... "the Hotel Crown Palace. Where is it?"

She cast a bony arm to the northeast. "Up thataways. It's gonna be thirty-six fifty."

It took a moment for Sharpy's soused synapses to process what "thirty-six fifty" meant. It wasn't a highway. It was his *bill.* He felt indignant again. Such small amounts seemed so much more devastating without the promise of a million dollars floating in the future.

"Would you look at that," he said, making a show of patting his pockets. "I think my wallet's in the car."

"You sure?" she said.

"Yeah," he said. "Be right back."

He casually pushed out the swinging screen door—then sprinted toward his car.

There was no problem in stiffing the woman at the tiki bar. He'd never come here again. He didn't even know where here *was.* She'd probably overcharged him anyways. Oh, he could hide behind thousands of rationalizations, could choose from a constellation of excuses. Sharpy slid into the rental minivan, punched the accelerator, and took off in a spray of pebbles.

The bartender appeared in the doorway. She watched the minivan disappear in a spray of pebbles. Then she pulled something from her apron pocket.

It was a credit card.

"You already gave me your Visa, dumbass," she said.

eighty-nine

. . .

AFTER D.L. LEFT, Tim didn't move for many minutes. His eyes were still rolled backwards behind their closed lids. The mattress was firm and supportive. At last his left hand began—

(*ding dong it's the paperboy give him the money ding dong it's the paperboy give him the*)

—to clench and unclench. Gradually it lowered to the mattress. If his sister had been there, she would've seen him open his eyes and awkwardly sit up. Outside, though cloaked in darkness, the hurricane wall billowed larger and larger as it plowed across the fields and swamps and hummocks.

Whump.

Tim jerked up.

Whump.

The sound wasn't caused by the weather. It was coming from the hallway. Despite the confusion floating through his head, Tim knew that sound. It was the same sound that he heard every afternoon at home in Indianapolis.

It was the sound of the local paper landing on his front stoop.

Whump.

It was the paperboy.

And because the paperboy was here, Tim needed—

(*ding dong it's the paperboy give him the money ding dong it's the paperboy give him the*)

—to pay him. With the money. From the safe.

The safe.

Where his father always kept the money for the paperboy.

Tim loped across the room with his weird gait, bent down at the armoire, and yanked open the door that concealed the safe. His fingers dialed—

(*7131*)

—the code his father had programmed the night before. The safe sprang open.

Inside the safe lay the envelope. Just as his father had left it.

Ten thousand dollars.

He removed the money and dug through the trash until he found the envelope that it had been stored in. He rewrapped the money inside the envelope and resealed it with same cellophane tape.

Then he went to the door.

———

In the fourteenth-floor hallway, Curtis had become a paper delivery machine. He was, as athletes and fighter pilots say, *in the zone*. Room number, check, drop paper, check, *whump*, check. The baggage cart, much lighter now, glided behind him noiselessly.

Room number 1410: check. He reached for a paper—

—and heard a bizarre, gurgling laugh behind the door. All the hairs on his arms pricked up. Curtis sensed that he was being watched. He peered into the peephole. "Hello? *Orlando Sentinel?*"

The gurgle-laugh soared into a high-pitched squeal. Then the door opened.

Standing before Curtis was a very startling twelve-year-old white boy. He had short, tousled hair the color of crab-cakes, a flood of freckles on his face and arms, and a wide pelvis that lent him a pear-shaped, womanish appearance. His arms were held out at unnatural angles from his body and the beautiful empty cornflower blue eyes housed pupils that were focused a mile away.

Entranced, Curtis held his breath without realizing it. Coming to his senses, he held out a copy of the *Sentinel*. The boy didn't notice it.

"Here," said Curtis, "take your paper."

The boy gurgle-laughed again. It sounded like a deranged seagull. When Curtis looked down at the package, he noticed the boy was holding out his own gift.

An envelope. Plain, unmarked.

"Is that for me?" said Curtis.

"Money for the paperboy," said Tim.

Curtis felt skeptical about that. Nobody had ever tipped him in this piddling little night job. When guests encountered him, they either ignored him or made a snarky comment about the lack of newsworthy news in Orlando. Plus, this boy was kooky. Judging from his looks, there could be *anything* in that envelope: the kid's homework, his mother's makeup kit, anthrax spores.

Still, Curtis watched his hand accept the envelope. Something rectangular and slightly bulky lay inside of it.

"Thank you," he said.

The boy hopped on one foot three times, clapped twice, then swung the door closed in his face.

Curtis felt oddly shaken, as though he'd just come face to face with God. He bobbled the package in his hand, feeling its heft, noting the slight stress it put on his forearms. It had to be a king-sized chocolate bar. Maybe two. Curtis chuckled to himself. He'd been tipped in Nestle.

Shaking his head, Curtis Marshall stowed the envelope in the pocket of his windbreaker. He would open it later. He needed to finish the job.

He leaned forward and pulled the cart to the next room.

ninety

. . .

THE GRAND BALLROOM of the Hotel Crown Palace had been designed by somebody whose very soul rejected decoration.

The room was large but dead, with gray carpeting and a collapsible gray accordion wall. The recessed lights cast conical pools of light onto the rows of seats below, which were stackable, foam-core, and upholstered in gray.

All told, the room had the personality of a dead carp.

It did, however, possess the virtue of cement-block construction, unbesmirched by any of those pesky openings known as windows. And that is why the hotel's guests, plus some shrewd locals, were being ushered into its flat gray bosom.

To wait out the hurricane.

In the lobby, D.L. primped her hair in the glossy belly of a statue of The Varmint. The wind had transformed her head into a tangled mess of locks. She took out the clip and shook her mane a few times. The mess bounced beautifully on her shoulders. Vivian would have been proud. She felt ready to make an entrance.

Striding casually through the open ballroom, she noticed

that the hotel staff was trying to make the calamity comfortable. She accepted a bright pink meal voucher, then was pointed towards a row of white-aproned chefs manning a set of hooded copper broilers on a banquet table. Nearby, a line of people queued up to graze upon the spread of salami, bologna, whole-grain breads, domestic cheeses, broccoli florets, mini-cauliflower heads, baby carrots, and ranch dip.

Very comfortable.

D.L. strolled towards the beverage table with a nonchalance that said this was merely the first stop in a night chock full of glamorous parties. Should she pour herself some coffee? No, she'd get too jumpy; besides, it might look pretentious. Lemonade? She reached for the nozzle, then changed her mind. Lemonade had too many childish connotations. She settled on a cup of iced tea drained from a stainless steel urn, then gazed across the ballroom.

Though the chairs had been arranged in neat rows facing the stage, the touron families had circled themselves in a hundred small clusters. The room had come to resemble a convocation of Native American drum circles.

D.L. moved her way through the tribes. One hand held her iced tea while the other hand self-consciously held her hair back. She tossed her head repeatedly, making small affected mannerisms. Nobody noticed. The mothers, fathers, brothers, sisters, cousins, friends of the family were preoccupied—playing cards, coloring in books, twiddling handheld video games, sending text messages, thumbing through drugstore novels, solving crossword puzzles, chatting on phones, snoring, drooling, bickering about intrusions upon personal space, or staring blankly at nothing whatsoever.

Weirdly enough, none of them seemed too upset by the idea that the decade's most intense hurricane was lumbering upon them with the ferocious hunger of a grizzly bear fresh out of hibernation.

Even worse, none of them was *him*. D.L. felt despondent.

The image of Arcade Boy—with his perfect floppy hair, his self-styled jeans, his insolent attitude—was driving her every step. And yet she had to engineer the encounter as though it were coincidence. The Italians called this *sprezzatura*, the art of artlessness. She called it being sneaky for a good purpose.

On her third lap around the arena, she finally spotted him. Arcade Boy.

Surrounded by *other girls*.

The affectations instantly ceased. Like a sniper, she dropped to the floor and crouched behind a chair. Her eyes peeked over the chairback.

There were five girls. Crosslegged on the carpet, their heads craned towards Arcade Boy as he ... what was he doing? *He was playing the guitar for them*! A Yamaha acoustic! D.L. gritted her teeth. How could he have *known* about her weakness for guitarists? It didn't matter if they could play, or if they flossed, or if they could even form sentences, really— they were *guitarists*. They could strike poses and pluck heart-strings with equal skill.

Inside her head, D.L. screamed and stamped her feet like a scorned woman. Who were these *ugly whores*? Fawning and cooing and eyelashes fluttering? She had been itching to toy with him, work him up into a lather. Now the tables were turned, and she was supposed to *fight* for his attention? Supposed to *compete* with these google-eyed boy-stealers? It was ludicrous.

She immediately knew what *not* to do. She would *not* sit at his feet with the others. That would leave her powerless.

How did a girl handle this?

What would *Vivian* do?

D.L. chewed on her fingernail. What if she *did* join his select little audience—but only to eliminate the competition? Maybe she would elbow them aside with a viperish smile, a discreet elbow, a scooted butt. But first she had to be invited. That was how Vivian would handle it.

Drawing a breath, she rose to her feet and sashayed past him, rolling her hips. Perfectly uninterested. Sure enough, Arcade Boy spotted her … and his strumming stopped.

"Hey," he said.

She kept walking.

"Hey," he said, more loudly. "You. From the arcade."

D.L. stopped and pivoted. Her hair pinwheeled radiantly across the air—a shameless display of her best asset. Its effect was immediate. Arcade Boy's tongue unrolled to the floor like a welcome mat.

"Oh," she said, "hi there. I didn't notice you." She frowned at his instrument. "Are you some kind of *guitarist*?"

Arcade Boy looked down at the instrument as though it were a dead infant. He tried to minimize it: "I play a little, you know … not much. Mostly during hurricanes."

"Do those happen in New Jersey?"

"All the time. New Jersey is actually the hurricane center of North America."

"Really."

"Yep. We get seven or eight each season."

She was inwardly ecstatic. Their repartee was exactly what she'd imagined. But she couldn't tip her hand yet. She glanced at the other girls. "Who are your admirers?"

She posed as five pairs of jealous eyes ruthlessly critiqued her hair, her face, her outfit, her figure.

"We're his *friends*," one of the girls said. "What about you?"

"I don't even know him," said D.L. "I was just passing by." The words tasted like strychnine pellets on her tongue, but she managed to choke them out.

Arcade Boy became very agitated. "Hey, don't leave," he said. "Why don't you chill for a little bit?"

"I don't really like guitar."

"That's okay. I was done anyways." He lifted the strap off his shoulder and set the guitar on a nearby chair. The girls were whispering madly into each other's ears. D.L. smiled to herself. It was unbelievable, but a little psychology went a long way. She had sailed in over these girls' heads! Worked them like a part-time job!

"Maybe just for a minute," she said.

"Do you have to get back to your brother?" he said.

"Yeah."

"Please," he said, "just for a minute." He actually pulled up a chair for her. Inwardly, D.L. was giggling with delight. He'd given her a *chair*. The other girls only had patches of carpet. Like preschoolers.

"Okay," she said. She lowered herself daintily onto the seat.

The way Vivian had taught her.

ninety-one

. . .

SHARPY TORE down the deadened road in his minivan. It was almost ten o'clock and his headlights cut a sharp hole in the quiet night and a dull thudding at the base of his skull reminded him that he was, in fact, still drunk. That was something he could easily handle. There were more pressing things to worry about.

Like the thing in his rearview mirror. It was, quite simply, an enormous blackness, and a deeply primitive tingle in his tailbone told him that if he didn't get to safety soon—*very* soon—his vehicle was going to be knocked around the fields like a pinball.

He blew through a flashing red light without pretending even a hint of brake pressure.

Then Sharpy smelled something strange. He felt a nonhuman presence in the air and a chorus of trumpet-like calls echoed through the sky. He rolled down his window and leaned his head outside the car. Above him was a sound like *flap flap flap flap flap*.

It was a cloud of dark skeletal shapes, flapping over his car. They were *birds*, sandhill cranes with seven-foot wingspans, and they were headed eastward—away from the hurricane.

Tilting his head upwards, he didn't see the yellow diamond-shaped sign, the one indicating a curve ahead, and when the road buckled sharply to the left, a true hairpin, Sharpy found his minivan sailing off the shoulder, rumbling over some dead wiregrass, careening between a pair of yuccas, and crashing into a shallow ditch with a terrific jolt.

His headlights shone onto a small embankment.

He had driven straight into ... a wall of dirt.

Sharpy cursed and popped open the door to inspect the damage. The air was now frighteningly calm. The last of the shapes had passed overhead, and there was no other wildlife within earshot, not even a whirring cicada. Everything that could move had either vacated the area or hidden underwater. The land was silent except for the random knocks and kinks of his cooling engine.

The minivan's front bumper and grill were pristine; they hadn't even touched the embankment. The front left wheel, however, was a different story. A viciously pointed piece of limestone had punctured both the rubber and the tube; now it was lopsided and deflated.

He spat in the dirt and wiped his face on the shoulder of his polo shirt. He'd never jacked a car up, certainly not in the dark, and definitely not with a hurricane approaching. But he couldn't wait for help either. With trembling fingers, he leaned against the side of the car and found a cigarette in his pocket and felt around his pockets for a book of matches.

Then Sharpy paused. Out of the west, out of the colossal billowing darkness, across the landscape ... a high-pitched whine reached his ears. It sounded like a thousand sanitation trucks compacting their garbage at the same time.

It sounded like a symphony of destruction.

His knees went soft and jittery. He suddenly knew something more certainly than he had ever known anything else in his life.

He knew he would die if he stayed in this field.

He tossed the cigarette onto the ground and slipped behind the wheel and started the engine. Throwing the gearshift into reverse, his front wheels spewed dirt and—miracle of miracles!—pushed him back up to level land and the road.

Problem was, the minivan listed horribly to the left. The weight of the front end was riding on a single rickety rim. The shredded rubber flapped against the pavement with each revolution.

It would have to hold. He hit the accelerator and tore down the road again.

———

Twenty minutes later, as the minivan turned into the Hotel Crown Palace, its carriage rained a shower of sparks onto the road.

He parked his car under the portico and inspected the damage. The wheel rim had been horribly flattened. No time for that. He needed to find Vivian and his children.

Sharpy stepped onto the rubber automatic door mat—and smashed his nose into the glass doors. Why hadn't they opened? Clutching his face, he saw a small hasp hooking the two together. Of course. The staff had locked the automatic doors in anticipation of the hurricane.

He went through the revolving doors instead. The increased air pressure practically exploded his inner eardrum.

The lobby was a ghost town. There were no valets, no doormen, no bellmen. Only one staffer—a food-and-beverage lackey wearing a purple polo shirt with the hotel's insignia stitched above the left breast and a radio clipped to his belt—waited patiently near the elevators next to a hastily-written sign reading "Ballroom This Way". Sharpy walked past the man and pressed the up arrow on the elevators.

"I sorry, joo can't go to your room now," the staffer said.

"Why not?" said Sharpy.

"Because all'e guests in the ballroom now."

"I have to get my kids."

"Maybe they already down 'ere, yeah?"

"We won't know unless I check."

The Cuban looked worried. "Sir, the 'urricane ees coming."

"I don't care."

The Cuban shifted unhappily and looked the other way. He wasn't going to pick a fight.

———

Sharpy stepped out of the elevator at the tenth floor and speedwalked down the muffled silence of the hallway. His footsteps died and were buried in the carpeting. He fished the keycard out of his wallet and slid it into the lock and waited for the green light. Click.

He pushed open the door and found Tim squatting on the floor stark naked. He was arranging his clothes in piles by color: white, blue, red, black, khaki, plaid, striped.

It barely registered on his father. "Snooker," he said, "get some clothing on."

"Colors."

"Snooker, there's a hurricane coming. Where's Vivian?"

The autistic boy made a shrill, keening noise. Then he stared at the wall with glassy eyes, his little prepubescent manparts dangling against the carpet.

That had been an odd sound. Sharpy entered the bathroom and washed his face and swallowed four Advils. He gazed at himself in the mirror. It looked as though he'd aged a year on this horrific vacation … pustules on his cheeks …

sagging jowls ... mussed hair ... a thin film of something on his eyeballs. To a stranger, he probably looked like some kind of an addict. That really wasn't too far from the truth. How long did you have to single-mindedly pursue something before you left reason and sanity behind?

He knew the truth. He knew the inheritance wasn't ever going to be his. He felt a colossal case of the-fox-and-the-grapes beginning to wash over him. He didn't need the million dollars. He shouldn't get the money. It would only bring jealousy and ruin. And if he ever did, Vivian's subtle machinations and infinite beggary would soak it all away anyways. She was smarter than he was. He knew that much.

He crinkled his nose and looked down at the backs of his hands. He remembered someone once saying that these were the parts of our bodies that we know the best because we spend most of our lives looking at them. His seemed old: thick hairy arthritic knuckles and stringy tendons and engorged green blood vessels, and ... what was that? ... something new, a small brown mark the size of a dime ... was it a liver spot? It couldn't be? But it *was*! His first one! Right there below the ring finger on his left hand! Jesus! *Liver* spots! He spread his hand out on the bare counter to have a better look.

The bare counter.

He paused. The counter hadn't been bare this morning. Vivian had been keeping a veritable battalion of beauty supplies on this counter.

He whirled around. Her cosmetic bag, the size of a steamer trunk, was gone.

He dashed back into the room. Her Louis Vuitton suitcase, gone. An empty luggage rack.

Brittany's matching suitcase, gone. An empty square on the carpet.

A red haze clouded Sharpy's eyes.

Vivian had left him.

ninety-two

. . .

SHARPY RUSHED OVER to the side table and began rifling through the pamphlets, brochures, receipts, and other family vacation paper detritus. She must've left a note explaining everything. Maybe how she had been transferred to another room, on the east-facing side of the hotel, where the hurricane wouldn't strike quite so hard. Maybe how she had taken all her luggage down to the ballroom to wait out the storm.

No, those were red herrings. If she'd transferred rooms, she would have brought along his luggage too, not to mention Tim, and there would be an official notice or a message waiting on the telephone. And try as he might, he was having difficulty visualizing Vivian, that queen of entitlement, that living memorial to exclusivity, sitting downstairs in the *ballroom*—a virus farm crowded with breathing, coughing, sneezing tourons. There was no earthly way. She wouldn't stand for it.

The wind was howling against the windows now. Sharpy sifted through the table's contents and found no evidence of anything resembling a note. His mood grew edgier. His eyes danced across the room, scanning for something, anything, a clue that he had *not* just been dumped by a woman wearing his seventeen-thousand-dollar engagement ring.

That's when he saw something else.

The safe.

Its door was slightly ajar and the pair of thick metal prongs were jutting out across the digital face. It was quite clearly *not* in the locked position.

He sprinted across the room, stampeding over Tim's precisely stacked piles of clothing. He knelt at the safe and jammed his hand inside. His fingers scrabbled around, feeling every inch of the small cubic space.

Empty.

Hyperventilating, Sharpy lowered his head sideways and looked inside. There was nothing inside.

The money was gone.

Had Vivian taken the money too?

That was impossible. How could she have opened the safe? Nobody had been in the room when he'd set the passcode last night.

That wasn't true. Tim had been in the room. Dimly he remembered having some drunken conversation with the boy about something ... what had it been? The tequila had obliterated his memory of everything.

Sharpy turned. From this vantage point he saw the mirror, and the perfect angle that it afforded anybody who was lying on the bed.

The bed was where Tim had been laying that night.

The night Sharpy'd set the passcode.

Licks of flaming rage roared in Sharpy's eyes. He flexed his arms and stalked towards his son: "You spied on me."

The naked boy gurgled. He was defenseless, stretched on his side.

"You saw my passcode," Sharpy said, "and you used it to give Vivian that money. Didn't you?"

Tim rolled over onto his back, grinning stupidly. Like a

freckled, happy dog lying on its back with its tongue hanging to the side of its mouth.

"Didn't you? Answer me!"

Sharpy suddenly kicked his son. The toe of his shoe connected with the boy's ribcage. It wasn't a particularly powerful kick. It wasn't particularly swift or expert. But it did connect.

Didn't some small part of the boy care what was happening to the family? The inheritance lost, the ten thousand in cash gone, Vivian vamoosed, his grandmother gone, his sister deserted, his very own mother dead?

Tim was a *victim*, he thought, naked on the floor like that. The kid was practically *asking* to be the scapegoat.

He felt the monster rise within.

Why was the boy still smiling? Didn't he know he'd been kicked? Sharpy watched his foot deliver another kick—a stronger one. It smashed into the boy's face and Sharpy watched the skin split open and the white of the cheekbone expose itself. He saw the boy's hand fly up and then he watched another kick connect with the boy's neck. Then his foot was raining kicks upon the naked flesh with vicious enthusiasm, one after another after another...

But abuse could be rationalized. It probably wasn't hurting the boy too badly, he thought, because of the soft rubber on the toe of his sneaker. He wasn't doing much damage. This could be a lot worse. He could be wearing a steel-toed workboot—that could really do some damage.

Sharpy could find fragments of excuses everywhere.

Finally the foot stopped kicking. He saw the boy scrambling away on all fours, a string of bloody drool trailing on the carpet, his ass up in the air, the little dangling scrotum under the darkened hole. Then he saw the terrible foot give a terrible push against the boy's buttocks, and the boy's head crushed against the night table, and it didn't move again.

He watched all of this from a great, safe distance. Like a

fourteenth-century noble observing a bloody battle from his picnic linen far from the slaughter.

Except that simile wasn't quite right. Because *he* was the one doing the slaughtering.

A loud clunk caught Sharpy's attention. He turned towards the window. Something had blown into the Thermopane. *Clunk.* He noticed that a voice had been yelling. His fingers touched his throat. He felt rawness.

Odd. It had been his voice.

He paused, his skin tingling. Sensing a terrible realization poised to leap upon him.

But before it could, he turned and fled from the room.

ninety-three

. . .

SHARPY LURCHED into the dimmed lobby, which was deserted except for the stray tourist scurrying through with a blanket in hand.

He paced between the planters with his head thrown back to the ceiling and the backs of his hands pressed against his eyes. Images of his shoe striking his son's naked body flipped through his mind's eye.

A horror reel.

Had he really kicked his own son? Like a dog in the street? The realization sent his head into dizzy circles. He lurched toward a low couch and sprawled across it. With one guilty foot planted on the terrazzo tile, he stared vacantly at the vaulted ceiling forty feet above. Self-loathing burbled in his chest and bubbled up malignantly onto his lips. What he'd done was flat-out unforgivable. To his list of sins—which already included *cheat*, *dupe*, and *greedhead*—he had officially added *child abuser*.

And poor Tim. He hadn't done anything wrong, Sharpy thought, except to first get saddled with an asshole dad and then get tangled up with some asshole chemical. Lead, mercury, pesticides, MMR vaccine—the rumors had been flying fast and furious for years, but the cause of autism was still as elusive as a jackalope.

No, there was no simple way out of this situation. Sharpy knew that he would pay an incredible price for his brutality. Even worse, he knew that he *deserved* punishment. This would be proper and just.

He curled into a fetal position and hugged his knees into his chest. He squinched his eyes shut until a single tear tracked sideways down his cheek.

When he opened his eyes again, the lobby was eerily silent. A heavy hush muffled the exterior doors.

Sharpy knifed up to a sitting position. His head was clear. He was feeling lighter, more purposeful.

He would retrieve his injured son from the room and carry him downstairs for medical attention. He wouldn't offer any explanations, but neither would he deny his responsibility, if asked. It was the first step towards redemption.

Sharpy moved towards the elevators, peeling his sweaty banlon shirt from his back. The elevator car whooshed soundlessly to the fourteenth floor. The carpet scrolled effortlessly beneath his heels. The doorknob opened beneath his hand.

Inside the room, he found Tim still sprawled unconscious on the floor. The force of the final crash had knocked the lamp off the night table, and now the bare light bulb was pressed into the pale skin of his lower back and searing him like a cattle iron.

Sharpy worked fast. He returned the lamp to the night table and replaced the shade. Then he lifted his son's inert body and placed it gently on the bedspread. He inspected the skin; it was already flushed with red marks from the force of Sharpy's shoes. Those would be bruises later.

The phone suddenly rang. He stepped away from Tim and lifted the receiver to his ear.

He heard Grandpa Frederick's voice. The voice was saying something about Grandma. It was talking about how these goddamn people barely lifted a finger, okay, maybe they used the paddles, and sure they *looked* frantic, but deep down these doctors can't be bothered, even with all that dough they're raking in, can you believe it, you watch, there's a malpractice suit here, she had a few more months left, we'll get something for this by God—

Sharpy chewed on his lip, while his round doe eyes blinked. He had expected this call for a long time.

He gazed out into the darkness. The landscape was holding its breath. His chest tightened in anticipation. He felt something awful, something gigantic, pulling itself across the lush fields like a disembodied hand struggling across the landscape, plowing through the swamps, lifting cars, tearing asphalt, battering mobile homes, spitting dirt. He felt it racing towards the window.

"She's gone, son," Grandpa Frederick said. His voice was tinny and tired. "Son, she wanted me to tell you—"

A sudden, enormous drop in barometric pressure sent a sharp crackling through Sharpy's ears, preventing him from hearing any more. His knees buckled as the entire building swayed beneath him.

The hurricane had arrived.

Still clutching the telephone, he flung himself upon Tim, shielding him with his body—

—just as the window exploded into a thousand tiny pieces.

An unbelievable force instantly flung both father and son across the room and tossed them into the closet like a pair of dirty towels. Then the mattress and boxspring flipped up on end. In his hand Sharpy still clutched the dead telephone, even as the unbelievable force held him against the wall, drove bits of glass into his face, and screamed into his ears like a bloodthirsty banshee.

He heard flying debris shredding into the mattress. He felt the warm spray of hurricane water pelting his ankles. And then he curled himself around his unconscious son in a final gesture of solidarity before he, too, joined Tim in the cloud of unknowingness.

ninety-four

. . .

IN THE BALLROOM, D.L. and Arcade Boy sat on the banquet chairs alone. Tired of being ignored, the last of the other girls had departed with a sassy swish of proverbial tail feathers. Now D.L. had this luscious, mysterious, but still totally relatable guy all to herself.

Between them sat a deck of well-worn playing cards that he had filched from a dozing family nearby. They were lazily pursuing a game of war.

"I think we should stop playing," Arcade Boy said.

"We can't just stop," she said. "We have to play until someone wins."

"It's been like, fifteen minutes, and the piles are still the same."

"What else do you want to play?"

"Casino."

"I don't know how."

"Blackjack."

"We need three people."

They lapsed into a silence. The awkwardness was a deformed baby wriggling on the floor between them. Her heart twittered worriedly. Was their attraction already fizzling out?

Then Arcade Boy caught D.L.'s eye. "I have a question," he said.

She waited.

"Can I ask you a question?" he said.

"*Duh*," she said. "I was waiting for it." Why couldn't he see that it was okay to do or say nearly anything he wanted? Why couldn't he just *know* this? Where was his *intuition*? Didn't he realize that she was *already* totally given over to him? That she would gnaw the head off a poisoned rat if he just said the word? Had she misjudged his skill in romance?

"In tennis," he said, "do you know why they say zero is love?"

"I have a feeling you're going to tell me."

"Because even when you've got nothing, you've still got that."

Her heart quivered a little. Years from now, it might have been a quiver of impatience with this kind of juvenile line. But right now, these were the crushingly sweetest words she'd ever heard.

"That sounds good," she said.

Arcade Boy's fingers twirled a pen expertly. She liked his hands: they were both rugged and sensitive. "Who do *you* love?" he said.

"My brother," she said. "But not tonight. That's why he's in the room."

"Is he safe there?"

"Maybe."

"Have you ever been in love?"

She looked away from him. "No."

"Have you thought about it?"

She felt her internals walls flinging themselves up. He was presuming too much. "What kind of question is that?"

Then Arcade Boy took her hand. D.L. tried to snatch it back, but he held fast. This was *the* moment. What would he do with it? She noticed that her palm was getting moist. She'd had this problem before, sweaty palms, had even used a prescription medication to dry them out. Would he get grossed out? It was too late. He was carefully lifting her hand to his face … and *kissing* it … he was *making out* with her hand … *here*, in this crowded ballroom full of *adults* … A surge of panic swept through her body.

Arcade Boy suddenly pulled back. "Do you trust me?" he said.

She froze. "I don't know."

Without a moment's hesitation, he said, "Then why don't you follow me and find out?" He stood up and offered both hands.

She watched his knuckles with suspicion. Where could he possibly take her? They were hemmed in this ballroom by hurricanes and hotel staffers. Still, she was intrigued by his plans. She wasn't going to say no.

D.L. clasped his hand. He pulled her to her feet in a fluid, effortless motion. He led her through the crowd towards the far end of the ballroom. It was fairly deserted here: only a few children dozing in their mothers' laps. Two fathers conked out unapologetically on the floor.

They stopped at an empty banquet table laid flush against the wall. Its most important feature, she noted, was a long curtain that reached to the floor. With a mischievous look, he dropped to his hands and knees—

—and crawled underneath the table.

"Are you coming?" his voice said.

She tapped her foot and glanced around. Part of her was nervous about diving under a heavy velvet sham with a strange boy. But a larger part of her was tempted to tear his shirt off and squeeze him like a python. She looked around again. Not a soul was paying them an ounce of attention.

The decision made itself. She dropped to her knees and crawled after him.

The air was dark and thick underneath the table. Arcade Boy was reclining on the floor already, his head propped up under some spare fabric, his arm flung open invitingly to his guest. She quickly lay down and nestled her head in the crook of his armpit. Her heart was pounding, but a smile was stamped on her face so hard that her cheeks hurt. She'd never, ever done anything like this in her entire life—and it was scaring the wits out of her. She inhaled deeply. His skin smelled like wood chips and spiced cider. She nestled closer against his body, feeling secure.

They lay there in silence, listening to each other breathe. "What should we talk about?" he said.

"We don't really know each other."

"Then we can talk about the important things," he said. "Did you ever notice that people will pour out their hearts and souls to total strangers, but never talk to their families?"

D.L. admitted that she knew something about that.

His fingers absently tapped the underside of the tabletop. "Do you ever wonder about the future?"

"Yeah."

"What do you wonder about?"

Her finger toyed with his button. "I want to know how to live my life."

"Yeah," he said. "Me too."

"There has to be a better way."

"Better than what?"

"Better than how my family lives." She was surprised by her own honesty.

"I don't see why we need so many *things*. My dad spends all this money on a big house, a big lawn, a big car—but other times, he's so cheap it's unbelievable. He'll bitch about fifty cents at a restaurant."

"That sucks," said Arcade Boy.

425

"Why is that?" She looked up at him. "Why do some people care so much about things?"

"Because they have a hole," Arcade Boy said. "They try to fill the hole with stuff, but it can't be filled with anything. Except love."

She felt her eyes drawn towards his face. He was looking at her with the faintest smile. As though she had rehearsed this moment a hundred times, D.L. swung her leg over his hips and hoisted her pelvis onto his skinny frame. She lowered her head and smushed her own lips onto his astonishingly soft lips—and then held them there. It wasn't very delicate. It felt like she was smothering him.

Her first kiss.

She became aware of his body shifting ever so slightly beneath her. She pulled her face away from his and opened her eyes. He looked frightened.

"Was I hurting you?"

"No."

"What's the matter?"

"Nothing. You're just easy to kiss," he said.

Her wall of suspicion immediately flung itself up. "Have you kissed a lot of girls?"

"Maybe." He said it so casually that it sounded like the most natural thing in the world. She had to admit that the idea of his tomcatting around didn't feel as repulsive as she'd imagined. Was it asking too much for a guy to have a little bit of expertise?

D.L. rolled halfway off his torso but kept one leg draped sideways across his hips. She could feel the bony jut of his iliac crests. She traced lazy circles on his shirt and watched his chest rise and fall with his breathing.

"What are you thinking about?" he said.

Before she could answer, a massive boom sounded upon the west side of the ballroom, a convulsive shudder that rippled across the walls and shook the structure down to its very foundations. Silverware clattered in its trays. Coffee cups tipped over. Children leapt into parents' laps.

Then a horrific whining, rising in pitch without reaching a crescendo, squeezed the ballroom.

The hurricane had arrived.

"Hold on to me," said Arcade Boy. She squeezed tightly.

Thunk. Then *screeeee.* Something heavy thudded against the west wall and scratched forty yards across the exterior of the wall. Like an enormous hand raking the outside of the building. Then a series of pops. *Thunk thunk thunk thunk thunk thunk.* Those would be branches, trunks, doors, street signs, twisted unrecognizable pieces of metal—who knows. All were barrelling through the sodden air and assaulting the sides of the hotel.

Touron heads swiveled around as if resting upon ball bearings.

Then there was a cracking sound from the roof. Throats, chins, and double chins were exposed as frightened eyes peered upwards. What the tourons saw was a ceiling that was slowly being peeled back like someone opening the top of a can of cat food. Chunks of gray plaster and particle board plummeted to the floor. In one corner, families screamed, shrieked, and scrambled for the doors, rubbing dust from their hair.

Beneath the banquet table, D.L. clutched Arcade Boy and gritted her teeth until her jaw muscles hurt.

"We're going to come out all right," he said.

"How do you know?"

"Because we have to," he said.

And so the small teenagers lay huddled there, under the heavy ruffled shams, listening to the demonic wind destroy everything outside, the girl's lips silently prayed that she would build a better way of life.

ninety-five

. . .

THE BATTERED LITTLE Civic blazed persistently down the road, heading eastward, racing the hurricane front.

Behind the wheel, Curtis ground his teeth and realized that he was holding his breath. He glanced nervously at the speedometer. Seventy miles an hour. That was way too much stress for the ninety-one tiny horses galloping underneath the hood. The engine's high whine sounded like a food processor about to blow vegetable pulp all over the walls.

As soon as he'd finished distributing papers at the Hotel Crown Palace, Curtis had shot downstairs, dove into his car, and hightailed it back to the main roads. There were three more hotels on his list, and four more newspaper bundles in his trunk, but a primitive tickle in his neck told him to get the hell out of there.

Suddenly a vicious gust of warm wind rushed beneath his compact car, lifted the back end off the cement, and dropped it several feet to the left. Curtis never picked his foot off the accelerator. He thanked an invisible deity for the remaining newspaper bundles in the trunk.

But the wind wasn't through toying with him. Another dizzying gust lifted his car even higher, and when it crashed down Curtis heard his undercarriage momentarily scrape against the cement. Even worse, he felt his bladder starting to weaken.

Then Curtis noticed objects whizzing through the air. Empty cans. Bits of wood. A garbage bag. A plaid shirt. A patio seat cushion. A cocker spaniel, its orange hair whipping. All of it told him one thing.

He had to get off the road.

He had to find shelter.

Now.

He wheeled off the freeway onto International Drive and hit the corner going almost fifty. It didn't matter since the roads were empty. Straight ahead stood a gas station, a Shell Food Mart. Curtis instantly found comfort in the familiar yellow logo. Even better, the lights were still on.

He careened to a stop and opened the driver's door. The wind was so strong that it swung the door out and smashed it forwards against the front left panel. Curtis didn't care. He fell out onto the concrete and staggered over to the station's front door. It was locked. He pounded on the glass.

Inside, a frightened pair of eyes peeked around the shelving. It was the attendant, a thin, dark-skinned Indian—probably a Dravidian, from the southern regions—crouched behind the Corn Nuts. He was literally shivering with fear.

"Can you let me in?" Curtis yelled. The words were unnecessary. Anybody on the planet could've guessed what he needed.

The Indian crept along the floor and lifted a trembling key. It took him several tries to fit the key in the lock. Finally the door opened. The chips, cupcakes, and magazines rippled and crinkled and fell off the shelves as the howling wind blew through the food mart. Curtis stepped inside, the attendant shut the door, locked it—

Just as the hurricane front arrived.

In full force.

The sound was deafening. At the pumps, all eight gasoline hoses were flung horizontally. The black squeegee blades skipped across the ground and disappeared. Curtis' two remaining hubcaps instantly detached from their tires and flew away.

That wasn't the worst. As the wind reached fever pitch, Curtis watched the back end of his pathetic little Civic raise up, a few inches at first, then several feet—as though drawn by an enormous magnet in the sky. Then it stood completely vertical, balanced on the tip of its front bumper ... and then toppled forward, onto its roof. The flimsy top was instantly flattened.

It didn't stop there. The car's momentum carried the nose up into the sky until it was vertical again—and then it landed on its tires. It kept somersaulting. His car had become a fifteen-foot-long tumbleweed. Soon the Civic had tumbled four times across the cement, like a carelessly tossed die, and smashed into a dumpster abutting a cement wall. Then it was lifted over the dumpster, over the wall, and up into the sky. It was gone.

His car had *flown away.*

Curtis didn't have time to think about it. The Dravidian was grabbing his sleeve and gesturing towards the bathroom: "Toilet, toilet!"

They dove into the ladies' restroom and shut the door and locked it and shrank down the far wall, shoulder to shoulder, until they hit the bottom. And then:

Crash.

Though they couldn't see it, a red octagonal sign bearing the word STOP had just shattered the glass walls of the Food Mart. Now the hurricane was fully inside the store.

The clerk's eyes were tight points of fear. He gazed at the ceiling and his lips worked themselves in some kind of frantic prayer. Outside was the sound of a thousand demons ripping, banging, crashing, smashing, shredding. The bathroom door rattled violently in its frame but held tight.

Curtis covered his ears, lifted his knees to his chest, and dropped his head inside his jacket. His annihilation was nearly complete. He had no home, no job, no money, no health, no wheels, and no hope. It couldn't get much worse than this. He prayed for Lucinda and their baby as he contemplated his own imminent death. What would it feel like? Would it be fast or slow? Merciful or tortured?

He decided to leave this world on a high note. He remembered the envelope in his inner pocket, the one that the weird teenage boy had handed to him. It was the chocolate bar. He would eat some chocolate. The last taste his tongue would ever record would be a sweet one.

"Do you want some chocolate?" Curtis shouted to the clerk. His voice could barely be heard over the pandemonium. *"I think I have some in my pocket."*

The Indian fixed him with a frightened stare.

"Do you want some chocolate?"

The clerk finally nodded very slightly.

Curtis pulled out the envelope. His shaking fingers slowly worked their way underneath the cellophane tape and opened the flap. He peeked inside—

At which point Curtis Marshall saw something that made him question his own sanity.

Inside the envelope was a stack of money. It was an inch high. He stuck his thumb inside the stack and leafed through it.

All were hundred-dollar bills.

He closed the envelope and tried to control the panic flooding his body. This wasn't possible. This didn't happen to people like him.

He opened the envelope again. The money was still there. He estimated several thousand dollars.

Curtis didn't have time to contemplate the who, the how, or the why. Not crouched in a gas station bathroom during a Category 5 hurricane. Instead, he folded the envelope carefully, stuffed it deep into his pocket, and clutched it close to his body.

"No chocolate?" said the clerk.

"No chocolate," Curtis said.

It couldn't be contained any longer. The madness, the frustration, the anger. He felt it rising from his soul, felt it scorching his throat, felt it leaving his body in giant sobs of uncontrollable laughter, felt it rolling down in his face in giant drops of salty wetness.

The clerk reached out for his hand and squeezed it tightly as the sound of the wind rose to an unsustainable volume.

ninety-six

. . .

A TELEVISION SCREEN displayed a reporter in a yellow rain slicker standing before a background of downed telephone poles and scattered palm fronds: "...the second-worst disaster in the state's history. Officials are estimating between three and four billion—"

Then the television abruptly snapped off. The finger on the remote control belonged to Vivian, her black mane soaking wet and her toned body swathed in a single white terrycloth towel. The gauzy white curtains on the window marked luxury.

She gazed at the blank screen, as her teeth chewed absentmindedly on her lower lip.

From the bathroom there was the sound of a shower hitting tile. Over it, a man's voice said, "Hoo boy, sounds like we got out of there just in time, baby. Can you see if I've got any clean white socks?"

Vivian shook off her mood. She rose and walked over to a worn leather suitcase. It was a battered, ugly thing, with a thick buckle that was about three decades out of fashion. Making a sour face, she raised the top of the case with two long fingernails.

"Baby?"

"I found them," she said.

"Hey—what time did you say we were meeting Breanna?"

She winced. "It's *Brittany*. And we're not *meeting* her. We're picking her up from the babysitting service."

The shower turned off. Finally the man waddled out of the bathroom. It was the plumber from the Hamburger Platter. He was wearing a gold chain around his neck and gold bracelets on his wrists. The terrycloth towel was hitched under his low-hanging belly.

"God, that tub drains slower than molasses through a pinhole. Wonder if the staff'd let me have a look." He thought about it. "Nah—they probably couldn't afford me." He splashed a handful of cologne onto his throat, then used a mirror to massage under his belly.

Vivian offered a forced smile. She'd dated worse than him. Lots worse. She could swallow her pride. His money was as good as anybody else's.

"I'm sure you're very good at what you do," she said.

The plumber reached into his wallet and peeled off a pair of hundreds. "That's for you, sweetheart. Buy yourself something pretty. I'm sure you know how this works."

She looked at the money and a spasm of nausea flashed across her face. But soon enough the cool mask hoisted itself again upon her hawkish features. Her sharp teeth revealed themselves behind a lethal smile.

Her long, sharp fingernails closed tightly around the cash.

"Yes, I do," she said.

epilogue

. . .

SIX MONTHS LATER, on a clear, bluish cold February morning, Sharpy calmly sipped a cup of coffee in a folding chair in the sunlit yellow atrium of a spacious physical rehabilitation clinic. There were twenty or so other people here, mostly parents like him. It was graduation day, of a sort.

On the dais before the small crowd stood five proudly reconditioned individuals, waiting to be awarded re-entry into society.

Tim was one of them.

During the hurricane, every window on the west-facing side of the Hotel Crown Palace had been imploded by the storm front. The rooms had been destroyed. Furniture shredded, carpet soaked. Rescuers combing the debris found fourteen injured, including Sharpy. He was treated for a concussion and multiple abrasions and was released from the hospital a day later.

The rescuers had also found Tim, naked on the carpet, flattened beneath the three-hundred-pound armoire. The television had crushed his legs. Even worse, his skull had been wedged into the base of the collapsed nightstand. He'd spent three weeks in intensive care with a closed-head injury that the doctors had logically but wrongly assumed had been inflicted by flying debris.

The odd purple bruises on his torso were assumed to have been made by debris.

These oversights had saved Sharpy's legal life but shattered his emotional one. Alone, the bitter taste of guilt filling his mouth, he'd been unable to sleep for weeks, loathing his own existence. Wracked by the memory of his terrible kicks. That final shove that had almost caved in his son's head like a rotten pumpkin.

He'd emerged a changed man. He'd eagerly paid for this rehab clinic, where his son had learned how to walk, talk, and feed himself again. Not that it made a whole bushel of difference. Tim would always be autistic. But that was seeming like less and less of a burden. In fact, seeing his son lurch across the stage with that familiar odd gait warmed the fibers of his heart. *This is my family*, he thought. *For better or worse*.

Sharpy thought back to Grandma Maya's funeral. One week after the hurricane, short and unremarkable. Not even twenty mourners. A quick service followed by a sense of relief that Grandma had finally joined the grand oversoul. Sharpy reflected that she'd always been there, always grasped some universality that none of the other family members had been able to comprehend.

He remembered how Grandpa Frederick had stoically watched his wife's casket, arms crossed. "I've prepared myself for this day for a long time," he'd said.

"I'm sure you have," Sharpy'd replied.

"Yes indeed. For a long time."

Sharpy'd sighed. "The director warned us not to take her out of the assisted-living home. We didn't listen."

Grandpa Frederick hadn't said anything to that.

"Did you hear me, Dad? We didn't listen."

Not a single line of regret in the granitic chin. Just two circles of light reflected off the lenses of his eyeglasses.

After the funeral, Grandpa had moved out of the assisted-living home. He'd left a note with a forwarding address, some apartment near Roanoke, but Sharpy had filed it in a drawer and promptly forgotten about it.

Then there was the matter of the departed mistress. Sharpy thought regretfully about what a fool he had been. Blinded by love, or at least the glitter of her jewelry. Truth be told, though, he'd *always* had his doubts. In the back of his mind, he'd always known that offering Vivian Talon a seventeen-thousand-dollar engagement ring was a giant steaming turd of a mistake. She just wasn't the marrying kind, in the same way that a jaguar just wasn't a housepet. No, to use was the function of her nature, and he didn't blame her for leaving.

After all, he'd lost the inheritance. Permanently. Montgomery had refused to yield even a micron, explaining that "no second chance" was an ironclad condition of the will.

Sharpy'd accepted the announcement and slunk out of the office, taking solace in the knowledge that his daughter was going to be a very rich girl someday. In the meantime, he was poorer than ever. He'd lost a seventeen-thousand-dollar engagement ring. He'd lost an expensive Swiss wristwatch (which he would eventually retrieve, at a cost of nine hundred dollars, through an attorney who threatened legal action against Gushbottom). And he'd mysteriously lost ten thousand dollars from his hotel room safe—relatively small potatoes that he'd shrugged off in the aftermath of the disaster.

Now the sacrifices had to be made. He'd cancelled the maid service and was scrubbing furniture and floors himself now, learning how to buff and polish with precision. He'd cancelled his golf club membership; for relaxation he'd taken to chipping balls across the scraggly, overgrown grass of his front yard, since he'd cancelled the lawn service too. But the biggest pill to swallow had been the debt consolidation. A blessing and a curse, it had him singing to the tune of a $974 payment every month for the next fifteen years. Simple and merciless. Sharpy paid each statement like an orphan swallowing a spoonful of castor oil.

But oh, Sharpy had changed. He exercised five days a week, running through the cold, flat soybean fields in the frigid dawn. He was listening to his daughter more—*active* listening too, not just thinking about food or money or sex while her little teenage voice buzzed distantly, the way he used to. He was determined that the three remaining Cravings would stay *together*—even if it meant eventually downsizing to a smaller house, which was looking ever more likely. They would treasure at least one more year, until D.L. left for college. That was an accomplishment.

Now, on the makeshift stage in the rehabilitation clinic, as Tim lumbered across the dais to accept his ribbon, Sharpy applauded loudly.

He wasn't the only one.

Next to him, D.L. clapped too, her eyes covered in a thin film of tears. Sharpy knew that she had felt some guilt about leaving her brother alone in the hotel room to be blown to smithereens. When they'd returned home, D.L. had spent all her waking hours tending to Tim's every need. She'd cooked meals, folded laundry, even shuttled him to rehab every morning before school using her new driver's license.

As Tim came up to accept his award, D.L. shoved a thumb and forefinger inside her lips and blew a loud wolf-whistle. Their secret signal. Onstage, Tim made a seagull-like squawk. Sharpy's eyebrows arched in surprise.

"He heard that?" said Sharpy.

"Of course."

"I didn't know you could whistle like that."
"You might if you paid more attention to me."
"Do you *want* me to pay more attention to you?"
She nodded ever so slightly. He nodded back.
His family was whole again.

plotworks publishing

Visit Plotworks Publishing and sign up for our newsletter! Stay up-to-date about our new releases, classics reprints, merchandise, and sales.

Now turn the page for a sneak peek at another title by J.A. Jernay!

THE URUGUAY AMETHYST

AN AINSLEY WALKER
GEMSTONE TRAVEL MYSTERY

J.A. JERNAY

the uruguay amethyst

The room felt ancient. Heavy red woven shades had been drawn against the morning light. There was an old settée at one end of the room, and a very heavy vanity edged in gold. Ainsley smelled unfamiliar creams and powders.

At the other end of the room was an elegant golden armchair.

In the chair was an elderly woman.

Her silver hair had been sprayed up until it resembled a wreath of smoke. Her wrists were a mass of delicate green veins. Her shirt was laden with sequins that glittered like reptilian scales. A heavy blanket had been tucked around her legs.

And inside the woman's face were a pair of black eyes, which were fixed upon Ainsley.

Watching.

Martina led the guest across the room. "Gugina, *tengo Ainsley*. Ainsley, this is Señora Gugina Carlotti."

"A pleasure meeting you," Ainsley said.

The old woman angled her head as her black eyes roved up and down the visitor. Ainsley stood uncomfortably.

Then her black eyes found Ainsley's purse. "Who gave

you that?" she asked. Her voice carried the same soft Latin accent.

"I bought it."

The old woman made a face. "It's ugly."

Ainsley didn't feel offended. This woman had the peculiar talent of making even the baldest insults sound like matters of fact. She could tell you that you were the bastard daughter of a truck stop whore, that your toes looked uglier than moldy pieces of fried tofu, and you would find yourself nodding in agreement.

"It's not my favorite purse either," said Ainsley.

"Why don't you bring your best today?"

"Because it doesn't match this outfit."

Gugina coughed, her small frame doubling up. Ainsley handed her a box of tissues. The old woman swatted it away. "My nurse will be here soon. Sit down."

She pointed at the matching chair next to her. Ainsley obeyed and perched on the edge of the cushion. The seat felt firm and unforgiving.

Gugina cleared her throat. "Something I have learned is that many Americans are afraid to travel. They are satisfied with their own lives."

"Not me."

"I have been to almost every country in the world," she finally said. "I have seen how many people live."

"I'm jealous."

"Have you ever travelled?"

"Yes."

"To where?"

Ainsley thought back to her father. He'd taken her on a vacation each of the first eight years of her life. She still had the foot photos to prove it. He'd snapped pictures of their four bare feet overlooking a cypress swamp in South Carolina, a canyon in New Mexico, a snowy mountain range in Alaska, a pine forest in Michigan.

Then the little carcinogenic masses had formed in his liver, hospice had appeared in the living room, and one morning there had been a trip to a nearby lake with a ceramic urn. The travelling had finished. But Ainsley still kept those foot photos, had stared at them for years until she'd forgotten his face but memorized every detail of the tops of his feet.

"Mostly around America," she said, "but I'm open to wherever."

The old lady didn't acknowledge the answer. Ainsley wasn't sure how the interview was going. Pleasing Gugina felt like practicing blindfolded archery.

The old woman's hand lifted a cup of water to her mouth. Ainsley watched her thin lips suck greedily from the rim.

When she was finished, Gugina set the cup down. She seemed refreshed. "You have a husband, Miss Ainsley?"

"No. He dumped me and moved out."

"Do you have children?"

Ainsley smirked. "Please."

A look of impatience flashed across Gugina's face. "Why *please*? I'm not a waitress. I can't bring you children like a pile of beans on a plate."

"I mean that I don't have any."

"That's very wise." The old lady fixed her eyes on the ceiling, as if her next words were etched in the woodwork. "There are too many people on the earth. And people are terrible anyways. I don't like them."

"I don't care about saving the earth," Ainsley said. "I just don't want kids."

Gugina's black eyes suddenly lit up. "Do you know Spanish?"

"Some."

"How much?"

"I studied for three years in school."

"And do you speak it?"

Ainsley swallowed hard. She hadn't for several years, except to talk to the maintenance men coming into her apartment to fix her shower. There'd been one long-ago boyfriend, a Venezuelan, who'd been a native speaker. But they hadn't really talked much at all, which is probably why the relationship had ended.

But she said, "Of course."

The old woman barked something to Martina, who quickly brought over a plate of fruit, placing it on the low coffee table.

Gugina pointed at a peach. "What is that called?"

"A peach."

"How do you say that in Spanish?"

Ainsley squinted at the fruit and thought hard. "*Melocotón*."

Gugina frowned and shook her head. "No, no. Let's try another. When you squeeze a peach, what do you get?"

"Juice."

"How do you say 'juice' in Spanish?"

She though back to her high school Spanish teacher. He'd been from Madrid. "*Zumo*," she said.

The old woman was angry now, but Ainsley didn't know why. "What is the Spanish word for 'street'?" she said.

Finally, an easy question. "*Calle*," replied Ainsley.

To her surprise, Gugina threw her arms into the air roared. She turned and breathed fiery bursts of rapid Spanish at Martina, who answered politely but with obvious frustration. It was clear they were arguing about her.

"Ainsley, can you excuse us for a moment?" said Martina.

She nodded, happy for the break from this testy old woman. Ainsley went back into the small warehouse and exhaled. Where were these women *from*? With their soft Spanish accents, Italian names, and white skin?

She roamed the aisle, hands clasped tightly behind her back, until she spotted a chalice, studded with blue stones, glittering in a cabinet under the light. It looked like chalcedony. Ainsley had just picked up the informational tag when Martina's voice cut across the floor.

"Please *don't* touch that."

She was standing in the doorway of Gugina's den, and the tone of her voice meant business.

Ainsley dropped the tag and backed away. "I was just curious."

"We are ready for you again."

The heavy scents enveloped Ainsley as she stepped inside the lair again. The old woman was still in her golden armchair, but now Martina sat beside her.

With no place to sit, Ainsley stood before them, trying to keep her knees still. This was an audition, these women her judges.

"We want to welcome you to Associated Industries," said Martina.

"I'm excited to be here," replied Ainsley.

"You're aware that this position involves travel."

"Yes."

"Would you like to know the location of your assignment?"

"Yes."

Martina paused. "You will be travelling to Uruguay."

Ainsley didn't know what to say.

"Do you know about Uruguay?"

Ainsley was drawing a blank. Try as she might, she couldn't think of *anything* she knew about Uruguay. She'd always confused it with Paraguay. And one of them had two capitals. Or was that Bolivia?

"No," she confessed. "Tell me."

She wondered if this would be the end of her employment. But her judges just smiled. "Good," hissed Gugina. "It is better that way."

"What will I be doing?"

Martina shook her head sadly. "We cannot tell you that yet. You must do something else first."

"What?"

"Learn Spanish."

"I already know—"

Martina silenced her. "No, you know Castellano. You don't know Rioplatense. That's the Spanish we speak in Uruguay."

So that's why Gugina had been testing her. And apparently she'd been answering wrong.

"How am I supposed to learn it?" asked Ainsley.

"We are going to send you to a private tutor. We will give you four weeks to learn from him. If you pass his tests, we will give you the mission. Is this clear?"

Ainsley nodded. "One problem."

"What?"

"I need to pay my rent."

The old woman sneered. Ainsley thought she glimpsed actual steam curling out of her nostrils.

"When you pass his test," said Martina, "we will deliver the first half of your money into your bank account. The speed of the learning is up to you."

Ainsley was floored. It was the nineteenth of the month. She didn't have four weeks to learn Rioplatense.

If she wanted to avoid eviction, she only had eleven days.

plotworks publishing

Visit Plotworks Publishing and sign up for our newsletter! Stay up-to-date about our new releases, classics reprints, merchandise, and sales.

bibliography

The following is a list of the texts used by the author during the course of his research.

Baron-Cohen, Simon. *Mindblindness: An Essay on Autism and the Theory of Mind.* Cambridge: MIT, 1995.

Beavers, Dorothy Johnson. *Autism: Nightmare Without End.* Port Washington, N.Y.: Ashley Books, 1982.

Churchill, Don W. *Language of Autistic Children.* New York: Halsted, 1978.

Classic Readings in Autism. Ed. Anne M. Donnellan. New York: Teachers College Press, 1985.

Clift, Jean Dalby and Wallace B. *The Archetype of Pilgrimage: Outer Action With Inner Meanings.* Paulist Press: 1996.

Delcato, Carl H. *The Ultimate Stranger: The Autistic Child.* Garden City, N.Y.: Doubleday, 1974.

Designing Disney's Theme Parks: The Architecture of Reassurance. Ed. Karal Ann Marling. New York: Flammarion, 1998.

Dunlop, Beth. *Building a Dream: The Art of Disney Architecture.* New York: Harry N. Abrams, 1996.

Dunn, Jancee. "The Secret Life of Teenage Girls." *Rolling Stone,* November 11, 1999, pp. 106-121.

Dusenbury, George and Jane. *How To Retire To Florida.* New York: Harper & Brothers, 1947.

Early Childhood Autism: Clinical, Educational, and Social Aspects. Ed. J.K. Wing. New York: Pergamon Press.

Egeria, Diary of a Pilgrimage. Ancient Christian Writers No. 38. Ed. W.J. Burghardt. Paulist Press, 1970.

Eliot, Marc. *Walt Disney: Hollywood's Dark Prince.* New York: Birch Lane Press, 1993.

Encounters With Autistic States. Ed. Theodore and Judith L. Mitrani. Northvale, NJ: Jason Aronson, 1997.

Flower, Joe. *Prince of the Magic Kingdom: Michael Eisner and the Re-Making of Disney.* New York: John Wiley, 1991.

Handbook of Autism and Pervasive Developmental Disorders. Ed. Donald J. Cohen and Anne M. Donnellan. Silver Spring, MD: Wiley, 1967.

Heuvelmans, Martin. *The River Killers.* Harrisburg, PA: Stackpole, 1974.

Hiassen, Carl. *Team Rodent: How Disney Devours the World.* The Library of Contemporary Thought. New York: Ballantine, 1998.

Howlin, Patricia, and Rutter, Michael. *Treatment of Autistic Children.* Chichester, NY: Wiley, 1987.

Bibliography

Inside the Mouse: Work and Play at Disney World. Ed. The Project on Disney. Duke University Press, 1995.

Janzen, Janice E. *Understanding the Nature of Autism: A Practical Guide*. San Antonio: Therapy Skills Builders, 1996.

Kasson, John F. *Amusing the Million: Coney Island at the Turn of the Century*. New York: Hill and Wang, 1978.

Koening, David. *More Mouse Tales: A Closer Peek Backstage at Disneyland*. Irvine, CA: Bonaventure, 1999.

-------. *Mouse Tales: A Behind-the-Ears Look at Disneyland*. Irvine, CA: Bonaventure, 1994.

-------. *Mouse Under Glass: Secrets of Disney Animation & Theme Parks*. Irvine, CA: Bonaventure, 1997.

Lane, Harlan L., and Pillard, Richard. *The Wild Boy of Burundi: The Story of an Outcast Child*.

Language and Treatment of Autistic and Developmentally Disordered Children. Ed. Thomas L. Layton. Springfield, IL: Thomas, 1987.

Lasn, Kalle. *Culture Jam: The Uncooling of America*. New York: William Morrow, 1999.

Lefort, Rosine. *Birth of the Other*. Trans. Marc du Ry, Lindsay Watson, and Leonardo Rodriguez. Urbana: University of Illinois, 1994.

Levinson, Boris M. *Autism: Myth or Reality?* Springfield, IL: C.C. Thomas, 1984.

Mesibov, Gary B.; Adams, Lynn W.; and Klinger, Laura G. *Autism: Understanding the Disorder*. New York: Plenum, 1997.

Mosley, Leonard. *Disney's World*. Briarcliff Manor, NY: Stein and Day, 1985.

The Neurobiology of Autism. Ed. Margaret L. Bauman and Thomas L. Kemper. Baltimore: Johns Hopkins, 1994.

Novak-Branch, Frances. *The Disney World Effect*. Self-published dissertation, 1983.

Rothenberg, Mira. *Children With Emerald Eyes: Histories of Extraordinary Boys and Girls*. New York: Dial, 1977.

Sacred Journeys: The Anthropology of Pilgrimage. Ed. Alan Morinis. Westport, CT: Greenwood, 1992.

Schickel, Richard. *The Disney Version: The Life, Times, Art and Commerce of Walt Disney*. New York: Simon & Schuster, 1968.

Shandler, Sara. *Ophelia Speaks*. New York: HarperCollins, 1999.

Siegel, Bryna. *The World of the Autistic Child*. New York, Oxford University Press, 1996.

Smith, Peter. *Handicapped in Walt Disney World: A Guide For Everyone*. Dallas: SouthPark, 1993.

Sperry, Virginia Walker. *Fragile Success: Nine Autistic Children, Childhood to Adulthood*. North Haven, Conn: Archon, 1995.

Stepp, Laura Sessions. "Beyond the Silver Spoon." *The Washington Post*, January 4, 2000.

Sumption, Jonathan. *Pilgrimage: An Image of Mediaeval Religion*. Totowa, NJ: Rowman and Littlefield, 1975.

Victor, George. *The Riddle of Autism*. Lexington, MA: LexingtonBooks, 1983.

Watts, Steven. *The Magic Kingdom: Walt Disney and the American Way of Life.* New York: Houghton Mifflin, 1997.

The Orlando Sentinel archives, Orange County Public Library, Florida.